THE LAST MARTYR

A THEOLOGICAL THRILLER

DR. JOHN DEE JEFFRIES

Edited by C. Genevieve Jeffries, MDiv

The Last Martyr
Copyright © 2015 by Dr. John Dee Jeffries

All rights reserved. No portion of this book may be reproduced, stored in a retrieval system, or transmitted in any form or by any means—electronic, mechanical, photocopy, recording, scanning, or other—except for brief quotations in reviews or articles, without the prior written permission of the author.

First edition, June 2015

ISBN: 978-0-692-45553-1

Printed in the United States of America

Readers should be aware that Internet Web sites offered as citations and/or sources for further information may have changed or disappeared between the time this was written and when it is read.

Illustration provided by ThinkStockImages.com

Dedication

To my wife, Genny, my love, my best friend and my wise editor; to my son, Sean, my daughters, Sheri and Courtney; and to my mom, Doris.

And to the wonderful congregations of...

First Baptist Church, Chalmette, Louisiana
First Baptist Church, Abita Springs, Louisiana
Lee Hill Baptist Church, Folsom, Louisiana
New Ireland Baptist Church, Union, Mississippi

I dedicate this work to each of you and especially to Him Who has created us one family.

I Salute Thee
The Noble Army of the Martyrs Salute Thee
TE DEUM
Thee, O God, We Praise

John the Younger, Son of Cosmas, Son of John from the Isle of Greece

TABLE OF CONTENTS

A Metaphor.

It's Beautiful.
Look. On God's Finger. Look.
A Butterfly.

I had a dream, which was not all a dream.
The bright sun was extinguish'd, and the stars
Did wander darkling in the eternal space,
Rayless, and pathless, and the icy earth
Swung blind and blackening in the moonless air;
Morn came and went--and came, and brought no day,
And men forgot their passions in the dread
Of this their desolation; and all hearts
Were chill'd into a selfish prayer for light…

Darkness
George Gordon, Lord
Byron[1]

PROLOGUE

A WORD FROM THE AUTHOR

He was a strange looking man, shabbily dressed. His dusty black jacket was fashioned like an old style drum major uniform. It was threadbare and had a double-breasted row of dull silver buttons running down its front. He wore a drab silvery-white cloak that had an insignia across the chest; an insignia that featured an eagle, a winged man, an ox and a lion, symbols of the *four evangelists.*[2]

He had strategically seated himself in the back of our church sanctuary. The area where he sat was not well lit. He sat there, in the shadows, staring at me, during the entire Sunday morning worship service.

I remember that service well, quite well. The children's message focused on the chorus of a song, *Bull Frogs and Butterflies – They've Both Been Born Again.* The message for the adult service focused on *Advancing through Adversity* and closed with the following encouragement....

> *"Fear strengthens Faith. God supplies faith to enable us to overcome our fears. He supplies grace to enable us to walk through life's most difficult valleys. Know this: God has appointed a time, a place and a circumstance for faith to ultimately triumph over fear. When that time comes you will see that God has used every event and experience of*

fear to strengthen your faith – to enable you to Advance through Adversity."

At the conclusion of the service the man emerged from the shadows and discretely pulled me aside, away from the congregation as they exited the sanctuary. He seemed distracted, disturbed, somewhat agitated, and worried. He also appeared to be frightened, yet keenly observant and decidedly sensitive to everything and everyone in the church building. He constantly turned his head one way, then another, scanning the crowds of people as they exited the church. He was looking for something. Or someone. He leaned close to me, placing his hand in the small of my back to draw me closer, and then he spoke, yet without ever really looking at me, his eyes constantly scanning the people as they exited the sanctuary.

"This is for you. Put it in your suit pocket, quickly."

He hurriedly pulled a manila envelop that contained what appeared to be a small ancient scroll, a rough, faded parchment, from under his coat and handed it to me. His hands were trembling.

"Listen carefully, but, please, do not show me any sign of special attention. We are less conspicuous here in the sanctuary. I think I'm being followed. Someone may be watching – both of us."

I quickly placed the document in my Bible. It was too large for my coat pocket. I did not know what else to do given the size of the document and the urgent tone and tenor of his voice.

"Do exactly as I say. Translate then transcribe this document into your laptop, then save it in multiple computers, in different formats, in different locations, for safety and security – then burn this document. Do exactly as I say. Burn it. The boy, John the Younger, who is now old and near death, told me to give this to you, and you alone. I am doing as he told me – you must do likewise."

He quickly shook my hand, smiled, and said, loudly, with an upbeat sounding voice: "Wonderful service, pastor. Wonderful message, too. Thank you. Thank you."

He then turned and walked away, quickly. As he walked away I noticed a clue as to his identity, though I did not see it as a clue at that time. There was a clump of silver spray paint on the back of his head, on the bottom curls of his hair, where his hair met his neck. As he walked away his body cast eerie shadows across the sanctuary walls and the church pews. I felt a shiver, a chill run up and down my spine, as a swirling cool rush of air danced in the very spot where he had once stood.

The whole clandestine conversation lasted less than a minute.

About an hour later, as I was seated at my desk in the church office working through some initial translations of the document, he telephoned me. He was emphatic that I do as instructed, quickly, without delay. He said that he was indeed being followed. He had little time left, and neither did I. He indicated that when I burned the original document, titled *A Psalm of the Apocalypse,* the flames and smoke from the burning would trigger the start of a series of events, catastrophic, eschatological end-time events. As these events unfolded I should write and record everything that happened – then get the written record, once completed – published without delay.

He shared many other things with me, gave me additional assignments, told me what to look for, and who to avoid. The first assignment was that which he had given in the sanctuary. I was to translate and eventually interpret *A Psalm of the Apocalypse,* written by a boy, John the Younger. It was originally written in New Testament *Koine Greek,* with some stanzas written in *Aramaic.* The translation revealed that the parchment was actually a sonnet, a psalm or psalter of the *Apocalypse,* comprised of a series of unbalanced verses and poetic stanzas. In substance, it was a faint foreshadowing of the end of what is and the beginning of what is yet to be. He also spoke of things that I will mention later, things about the boy, things about myself, things about the future, the end of the age, and many other things theological, philosophical and prophetic in nature. I asked if we would meet again. He said that he would always be near, even though I would be unaware of his presence.

When I asked his name he replied, *"Leitourgós."* I later discovered that the word *lietourgós* is used once, and only once, in the Bible; in the New Testament book of Hebrews, where it is translated as *"ministering spirits" – there are ministering spirits – lietourgós – sent out to serve for the sake of those who are to inherit salvation."*

His last words were a warning. "Beware of the man with one shoe."

With those words a smile came across my face. This was evidently some type of hoax or a well planned prank. In Virgil's *Aeneid* an oracle had warned King Pelias to beware of the man with one sandal. The search for the Golden Fleece was actually launched when Jason appeared before King Pelias – wearing one sandal. The next shoe to drop in this prank, I reasoned, would be the appearance of someone wearing one shoe.

Nevertheless, with a smile on my face I continued translating *A Psalm of the Apocalypse.* I was really not sure about whether or not I should actually burn the document. I was sure of one thing; however, I was definitely going to translate it. The initial translations proved to be rather unusual, unique – and intriguing, with its frequent references to *apocalyptic imagery* and *biblical numerology.* Finally, while praying and seeking God's guidance as I continued translating, I felt impressed to do as *Leitourgós* had instructed – and burn the document once the translation was complete.

I reasoned that if I chose to do nothing, other than simply translate, then nothing would happen since *Leitourgós* had indicated that the actual burning of the document would trigger the beginning of end time prophetic events. I also reasoned that if I chose to do as instructed and nothing happened, then, nothing would happen. Someone would have enjoyed their hoax and the joke would have been on me. On the other hand, if I chose to do as instructed, translated, transcribed, then burned the original document, well, if the flames and smoke then triggered the start of a series of yet unknown prophetic events, well, *the steps of the righteous are ordained by the Lord.* So what have I to fear? Anyway, it just might be that I am predestined -- predestined in the old Calvinist sense – to do this.

Even so, as I continued translating I was vacillating back and forth, wondering and worrying. Was the decision to burn the document the right decision? Or, should I wait, and perhaps consult with others -- *I was not sure.*

Later that evening the translation was complete. I then transcribed and saved the document into my laptop, then saved it in multiple computers, in different formats, in different locations via the internet. I was deep in thought, totally preoccupied with the task at hand, when the telephone rang. It was my wife, Emma.

"John, I'm at home and there's an elderly man, a really old man actually, that I've invited into the foyer. It's raining outside so I invited him in to get him out of the rain. Once inside he said he needed to see you immediately. He's mumbling that you have something that belongs to him and he wants it back. He appears to have a hearing problem. John, he's a pitiful looking old man, looks like he's at least a hundred years old and he walks with a walker. It looks like he suffering with the gout or something. Anyway, he seemed harmless enough when I invited him into the foyer but he's becoming quite agitated about whatever you have that belongs to him."

"Aw, Emma. I can't believe this. What would possess you to invite a stranger into our home – even if it's raining outside? Ask the old fellow his name. Who is he? What's his name?"

I was barely able to hear Emma's voice as she spoke with him. I could hear him, however, as he answered her with a very loud angry voice.

"Albert. My name is Albert. Tell him I want what is mine and I want it now. Tell him."

The hostility in his voice gave me shivers; and though his name, Albert, is not a frightful sounding name, it caused inexplicable waves of fear to rise within me.

"John, he said his name is…"

"Yes. His name is Albert. I heard him. Emma, a moment ago you said he has the gout or something. How do you know that? Why would you say that?"

"Well, he walks or should I say he limps with the aid of a walker. He constantly keeps his left leg bent at the knee and he slightly drags his left foot along without allowing it to touch the ground….and, just like my dad when he had the gout, the old man's wearing only one shoe."

I felt a dull ache in the pit of my stomach as I feared greatly what I subconsciously already knew: this was no prank.

"Emma. Listen carefully. I have reason to believe that this Albert fellow is dangerous. I want you to give him the telephone. As he and I talk I want you to leave the house immediately. I'll telephone you later this evening. Now, please, give the phone to Albert."

"Hello. This is Albert."

"Albert," I said loudly, "if you want what I have you will have to come to my church office to get it."

"What'd you say? Speak loudly so I can hear you."

"If you want what I have," I shouted, "you will have to come to my church office to get it."

Less than an hour later as the church elevator lifted Albert to my third floor office, I made a decision. The Bible speaks of the *"Valley of Decision."* This was my valley, this was my decision. A decision absolutely had to be made – at that very moment. The choice was mine – and so were the consequences.

Even as I write this, I wonder: What would you have done, reader? Put yourself, if you will, in my shoes. See through my eyes. What would you do? There is no time to wonder and no time to worry – *a decision must be made.*

As the elevator doors opened in the glare of light a figure emerged – it was Albert. His agitated voice filled my office as he limped toward me....

"I want what is mine and I want it now."

I pitched the original parchment -- *A Psalm of the Apocalypse* -- into the flames of an open fireplace. I had no idea at the time, however, of the high price that would have to be paid for that decision. As the flames rapidly consumed the parchment in the distance I heard a lonesome sound, the faint cry of a fog horn – the sound of a ship leaving the port of St. Bernard on the banks of the Mississippi River – taking passengers to an unknown destination.

Rain started falling, a hard-beating kind of rain, as lightning flashed across the black sky. Thunder rumbled repeatedly in the distance signaling distress as a dreaded storm approached.

My editor and publisher, as well as a few family members, friends and ministerial colleagues who have read advanced copies of this work have asked me, "Did these things really happen?"

My answer is simple: I have lived long enough to know that people believe what they want to believe. And, you too, dear reader, will believe what you want to believe. Whatever. I know what I know and I know what happened to me. After all, I was there, stranded on the roof top of *Christ Cathedral - The Church of the Last Judgment,* in the midst of the storm.

As my wife, Emma, once said, "Truth is sometimes stranger than fiction. Sometimes, what actually happens is more bizarre than anything imagined." The English novelist and poet Thomas Hardy, in a similar vein, once said that "while many things are too strange to be believed, nothing is too strange to have happened."[3] Again, I know what I know and I know what happened to me.

Do know this: everything that I have written has been written for a reason. Within that reason lies the kernel of cause and effect, which in turn leads to yet another effect which becomes the next cause. Think on this. Nothing that is written is written incidentally or accidentally. Everything that is written has a reason. Some of what is written may appear as a *riddle,* or as a *paradox* or *symbolic,* or even *antinomy.* Remember, in life and in literature things aren't always what they seem to be. Then again, sometimes they are. Wisdom discerns the difference, the difference between the story of what has happened and the story of what appears to have happened. What's really important is the moment at hand, the choices that flow from that moment and the consequential moments following choice.

As I write these words I can share that *A Psalm of the Apocalypse* has been translated, transcribed, and the original was burned, just as instructed. (A copy of the translation is printed in the pages immediately following this prologue). Its interpretation and meaning was eventually gained through the events that it triggered, events recorded in this book.

May God open your eyes that you may see His deeds,
and your ears that you may hear His voice as
He speaks to you.

There is something that must be established at this point, something vital. In the writing of and in the reading of a work such as this, you, the reader, and I, the writer, bring certain convictions with us. On some points, our convictions may be compatible. On other points, our convictions may differ. On still other points, our convictions may clash. This is the common experience of all people of faith. It seems that we can agree on many things but not all things.

Because this is so there is something that must be interjected at this point, some fundamental convictions that I embrace and bring with me to this work:

First, the Bible is Truth, God's Truth. It is Truth without any mixture of error. The Bible, and the Bible alone, is the standard of measure for all things pertaining to faith and practice – life and righteousness. People of biblical faith will embrace this fundamental conviction and be nurtured and challenged by what I have written. People of unbelief will be challenged too – as they explore and examine their unbelief.

Second, people of biblical faith have *convictions* built upon the Truth of God's Word. Hear me. He who writes what you are reading knows what he is talking about: *God's Truth is greater than our convictions. Convictions* grip us. They give us spiritual backbone. They help us to stand in the midst of swirling theological controversy, troubling trials and adversity. Nevertheless, even though we value our *convictions* and, indeed, even though our *convictions* are valuable, God's Word, God's Truth, is greater than our *convictions.* Our *convictions* are subservient, always subservient, to the Truth of God's Word; not the other way around. The Truth – God's Word -- is the standard of measure – not our *convictions.* May you discern the difference and be transformed by the renewing of your mind as you put on the mind of Christ.

Third, proceeding from *convictions* are *principles. Convictions* grip us. *Principles* guide us. *Principles* add flavor, shape and color to our *convictions* and their expression in life.

Fourth, flowing out of our *principles* are *predilections* and *preferences, options* and *opinions* – and from all of these -- *choices* -- and, that is where the rubber meets the road: we make *choices* and *choices have consequences.* And, it is here, in the consequences, that our destinies are shaped and our testimonies are shared.

Remember, when those who carry the torch tarnish or taint God's Truth, the Word of God is injured, violence is done to the church, and injustice is done to the common man.

Injury to the Word of God, because we have trivialized the eternal.

Violence to the church, because we have diminished the quality of the high standard of the biblical revelation.

Injustice to the common man, because he is led to embrace a brackish truth set forth by one who is disqualified by the Spirit of God for his failure to fulfill the first, basic, fundamental requirement: an unwavering allegiance to the Truth of God's revelation.

Finally, *Google is your friend.* Use it or the search engine of your choice to clarify any technical terms you may encounter as you read this document. Some words and phrases are *written in italics* as an interpretive aid to facilitate your reading and search engine experience.

In closing, I am and I remain…

Still Running the Race, In Christ
The Noble Army of the Martyrs Salute Thee
TE DEUM
Thee, O God, We Praise

A PSALM OF THE APOCALYPSE

THAT WHICH WAS, WHICH IS, AND IS YET TO COME

May God Open Your Eyes That You May See His Deeds,
and Your Ears That You May Hear His Voice

John the Younger, Son of Cosmas,
Son of John from the Isle of Greece

A Translation

In *the Candle* – in the darkness
A slender flame leaps – in solitude.
Its flame. Its flame.
With fiery mouth thunders.
Eschatos. Eschatos.
It Hungers. Hungers.
Its tongue, a flame, hungers.
Eschatos. Eschatos.
Shiv`a

Jezreel. Jezreel.
Stained with Blood. Graves, Open, Bone-Filled.

Widen their jaws.
A Gathering of Armies. Falling Stars.
Merj ibn-'Amir, the *Plain of Megiddo.*
War Men at the End of Time
Broken Seals. An Ancient Rhyme.
The Wound of Death. Blood, Bridle Deep.
Infidels Salute. Angels Weep.
TE DEUM.

Six, Imperfection, the Number of Man
Six thrice, Woe unto the Earth, the Beast
In the Latter Day, his Feast –
Six, Imperfection, the Number of Man
War Man at the End of Time
Zarathustra
An Image – A Symbol -- Who will understand?
Six thrice, the Number, the Beast, a Man
Shiv`a.

Zarathustra
A Dark Seed Blossoms
Flowers, Black, Three in Number, Stand Tall
Shadows, Bleak, a Terrible Fall.
Kyrie Boethei. Lord Help.
Lord Help Us All.
Trisagion – Holy, Holy, Holy
Thrice Holy -- Agios O Theos – Tersanctus.
TE DEUM.

Three. Three. Shaped by the Pen.
Recurrence. Recurring, Again and Again.
Philosophers Three – All Agree
What Ill Hath Befallen Thee
Camus' Foul Sons, Foul Sons Thou Art
Who are, will be, yet are not --

A Devious Plot.
He Who Has Eyes, See.
Unholy Trinity. – Unholy Three.
Avel.

Seven, the Number of Perfection
And of Weeks
Daniel saw Seventy, of Years
One Disappears, Cut Off – Eternal Tears
Yet, Once More, In the Holy Land
The Unholy *Zarathustra*
He Will Stand
Seven, Perfection. Six thrice, a Man.
Keriah.

One Week Remains, Singular. Alone.
Earth's Final Judgment – The Great White Throne
In *the Candle* – in the darkness
A slender flame leaps – in solitude.
Like a Sheep led to Slaughter
He Died for His Own
One Remains, Singular. Alone.
Shiv`a. Keriah. Avel. Keriah. Shiv`a.

One remains
Only One, One Week of Years
The Lamb, The Lion -- Final Tears
Jacob's Time of Trouble.
It now appears.
A labyrinth leads the way,
But not in the light of day.
The time is fulfilled.
Final Trump.
Shiv`a.

The horsemen. The horsemen.
Four in number.
Apocalypse. Apocalypse.
Do not slumber.
Burning Winds. Twisted Land.
Waters Rise and Rage.
Eschatos. Eschatos.
The Lion. The Lamb. The Cage.
Avel

Seven Cities Rise, Seven Cities Fall
One, On Seven Hills -- The Leader of All
Like A Rope Stretched O'er the Abyss
Unholy Pope. Something Amis.
Secular City, Once Sacred, Sterile, Stained Within
Antiochus. That Swine.
Flee Babylon, the Harlot, the Whore
The Closed Door.
Avel.

The Sound of Weeping
The Feel of Fear,
Jacob's Day of Trouble, Drawing Near
Nations Rejoice,
Blinded, No Choice
The Righteous, Few,
Beat The Breast, Bow The Head
Find A Pew
Shiv`a.

Seven Final Thunders
The Nations, They Shudder, They Cry
Mountains fall on us, lest we die
Seven Heads Turn, Seven Crowns Fall
Seven Kings Weep – Earth, Final Call

Can these bones live?
God's Scepter Shall Bless.
1000 years. A Holy Rest.
Selah.

Zarathustra. Zarathustra.
Overman, Underman, An Unholy Jeer.
A Divine Funeral,
The Procession Draws Near
The Sound of Weeping
Sharia law(less) Unholy Dread
Who Will Bow The Head
God Is Dead
Shiv`a. Keriah. Avel. Keriah. Shiv`a.

God Is Dead. God Is Dead.
Thus Spake Zarathustra –
His scandalous tongue seduces many
The Nations Shout with Glee
An Unholy Harmony
God Is Dead.
Say The Unholy Three
God Is Dead. God Is Dead.
Templum aedificavit – Build A Temple
TE DEUM.

Fiery Trial. Fiery Trial. A Hard Example.
Sacred Blood through Flames Trample.
Learn Patience Beneath their Altar
As they sing Retribution's Psalter
How long, O Lord, How long shall we wait?
The last living Martyr at *Menorah's Gate --*
His death will soon pass
The last shall be first and the first last
Shiv`a.

See -- The Just Man –
Struggling For Breath
Running to Certain Death
He, a Martyr, the Last, Runs, Yet Not Alone
Nor for sin does he Atone -- But for Fear
It crawls down his cheek, a tear
At his Death, Two Olive Trees, They Appear.
End Time Prophets. Slain. The Second Woe.
The first shall be last and the last first
Shiv`a.

Strong Nails, God's Men,
Refugees From The Past
Hold the Church Together, Stand, Steadfast
Through Pen, Through Pulpit
Astonish. Awaken. Arouse.
Knowing therefore the terror of the Lord
Soon Judgment Will Fall
The Wall, The Wall
On Which Ancient Prophets Wrote
Cracking at the Seams
Hell's Final Stroke

The Trump, The Trump
The Last, The Final Call
Even So, Come Quickly, Lord Jesus,
Come, Come for All
Pause. Praise.
His Anthem Raise.
Selah.

RESTORE POINT 1:

DARKNESS AND CONFUSION

It's Beautiful.
Look. On God's Finger. Look.
A Butterfly.

Darkness. Confusion.
A Distant Flash of Light.
Men Whispering. Men Cursing. Shouting. Crying.
Echoing. Echoing Inside My Head. Echoing.
Part Of A Fading Past. Part Of A Fuzzy Future.

Then, in muffled tones I heard myself speak…

"Where am I? Where am I?"
"I saw the Souls of the Martyrs."

Applause. Loud Applause. Cheers. More Applause.
The Sound, the Echoing Sound, of Fading Distant Applause.
A Distant Flash of Light.

"Propofol. Lorazepam. Midazolam."
"How much Sevo does he have on board?"

"Quickly. He's Light. He's Moving. Regaining Consciousness."
"The anesthesia is wearing off."
"Sevoflurane."

Blinded, I could not see, yet I could hear, vaguely, and once again, I heard my voice…

"I saw the Souls of the Martyrs."

"Calm Down, John. Calm Down. Calm Down, John. Calm Down."

"I saw the Souls of the Martyrs under the Altar."
"White Robes. White Robes were given unto every one of them. White Robes."

"Tighten his straps. He'll hurt himself."
"We've been monitoring you, John, Tracking you, every step of the Way."

"Where am I? And, and, who are you?"

"I am Dr. Bernard Rieux, Chief of Neurology, *Defense Advanced Research Projects Agency*"
"We're in an underground medical facility near Blacksburg, Virginia"

"Bernard. Bernard. Shut UP. SHUT UP. What are you doing? That's classified information."
"Don't Worry, Dr. Castel. He won't remember. Just having some fun. Mixing in a little *Déjà vu.*"

"Shut up, Bernard. SHUT UP. None of this is fun. NONE OF IT."
"Get a sense of humor, Dr. Castel. The versed will block the formation of memories."

"Where am I? Neurology? What are you talking about?"

The Strange Sound of a Distant, yet Familiar Voice
"You reached the Fifth Seal, John, you reached the Fifth Seal."

"Neurology? Fifth Seal? I don't understand."

Applause. Applause.
The Sound, the Echoing Sound, of Distant Applause.

"I saw the Souls of the Martyrs under the Altar."
"White Robes."

Darkness. Confusion.
A Distant Flash of Light.

"What are you talking about? Fifth Seal? What are you talking about?"

"Choices have Consequences, John. Choices have Consequences."

"Choices? Consequences? What are you talking about? Where am I? Who are you?"

"You must go back, John. You must go back."

"Go back? Go back where? What are you talking about?"

"You're going back, John, listen to me, you're going back to where it all began."

"Where it all began? Beginning? What are you talking about? I'm Confused."

"Propofol. Lorazepam. Midazolam."
"Give 'em more Sevo."
"Push the Propofol. Push the Propofol."
"Quickly. Memory Depletion. Limited Connectivity. Quickly."

"I saw the Souls of the Martyrs under the Altar."
"White Robes."

"Make a Faith Choice. John, Make a Faith Choice. Fear held you back."

Darkness. Confusion.
"Increase his dosage. Re-Boot. Re-Boot. Restore. Restore. Restore. Quickly."

Darkness. Confusion.
A Distant Flash of Light.

"He's Totally Sedated. Unconscious. Dr. Rieux, He's Totally Sedated."

"I HEARD You. Hand me the Drill, please….and the Tracer MC Device."
"Drill and Tracer MC Device."
I felt a stabbing in my head. Pain Danced and Drilled in my Brain.

"Hold His Mouth Open, Wide. I Need to Plant the Tracer in the back of his Jaw Bone."
"Good job, Bernard, Good job."

The Sound, The Sound, Of A Grinding Drill.
The Smell, The Smell, Of Burning Bone.

The Sound, the Echoing Sound, of Fading Distant Applause.
A Distant Flash of Light.

"Hand me the Cranial Metaphoric Imager, please… and the Cranial Inserter."
"Cranial Inserter and Metaphoric Imager."
"Thank you. Darn, the Imager is larger than I anticipated. Where's Grand?"

"Here sir, Grand here sir. Upper balcony, right concourse, sir."

"Grand, why is this Imager so large? I'll have to create a larger cranial cavity to make it fit."

"It's a Metaphoric MC 12,000, sir, the most powerful imager available at this time."

"Why so large?"

"It's needful, sir, he's a man of strong conviction, sir, very strong conviction."

A Distant Flash of Light.
Applause. Loud Applause. Cheers. More Applause.
Echoing. Echoing Inside My Head. Echoing.
Part of a Fading Past. Part of a Fuzzy Future.

"Truth is sometimes stranger than fiction. Sometimes, what actually happens is more bizarre than anything imagined." -- Emma

RESTORE POINT 2:

OCCAM'S RAZOR

I know. I know. It seemed crazy, absolutely crazy, insane, that this guy from Templeton was here, sitting across the table from my wife and me, sipping coffee. The irony of that statement is that, well, he just might think that I really am crazy. He really might.

Some people, when they hear my story, think I'm crazy and others think that those who think I'm crazy just might be right; and this guy from Templeton just might think the same thing. He really might.

Nevertheless, this is my story and I'm sticking with it.

Historically, the John Templeton Foundation is a religious grant writing organization. They provide grants and financial underwriting to individuals and organizations seeking to answer what they call, by their understanding, the "big questions" of human purpose, cosmic design, destiny and ultimate reality.

Templeton represents, at least in their minds, the saner voices seeking sanity in an insane world. Consequently, the Foundation is continuously engaged in relentless intellectual combat against the absurdist philosophical school of thought which believes that all efforts to find inherent meaning in life will ultimately fail.

Templeton's primary mission, according to their literature, is to foster informed dialogue among scientists, philosophers, theologians and the public at large. The Foundation's motto, "How little we know, how eager to learn," signals, according to their web page, "an open-minded sense of inquiry."

Implication: They're a left wing, theologically liberal, philosophical think tank. Templeton would probably disagree with that description but when the chips are down, you know which way they're going to go – to the left.

That "open-minded sense of inquiry" made me wonder all the more: Why was *their* representative here? Why did he want to interview *me*? Why did he want to hear *my* story? If anything the liberal crowd typically associated with Templeton would cast a suspicious eye at me, label me as a "closed-minded" Bible-thumping fundamentalist – probably call me names, like "crazy" and promptly dismiss me as insane.

Whatever. I know what I know. I know a day is coming when the wolf and the lamb shall graze together, the leopard will lie down with the goat[4] and the lion shall lay down with the lamb. In that day all things shall subsist in harmony in Christ. There shall be no divisive liberal standing against the fundamentalist, nor shall moderates vilify conservatives. All things shall be one in Christ – without any heretical overtone of oneism. *But, not yet.* That day is not yet. And, so, until that day, we may agree on many things but not all things. Polarization.

He who writes this knows this because of what happened. After all, I was there, stranded at *Christ Cathedral - The Church Of The Last Judgment,* in the midst of the storm. They weren't. What did Templeton know? And, so what if they might think that I was crazy, or insane, or the victim of some sort of psychotic break. *Christ Cathedral* was real. Dr. Bernard Rieux was there. Albert Camus was there. Other people were there too – inside the cathedral -- and I was one of them.

So here we were, Emma and me and Mr. Joseph Grand, a representative of the John Templeton Foundation, muddling through perfunctory introductions. I said nothing, silently nodded my head, shook Mr. Grand's hand, helped Emma with her chair, then quietly sat down – and waited for the conversation to begin. My head trembled for just a second, as I sipped the strong, dark, caffeine-laced coffee at *Café' du Monde* in New Orleans, Louisiana. *Wow. This coffee is strong.*

The *French Market,* where the coffee stand is located, is comprised of six blocks of European style shops and restaurants, a massive *Flea Market* and a recently renovated distinctively *French Market* place that sells fresh fish, vegetables, pottery, jewelry, imported goods and the like. Even though it was February, the Quarter was hot and sweaty, filled with people, plenty of people, and plenty of sights and sounds, odors and smells.

A unruly man, seated at a table across from us, kept loudly blowing his nose as he unpacked a sandwich wrapped in aluminum foil. He grunted with each sip of coffee and actually moaned while eating his sandwich.

The Quarter always seemed provocative, tantalizing, teasing the senses, intentionally appealing to the sensual. Raymond Rambert was a journalist from Paris that I'd met at *Christ Cathedral.* Rambert, with his strong sensual longing for lost love would have been most comfortable here in the French Quarter. Not so, however, for Dr. Rieux. Dr. Castel? No. The priest Father Paneloux? No. Definitely no.

The famed *Jackson Square,* also known as *Place d'Armes*, the most historic park in New Orleans, was directly across the street from our table at *Café' Du Monde.* The Square, as always, was a hub of activity, with artists, street vendors, musicians, horse drawn carriages and more – all competing for tourist dollars. The outstretched branches of moss covered dark oak trees wrapped around one another, providing shade and character to the square; and, a safe haven for pigeons. "Pigeons," the jovial Monsieur Jean Tarrou would say, "are winged-rats. Rats with wings, that's what pigeons are: rats with wings."

The Cathedral-Basilica of St. Louis King of France, better known as St. Louis Cathedral, is the oldest Cathedral in North America. Just as the oak tree branches of *Jackson Square* wrapped around one another so too had the Cathedral become entangled, deeply entangled, with the life of the city. The Cathedral serves as a towering spiritual backdrop for *Jackson Square,* the *French Quarter* and the city of New Orleans. The nostalgic tolling of the cathedral bells, hidden behind a grey stone bell tower, drifted across the city while Gregorian Chant echoed throughout the empty spaces of the cathedral. Kierkegaard, the prominent theologian and prolific theological writer during the Danish "golden age" of philosophical inquiry would have found strength in the shadow of the Cathedral's three crosses.

The towering crosses atop *St. Louis Cathedral* and my passing memory of Kierkegaard triggered a quick flashing thought of despair. It provoked an unpleasant memory and an uncomfortable feeling of despondency that

I encountered during my stay at *Christ Cathedral.* Albert Camus, Sarte, Feuerbach, Nietzesche, and their existential companions were more suited for that desolate place than I.

"Let me be clear about this, Mr. Grand. We're not exactly sure why you're here. Obviously, we know your visit is connected with what happened during the hurricane – at *Christ Cathedral.* We do not, however, fully understand the specific intention and purpose of your visit."

As Emma spoke, focusing on the purpose of our meeting, she moved forward slightly, adjusting her chair, and wrapping her hands around her cup of coffee, before continuing.

"At the very onset, Mr. Grand, I want you and the people at Templeton to know, and I want anyone who hears about or reads what you write about my husband's incident to know, that he is a truthful man. His integrity is solid. There's not a dishonest bone in his body."

Emma was passionate, forceful and firm as she spoke, undaunted and undeterred by the chatter of coffee drinkers at the surrounding tables and the clatter of their cups. We married nearly forty-four years ago, raised three college educated children, and attended both college and completed our master's level work in theology together at the New Orleans seminary. Only later, did I go it alone to complete the theological studies necessary to receive my doctorate.

As far as I am concerned, and I'm fairly well read, Emma is one of the finest theologians I have ever encountered. Her only shortcoming is her lack of discipline in devoting time to complete her theological writings. If anyone would have asked me, say twenty years ago, which of us would be interviewed by the John Templeton Foundation my vote would have been cast for Emma.

"Mr. Grand, as far as my husband's altered thinking in the aftermath of his *Christ Cathedral* experience, I've listened very carefully to what he has had to say. I've read what he has written. We've talked and talked and talked, over and over again, about the content and implications of his reflections. His premises *are* theologically solid. His philosophical conclusions *are* biblically consistent, rational, logical – and intuitive, very intuitive. There's only one problem, one major problem, Mr. Grand, as you are well aware -- none of what my husband says happened actually happened. Think about it. *The Church of the Last Judgment.* Dr. Bernard Rieux. *A Psalm of the Apocalypse. The Souls of the Martyrs under the Altar.* None, absolutely none of what my husband says happened occurred. It's simply impossible."

She paused for just a moment to take a sip of coffee, focus her thoughts and catch her breath. She was very much like a she-bear defending her cub, forcefully protective, a modern-day Artemis, with her bows fully drawn, ready to strike with the least provocation.

In my line of sight behind Emma, directly across the street by *Jackson Square*, I saw a waiter wearing a long white apron sweeping sawdust in an empty restaurant. I also caught a glimpse of the ever-present silver spray-painted Silver Statue man. Like an eternal sentinel, he can always be found on Decatur Street across from *Café' Du Monde*, standing there at the corner of the *Square,* motionless.

Across from the Silver Statue man stood a pan handler, capitalizing on his disability. He had a wooden peg leg and was dressed as a pirate. He had a black patch over one eye, wore a red bandana knotted over one part of his head, a large gold earring – and demanded loot from friendly tourists.

The *French Quarter* has a ton of street performers. Some play musical instruments. Others sing, or dance, or juggle. Street performers do just about anything to half-way entertain in an effort to earn a few dollars. If a street performer can't do anything that requires talent then he can spray paint himself silver from head to toe, stand motionless, and become a human statue. There are a lot of Silver Statue men in the quarter who simply stand there. Tourists pose with them for souvenir photographs and then drop a dollar or two in their silver painted bucket. Crazy world, isn't it?

"Mr. Grand, my husband is lucid, coherent and sane, but, none of what he says happened actually happened. Yes, there was a storm, a terrible hurricane, but, there was not and never has been a *Christ Cathedral* in lower St. Bernard parish. There was no Dr. Bernard Rieux on the roof top of a non-existent *Christ Cathedral* and he was not treating diseased people stranded on the roof top, on inside of or in the shadow of *Christ Cathedral* during the storm. No one died on the roof top because there was no roof top and there were no sick, dying people infected with some type of deadly plague. There was no suicide attempt by a fictitious Cottard who tried to hang himself. He didn't exist either. Mr. Grand, there was no Jean Tarrou from the University of Paris, France, who vehemently objected to what he called 'metaphysical madness.'"

Emma paused temporarily, took another sip of coffee, then continued speaking.

"You see, Mr. Grand, there's a real problem here for my husband. None of what he says happened actually happened. These people did not and do not exist. These are not flesh and blood real people. Each one of them, as you well know, are actually fictitious characters in a novel written by the existentialist Albert Camus. The events associated with my husband and these people never occurred. The *Christ Cathedral* incident never happened. The events inside the cathedral never happened. Everything about *Christ Cathedral*, everything that has been told and retold again and again – these things simply *did not happen.*"

"Well, actually" replied Mr. Grand, as he looked directly at Emma, "the context that spawned and gave birth to your husband's understandings, that context, whether real or imagined, is not as germane as the content of his thought."

Mr. Grand was tall, lanky and thin, with smallish shoulders. Some would say that he was skinny. He had blondish-red, shoulder length hair and a large yellowish mustache. He looked rather eccentric, wearing a bow tie and a sweater vest, even though it was a hot, sweaty day. I wonder what image Mr. Grand was seeking to convey.

"Somewhere, somehow, in the theological, therapeutic understandings that have emerged from the infamous *Christ Cathedral*, a rather simplistic, yet profound new way of thinking has surfaced. Large portions of both the American and European population have begun to employ that therapeutic way of thinking to safety navigate the complexities of life. That phenomena and the content of this new way of thinking is of great interest to our Foundation. Our primary goal is to better understand the deeper implications of these new theological therapies. We have no interest in how they were procured. Our interest is in how they are deployed."

"Yes, but...." interjected Emma, before being quickly cut off by Mr. Grand.

"No. No. Please allow me to continue, Emma. Let me add that I'm not a physician, nor am I a neurologist and I am certainly not a scientist. I don't know if something physiological happened or if something neurological occurred or if we are dealing with some kind of atmospheric phenomenon. I'm not qualified to offer a diagnosis or a prognosis or to differentiate from these and other options. I don't know what happened. But this I do know: something happened, something very strange – with an apparent positive outcome."

Mr. Grand paused for a moment, scanning our faces, seeking to determine our reaction to what he was saying. I was feeling comfortable, very comfortable, sipping my coffee, listening to Mr. Grand and Emma talk. The coffee was warm and the caffeine was strong; and so was the conversation.

"I'm also not a philosopher nor am I a theologian, at least not in the strictest sense. I'm actually a retired civil servant under contract to Templeton, writing a series of articles on philosophical and theological issues. My assignment is to analyze the conflicts within and the compatibilities between various competing therapeutic schools of thought. So, I'm simply a writer serving at the bequest of the Foundation."

Mr. Grand paused, just for a second, adjusted his bow tie, and cleared his throat before he continued speaking. It was during that brief pause that he felt an intense stab of anxiety. He was no writer and he knew it. He was a gifted conversationalist and speaker; but, he simply could not write. Grand had been trying, unsuccessfully, for years, to write a book; but, he had never gotten past the opening line. He just couldn't express himself in written formats. And Templeton? And this assignment? This was his last chance, his final opportunity, as a writer, and he knew it.

As he cleared his throat again, he struggled to move beyond his anxiety.

"I do remember, however, while attending college," he continued, "I remember something called *Occam's Razor*, a philosophical tool utilized to validate and verify conclusions. *Occam's Razor* essentially states that when you have two or more competing theories about something and they're heading toward the same conclusion, the simpler theory is better. My simple theory and conclusion is this – something happened. I'm not here to determine what happened. Whatever happened, however, seems to have caused your husband to see things in a way that he hadn't seen things before, to understand things in a different way. That's why I'm here; to explore that different way of thinking, that different way of seeing. Your husband, from what I understand, calls this…."

"*Metaphorics*," I finally spoke, finishing his sentence.

He appeared startled when I spoke. He was so engrossed with what he had to say about me that he seemed to have forgotten me. I don't know. Maybe I was like that Silver Statue man. He wasn't supposed to move… and I wasn't supposed to speak, at least not until the appropriate time. Perhaps when called upon to speak, like a child, or like someone who was mentally impaired, perhaps insane.

But, I spoke.

"Mr. Grand, *metaphorics* or the practice of *metaphorical thinking* has been around since the dawn of time. It is not a new way of thinking. It's a biblical way of thinking, a way of thinking that enables one to see – utilizing images -- the reality of what is unfolding and why it is unfolding within the context of one's life. This way of thinking, as I share with my pen and through my pulpit, might be compared to the childhood challenge of discovering the 'hidden pictures' in children's magazines. When I was a boy these 'hidden picture' sketches were popular."

I shifted my position on my chair, stiffened my back, and positioned myself so as to look directly into the eyes of Mr. Grand.

"Mr. Grand, in these childhood pen and ink sketches an image was presented to the reader, perhaps of a cloud-covered mountain surrounded by tall trees and a calm lake. Beneath the cleverly drawn sketch were instructions challenging the reader to examine the sketch closely -- to search for certain things that no rational mind would have reason to believe were in the sketch – 'hidden pictures.' Camouflaged within the sketch were objects. The mountain hid a hamburger. A tree branch was actually a toothbrush. The lines around the lake formed a baseball bat. 'Hidden images,' on closer inspection, would suddenly emerge. The reader could not be talked into seeing these 'hidden pictures' -- they had to be seen. They were either seen or they were not. That was the challenge of the game: to see that which was not readily seen, that which no one expected to see. Once the 'hidden pictures' were seen, however, they became plainly visible whenever the sketch was viewed."

The hook had been baited. The line had been cast. Mr. Grand bit. He was intrigued by the utter simplicity of the analogy of the 'hidden pictures.' I sensed it as he leaned forward toward me. I could see it in his eyes.

"People do not fall into crisis because truth has failed," I continued. "Mr. Grand, people fail because they simply do not see the false 'hidden pictures' sketched and imbedded in the mental images that guide their lives."

He moved.

He moved. I've never seen that happen before...the motionless Silver Statue man suddenly moved. He reached down to pick up his silver-painted cash box, crossed the street, sat at a table directly across from us, and ordered a cup of coffee.

I'd never seen that before...he moved. The Silver Statue man moved.

And, just as quickly I moved. Placing my hands in my pockets I walked around the coffee tables, squeezed between the crowds, and started walking toward the parking lot to retrieve our car.

"Emma. Mr. Grand. Let's go to Chalmette."

Mr. Grand was caught off guard. Emma was startled. One of them quickly paid the waiter and just as quickly they squeezed through the crowded tables of coffee drinkers to fall in line behind me. I smiled a silly smile as I quickly walked out of *Café' du Monde* toward the parking lot. The proverbial worm had turned. They were now like small children, hurriedly racing with short legs to catch up and keep up.

As we walked away I turned to catch a final glimpse of the Silver Statue man. Our eyes met. I nodded my head in gesture toward him, smiled again – and winked. He in turn nodded his head toward me, smiled a sly knowing smile – and winked back. – *Déjà vu.*

RESTORE POINT 3:

POLARIZATION

As Emma drove our vehicle through the main *French Market* parking lot behind *Café' du Monde,* which runs parallel to the Mississippi River, we passed by the *Moonwalk*, named after a former mayor of New Orleans. We then drove through the connecting *Farmer's Market* parking lot that exits near the historic Esplanade Avenue.

This segment of Esplanade Avenue, blessed with beautiful large oak trees that shadow neighborhood homes, runs from the Mississippi River to N. Rampart Street. Esplanade Avenue separates the *French Quarter* from the storied *Faubourg Marigny.* The Marigny was at one time a segregated Louisiana Creole area where white Creole gentlemen set up households for their mistresses of color.

Gentle winds, like soft whispers, began to rustle and blow through the massive oaks, signaling an approaching rain. The skies began to darken as grey clouds gathered overhead. A faint echo of thunder softly rumbled in the distance.

"Mr. Grand, do you have children?"

"Yes, I do, but they're adults, married, making their way in the world, as they say."

Grand wouldn't say it, couldn't say it, but even though his children were indeed now grown, with children of their own, something was wrong with their relationship. Either his children were essentially unlovable, or he was. They weren't interested in him and he wasn't interested in them. They disregarded his opinions and he did likewise. To make matters worst it bothered him that it didn't bother him that things were as they were. *Que Sera Sera. Whatever Will Be Will Be.*

"Wonderful. We have something in common," I said. "Our children are grown too."

Grand smiled a fake smile. We had nothing in common.

"When we were in *Café' Du Monde*," I continued, "you indicated that one of your primary goals was to better understand the biblical concept of *metaphorical thinking*. I'd like to tell you how I originally came across this concept. It might be helpful for your articles."

"Sounds like a good place to begin. Tell me about it."

Grand took out a small iPad, created several folders and started typing notes to detail and record our conversations.

"Good, my earliest exposure to *metaphorical thinking* began with an incident that happened with our youngest daughter many years ago. She was but a child, a little girl who usually wore pig tails and always sat quietly in church. Sometimes, I can close my eyes and still see her, sitting crossed-legged on the back pew of the church; and sometimes I can still hear her soft, excitable child's voice."

"I like him daddy. When he preaches, I see cartoons."

"Our youngest daughter spoke those words nearly thirty years ago. I've never forgotten our conversation as she explained what she meant by *cartoons*. Somehow, in ways that are beyond my ability to explain, I grabbed a hold of her childlike cartoon analogy and her cartoon analogy grabbed a hold of me."

"What she was saying then," said Grand, "is that the preacher used language in such a way that she could see or visualize what he was saying."

Grand tilted his head, thought within himself, then said…

"I wish I could use language like that."

Slowly, Emma drove past the old New Orleans branch of *the U.S. Mint building*. Its tall pillars towered above the French-styled black wrought iron fence that surrounded the stone courtyard facing the *French Market*. Structural damage to *the Mint* from the hurricane was limited. A large piece of the copper roof was blown off, causing only minor water damage in the office areas below.

I nodded my head in the direction of *the Mint* building and continued talking. Mr. Grand turned his head toward the stately old building, nodded his head and continued listening.

"You wish you could use language like that? Well, you can and you will, Mr. Grand. We'll make that one of our goals as we discuss *metaphorical thinking.*"

"I like him daddy. When he preaches, I see cartoons."

"What she was saying, Mr. Grand, was that the preacher, a master story-teller, a Rev. Daniel Lanier, somehow created mental images, word pictures, metaphors – *cartoons* -- she called them – that enabled her to understand biblical truth."

For Grand using language that way would be a dream come true. Ever since his ex-wife, Jeanne, left him, years ago, he had tried to write her a letter, but he failed in his efforts to find words that expressed what he felt. This problem – *verbal paralysis* – evidently was rooted in a dysfunctional childhood. It was a childhood disorder that he had not yet overcome.

I was familiar with language disorders and speech impediments. When I was a child I too had a rare speech disorder that caused me to repeat sentences and speak in rhyme. My relief came in a rather miraculous way through a strange legless man. Everyone in our neighborhood knew the legless man. He sat on a wooden board that had casters, little wheels, mounted on the bottom. The casters were his legs, his means of transportation. He could usually be found seated by a grocery store on the corner of Washington Avenue and Annunciation Street in the Irish Channel section of New Orleans. That's where I lived when I was a child.

The legless man always had an old tin can stuffed with yellow pencils in front of him and beside it, an empty cigar box where people would toss a few coins or a couple of dollars in return for a pencil. I can still hear the legless man's voice as he called out to passersby, "Pencils. Ten cents. Pencils. Ten cents."

The neighborhood rumor was that once a year the legless man would go to church and give away two special pencils, two miracle pencils. Whoever received these two pencils would have to give one away which would then trigger a miracle for two people, rather than just one.

One day, while I was helping at church the legless man, who was also at church, gave two pencils to a stranger, an older man who was very upset with God. I did not know the older man, at least not at that time. I only remember that he was crying and calling for God to help him.

"Kyrie Boethei. Lord Help. Kyrie Boethei. Lord Help."

The priest talked with the man for a little while and then the man left. Later, I don't remember when, I don't remember why, but later I met the man when he came back to church. We talked a little while. He noticed that I had a speech impediment. He gave me one of his pencils, told me to place it crosswise in my mouth and then he told me to bite as hard as I could until the pencil broke. I did and from that day forward my speech disorder disappeared. So, Mr. Grand did not know it but I was quite familiar with language disorders and speech impediments.

"Drive slowly, Emma, dear. Let's enjoy the sights, the sounds and the shade. And if a parking place is available pull the car over when you get to N. Rampart Street. There's something there that I'd like Mr. Grand to see."

The hurricane, which had a disastrous effect on large portions of New Orleans, did less damage in the Esplanade area than in other parts of the city. This section of Esplanade Avenue, on the river side of N. Rampart, suffered some wind damage but very little flooding, especially in comparison to the flooding which inundated St. Bernard parish. Nevertheless, tragedy had touched this area too – Esplanade was not exempt from nor escaped the suffering caused by the storm.

"I did not realize it then, Mr. Grand, but my daughter's cartoon analogy was serving as the initial catalyst for *metaphorics*. The mental image of my daughter being impacted in a profound way by mental images became an image within itself that shaped my early understanding of the power of metaphors. Many other experiences and exposures, especially the experiences related to *Christ Cathedral*, fleshed out and firmed up my positions concerning *metaphorics*."

The flush of pink and red azaleas beneath the large oaks on the neutral ground of Esplanade Avenue danced in the gentle twisting winds. The phrase *neutral ground* in New Orleans is our phrase for the median in the middle of a street or avenue. Many years ago, perhaps a century or so, there were serious ethnic tensions between several immigrant groups because of their different nationalities, lifestyles, manners, and values. The neutral grounds were the safe places where these groups would meet, transact business, and sometimes socialize, without tension, fist fights, or physical violence. Today even newer streets that didn't exist until long after those ethnic tensions ceased have neutral grounds - never "medians," at least not in New Orleans.

"Though the image of my daughter's *cartoon* experience served as a personal catalyst for me, I soon discovered that the use of metaphors to convey truth is rooted in biblical antiquity – and came to flower through the New Testament teachings of Jesus."

As Emma continued driving I shared with Mr. Grand that the language of Genesis, the first book of the Bible, especially concerning the fourth day of creation, goes far beyond the physical event of God creating the sun, moon and stars. These celestial objects have several natural, astronomical functions, one of which, of course, is to govern the seasons.

"However, the sun, moon, and stars were not only given for seasons, Mr. Grand. God says they are given *'for signs.'* As *signs* they convey a message and, the message has a meaning."

Grand cocked his head to the side, stared at me, just for a moment, and then allowed a half-smile to play across his face. That half-smile; it triggered something within me, an eerie feeling. I felt a cold shiver running through my body, accompanied by a strange compelling sense of familiarity. A feeling of *Déjà vu.* quickly surfaced, then just as quickly vanished. It felt like I'd been here before, with Mr. Grand, in this automobile, on this very street. *Strange. The feeling was not a pleasant experience.*

"You know," said Mr. Grand, "I've read that Genesis passage many times and I was aware of that wording – *'for seasons and for signs'* – yet I've never really given serious thought to the implications of the word *'signs'* until I began preparing for this assignment from Templeton."

Because of its proximity to the *French Quarter* this section of Esplanade Avenue always produces a carnival of Bohemian sights and sounds. It might just be that the sights, sounds, and scents of this section of the city are cultural signs or *cultural metaphors* indicating that life is lived a little differently here. As we continued to drive up Esplanade, the competing sounds of Dixie Land jazz, rhythmic blues and other types of music poured out of open barroom doors and the open windows of sidewalk restaurants and coffee houses.

On the other side of the *neutral ground* an array of colorful characters sat on the concrete sidewalks, called *banquettes* in New Orleans. They leaned against the outside walls of several of the buildings. A scrawny, gawky framed tall girl wearing a decorative patch over her right eye and a loose-fitting bohemian outfit strummed a banjo. Across from her a bare-footed male wearing a yellow bandana, bobbed his head up and down to an imaginary beat. A strange mix of eclectic and eccentric locals and tourists walked by; an unusual mixture of ordinary looking people who mingled and meandered through a thin crowd of weirdoes, shoppers, and homeless people – the whole shebang.

Looking across the *neutral ground* brought to mind a statement by C. S. Lewis, "There is no neutral ground in the universe. Every square inch, every split second is claimed by God, and counterclaimed by Satan." [5]

I thought about Lewis, looked at the neutral ground, then at Grand, then at the boy with the bandana – and felt a stirring, a stirring like a fire in my bones.

"Now, at this point in our conversation, let me be clear about something, Mr. Grand. Just as you and I are different, say, from that young man by that coffee shop over there. I'm talking about the bare-footed guy with the yellow bandana on his head leaning against the wall of the coffee shop. Just as you and I are different from him in the way we think, feel and make choices in life – so too are you and I different, one from another, in our theological positions and persuasions."

Grand appeared startled at this change of direction in our conversation. He knew we were on opposite ends of the theological spectrum when he accepted this assignment. He hadn't anticipated, however, that he would be forced to deal with our differing theological positions, at least not so early in the interview.

"We both know, Mr. Grand, that I am a biblical fundamentalist deeply entrenched in the fundamentalist theological camp. I want to be clear about this *metaphor* business. I and others like me are convinced, it is our conviction, that the Genesis creation account is literal history and not *metaphorical* in any sense of the word. I make no apology for what I believe, no apology for where I stand, and no apology concerning whom I stand with in matters of faith, practice and biblical interpretation. I don't want to be ornery or contentious, Mr. Grand, but I also don't want to be misrepresented or misunderstood on this point."

As we drove down Esplanade Avenue, one of the major avenues of the *Big Easy,* there was nothing easy about our conversation at this point. We were dealing with the inevitable at the very start of our conversation -- our theological differences and our theological distinctions.

"Templeton has taught me," related Grand, "that the place where people deal with differences is the place where true compatibility begins. Nevertheless, theological debate, as you already know, is always complicated and has the potential to become deeply personal, especially when two people seek to close the gap between the *possible* and the *actual*, without compromise."

"Well, Mr. Grand, from my perspective, I'm not sure about your definitions of *possibilities* or *actualities.* What I do know is that compromise is the negation of conviction and creates a false compatibility that will eventually self-destruct. As for myself, I know who I am. I know where I have been, where I am, and where I'm going with the Lord. I have convictions about that, Mr. Grand -- and, there's no room for compromise and certainly no room for false compatibilities."

The tension was escalating. While the tone of our voices was civil, civility could not hide the stress created by our conflicting theological positions.

"Well, from my point of view," interjected Mr. Grand, "philosophical and theological questions, which contrast and compare *possibilities* and *actualities*, can never be answered with complete finality. And therein lies the necessity of compromise. Because there can be no complete finality there must be compromise. All of our *possibilities* and *actualities* create philosophical and theological questions which are processed by reason, which is fallible, and fallible reason necessitates compromise."

"Now, you may think I'm bull headed, Mr. Grand, but I do know this: problems arise when men compromise God's biblical revelation. Reason may be fallible but God's revelation is not. And, Mr. Grand, fallible reason does not necessitate compromise; fallible reason necessitates revelation.

"Well, as you are aware," said Grand arrogantly, "the relationship between revelation and reason has always been a theological concern. Does faith seek understanding or does understanding seek faith? Which is it? Either/Or? Both/And? Some theologians completely eliminate one or the other from their theological systems. Others tend to favor one over the other. Still others treat both with equal emphasis. The amusing thing, from the way I see it, is that each feels that the other is, as you said, bull headed."

Grand, bending his face into a single wrinkle, had the look of composed satisfaction. It was as if he was saying through his facial expression that he was not bull headed, but rather a contented compromiser.

"It is the function of philosophy to ask questions," asserted Grand with a quick, sharp nod of his head.

"And it is the function of theology to give answers,' I replied. "Ask your philosophical questions, Mr. Grand, and the Bible will be as a map with an X marking the spot where your head needs to be buried to find your answer."

Grand sat with his arms folded across his chest and didn't answer. The muscles of his face were strained, tightly contorted. He was either pouting or biting his tongue.

"I guess you're going to tell me now that God created everything out of nothing," snorted Grand.

"Quite honestly, that was not my intention, but, since you brought it up, God did create everything out of nothing -- *ex nihilo* is the theological term."

"Ex nihilo. Ex nihilo. Ex nihilo." mocked Grand. "Metaphysical Madness. Sheer Metaphysical Madness."

"Who is mad, Mr. Grand, "the man who believes that the world was created *by nothing* or the man who believes that the world was created *by Someone?* Your atheistic view of creation – *nothing created something from nothing* – requires a greater miracle and greater faith that the theist view – *Someone creating something from nothing.*

"You and your metaphysical magicians declare the world came into existence by *chance,* Mr. Grand. But, really, what is this thing you call *chance?* Can you tell me the color of this thing you call chance? How much does this thing called *chance* weight? What is the size of this thing called *chance?* You cannot answer any of these questions, Mr. Grand, because *chance* is not a thing. It is a no thing, Mr. Grand, a no thing. A no thing is *nothing* and according to your own definition of terms the world was created by a no thing, by *nothing.* Your atheistic view of creation – *Nothing (chance) creating something from nothing* requires a greater miracle and greater faith, Mr. Grand, that the theistic view – *Someone creating something from nothing.* There is metaphysical madness, much metaphysical madness in the atheistic position, Mr. Grand. A man would have to turn his brains off to believe such nonsense.

"Listen, Mr. Grand," I said intentionally softening the tone of my voice. "Being a biblical fundamentalist does not mean I have to turn my brains off when I open my Bible. God gives us the ability to think and the ability to use reason to contemplate His revelation…and, they both come into play when I study my Bible. Nevertheless, God's revelation always has precedence over man's reason and reasoning ability. God's revelation enables a person who receives it to suddenly see what has always been available for every one to see. Faith in this revelation allows us to know the unknowable, see the unseeable, think the unthinkable, hear the inaudible and plumb the depths of God's revelation.

"It's not that I reject reason and *rational arguments* to prove the existence of God or *theistic creation.* It's that I do not rely on *rational arguments* to substantiate my faith.

"God, Mr. Grand, can never be defined. He who is *infinite* cannot be defined because to define is to *'de' 'finite'.* That, dear sir, is not only a contradiction of terms but an impossibility. No one and nothing can *'de' 'finite'* the *infinite.* Thus, He who is *Infinite* cannot be defined, nor can our limited, rational understanding contain or fully grasp the *Infinite One.* Such is the life of faith in God and in His self-revelation. God, Mr. Grand, cannot be made to fit within the limits of our rational understanding. God is beyond the scope of rational thought – thus, God makes Himself known -- *revelation, with Christ as the Interpreter of God.*"

Emma sat straight, gripping the steering wheel as she continued to drive down Esplanade Avenue. Her neck was delicate, graceful as she nodded her head in agreement as I spoke.

"When I open my Bible, Grand, I find that the traditional tools of biblical interpretation, tools such as *literary analysis, language studies, word studies, syntax* and *etymology,* when applied to the linguistic structure of Genesis – these tools verify that the Genesis account is actually a historical narrative. There is absolutely no evidence, internal, external or otherwise, to suggest that there is anything non-literal or figurative in the Genesis creation narrative. Adam is not a *metaphor.* Neither is Eve, nor Eden. Adam and Eve were both real people, created by God, at a particular point in time, at a specific place. There is nothing mythical, nothing metaphorical, and nothing symbolic about either of them or about the historic acts of creation."

"You do realize that other theologians do not see it that way," said Mr. Grand.

"Well, I'll tell you how I feel about that. There is, indeed, a pitiable shallowness today that is mixing Truth with the murky waters of evolutionary thought. These cognitive wanderers, these other theologians, as you called them, with their minds steeled against the truth, dot the historical landscape, primarily of the last century. These confused modern day theological mavericks who attempt to marry Moses and Darwin to accommodate some kind of spiritualized evolutionary union stand guilty of exegetical folly and foolishness...and, as a consequence, many salt-of-the-earth people sit in the shadow of their confusion, totally confused."

"You seem to feel very strongly then that there is some sort of theological conspiracy and some type of theological betrayal at work," Grand said with a look of peevish satisfaction.

"Mr. Grand," I said sharply, "you well know that words like *conspiracy* and *betrayal* are inflammatory. The word *inflammatory* comes from the Latin word *'inflammare'* which means *to set on fire.* It is not my intention to inflame anyone, nor is it my intention to judge anyone. It is, however, my responsibility to *discern,* another Latin word, Mr. Grand, another Latin word that means *to separate,* as in separating that which is true from that which is false. And, here, Mr. Grand, is what I have discerned: When those who carry the torch tarnish or taint truth, the Word of God is injured, violence is done to the church, and injustice is done to the common man. Injury to the Word of God, because we have trivialized the eternal. Violence to the church, because we have diminished the quality of the high standard of the biblical revelation. Injustice to the common man, because he is led to embrace a brackish truth set forth by one who is disqualified by the Spirit of God for his failure to fulfill the first, basic, fundamental requirement: an unwavering allegiance to the Truth of God's revelation."

Grand listened and stared intently. He knew, deep within himself, that there was a reason as to why we were here, a reason that went beyond the Templeton assignment. Though I did not know it at the time Grand knew that this was his last opportunity, his last chance. The choices he made from this point forward were irreversible. If he was not careful he would become like Esau who found no place for repentance, though he sought it diligently with tears – *Déjà vu.*

"People today are seeking and longing for, not a modern God made in the image of man, Mr. Grand, but the ancient God of Scripture, the God of Abraham, Isaac and Jacob, the God and Father revealed through the Son and confirmed by the Spirit."

Grand listened silently, yet a little anxiously. His mood had changed, softened. He was fascinated with this conversation, yet, he hadn't anticipated it. On the inside he knew somehow that he was supposed to be here, yet, he felt queasy, unsettled. He was a liberal, a theological liberal. He had built his theological house on sand and he was beginning to sense that he was sinking. Once or twice he had sung *On Christ the Solid Rock I Stand* – but he had never really stood on that Rock. Even so, he somehow found himself strangely attracted to and intrigued by fundamentalism allegiance to Christ and the Bible.

Grand shifted his position, then wiped his forehead with his handkerchief. There was something missing in Grand's life. He had known that for quite some time. There was this sense of ambiguity, a lack of certitude, which always surfaced when Grand was forced to confront Christ and the Bible.

"I'd rather not talk about this. My time with you is limited and I must complete my assignment for Templeton."

"I understand. Perhaps we can find time to talk more personally later."

"Perhaps."

RESTORE POINT 4:

THE WORLD OF ART

Sometimes, the world of art is more like a mysterious journey than a set of techniques. The brush, the flush of color, the stroke of paint, combined with the contrasting intrigue of shadows and light on a canvas have powerful potential. True art speaks its own language, without words. The canvas can take us back in time, and speak of yesterday, or forward, and speak of tomorrow. The image on the canvas can take us to distant lands, to places where we have never been to meet people we otherwise would never have known. The mystery of the canvas lies in its ability to cause us to step back for a moment, to get out of the stream of daily life, and to see, not only through the eyes of the artist -- but to see the artist himself – so that we may see what he saw, hear what he heard, and feel what he felt as his brush touched the canvas.

New Orleans, of course, has a large community of artists. Many artists, who cater primarily to tourists, hang their canvases and display their oil paintings, watercolors, prints and etchings on a large black wrought iron fence that surrounds *Jackson Square. Pirates Alley* and other romantic, narrow side streets behind and around *St. Louis Cathedral* are cluttered with art galleries filled with fine works of art from New Orleans and around the world for the serious minded collector. But, there's something about art produced in this city. It has the mysterious power and ability to take hold of you.

The threatening rain shower suddenly began to fall as Emma parked the car on Esplanade Avenue near N. Rampart Street. It looked like chaos on the Esplanade as people ran in different directions trying to avoid the sudden downpour. Thin sheer sheets of plastic suddenly covered everything and everyone. People huddled under these makeshift plastic tarps while others stood under the overhanging canvas awnings to avoid the rain.

As we waited for the rain showers to pass Emma and I shared some of our thoughts about art with Mr. Grand. We talked about artistic symbolism, visual images and their relationship to *metaphorical thinking*. Then I shared with Grand the strange, melancholic story of a New Orleans artist, an unusually gifted painter named Bill.

"Bill always had a little nostalgia in his heart and a little art in his eyes but neither ever reached the canvas. He was a retired window dresser, Mr. Grand, a retired window dresser for Sears & Roebuck. He lived in poverty, as a recluse, in a back-a-town shack in rural Tangipahoa Parish, about 60 miles north of New Orleans. He had a brief, prolific, unbelievably meteoric art career which began in 2002 – then, abruptly, in 2009 Bill Hemmerling died. Cancer. His captivating life portraits, dominated by soft images of rural African American rituals and religion were unique in that they were painted with left-over house paint on discarded pieces of scrap wood and ply-board. Hemmerling's paintings have hung alongside works of art by Salvador Dali, Fernando Botero and other renowned artists from around the world."

"I don't believe I've ever heard of this Hemmerling fellow," said Mr. Grand. "And, I don't believe I've ever viewed any of his art."

"Then you have indeed missed a blessing. Perhaps we can find time to visit a gallery or two. One of the reasons his paintings are so cherished is their simplicity. His paintings were simple, one-dimensional images, flat dark silhouettes of young black girls wearing bright white dresses. They were always painted with plain, yet expressive faces; yet they had no facial features, other than an outline of lips. As a final touch Hemmerling would hand paint words and sayings with his brush right on the paintings, words of wisdom, or comfort, or inspiration."

"I remember how deeply my husband and I were touched by one of his paintings," said Emma "It was a sad, soft image of a sorrowful old black woman with the traditional Hemmerling inscription beneath her portrait – *'if I could only hear my mother pray again.'* There was something touching, yet sad, something deeply moving about that painting – *'if I could only hear my mother pray again.'* The inscription added to that painting brought back memories of my own dear mother praying. Hemmerling's painting and his inscription actually brought tears to my eyes."

"There was something," I added, "something *existential,* something incredibly deep that could be felt through that painting, the devastating numbness of deep loss. And, there was something terribly sad, despondency and dark despair, hidden in the black traces of Hemmerling's brush. And, there was something sorrowful in Hemmerling's inscription, the silent anguished sound of mourning, the secret longing that no one sees but everyone feels, the unseen feeling of aloneness, of separation. Like Emma, I don't think I have ever been so moved, or so touched, or felt so deeply stirred before or after viewing that Hemmerling painting – until now."

As I shifted myself forward in the back seat of the car Mr. Grand looked in the direction that I was pointing toward – a small make-shift plaza on the neutral ground at Esplanade and N. Rampart Street.

"Right over there, Mr. Grand, on that neutral ground under the canopy of the oak trees, is a small outdoor plaza. The centerpiece of that plaza is a large painting on a sheet of old, discarded ply-board. In my opinion this painting is the most gripping, compelling work of art I have ever seen. The locals, the media, and city government, embroiled in controversy about the painting and the outdoor plaza, call the area *Paw Paw's Plaza.* The plaza is slated for destruction by the city, if the city has its way, because it has become an eyesore, attracts beggars by day and drug users by night. Most people who live on Esplanade Avenue are also opposed to *Paw Paw's Plaza* being located on the Esplanade.

"No one knows what will happen to the painting if and when *Paw Paw's Plaza* is demolished. And, no one knows who painted the painting or where it came from; it unexpectedly appeared on the neutral ground one day and the plaza suddenly came into existence a few days later, shortly before the seventh anniversary of the hurricane. One thing is known for sure – Hemmerling is not the artist.

The rain, which had been falling steadily for roughly thirty minutes, suddenly stopped. *Paw Paw's Plaza* and the Esplanade, which appeared to be pretty much locked down because of the rain, suddenly came back to life. The scrawny, gawky tall girl resumed her banjo playing while the young man with the yellow bandana returned to the security of his spot against the wall of the coffee house, once again, bobbing his head up, then down; up, then down.

An unusual couple, in unison, closed their umbrellas and began walking toward the plaza. She, a rather refined-looking elderly white-haired lady dressed in white and he, a poorly dressed younger man with long hair wrapped in a pony tail, stood together, distributing printed material explaining the plight of *Paw Paw's Plaza.* The people whom the media derisively described as hippies, punks, and homeless picked up and then folded their plastic rain covers while tourist milled about taking photographs. The buzz of human activity began to reverberate up and down the Esplanade. The rain had passed.

"*Paw Paw's Plaza*, Mr. Grand, has become a place where people come, some homeless, some hopeless, and some helpless. Some are still troubled and afflicted by the storm. Others are crushed by the harsh rigors of life. Most people come, not so much to find relief as to immerse themselves in sorrow, surrounded by the sorrowful. To be disheartened is a dismal affair, Mr. Grand. It seems to be despair's duty to attract despair; and that of affliction to attract affliction. Sorrow has few cheerful friends."

"Well, I've heard it said that 'Misery loves company,'" said Grand.

"No. No. That's only half true," I interjected, shaking my head. "Misery loves miserable company."

The plaza was nothing fancy. It had two rather large old sofa's facing one another, with a discarded, well worn, twelve foot by twelve foot square linoleum rug between them. Several, less than a dozen, brown folding metal chairs were behind each of the sofas and another dozen or so were at the opposite end of the painting. There was additional standing space for roughly another thirty or so people behind the group of folding chairs at the opposite end, facing the painting.

Quite a few old photographs, perhaps a hundred or so, reportedly of people who died in the hurricane, were scattered on the ground, strategically placed at the foot of the painting. Some had frames. Some didn't. Most were faded. Several were ruined by rain. A few potted plants were scattered about, near the edge of the linoleum rug. A funeral spray that stood nearly six feet tall, mounted on a thin metal tripod, covered with dried dead flowers, stood to one side of the large painting. In a place of prominence, on the opposite end beside the painting, was an empty grocery cart. It had a large, round unlit blackish-brown candle placed in the child's seat and a small hand-painted wooden plaque that simply said, *"In Memory Of Paw Paw."*

Someone had propped up an old, rusted metal music stand beside the grocery cart. It served as an impromptu speaker's podium and sometimes as a platform for new age readings, haiku poetry or quiet testimonies. Behind the metal music stand, a three-foot aluminum cross was perched atop an empty wooden crate. The cross was held upright by a metal Christmas tree stand, which was screwed to the cross at its base. It did not look very safe and did not appear to be very stable. On the opposite side, beside the funeral spray of dried flowers, standing motionless, like a silent sentinel, was yet another silver spray-painted Silver Statue man. On behalf of the arts community he and a coalition of other Silver Statue men guarded, in rotating shifts, the painting against the wiles of an insensitive city government.

Across the street, a policeman in uniform sat in his marked patrol car. Quietly, oblivious to the world around him, he pulled out some tobacco and began rolling his own cigarettes. With his patrol car windows rolled down, the soulful sound of New Orleans jazz playing on his patrol car radio served as a musical backdrop for that section of Esplanade. With a keen eye, however, he too watched the painting, protecting it from the wiles of the arts community.

Bolted to a wrought iron fence that surrounded a second story porch above the coffee shop across from *Paw Paw's Plaza* the local NBC news affiliate had secured a live camera, as an additional security device. The news media did not trust either the local government or the arts community and regarded their surveillance activities as a service to the larger community.

The large painting, which was the center of attention, was painted on an old, discarded sheet of rough hewn ply-board. It stood, in my opinion, as a mute post-modern monument to *existential despair*. As a work of art it contained many, if not all, of the elements of existentialism. On one level it portrayed the *emotional components* of existentialism: frenzied feelings of desolation, disorientation, displacement, alienation, estrangement, futility, desperation and despair. On another level it conveyed the *rational component,* or should I say the irrational, conclusions of existentialism: cynicism, pessimism, nihilism, atheism and the conclusion that life is absurd because it is always terminated by death. On the *volitional level* it represented man as lacking freedom, with options for liberty denied, with meaning obliterated and morals negated creating meaningless choices with tragic conclusions about life.

The background or base color of the painting that was used to accomplish these dismal purposes was a stained, streaked shade of darkened ivory, with the ivory dulled by the elements and somewhat soiled by exposure. The painting was a dull, dismal, horrid blend of bland color – darkened ivory, blemished grays and grime – creating a drab backdrop that suggested *existential hopelessness.*

The female figures, in the style of Hemmerling, were black girls, but unlike Hemmerling, the white dresses worn by these girls were soiled, horribly soiled, and dismally stained. Each of the seventeen or eighteen girls, with the exception of one, held their heads downward, sorrowfully resting their chins in their hands. With no eyes, and no facial features, other than lips, they sat there, nameless, faceless, their identity unknown to any of us, yet looking out at us – locked in a look of eternal despair.

The unknown artist of the ply-board painting, whoever he or she was, brushed the painted word "Desolation" at the very top of the painting in large letters, utilizing a distressed hand painted type of font. The word "Desolation" was also painted in the style of Hemmerling with smaller letters at the bottom and along the sides of the painting, creating the image of a frame.

Strategically placed beside the silhouettes of the young black girls, creating an illusion of aloneness, separation and isolation, were the words *Refugee. Refugee. Refugee.*

This title – *Refugee.* – was one that we locals could unfortunately identify with in the aftermath of the hurricane. *Refugee.* was a title given by an insensitive national news media to us and to those tens of thousands of people like Emma and me who were displaced by the storm. We who had lost everything through the storm felt so alone, so terribly, terribly alone, estranged and alienated from everyone and everything that gave life value, substance and meaning.

In St. Bernard parish (county), where Emma and I live, for the first time in American history an entire parish was completely destroyed. Not just one or two towns within the parish, but every town, every community and every neighborhood that comprised the entire parish -- flooded and destroyed. Every building and every structure – every business, every school, every home, every church – were all flooded, wind damaged and destroyed. Everything that formed the backdrop of our lives, gone, destroyed. The entire St. Bernard population of 63,000+ were gone, displaced, with 50,000+ of the original residents permanently relocating somewhere else, never to return to St. Bernard.

Everyone who stood in the foreground and the background of our lives were now gone. Our families were broken, fractured and scattered across the United States from the Atlantic coast to the Pacific seaboard and all points in between. All of our friends too were displaced, many never to be seen or heard from again. We would wonder, what became of the other people who stood in the shadows of our lives? We mourned the absence of the young boy who once served hamburgers at the malt shop? He was gone, like the malt shop, no longer there. And, what became of the hairdresser, where did she go? And our mailman, did he survive? And that older man who delivered our newspaper early each morning, whatever happened to him? All of these and a host of others -- displaced, gone. And we, we who were so alienated, so estranged, who or what were we? The national news media gave us an answer, *Refugees.*

Yes, in the midst of the anguish of separation and uncertainty, in the midst of disorientation, chaos and disorder, this disheartening title – *Refugee.* – assigned to us by the national media seemed to somehow make our isolation and our aloneness official. This one singular word validated the validity of the conflicting dark emotions that worked within and flowed from each of us. The presence of absence was so real, so terribly real. *Refugee.* It had existentialism's color, existentialism's flavor, its coldness, and its poisonous despair. And what of God? The presence of God is difficult to define but His absence is easy, very easy to detect.

Above the painted silhouettes of the girls were images of rolling dark storm clouds surrounding the now familiar satellite image of the hurricane consuming the Gulf of Mexico. Above the clouds, near the upper right of the ply-board, was the image of what appeared to be a dull, white castle, with its once brilliant halo faded, and its once bright holy glow growing dim. It was very obviously the artist's visual representation of heaven. Beneath the images of the girls was an inscription, written rather largely, in the same distressed hand painted type of font: *"If there is a God He ain't here."* The absence of God, as felt by the artist, was indeed easy to detect. His absence – the sense of His absence -- created a feeling of emptiness that was felt -- especially by the *Refugee.*

If Camus were a painter – this would be his atheistic seal. If Sarte held a brush – this would be his atheistic sign. If Nietzsche, the mentally deranged antagonist of Christianity, who died by his own hand – if Nietzsche read the inscription – he would stand and salute. They would, but they cannot. For they have all been swallowed up in death.

Beneath the heavenly castle, standing beside her black sisters, was the one black girl looking upward. Her arms were raised heavenward, with her hands frantically pointing to the heavenly castle. With her jaw dropped and her narrow mouth painted in the shape of an oblong, wailing kind of circle, she conveyed a look of dismay, anxiety and fear, bewilderment and utter disbelief. The cause? A small, troubling sign hanging on the gate to heaven: "No One Home."

The sound of air brakes locking and releasing air pressure on a *Big Easy* double-decker tour bus momentarily drew my attention away from the large painting. The power-operated mechanism that controlled the double-wide exit doors on the bus suddenly opened. One by one, a group of tourist stepped out of the bus onto the curb of the street that was still damp and wet from the rain. As the bus operator lit a cigarette the tour guide stepped forward to the front of the tour group. He then pointed his finger in our direction, an obvious sign that he was guiding the tour group toward the coffee houses, gift shops, restaurants and *Paw Paw's Plaza.* They would soon be milling around, taking photographs, and, no doubt, uploading them to Facebook, Twitter and their internet blogs to record and share the sights and their experiences while vacationing in New Orleans.

A young man, seemingly coming from nowhere, strangely, without reason or provocation, began kicking his legs high in the air like a prancing horse as he ran across the neutral ground toward the tour group as they exited the bus. He stopped running, rather abruptly as he reached the very edge of the neutral ground. Like a proud stallion marching in place, he continued moving his legs up and down, prancing without any forward movement. As he continued his in place parade, constantly moving his legs, he pulled on imaginary reins and began making neighing sounds, like an excitable horse. As the tour group stared at this unusual spectacle the young man suddenly raised a rebellious fist high in the air, then, for some unknown reason, he began taunting the tourists, shouting obscenities, all the while lifting his legs up and down, up and down. It was that bare-footed guy, the one with the yellow bandana on his head, the young fellow who was leaning against the wall of the coffee shop as we drove down Esplanade Avenue. Just as his shouting reached a fever pitch, the lights of the police car came on and began flashing. In an instant, the young man's voice was silenced. He literally stopped, mid-sentence, and turned and started walking, calmly and nonchalantly, toward Mr. Grand, Emma and me.

He came right next to me, stopping so as to stand just a few feet away, between me and the painting. He looked first at the painting, then at me, then back at the painting, then back at me. With a defiant, yet frightened look, the look of a little child trying to be brave, he stared directly into my eyes before he spoke. It was, however, with a surprisingly calm, quivering, soft voice of a child that he spoke, almost in a whisper.

"Know what it means, dude? Do you know what this painting really means?"

There was a note of inquisitive sorrow, an anxious kind of sadness within his voice, as the young man answered his question before either Grand, Emma or I could respond.

"It means we're on our own. That's what it means, dude. That's what it means."

He looked down, then he looked up, then he took a deep breath and looked directly into my eyes.

"Ain't that a bummer, dude? It's just us, man, just us. You look after you. I look after me. That's all we got, just us, man, just us. Look around you, dude, look around you. This is all there is. This is all there ever will be. That's it. Ain't nothing else, nothing before, nothing after, nothing beyond. None of that brother's keeper stuff, know what I mean?"

There was a cry of outrage deep within my spirit, a shouting silent protest. The image of this broken, bewildered boy brought forth a torrent of silent shouts:

> *Here is the fruit of your poison, Nietzsche. And what say you, Camus? What say you, Sarte? We call you. Give account. What is your legacy? What joyless mantle have you cast upon us? Here is your gift to the ages: a joyless man amid joyless men who have lost their way in the dark despair of a world emptied of God.*

RESTORE POINT 5:

PAW PAW'S PLAZA

Breaking away from my raging thoughts, I was about to speak to the young man in an effort to reach out to him when he spoke again before I could say anything.

"What say? Can ya spare a few bucks, dude? Whatcha think? Can ya spare some pocket change? Anything will do, ya know. Anything."

"Well, I'd rather talk to you about how you see this painting first. You see, according to your way of seeing things – your paradigm -- you just might be right in how you see this painting, but that doesn't mean that you're correct -- in either your assumptions or your conclusions."

"Dude, ya sound like one of my old college professors," he said with nervous laughter as he lifted his hands high above his head, then lowered them quickly to slap his thighs. "Assumptions. Conclusions. Paradigm? What's with that, dude, what in the world's with that?"

He quickly turned away from me, and once again, like a high kicking stallion he galloped back to the coffee shop. An older couple, wearing yellow Missouri Volunteer t-shirts with matching yellow baseball caps, were evidently amused by the antics of the young man. Laughing and shaking their heads, they quietly sat on the sofa opposite Mr. Grand and Emma. They smiled at Grand and Emma, then glanced toward the painting, then turned to smile at me.

"Aren't you that preacher that was on the FOX news network a few weeks ago? I'd be willing to bet you are, and if you're not, you're a dead ringer or have a twin," asked the man.

"No. No," interrupted the woman, who was his wife, "It was PBS. I definitely remember -- it was PBS."

"Thanks for watching," I replied quickly, not mentioning the *PBS Religion and Ethics* program or the PBS network, in an effort to ease the sudden appearance of tension in their conversation and to avoid potential conflict. I could discern an undercurrent of disharmony between them, an irritation, a symptom of something far deeper than our brief conversation revealed.

"And thanks for remembering. Are you from this area?"

"Naw. We're from Missouri. We came down a week after the storm…"

"No. No," interrupted the wife again, "it was two weeks after the storm. I definitely remember, it was two weeks after the storm."

"The wife and I came down, ah, two weeks after the hurricane," he said with emphasis as he rolled his eyes upward, "we came down two weeks after the hurricane to work in a feeding station to help with disaster relief efforts. Been here ever since. I'm Gary, Gary Grove, and this is my wife Myrtle."

"Glad to meet you," snapped Myrtle in a terse tone.

As Gary, Myrtle, Emma, Mr. Grand and I shook hands and exchanged pleasantries, an old man, a man who looked like he must have been at least a hundred years old, began walking across the neutral ground toward *Paw Paw's Plaza.* He held tightly onto his lightweight walker as he slowly made his way on one foot across the neutral ground, carefully keeping his left foot from touching the ground. Eventually he made his way across the linoleum rug, then plopped himself onto the sofa, breathing with loud sounds until his breath calmed down.

"Are you going to give a speech or preach or something?" asked Myrtle.

"Well, I was going to share about *Paw Paw's Plaza* and about the hurricane with Mr. Grand," I said pointing toward Grand. "He's visiting our city, seeking to gather information for a series of articles he's writing. If it doesn't matter to Mr. Grand it's OK with me for you to stay and hear some thoughts that I'll be sharing."

Before Grand could say anything the old man with the walker, who evidently had a hearing problem, spoke rather loudly to no one in particular.

"What'd he say? Is he going to give a speech or something? Tell him to speak loud so I can hear what he's saying. Tell him I said to please speak loud."

As I nodded my head in the old man's direction to indicate that I would speak loudly, other people came by and joined our small, yet growing crowd. A few people from the tour bus group sat in the folding chairs, while others stood behind the chairs stretching their legs. Most of the tour group, however, walked past *Paw Paw's Plaza* toward the gift shops and the coffee house. The couple distributing literature began working the small crowd, softly talking about the plight of *Paw Paw's Plaza* to anyone who would listen.

A preppy-looking 20-something young man with amazing curly hair, parked and locked his bicycle in a bike rack in front of the coffee shop, then briskly walked over to the plaza, taking a seat in one of the brown folding chairs behind Mr. Grand and Emma. Sitting directly across from me, directly opposite the painting, was a rather large, round, stocky, obviously drunk man who tightly held onto a full plastic cup of beer in one hand and a thin black cell phone in the other. Another couple, a middle-aged man and his wife, sat beside the drunk, a few seats away, on the brown folding chairs.

"Want to see a picture of my grandson, Madame?" the drunk asked the couple. He raised his large, deeply creased face and his bushy eyebrows simultaneously as he flipped open his cell phone, poked some buttons, then leaned forward toward the couple to show the image of his grandchild on the phone's screen. He had a heavy French accent, sounding somewhat like a slurred version of the French actor Maurice Chevalier.

"No," replied the wife sharply as she turned her nose upward and away from the drunk. "We would like to simply sit, enjoy the shade and hear about this painting, if you don't mind."

"Well, *pardonner, Mademoiselle.* Certainly I know not what I utter," snapped the drunk. *"Pardonner. Oh, mon Dieu."*

I placed my open cell phone on the music stand to use it as a clock then introduced myself, Emma and Mr. Grand to those who had come to the plaza. I then offered some impromptu introductory remarks explaining that I was not an art critic but a local pastor. I briefly detailed my experience working with visual and mental images and their impact on human behavior, behavior modification and change.

More people joined our small, but growing audience. Some sat on folding chairs, while others chose to stand. I cleared my throat then began to share with the audience what I had intended to share with Mr. Grand, but in a more professional manner as opposed to the casual style of general one-on-one conversation that I would normally employ.

"Here, my friends, is art born of sorrow. Here we see, not only what the artist saw, but, on a deeper level; we see the artist himself. Like Christ, our artist is a man of sorrows, acquainted with grief. [6] Like the Old Testament prophet Jeremiah, our artist is one who weeps – not through the traditional prophetic pen, but through his more contemporary prophetic brush and canvas.

"Jeremiah and our unknown artist cry the cry of abandonment. With a singular voice, in unison, from different generations, different cultures, they both ask one of mankind's most vexing questions: 'In times of trouble why is God a stranger in the land?' [7] Together Jeremiah and our unknown artist mourn the sad absence of God and together they join Jesus in crying the cry of estrangement: 'My God, My God, why…why…why hast Thou forsaken me?' Wounded, weary, feeling forsaken and abandoned, our artist mourned and despaired over a desolate world seemingly emptied of God, a world where God could no longer be found.

"The answers, the answers to these vexing questions are first and foremost, theological, between God and man. Yet, the answers are also sociological, between man and man; and psychological, between a man and himself. And, finally, they are ecological, between man and his world.

"Let me ask, dear friends, today, what did you come to see? A curious piece of art planted on a controversial spate of land? Good. May you be blessed in the viewing. But do not fail to see the bereaved, broken artist who could not find God in the mist of calamity, desolation and despair. Do not fail to feel the alienation of this anguished artist who gave birth to this curious piece of art. His anguish, his sorrow, his grief and his tears labored together to produce this artistic image, an image captured on this rough hewn wooden canvas – art born of sorrow.

"Several years ago, in the immediate aftermath of this terrible hurricane, through the medium of television, each of you and millions across our nation and around the world, saw the outer physical effects of the storm. Today, through the medium of this particular piece of art an unknown artist has touched upon and captured with paint and brush the delicate inner effects of that storm. His is a inner portrait of a place, a place of sorrow where the mind could find no rest; where the heart could find no peace; and, where the spirit could find no solace. Sorrow, like a vice, squeezed him tighter and tighter, splashing sad, sorrowful color on canvas – again, art born of sorrow.

"Such is the power of image. Image grips us, seizes us, and paints its indelible impression on memory, on the canvas of the mind, never to be forgotten."

Across the street small groups of people, preoccupied with their own agendas, were dodging one another as they walked in opposite directions, up and down Esplanade. Some, going back to work after a quick lunch, wore business suits and more dressy wear. Others, perhaps tourists, perhaps locals, were dressed more casually. Mingled among both groups were the homeless and hippies, both young and old, male and female.

The winds began to rustle yet again, softly blowing through the massive oaks that shaded *Paw Paw's Plaza.* Another approaching rain labored in the distance as a faint echo of thunder gently rumbled yet again. Once again I spoke.

"Here again, my friends, behind me, is art born of sorrow. August 29, 2005 is for many, just a date on a calendar; for others, it is a point of division, a definitive line of demarcation. Before that date is the New Orleans we once knew. After that date is the New Orleans that is still yet to be. In a sense our city will forever exist, at least in the minds of this generation, it will exist as two cities: The one that existed before and the one that exists after August 29, 2005.

"That date -- August 29, 2005 -- gave birth to this art, thus my reference to art born of sorrow. Here we see in symbolic imagery that which the artist saw. A devastating storm. A catastrophic event. And we feel, not only do we see, but we feel what the artist felt. Devastation. Destruction. Desolation. And like the artist we too wrestle with the most vexing of human problems: pain, human tragedy, suffering and death. This you have seen and this you have experienced from afar. And this you have viewed, through the medium of television, from a distance. And the images, images of what you have seen, images of what you have felt, they remain with you still.

"For others the horror of what happened was not distant, but near, very near. See them. See the people who have labored in the shadow of death, weighed down by the burden of despair."

As I paused speaking the skies once again began to darken slightly as grey clouds slowly gathered overhead.

"The Bible says that 'the people who sat in darkness have seen a great light.' [8] Do notice, however, that the Bible says that before the light appears there is first darkness. And this light that appears, what is it? It is God's light, the invisible made visible, shining in the darkness."

The screen on my cell phone began to flash. It was a short text message from Emma. While I continued to speak I punched the *receive message key* to glance at Emma's message.

"Good job. You're explaining this well. I love you."

"Again, here we see art born of sorrow, sorrow that is expressed, sorrow that is felt through an existential image painted on this large wooden canvas. Yes. Art born of sorrow, the sorrow of multiplied dark devastating images of storm despair, exploding all around us, impressed indelibly on the canvas of our mind – and the mind of this artist.

"See the image of the Super Dome with its beleaguered thousands seeking shelter in the darkness. Yes. Darkness was there. Suicide was there. Hunger and thirst were there. Criminals and pedophiles were there. And, fear, anxiety, desperation and despair – tightening its grip on a broken people.

"Lay hold of the image of the huddled masses at the New Orleans Convention Center. Allow the brush of thought to paint an image of a modern-day exodus of people, wearily walking across the Mississippi River Bridge seeking safety, only to be turned back toward desolation. See them as they walk with heavy hearts down the I-10 corridor to Metairie. Darkness was there. Suicide was there. Hunger and thirst were there. And, loneliness and despair. And, fear and anxiety.

"Images explode across our minds, do they not? Images of people stranded on the roof tops of homes surrounded by treacherous, deep water. See their distress. Hear their pitiable cries for help. See their crudely made signs pointed heavenward to military rescue helicopters and news copters recording the event. Darkness was there. Suicide was there. Hunger and thirst were there. And, fear, anxiety, desperation and despair. Darkness was there.

"And here, in this place, *Paw Paw's Plaza* is yet another despairing tale of woe, death and devastation. A local radio newsman, reporting on the parking lot suicide of a police officer, noticed a shopping cart, right here, on this very spot. Broadcasting live he explained that something was inside the grocery cart, but he could not see, nor determine what it was. Upon closer inspection, visibly shaken, with a broken, weepy voice, he reported that a corpse was inside the grocery cart, the dead body of a white-haired, elderly black man....and, attached to the side of the grocery cart with duct tape was a frantic hand written note, written in crayon: 'This is our paw paw. Please take care of him. We cannot.'

"Here are images, images of desolation and despair multiplied, images of a people seated in darkness....and here is art, art born of sorrow.... and..."

As I continued speaking I noticed a man, a rather unusual looking man walking with slow, cautious, deliberate steps behind the crowd. He was wearing a tight cut black suit with a black designer shirt and a black tie. Thin black sunglasses camouflaged his face. He was wearing a black hat, a black fedora hat to be exact, pinched at the front and pushed back on his head. Over the suit he wore a heavy full length dark wool overcoat that reached down to his ankles. Though the overcoat was dark in color, it was not very clean. It looked as if he had been wearing the overcoat for quite some time; which was strange because, even though it was February the humidity was high and it was very hot. His hair was black. He looked sinister and unfriendly as he stood on the fringe of the crowd, looking one way, then another, as he surveyed different groups of people in the crowd. The sight of him, the sight of his unfriendly mannerisms and his sinister movements, made me uncomfortable, suspicious. Yet, there was something familiar about this man in black. I felt like I knew him. I felt like we had met before, somewhere.

Ominous, intimidating and overbearing in appearance, he continued slowly walking behind the crowd. Occasionally he would use his cell phone as a camera to take a photograph. He was making feeble, unsuccessful attempts to act like a tourist; but, he looked and acted more like a covert operative. He was inconspicuous to the crowd as he slowly walked behind them. It was as if he wore a cloak of invisibility that hid him from the people in the plaza. Both he and his movements, however, were easily seen by me. My vantage point made him more visible.

As I continued speaking, watching as he quietly walked alongside the back edge of the crowd, he occasionally stared straight at me through his dark sunglasses then appeared to whisper something into his cell phone. He was definitely talking to someone.

Suddenly, around the outer edge of the crowd in all directions, I saw six or seven other men, all dressed in the same black attire. A Jesuit priest, dressed in black, was with them. Each of the men, other than the priest, wore black fedora hats and black sun glasses. Most of them held thin black cell phones to their ears. Something was up, I couldn't tell what, but something was definitely being coordinated by these people.

The crowd probably thought I was silent for effect as I quietly pointed to each of the words painted on the large wooden canvas. I was silent, however, in an attempt to collect my thoughts. It was as if I was frozen in time. I again resumed speaking to the crowd. As I turned again to face the people the first man in black was standing still, perfectly still, staring intently at me. I was shocked as he removed his hat and his sun glasses to wipe sweat from his forehead.

It was Dr. Bernard Rieux.

The words that Emma spoke earlier to Mr. Grand suddenly raced across my mind....

> *"You see, Mr. Grand, there's a real problem here for my husband. None of what he says happened actually happened. These people did not and do not exist. These are not flesh and blood real people. Each one of them, as you well know, are actually fictitious characters in a novel written by the existentialist Albert Camus"*

Suddenly, the screen on my cell phone flashed again, another text message from Emma. I punched the *receive message key* to retrieve Emma's new message. Dr. Rieux stood with his arms folded, looking intently at me as I read Emma's message.

"Do not be afraid. Do what they say."

As I looked away from Emma's text message Dr. Rieux began walking again, cautiously, behind the crowd, keenly observant. He didn't say anything to anyone other than through his cell phone.

Then, in an instant, he put his hat and glasses back on and once again stood still, staring at me. He resumed talking in his phone. Then he pulled his phone away from his ear, looked at me again then at his phone as he began punching keys on the phone.

The screen on my cell phone immediately indicated that I had received another text message, but not from Emma. The cell simply reported that the origin was "Unknown." I punched the receive key.

"The man who wants to lead the orchestra must turn his back on the crowd"

As I lifted my head Dr. Rieux began moving his finger in a circular motion, indicating that I should turn around, away from the crowd. I glanced quickly toward Emma and Mr. Grand. Another man dressed in black, had strategically placed his hand on Emma's shoulder. I recognized him. It was Garcia, a smuggler from Dr. Rieux's city of Oran. Emma's face was ashen. She looked worried. Mr. Grand sat silently. His wide eyes conveyed fright. Both nodded their heads ever so slightly so as to say "Do what they say."

I briefly caught a glimpse of the Silver Statue man. Our eyes met. He nodded his head toward me, ever so slightly, smiled a sly knowing smile – and winked. He too appeared to be saying "Do what they say."

Dr. Rieux was still moving his finger in a circular motion, indicating that I should turn away from the crowd toward the cross.

As I slowly began turning away from the crowd I heard myself saying once again for the benefit of the crowd that now familiar passage of Scripture: "'The people who sat in darkness have seen a great light.' And, here is that Light; the Light is Christ, symbolized by this cross."

Pointing to the cross then back to the large wooden canvas I began to ask a series of rhetorical questions: "But, where do you go when the darkness is so great that you cannot find that Light? Where do you go and what do you do when God is nowhere to be found?"

Everything that happened next appeared to the crowd to be spontaneous. But it was not. It was a well-coordinated series of events, and they happened fast, very fast.

As I stood facing the cross, the preppy-looking young man with the curly hair suddenly sprang to his feet. As he raised his arm he pointed toward his bicycle in front of the coffee shop and began shouting with a high-pitched, shrill voice, "He's stealing my bike. He's stealing my bike." The people in the crowd turned their heads, simultaneously, in unison, in the direction of the coffee shop and the bike. It was Gonzales, another smuggler and friend of Garcia's, from Oran, stealing the bike.

Almost immediately, the drunk stood up, making a clumsy effort to see who was stealing the bicycle. With a silly smile on his face, he laughed as he spilled his cup of beer, drenching the woman who earlier rejected his attempts to share the photo of his grandson. It was the jovial Monsieur Jean Tarrou, also from Oran. Monsieur Tarrou was a loud, boisterous man. He always smiled a lot. Before the plague came to Oran, he would laugh, and dance and make jokes – usually about Spanish dancers and musicians.

The woman, drenched in beer let out a shrill, high pitched yell. Then she began repeatedly hitting the smiling Monsieur Tarrou with her purse. The people in the crowd turned their heads once again, this time toward the spectacle of the woman shouting and beating the drunken Tarrou with her purse.

The old man with the walker began shouting, repeatedly, "What'd he say? What'd he say? What'd he say?" Simultaneously, the young man with the yellow bandana stood and began shouting obscenities at no one in particular. He was prancing like a horse again, loudly shouting obscenities, with his voice rising above the noise of the crowd.

The policeman across the street threw his cigarette to the ground and began running toward us, blowing his high pitched whistle, over and over again. It was Raoul. I recognized him too. Raoul was a corrupt sentry from Oran who arranged Monsieur Raymond Rambert's escape from that quarantined city during the plague for a fee of ten thousand dollars. As if from nowhere four or five horse mounted policeman raced toward the crowd, causing people to run in several different directions. In the confusion of everything that was happening I could see Emma and Mr. Grand walking across the neutral ground away from *Paw Paw's Plaza* with Garcia. He had his hand firmly gripping Emma's arm as they walked toward our automobile. With them was the priest, Father Paneloux, the well-respected Jesuit from Oran. Laughing and smiling as he talked with Emma he appeared to be oblivious to what was actually happening.

Suddenly, I heard Emma's voice again, in my head…

"There's only one problem, one major problem, Mr. Grand, as you are well aware -- none of what my husband says happened actually happened.

But this was happening. The fear on Emma's face conveyed what words lacked the power to convey – she was frightened, very frightened and fearful because something beyond our ability to control was actually happening.

The sound of Emma's voice flashed again….

"These are not flesh and blood real people. Each one of them, as you well know, are actually fictitious characters in a novel written by the existentialist writer Albert Camus."

Just then there was the crashing, clapping sound of thunder, several flashes of lightening, and a sudden hard downpour of rain. People again were running in different directions. I don't know exactly how it happened but someone bumped against the cross. The wooden crate tumbled backward causing the cross to fall forward. Even though I grabbed at the cross in an attempt to protect myself, my attempt was unsuccessful. The cross fell, hitting me on the head. I somehow managed to hold to the cross as I tumbled to the ground. My head was spinning as someone dressed in black helped me to my feet. As we walked away, my legs were wobbly. I was dizzy and disoriented.

RESTORE POINT 6:

ECHOES OF A FADING PAST

Darkness. Confusion.
A Distant Flash of Light.
Italian voices, singing --
"Te Deum. Te Deum. Te Deum."
Echoes Of A Fading Past.
Spinning Sounds. Rapidly Spinning. Spinning Sounds.

"Where am I? Where am I?"

I Woke Up to Find Myself Strapped to a Chair
A Rotating Circular Surgical Chair.

"Where am I? Where am I?"
"Calm Down, John, Calm Down."

"Where am I? Where am I?"

"Propofol. Lorazepam. Midazolam."

Darkness. Confusion.
A Distant Flash of Light.
Echoing. Echoing. Echoing Inside My Head.
Torches. Muffled sounds. Voices. A clap of thunder.

RESTORE POINT 7:

MENTAL TURBULENCE

As the rain continued to fall, I was in a mental fog, confused and disoriented. The Italian voices singing *Te Deum.* had ceased their song of praise. I no longer heard the sound of rotating rectangles and squares. The final sound, a strangely familiar sound -- of deceleration -- baffled me. I was not sure about where I was or what was happening – but I did have a deep sense of having been here before – *Déjà vu.*

I staggered, or I should say, stumbled, directionless, with halting, hesitating steps. I was shivering, cold, and wet as the rain continued to fall. I could not see clearly and it seemed like my hearing had become dull, with sound fading in and out. Each uncertain step felt like amplified movement, yet in slow motion, so much so that I couldn't walk without assistance. Someone, apparently a man dressed in black who looked like a dark blur, wrapped one of his arms around my waist. I draped one of my arms over his shoulder. He became a human crutch for me as I slowly and dizzily stumbled through the falling rain. With my other hand I instinctively held tightly to the cross which hit me in the head when it toppled from its wooden crate.

Unbelievable. Incredible. A cross. My head. A painful blow.

My sight was severely impaired. I felt like I was looking at the world through dull cataracts or suffering with macular degeneration that colored everything with a smear. Everything was hazy, foggy, visually distorted, double-visioned, one big blur. I could discern, however, that the immediate area around me was alive, alive with movement, shadowy movements, but movements nonetheless.

Torches. Muffled sounds. Voices. A clap of thunder. A flash of lightening. Everything was like a strange, frightening recurring dream, filled with mysterious yet familiar sounds and surreal movements, shadows and images. I kept sensing that I had been here before. – *Déjà vu.*

I heard myself speaking to myself in a nonsensical, monotonous, repetitious way: "Where do you go and what do you do…? Where do you go and what do you do…?"

As the man in black and I stumbled through the rain and darkness, my voice, mingled with the muffled sounds and noises, constantly repeated the question.

"Where do you go and what do you do…? Where do you go and what do you do… when God is nowhere to be found? Where do you go and what do you do when God is nowhere to be found?"

"Head injury," I heard someone say. "No broken bones."

High above me, I could barely see the outline of a very tall steeple against the backdrop of a lime green sky. The steeple appeared to be resting atop a great stone wall, crowned with the soft glow of stained glass windows. It stood there, in the midst of the falling rain holding high a tall cross -- *a symbol of hope.*

"You there. Are you OK? Can you hear me?"

"Where do you go and what do you do when God is nowhere to be found? Where do you go and what do you do when God is nowhere to be found?"

"I don't know the answer to that question," the man in black said. "You'll have to ask Father Paneloux. He knows about that kind of stuff."

Father Paneloux? At the sound of his name, I squinted my eyes, attempting to stare through the rain and the mental midst that clouded my thinking. My mind was in a fog. I couldn't think clearly, yet, the name Father Paneloux -- I knew that name. Father Paneloux. Paneloux?

"Father Paneloux?" I heard myself shout loudly. "Are you talking about Father Paneloux, from Oran, on the Mediterranean coast of Algeria?"

"Yes. Paneloux was once at Oran."

Paneloux. Father Paneloux. It has a ring of familiarity, that name; but, I was too dazed to figure out how or why it was that I knew his name or how it was that I knew that he was once at Oran, in Algeria.

"Can you tell me, sir, where am I?"

The thunder sounded again, causing the man to hesitate before he replied.

"You're on the roof top of *Christ Cathedra. The Church Of The Last Judgment* in lower St. Bernard, Louisiana. It's the oldest Cathedral in the new world, built around the time of the *Louisiana Purchase.* That's where you are. *Christ Cathedral. The Church Of The Last Judgment*"

> *Christ Cathedral. The Church Of The Last Judgment? Maybe I am insane. I don't know where I am. I don't know how I got here. I don't know what to do. Maybe I really am crazy. There is no Christ Cathedral. The Church Of The Last Judgment in lower St. Bernard, Louisiana? There never has been any such church.*

In the midst of my confused thinking I somehow heard the calming voice of Emma, like a whisper speaking comfort to me, comforting words that she had spoken to me at some point in the past…

> *"Remember, some things are too great for us to understand. That's when we need to shift from what we know to what we believe."*

"May I," I heard myself ask the man in black, "May I ask your name sir?"

"My name? My name is Rieux, Dr. Bernard Rieux."

> *Was this a trick of my mind? Rieux? Paneloux? Why are these names so familiar? Why does the voice of this Dr. Rieux sound so familiar? How can these things be? This is absolutely insane. If I am crazy or insane then I must, I must somehow remain calm. This physician, this Dr. Rieux, must not know of my insanity. The last thing I need is to be placed in an insane asylum.*

"Dr. Rieux, I could really use a cup of coffee to clear my head. You wouldn't be able to get me a cup of coffee, would you?"

"No coffee for you, sir, not just yet. Dizziness, impaired vision, loss of consciousness and a large knot on your head indicates possible brain trauma."

"May I ask your name again sir?"

"My name? My name is Rieux, Dr. Bernard Rieux. You'll be bedridden for at least three days. My friend, Father Paneloux, has a guest bedroom in the cathedral's living quarters, a beautiful room usually reserved for theologians, scholars, missionaries, and visiting clergy. You can recover there."

"Did you say Father Paneloux, sir?"

"Yes, I did. Paneloux, a Jesuit priest, is senior pastor of *Christ Cathedral. The Church Of The Last Judgment.* Now, as a safety precaution we'll not allow you to sleep, eat or drink for the first twenty-four hours. And that definitely means no coffee. Stay away from caffeine. Caffeine is not your friend. Coffee is a harsh mistress."

RESTORE POINT 8:

SPIRITUAL TURBULENCE

I tossed and turned, staying awake for the required twenty-four hours, hungry and thirsty, tired and very much awake. Staying awake was no great accomplishment. I could not sleep. I was anxious. I was consumed with thinking, thinking, thinking, constantly wrestling with my thoughts.

As I lay on the bed tossing from side to side, my thoughts were racing. My mind simply could not stop thinking. The more I tried to turn thinking off, the more my anxious thoughts continued, constantly escalating, racing – rapidly asking questions, seeking answers – finding none.

I could feel myself sinking lower and lower, into despair, depression, and fear, yet struggling to hold it together. The first time I really suspected something was mentally wrong with me as I lay in that bed was when I saw a young boy dressed in white standing at the foot of my bed. He did nothing. He said nothing. He was silent. Without uttering a word he simply stood there, staring at me, slowly nodding his head as a single tear crawled down his cheek. While he stood there I heard a voice, not his voice, not the voice of the boy, but the whispering voice of a man, an unseen man...

"In the Candle – in the darkness –
A slender flame leaps – in solitude.
One becomes many, burning bright.
A labyrinth leads the way,
But not in the light of day.

Beware. The man with one shoe.
Even now he searches for you."

"Who are you? What do you want?"

A thin half-starved rat quickly scurried across the room as the boy disappeared. He simply dissolved before my very eyes. I was startled, frightened, and felt a shudder of fear as I pulled my covers around me.

Rats. A boy in white. Strange sounding whispers. The man with one shoe.

Slowly, very slowly, I calmed myself down. My mind, disturbed, and my thinking, chaotic, and my mental ability began to gradually clear – but only slightly. Even when I tried really hard, the pieces of thought that I gathered and put together were like pieces from two different puzzles. They matched but didn't fit together.

My short-term memory, one puzzle, seemed to be slowly returning. Memories of *Paw Paw's Plaza,* Mr. Grand, and the recent chaos at the plaza began to surface. Thoughts about that, about recent events, seemed to be gradually reconnecting. Yet, yesterday, was somehow severed from today.

It seemed that my long-term memory, the other puzzle, was not as affected by the blow to my head as was my short-term memory. I had no difficulty remembering Emma, or the storm, or my seminary training, or other more distant events of my life. It was my limited functionality with turbulent short-term memory that was more problematic.

The more recent events at *Paw Paw's Plaza* and the more distant events of the hurricane eventually began to merge as the hours of the first day passed. Mountains of memories, leveled, then began to rise while valleys of thought reestablished their boundaries. Slowly, the ambiguities of thought dissipated, but not without great mental effort.

Exhausted, I took my troubled thoughts to bed with me. As I lay in bed during that first twenty-four hours, my mind and its thoughts and my heart and its anxieties raced incessantly, striving for resolution and mental clarity.

No matter how hard I tried I simply could not stop thinking. My initial inability to make appropriate mental connections was very discouraging, devastating, actually. To doubt your sanity while knowing that you're on the edge of insanity is frightening. I constantly found myself falling into a dark mental abyss, entertaining patterns of thinking that reinforced feelings of insanity.

Then I began to hear a low constant sound of 'white noise' in my skull. I held my hands over my ears and buried my face into my pillow, trembling and crying. In the midst of the static white noise I heard Emma's words echoing in my mind…

> *"You see, Mr. Grand, there's a real problem here for my husband. None of what he says happened actually happened. These people did not and do not exist. These are not flesh and blood real people. Each one of them, as you well know, are actually fictitious characters in a novel written by the existentialist Albert Camus"*

> *Oh. Emma. If the earlier events did not happen, tell me, Emma, tell me, what about this event? What about the event at Paw Paw's Plaza? Did that not happen? And, what of your text message urging me to do what they say?*

As the hours passed that first day then into and through the first night I grew more restless and more exhausted, physically, mentally and emotionally.

"Hello. Hello. Is anybody there? Hello. Dr. Rieux, are you there? Can anybody hear me?"

One moment I was thinking logically, or so I thought, with great clarity. Then, the next moment, I found myself in the grip of mania, fearful, fretful, thinking like a crazy man. On more than one occasion I saw butterflies, hundreds of butterflies, hovering outside my window… *and caterpillars building cocoon's, intent on joining the party.*

"Shooo. Shooo. Get outta here. Get outta here."

Interspersed between clarity and crazy I was agitated, frazzled, punching my pillow. I would often find myself talking to myself and shouting loudly, at no one in particular. I was constantly getting out of bed to pace the floor, then jumping back into bed.

The night was filled with brief, sporadic fits of crying and long episodes of anxiety and fear, as I tossed back and forth on the bed; always, always hearing Emma's incessant voice through the darkness....

> *"These people do not exist, other than on the pages of the novel written by Camus.*

> *Oh. Emma. If the people associated with my earlier experience do not exist, other than on the pages of the novel written by Camus, then how did Dr. Bernard Rieux, and Father Paneloux, and Garcia, the smuggler and Raoul, the corrupt sentry and the drunken Monsieur Jean Tarrou – how did these people who do not exist suddenly appear at Paw Paw's Plaza?*

Everything was so extreme. In my heightened state of paranoia I believed that I was being pursued by a strange mystery stalker, an old man with a walker. He stood before me, often, with his body rigid and fixed. Fear and flashes of anxiety raced through me as the head atop his shoulders slowly turned toward me. Rigidity kept me from moving any part of my body but I could see and I could hear. We looked at each other. His eyes met mine.

> *"I want what is mine and I want it now."*
> *"I want what is mine and I want it now."*

Somehow, in the onslaught of this mental turbulence, I made up my mind that I had to put the pieces of this puzzle together. This confusion, this disorientation, was intolerable. I wanted to yell, to scream, to cry. Hallucinations, paranoia, and voices taunted me, suggesting mental breakdown. I was falling deeper and deeper into a black pit of exhaustion-induced despair.

As the battle raged, nothing could drown out the tormenting voices in my head. A strange, terrifying line from the poet T. S. Eliot suddenly came upon me, repeatedly, mingled with my own dark, whispering thoughts.

Be still, and let the dark come upon you [9]
Be still, and let the dark come upon you

I couldn't continue this way. I just couldn't. It was intolerable. Intolerable. I had to somehow sort things out, to think my way through, to develop some conclusions, to make choices. I was so desperate. It felt like my sanity was slipping through my fingers. I felt trapped in a world from which I'd never escape.

Memories passed before me. Good memories. Bad memories. Memories of wasted moments. Memories of choices, wise and unwise, with the consequences of those choices suddenly apparent. And questions, incessant questions. I did not know how much longer I could endure this.

> *"These people did not exist. These are not flesh and blood real people. Each one of them, as you well know, are actually fictitious characters in a novel written by the existentialist writer Albert Camus."*

So I struggled, struggled to make sense out of the insensible. I heard myself speaking to myself yet again: "Where do you go and what do you do…? Where do you go and what do you do…? Where do you go and what do you do when God is nowhere to be found?"

RESTORE POINT 9:

THE GRAND LIBRARY

"The righteous cry out, and the Lord hears, and delivers them out of all their troubles."[10]

I prayed. I cried out to God. I was terrified. I was scared, worried, frantic, nervous. Did the Lord hear? Would He deliver me out of my troubles? Then, I grew silent and simply listened; but, I heard nothing. No voice, no message from God, nothing but silence, a devastating, deafening silence. God's silence left me feeling more frightened and helpless than before I had prayed. I found myself crying and pleading and praying Scripture, "Keep not thou silence, O God: hold not thy peace, and be not still, O God." [11]

Then a word came, not a word from God, but a word about God. I remembered something a pastor friend once said, "Never forget in the dark what God taught you while in the light."

Never forget. Never forget. Somehow, I recalled the words of Corrie ten Boom, a famous Dutch Christian, who suffered imprisonment during World War II, "There is no pit so deep that God is not there." [12]

"Never forget. Never forget."

Then I remembered the words of a mother, a mother who spoke to me during the funeral of her teenaged son. Her son was killed in a hit-and-run auto accident while driving his bicycle in Chalmette, "Oh. Pastor. My heart is so troubled. Yet in my heart I do know one thing: *"God can do anything except make a mistake."*

I was surrounded by question marks. The distressing questions dug deeper and deeper into the darkness of my troubled heart.

"Never forget. Never forget."

"God can do anything except make a mistake."

Questions on top of questions were bubbling to the surface, coming to the light as the light of day approached.

"Never forget. Never forget."

"There is no pit so deep that God is not there."

Where was I? Who were these people? Who was this Dr. Bernard Rieux? And what of this Father Paneloux, who was he?

"Never forget. Never forget."

"God can do anything except make a mistake."

The boy in white? The starker? Why were they here? Why was I here?

Butterflies? Rats. Caterpillars. Cocoons? Why is this happening to me? What about Emma? Where was she? How was she?

"Never forget. Never forget."

"There is no pit so deep that God is not there."

I simply had to, had to, had to find some rhyme or reason, some light in the midst of the darkness, some rhythm that brought harmony out of the chaos. One thought came after another as the hours of the first day and night slowly passed, with one thought dominating all others…

> *"These people do not exist, other than on the pages of the novel written by Camus."*

Dr. Rieux visited a second time, briefly, then instructed an aid to have someone from the kitchen bring me a cup of warm milk. As he walked away I wondered, *Is he real? Or, is he a figment of a disordered mind? My disordered mind?*

Shortly after Dr. Rieux concluded his visit, a rather sickly looking old woman with tired, yellowed eyes glared at me as she slowly and carefully placed one foot in front of another in an effort to carry the cup of warm milk to a small table next to my bed. When she walked she actually wobbled, wobbled with slow, dull movement. Her tongue lay slightly over her bottom lip, as if her face were partially paralyzed. When I nodded to her

I smiled and said "Thanks" -- she jerked her head from side to side, then smiled a sly smile, and winked.

"Welcome, Monsieur."

As she walked away, I turned and looked through an open window at the evening sky. A star, a single star, silently winked in the darkness. As I looked out the window I recalled the words of Vincent van Gogh, "Looking at the stars always makes me dream…" [13]

I thought again about the old lady and the cup of warm milk and turned toward her again. She was gone. I heard the troubling voice of Emma speaking once again….

> *"These people did not exist. These are not flesh and blood real people."*

> *If these people do not exist then how is it that I have this cup of warm milk by my bedside? Was the old woman with the milk a figment of my imagination? How is it that these people who do not exist suddenly appear? There must be a sane explanation. And, if not…*

After drinking the cup of milk I passed into light sleep, a sort of twilight kind of sleep, half here, half there. It was as if I had wandered into that secret place where dreams lie in waiting.

The night was filled with dreams as I slept, dreams of butterflies drifting through the open window, shuttling weightlessly back and forth, flashing color as they danced on delightful flowers that climbed across a massive oak trees' branches just outside my open window.

Then I awoke. I was stunned by what I saw. Outside my window, struggling to stand, was a decaying, hollow dead oak, with gray moss crawling, climbing and choking the tree limbs.

Before it flew away I caught a fleeting glimpse of one single butterfly as it slowly crawled across the window sill – *then it quickly disappeared.*

The sight of the butterflies triggered thoughts of the Chinese philosopher Zhuangzi. He once dreamed he was a butterfly. He was happy being a butterfly and happy doing whatever it is that butterfly's do. In his dream he didn't know he was Zhuangzi. He thought he was a butterfly. Then he woke up. He was no longer a butterfly. He was Zhuangzi. But he didn't know if he was Zhuangzi who had dreamt he was a butterfly, or a butterfly dreaming he was Zhuangzi. What a crazy thought? Or, is it?

If these people do not exist, could I be dreaming, could I actually be dreaming that they exist? Could everything that has been happening be a dream? Nothing more? If these people who do not exist are a dream and I too am in the dream with them – am I dreaming of them or are they dreaming of me? Who or what is real here? What is reality? Who has and who does not have existence? *There must be a sane explanation.*

Several hours later, feeling somewhat rested, I knelt beside the bed and began to pray. It was in that moment of prayer that I remembered a verse of Scripture: "Thy word is a lamp unto my feet and a light unto my path."[14]

The old woman from the kitchen returned again, early, on the morning of the second day. She smiled another tired smile as she slowly walked across my room to set a cup of coffee and a biscuit on the table next to my bed.

"Monsieur," she said with a heavy French accent through a scratchy voice, "Dr. Rieux say you now coffee drink, now can eat."

"Thank you, Mademoiselle. Tell me, Mademoiselle, do you know if there might be a Bible somewhere for me to read?"

"Read? I old woman, Monsieur, foolish old woman. My eyes dim and is my mind. I know nothing how read."

It was obvious from the way she spoke that she was mentally challenged. It appeared that some affliction had impaired her both mentally and physically. Her reply to my question about the Bible was very short and quick, somewhat ill-tempered. She then began to repeat her answer to my question, but as a low, mumbling murmur…. .

"I old woman, foolish old woman. My eyes dim and is my mind. I know nothing……"

With an air of what appeared to be simmering hostility she moved with deliberate, yet faltering steps, one step at a time, slowly crossing the room, until she stood in front of a large antique book case. Slowly, she turned to face me, raising one of her hands upward to her face. Putting one long thin finger across her mouth to indicate that we should be silent she then waved with her other hand for me to follow.

"Shhh. Shhh. Shhh. Quiet, Monsieur, quiet. Shhh. I old woman, foolish old woman."

With her free hand she gently pushed against the book case until it moved aside, revealing a hidden doorway, an entrance to a large secret chamber.

"This, Monsieur, great library of *Christ Cathedral.* Has secret entrances to seven rooms, including door your bedroom. Father Paneloux here often. He read. He pray. He curator of library. He not know I know about library. I sure Bible here."

She laughed a low, disturbing kind of laugh, raised her hand to direct me to the main chamber, then turned and winked a sly wink at me as she left to return to the kitchen.

"I old woman." she repeated, several times, as she walked through the secret door. "I old woman. I old woman, foolish old woman."

Her voice faded in the distance as she left the Great Library. As I walked through the secret passageway I could see the main chamber of the great library up ahead, awash in light, a pulsating, golden glowing kind of light. It had the appearance of a 16th century medieval library, filled with dark corners, rough hewn dark beams, and tall vaulted ceilings. I was overcome by the majestic appearance of this room dedicated to knowledge. Biblical historians, Bible scholars, theologians and philosophers would flock here, if given the opportunity.

Standing at the edge of the main chamber I could see that it was surrounded by seven smaller rooms that were connected to the main chamber. Each of the seven rooms had short beautiful halls decorated with gilt laurels and Escher-like inlaid marquetry, which formed decorative patterns. The hallways to each of the seven rooms served as mini-repositories of rare books. The hallways and rooms appeared to be off-limits to the public as each had a thick velvet rope draped across the entrance, symbolically blocking access to each of the seven rooms.

Each room began to glow as I approached their individual entrance. Not a physical glowing, as if someone had turned on a light, but a radiance, a presence that words fail to describe. Beyond each of the short hallways, inside each of the seven rooms were tall shelves, stretching to the high vaulted ceilings, filled with more rare books, commentaries, small ornate statues, elaborate paintings and other historical artifacts.

As I backed away from each particular room into the main chamber, the smaller rooms would darken. It was then that I noticed that above the doorway to each particular room there was a large carved beam, made of cedar. On each facing of the beam, on the right and on the left, were carved woodcuts of cherubim and palm trees. Between the cherubim and palm trees were woodcut inscriptions carved into the face of the beam, phrases to designate and describe the category of old and rare books and other artifacts found in each particular room. The rooms were designated as follows: The Gallery of Treasures, The Theologians Porch, The Philosophers Porch, The Apologists Porch, The Gallery of History, The Poet's Square, and, The Psalmist's Corner, which contained musical works from antiquity.

As I moved from room to room with each turn of a corner I would bump into antiquity, a vast collection of historic treasures beyond compare. The grand library contained valuable books, commentaries, documents, and much more. There were historical church documents, manuscripts and collections of manuscripts. Some were more than 2,000 years old dealing with biblical studies, theological treatises, philosophical works, music and science, even warfare. The library of *Christ Cathedral* was filled with hand written manuscripts from before the invention of the printing press and the shelves were lined with thousands of printed books, Christian and pagan, sacred and profane, in virtually every language known to man, including Greek, Arabic, Armenian, Hebrew, Georgian, Syriac and old Udi texts.

Each room was filled with ancient engravings, wood cuts, etchings, drawings, and images of Old and New Testament saints, theologians, poets and philosophers. Strangely, each of the books had brand new covers, spines and gold-leafed lettering with the titles and author's names clearly visible. Everything appeared to be carefully catalogued with the original contents protected and preserved by the new covers. I was especially careful not to touch or remove any of the volumes or their protective covers.

I held my head to one side as I scanned the titles of the books on each of the shelves in each of the individual rooms. I carefully traced my fingers over the spines of the commentaries, books and collections moving my hand

and my eyes back and forth across the rows, working my way downward, as I read the various titles and authors.

There are far too many books and manuscripts for me to name, but some of the titles that I remember were: Epistles on the Arian Heresy and the Deposition of Arius by Alexander of Alexandria: On the Christian Faith (De fide) by Ambrose ; The Complete Works of Athanasius; plus works by Augustine, Basil the Great, Ignatius of Antioch, Jerome, John Chrysostom, Justin Martyr, Origen, Polycarp, and more. Novatian's Treatise Concerning the Trinity was there as was a mint condition 25-volume collection of the writings of Tertullian: The Didache (c. 100), Apostolic Constitutions, The Legend of Barlaam and Josaphat, The Passion of the Scillitan Martyrs and a 38-volume collection of writings from the first 800 years of the church entitled The Early Church Fathers were also there. Corpus Thomisticum, Summa contra Gentiles and Summa Theologica byThomas Aquinas, Desiderius Erasmus, Peter Faber, Pilgrim's Progress by John Bunyan and many more works were there.

Every rare book imaginable that a historian, biblical scholar, theologian or philosopher could ever hope to read seemed to be here -- in this wonderfully grand library. Every book, that is, except the one that I was looking for – the Bible.

As I walked to the center of the main chamber, slowly, yet suddenly, the environment became different, obviously different, electric. Poetic images of radiant light, contemporary words, phrases and modern terminology descriptive of light, even Hebrew, the language of Light -- all fail to capture the essence of the experience of walking through the main chamber.

Luminous. Resplendent. Glowing. Words fail. Language fails.

Soft circular patterns of gentle golden light flowed across everything in the main chamber of the grand library. It was as if everything in the main chamber — the elaborate walls, the seven ornate statues of biblical figures that stood at each entrance to the seven adjoining rooms, the seven-branched candle stick, even the massive ceiling with its ancient fresco — all shimmered with soft circulating, pulsating golden light.

The massive, ancient fresco, a painting executed in plaster on the ceiling of the main chamber, depicted and traced the spiritual pilgrimage of man, from creation to the final judgment. The painting is dominated by scenes of the final and eternal judgment by God of all mankind. Souls rise and descend to their fate, as judged by Christ. An unknown French artist, the painter, from the School of Paris, filled the fresco with renditions of dozens of historical and religious figures. In the painting Christ is positioned at the center, seated upon a Great White Throne in the midst of seven golden lamp stands, with patterns of horizontal layers depicting heaven, earth and hell. Twelve patriarchs, one for each of the twelve tribes of Israel, and the twelve Apostles were represented as were the four and twenty elders. They were all positioned at the highest level, followed by the pastor's, theologians, apologists, and other children of Light. These all glowed, both body and face, with the flush of eternal life. Those who populated the lower level were shadowed by darkness. Lurking there were the heretics, secular philosophers, sorcerers, followers of dark spirits and such. Their image was the epitome of eternal separation from God, with faces filled with fright, and stressful images of weeping, wailing and gnashing their teeth.

While I silently stood looking upward at the fresco, I was startled by a sudden sight, a triple flash of white; and sound, the sound of wings flapping, as three pure white doves, winged their way overhead in circular patterns. As they flew their circular patterns within the oval confines of the large chamber, I recalled a dove release during a wedding ceremony, many years ago. The breathtaking sight of the release of three doves in that wedding ceremony was intended to represent the presence of the Father, the Son and the Holy Spirit. Could these three doves be a signal of God's triune presence?

In unison, as if guided by divine providence, all three landed on a small, antique bookshelf, separate from all others, mounted on a wall. On the upper shelf were four white candles, with one of the four a larger candle, unlit, in the center, surrounded by three smaller candles, which were lit. Each dove stood next to one of the smaller candles, then, in a flash they each flew into the flame of their candle, then crashing into one another, merging, miraculously becoming one singular dove. The three became one, then, as one spiraled upward disappearing into the fresco. The center candle suddenly lit, with a lively flame dancing and flickering joyously.

In my mind I heard ancient, strange sounding words, words that echoed the sentiment of the sacred *Trisagion*. They were repeated several times, in unison… .

> *Thrice Holy. Thrice Holy. Thrice Holy Is Our One God.*
> *Thrice Holy. Thrice Holy. Thrice Holy Is Our One God.*

As the singing subsided, the glow from the large singular candle cast a holy glow on the book shelf. There, in the light of the golden glow of the large candle I saw several antique Bibles, ancient manuscripts, a Douay-Rheims Bible published in the 1500's, plus a copy of the more recent Jerusalem Bible….and the authorized version, the King James Bible.

In the soft light of the singular candle I saw my hand reach for the authorized King James version of the Bible. Trembling, I cradled the Bible in my hands like a child, smiling as a favorite Scripture came once again to mind….

> *"Thy word is a lamp unto my feet and a light unto my path."*[15]

The three doves. The secret chamber. The old woman showing me the way. The grand libraries. The ancient artwork. The wondrous fresco. The Bible. God's Lamp. His Word. A light unto my path. My heart was pounding. God in His providence definitely had heard and was now answering my prayer. And here, in His Word, I would find answers to my questions. He had something, something special, some special revelation – just for me.

Surrounded by the soft golden glow of the large chamber, in the midst of swirling golden light, beneath the fresco, I sat on the floor and prayed a silent prayer.

I gently opened the thick black leather cover of the Bible and there was – *NOTHING.* – nothing but a blank page followed by more blank pages. The pages of the Bible, every one of them, were blank. There was no text. No print. *NOTHING.*

I was stunned. Speechless. Shocked.

The room suddenly filled with the noise of shouting. Angry, hostile shouting, shouting as cold as ice. It was my voice – cold, hard, angry, hostile -- shouting and echoing throughout the large chamber, through the seven hallways into the seven smaller rooms....

"The pages are blank." I shouted. I was frantic.

"The pages are blank. Dear God. The pages are blank. I have no lamp for my feet. There is no light for my path. Oh. God. The pages are blank. The pages are blank."

I found myself trembling, half sitting, half lying, on the floor. I was frantically flipping through page after page of the Bible. Weeping and angrily shouting. There was no text; no index of the Old or New Testament books -- nothing.

The outside spine indicated that this was a red letter edition of the authorized King James Bible – but there was no lettering at all, nothing. No red ink. No black ink. No text. No lettering. No print. No maps. *NOTHING. NOTHING. NOTHING.* The pages were blank. *NOTHING.*

"God. Oh. God. The pages are blank. I have no lamp for my feet. There is no light for my path. Oh. God. Where are You, God? Where are You? Help me, God. The pages are blank."

My hand was trembling as I stood and placed the authorized version of the Bible back on the shelf. I then reached for the New Jerusalem Bible. I had a crazed, blank stare as I opened this Bible.

The pages were blank.

This is a nightmare. This is a cruel joke. This is insanity. Something inside me snapped. I hurled the New Jerusalem Bible across the room. I then took the authorized version from the shelf and began ripping pages from it, leaving them scattered on the floor.

I ran into The Theologians Porch and grabbed the first volume of Corpus Thomisticum, Summa contra Gentiles and Summa Theologica by Thomas Aquinas. Opened it. The pages were blank. The second volume, the pages were blank. I was too stunned to scream, to angry to be silent. With one broad, angry sweep of my arm the entire section of books by Aquinas came crashing to the ground.

I was like a dog rummanging through garbage cans – making a mess of everything.

The works by Augustine -- blank. Basil the Great, blank. Ignatius of Antioch, blank. Jerome, John Chrysostom, Justin Martyr, Origen, Polycarp -- blank. -- blank. -- blank.

As quick as I touched a volume, saw that it was blank, it was thrown to the floor.

And more. Novatian's Treatise Concerning the Trinity – all of the pages -- blank. The 25-volume collection of the writings of Tertullian – every page of every volume – blank.

Page after page, front and back, volume after volume -- no black ink; no colored ink. No fancy lettering. Nothing. The pages were blank. Every place I turned. Every room I entered. Every book I opened. – blank. Nothing. All blank pages. The Philosophers Porch, The Apologists Porch, The Gallery of History, The Poet's Square, and, The Psalmist's Corner – it was all a charade. There were no words printed on any of the pages of the thousands of books that were now all over the floor.

I wandered through the library, stunned, shocked, too confused to entertain questions and too despondent to pray. In one final act of desperation I reached for another book – another Bible. Trembling, I once again cradled it in my hands and gently opened its cover – nothing – the pages were blank.

Dr. Rieux and Father Paneloux will think I'm either insane or that I've suffered some type of brain damage. I was frightened. Worried. Anxious. Afraid. Then I heard a familiar voice....

> *"These people do not exist, other than on the pages of the novel written by Camus."*

RESTORE POINT 10:

THE LIGHT OF DARKNESS

Sometimes, life is difficult. Sometimes, life is incredibly cruel. Questions, ultimate questions, gut-wrenching questions, confront us, taunt us, and frustrate us. Answers, often so elusive, are sometimes closed to us, like tightly locked rooms. Finding, not just answers, but right answers, is crucial. Choices have consequences. Like the proverbial pot of gold at the end of the rainbow right answers can change everything in an instant.

Life has a mysterious way of rearranging things in incredible ways, swiftly.

Adversity, at least the kind that I was dealing with, demands that we take deliberate steps. My steps took me out of the main chamber of the great library, down a very narrow spiral staircase, into a vestibule at the rear of the sanctuary of *Christ Cathedral.*

I was there for one reason and one reason only – *to confront God.*

I paused at the rear of the sanctuary, drew a deep breath – and stood motionless. Before me, I must confess, was beauty, stunning beauty in every direction.

In the very front of the sanctuary of *Christ Cathedral,* soft colorful shades of light were streaming through a large, stained glass circular dome positioned high above the altar.

On the massive front wall, beneath the dome, above the altar, was a large work of art, a fresco depicting a weeping angel, with huge white feather wings, towering high in the heavens, holding an open book, the *Lamb's Book of Life.* Seven angels, ready to distribute divine retribution, stood behind the large weeping angel. They were ready to sound seven trumpets that would signal *earth's final call -- the seven trumpet judgments.*

There was something fascinating, something beautiful, yet horrifying and frightening about the weeping angel and the image of the open book that he held. The angelic fresco created a sense of awe, and a contrasting feeling of fear and trembling. My eyes were so fixed on the totality of the images conveyed through the fresco that I could not move. I could only look, and wonder – and stare.

The weeping angel holding the open book had another arm, a long, outstretched arm, with its hand and a long finger pointed downward, indicating judgment and banishment. Beneath the angel's frightening outstretched hand, a condemned heretic, an atheistic philosopher, and behind him, two of his atheistic peers. The first philosopher cowered and trembled, his face wet with tears, filled with eternal fright. *His name was not written* in the *Lamb's Book of Life.* There was something sad and something strange about this atheistic philosopher – *I felt like I knew him. And I did.*

I also knew the other two atheistic philosophers, who, with equal fright, fear and trembling, stood behind him. Here, cowering before the *Great White Throne,* were three, three who were referred to in several lines of *A Psalm of The Apocalypse…*

Three. Three. Shaped by the Pen.
Recurrence. Recurring, Again and Again.
Philosophers Three – All Agree
What Ill Hath Befallen Thee

As I stood there I heard my voice, speaking harshly, inside of my head.

You're here for one reason and one reason only – to confront God.

Standing there I remembered something that the philosopher Thoreau said. He said something about *most men living their lives in quiet desperation.*[16] The palms of my hands were sweating. My heart was racing – as were my thoughts. I was about to take a drastic step, a step of desperation that would far exceeds anything that Thoreau referenced.

I was here for one reason and one reason only. My intent was to confront God. An act of desperation? Yes. But, there would be nothing *quiet* about my confrontation.

Desperation. Rebellious thoughts began to spike, speak and rage within my head. Once again I heard my angry inner voice, demanding confrontation….

You're here for one reason and one reason only – to
confront God.
Confront God. Confront Him. Confront God.
You asked for Light. God gave you blank pages.
You have no options. You have no choice.
Confront God. Confront Him. Confront Him now.

I was standing motionless amid the soft shadows of the vestibule, immobilized by spiritual confusion and the thrust of a raging spiritual conflict that was working within me.

Am I wrestling against God? Am I doing battle with myself? Or, is this turbulent inner clash a fight to the death with spiritual forces arrayed against me?

The Bible speaks of *waging a good warfare,*[17] *of fighting a good fight of faith.*[18] It speaks of *being steadfast, unmovable.*[19] I wondered, was I waging a good warfare? Fighting a good fight of faith? Was I being steadfast? I was not sure. What I did know is that a war was being waged within me, a war that pitted my flesh against my spirit -- *and pitted me against God.*

Be still, and let the dark come upon you[20]
Be still, and let the dark come upon you
Confront God. Confront Him. Confront Him now.
Be still, and let the dark come upon you

I was immobilized by the violence of the voices raging around and within me. I was playing a game that I could not win. I didn't know what to do. I didn't know what to say. I simply stood there with my two fists clenched, my chest heaving, sweat on my brow, sweat running down both sides of my face, enduring unbelievable inner pain and suffering.

Be still, and let the dark come upon you
Be still, and let the dark come upon you
Confront God. Confront Him. Confront Him now.
Be still, and let the dark come upon you

No. I will not be still. And, No. I will not let the dark come upon me. I am a soldier of light. My struggle is not against God. My wrestling is a struggle to hear from God and receive God's blessing. Be rebuked ye evil ones. In the name of Christ be rebuked. Jacob wrestled with God and gained a blessing. He heard the voice of God. Light came upon him – not darkness.

No. I will not be still. And, No. I will not let the dark come upon me. I will not walk in darkness. I will not. I will not. I will not.

At the sound of the name Jesus Christ, suddenly, my eyes once again were opened and focused on the image of the weeping angel. I felt an uncontrollably strong urge to cry, but could not. The tears would not come. I was learning a very painful lesson: the absence of tears does not mean the absence of suffering.

Psychological pain, spiritual anguish, desperation – the definition of these words can be found in a dictionary. The inward suffering and agony they create, however, are impossible to define. The wise chase away this kind of inward suffering. They root it out as a poisonous weed, yet the spot, like a gaping wound where the weed once stood, remains. Some scars are visible. Some are not. Some wounds heal. Others, never. And, sometimes, even though you can't see the pain you can feel its pull as it takes you where you do not want to go and causes you to become what you never intended.

Where are the wise men? Where are the sages? Who is wise enough for this hour? Who is sufficient for this agony? *My God. My God. Why hast Thou forsaken me?*[21] *You alone are my everlasting hope.*

I stood there, a lonely, alienated, isolated man with a troubled heart, a deeply scarred, troubled heart. Frail, without strength, I had come to the end of my rope. With my fist held tightly in a round ball and my forehead pulsating and throbbing, I could feel the pressure of blood coursing though the veins on my neck and forehead.

Tears cannot, no, tears cannot cause this kind of suffering's demise. Nor can philosophy or psychology end its reign. No novelist, no author, no poet, no literary giant can deal a death blow to the pain of abandonment by God -- and the gut-wrenching suffering that accompanies that abandonment.

The pen is powerful, but not powerful enough. Desperation and its pain, the pain of alienation, abandonment, *Divine Abandonment* – do they not claw more deeply and more cruelly than any other pain? Does its pain not wound more deeply than any other? Does its pain not endure longer, infinitely longer? Does it not take longer to heal? Can it ever heal? O God, where are You?

And, so, there I stood, filled with troubling questions, silently weeping as I stared at a weeping angel. I was desperate for God, yet I felt abandoned by God. I could not find Him. I could not find God. And, to make matters worse, if I found Him I had nothing to offer Him but a confused, mangled heart – *and my anger.*

With eyes I saw, yet I did not see. As I moved my gaze across the fresco of the weeping angel, there, downward, below that horrific scene of divine judgment and banishment, surrounded by clouds, was the image of a frail, white-haired old man with a medieval-like halo wrapped around the back of his head. He was dressed in long flowing robes of white, seated, looking upward at the weeping angel and the condemned atheistic philosophers. The frail, white-haired old man with the halo was writing on a scroll. Here was the artist's rendition of the last living apostle, John, exiled to the aisle of Patmos for his faithfulness to the Word of God. He was recording on his parchment scroll all that he saw from his vantage point in the heavens. With eyes filled with wonder he looked, he pondered, and he recorded the mysteries of the heavenly vision of everlasting judgment.

A spirit of utter calmness came over me, a great peace as I looked at the portrait of John. The calmness was strange and mysterious. Just a few moments ago I was frantic, acting out of inner anguish and desperation. And now, calmness.

I knew, I knew, that this was the place where I would meet God. I suddenly remembered what it felt like to be me again. I felt a flush of faith rise within me. I was very aware that I was in exactly the right place where I needed to be.

Once again I glanced across the sanctuary. It was filled with apocalyptic imagery. There was a breathless mesmerizing beauty in the apocalyptic imagery of the architecture of the sanctuary of *Christ Cathedral.* Apocalyptic imagery and imagination has nurtured generations of mystics, seers, prophets, theologians and everyday believers across the ages. The elaborate symbolism of the architecture and the prophetic imagery of the primitive art displayed throughout the sanctuary focused on biblical numerology, in particular, the number seven, the number of perfection: artists and architects filled the sanctuary with images of the Seven Churches, the Seven Angels, the Seven Stars, the Seven Golden Candlesticks, Seven trumpets, seven, seven, seven, everywhere seven.

The long, center aisle from the vestibule to the front of the sanctuary was lined with seven columns on the right and seven columns on the left. There were seven circular stained glass windows on the outer wall on the right and on the outer wall on the left. The traditional plaques representing the Seven Stations of the Cross, sometimes called the Way of Sorrows, depicting the final hours of the passion of Jesus were present, but complimented by a visual scheme that amplified Jesus and His role as Judge in relation to the seven churches of Revelation.

Near the display dedicated to the first of the Seven Lamps of Fire a little crowd, pious and emotional, knelt and prayed, made the sign of the cross, then moved to the next display dedicated to the second of the Seven Lamps of Fire. An arrogant, smug looking young man stood behind the little crowd. He was strong and healthy in appearance, yet too proud to kneel. Beside him a weary, older, silver-haired man, leaning on a dull wooden cane, also stood. Unable to kneel, he held his hat in his free hand with his head slightly bent, signaling deference and reverence. As the group moved from display to display a small boy in a white robe carried a golden vessel filled with incense. He would shake the golden vessel, seven times, toward the small crowd then shake it again, seven times, toward the display, reciting a brief prayer in Latin, seven times. The crowd would then move to the next display.

To the right of the sanctuary, near the front, in a place of prominence, was a very large, elevated, crucifix, an icon. An older woman, wearing a thin silk scarf over her head, knelt before the crucifix. She was looking upward, gazing at the dying figure of Christ, carved in stone, fastened to the cross. She would then lower her head, lightly touch her hand to her chest, then pray a bead on her prayer chain. After she completed her prayer, she repeated the process, moving to the next bead until she had prayed all of the beads on her prayer chain. The repetition in her prayer was intentional, a type of memorized way of talking to God.

Looking down at the woman from the crucifix was the Suffering Servant, Jesus. His larger than life stone body was fastened to two large wooden beams, portraying his death for her sins and for the sins of the world. As she prayed the last bead on her prayer chain she genuflected, slowly bending one knee to the ground, as a gesture of respect for the stone Jesus. She then went to a rack of candles on the left where she would light candles, one at a time, with each lighting of a candle followed by a prayer read from a prayer book. She would then light another candle, then pray once again from the prayer book.

There were supposedly seven mysteries attached to each set of seven prayers that she would pray and each of the seven candles that she would eventually light. Each of the seven mysteries focused on one of the seven seals of the seven sealed scroll of the *apocalypse.*

I heard the older woman make a faint sort of choking murmur, a final prayer, followed by the sound of low muffled sobbing. Once again she genuflected, making *the sign of the cross* while slowly bending one knee to the ground, then she left the sanctuary.

Beside the crucifix, to the right, suspended from the high, vaulted ceiling was an oil-filled sanctuary lamp, with its holy glow encased in a red glass globe. Inside, the "eternal flame" danced atop the oil-filled wick, continuously, signifying the eternal presence of God. Embedded in the gold rings that circled the golden lamp was engraved images of the seven eyes of the Spirit of God.

A young boy, dressed in a plain white robe, was to the right side of the sanctuary, beneath the sanctuary lamp. He was working with a second rack filled with candles. Candles, in most churches, are a symbol of the Christ Who has come. In *Christ Cathedral* they symbolize the Christ Who was yet to come – *in judgment.*

The young boy was having difficulty lighting candles and appeared to be frustrated. He lowered his head, tensed his body and clenched his fists, evidently to better control his frustration. For reasons unknown to me the boy suddenly and slowly turned around. He looked at me, directly at me. Our eyes met. We both stood still, not moving an inch, nor blinking our eyes. It was as if there was some indefinable connection, a kinship between us. He quickly, yet calmly and quietly, turned away to resume working with the rack of candles.

Another boy dressed in a white robe was walking up the steps that led to the altar beneath the fresco of the weeping angel with the *Lamb's Book of Life.* The boy was carrying a bundle of long, thin white candles, placing them, one by one, atop two large seven branched candelabras on either side of the altar. Another boy, also dressed in white, was close behind, carrying a brass pole with a lighted wick at the end. He carefully held the pole up, gently touching the tip of each of the slender candles, methodically lighting each one, until all seven on each side of the altar were lit.

A group of men, seven in number, were all dressed alike in long black flowing robes, ritual garments. They had shaven the crowns of their heads as a symbol of renunciation of earthly things and submission to God. They whispered among themselves, softly, yet excitedly, as they debated various interpretations of woodcuts depicting the Seven Last Plagues.

A massive, ancient fresco, a monumental composition much larger than the one in the great library, and much larger than the one above the altar, ran the full length of the sanctuary of *Christ Cathedral,* high above the long center aisle. The massive painting was dominated by various aspects of *the bema judgment, the Judgment Seat of Christ,* one of the central doctrines of the New Testament. Though salvation is by grace through faith, the doctrine of *the Judgment Seat of Christ* focuses on the blessings and rewards that Christ bestows on believers for their faithfulness. The Bible teaches that *the Judgment Seat of Christ* is a place where believers will receive or forfeit rewards depending on how one has lived his or her life for Christ.

In *the Judgment Seat of Christ* fresco, Jesus is seated on a Throne surrounded by a large circular rainbow, a rainbow that has no beginning or end. His feet are resting on the earth, which serves as His footstool. An upward gesture of blessing, made by his right hand, has two fingers pointed upward, the traditional medieval symbol of reward and blessing. The two upward pointing fingers also represent the two natures of Christ, that of man and that of God.

At the base of the rainbow the artist depicted the reception of the righteous into heaven. On the left of the painting a small band of Old Testament believers were being ushered forward by leaders representing the twelve tribes of Israel to receive their blessing. On the opposite side, in a similar position another small group of New Testament believers were being escorted by the twelve apostles to receive their rewards. Both groups, after receiving their rewards and blessings, were clothed with white robes by angels, then, together they passed through large golden gates into the heavenly paradise. Surrounding the earth, at the four points of the compass, four angels were preparing to blow their apocalyptic trumpets.

There was one big mystery for me as I looked at and studied the massive fresco – the upward gesture of blessing, made by the right hand of Christ, with His two fingers pointed upward. I found myself staring intently at the soft rays of light as they danced across the two-fingered symbol of blessing. It was a moment of sacred silence, reverent silence, a silence that was suddenly interrupted by an inward mocking whisper.

> *"Thy word is a lamp unto my feet and a light unto my path*[22] *-- I sought Light; I sought Blessings -- yet you gave me darkness."*

As I heard those words I could feel anger, rebellious anger, welling up inside of me, rushing over me. As I looked above at the fresco, at the hand of blessing, my hostility toward God increased. Earlier, angry steps had taken me out of the main chamber of the library – *to confront God.*

With deliberate, angry steps I descended the spiral staircase. I had come into this vestibule at the rear of the sanctuary of *Christ Cathedral* for one reason and one reason only – *to confront God.*

> *Be still, and let the dark come upon you*[23]
> *Be still, and let the dark come upon you*
>   *Confront God. Confront Him. Confront Him now.*
> *Be still, and let the dark come upon you*

They say you need to pray, when you need a word from God. But they don't tell you what to do when you pray and God is silent. Once again, out of desperation, I silently cried out for God. From deep within I cried out, again and again, for God to speak to me. *Nothing. No response. Nothing but silence.*

Is this the wine of God's fury? Must I drink from the cup of God's wrath? *"Cursed is He that hangeth on a tree."*[24] When Christ hung on the cross, on Calvary's tree, He took upon Himself our curse that we might share in His blessing. Where is my blessing? Why this mocking from above? Why this silence? Why, why was I given blank pages? Here, above me, the raised hand of Christ. A promised blessing? Where is my promised blessing? Why this deafening silence? Why? Why? Why?

> *My God, my God, why has Thou forsaken me?*[25]

The cry of Jesus was angrily shouted within me, protesting this horrid Divine abandonment. When Christ shouted those words His shout was a shout of victory. My shout was one of anger, hostility, desperation and defeat. I was angry and confused, unable to think clearly. As I slowly walked the long center aisle my mind was filled with troubling, questioning thoughts.

> *Be still, and let the dark come upon you*[26]
> *Be still, and let the dark come upon you*
>   *Confront God. Confront Him. Confront Him now.*
> *Be still, and let the dark come upon you*

"A light unto my path?"
Did I not ask for light? What did I receive? *Blank pages. Silence.*
"A lamp unto my feet?"
Did I not reach for His lamp? What was I given? *Silence. Blank pages.*

Jesus said, *"Ask and it shall be given unto you."* [27]
Did I not ask? Yet, what was I given? *Blank pages. Silence.*
Jesus said, *"Seek, and ye shall find."* [28]
Did I not seek? Yet what did I find? *Nothing.*
Jesus said, *"Knock and it shall be opened unto you."* [29]
Did I not knock? What was opened to me? *Nothing. Blank pages. Silence.*

Heaven's doors were locked, shut tight. The shutters were closed. The blinds were drawn. Providence was slanted against me. I felt helpless, abandoned, terribly alone – *without hope.* In the midst of the inward turbulence and turmoil the words of an unknown first century Christian came to mind....

> *There are times when the things of God appear to be opposed to the things of God, when the things of faith appear to be opposed to the things of faith, when we hope against all hope and all hope disappears.*[30]

The plaintive cry of that unknown Christian from long ago was followed by my own...

> *"Where do you go and what do you do when God is nowhere to be found?"*

I began to think: there is only one thing worse then being hated by God. It is being ignored by Him. At least when He hates you He treats you like you exist. To be ignored by God is harsher than any man can bear. It is as if you do not exist.

I was still standing motionless amid the soft shadows of the vestibule. I could feel the pressure of blood pulsating though the veins on my neck and forehead. I was filled with despair toward God, still immobilized by spiritual confusion and the thrust of a raging spiritual conflict that was working within me.

Here, indeed, was my sorrowful portrait -- *my art born of sorrow.* I stood there, a lonely man with a troubled heart. Frail, without strength, I had come to the end of my rope. I had seen things that others have not seen. I had felt things that others had not felt. I had experienced things that others had not experienced. Yet, here I stood a frail lonely man who had witnessed the collapse of everything that gave life substance, value and meaning. And my faith was disappointed, devastated. The bitter taste of spiritual and emotional despair soured, not only my stomach, but deep down into the very pit of my soul. By all outward circumstances, by all outward appearances, God had failed me in my hour of great need. God had let me down…and, I was filled with despair, disappointment, anger and rage.

Give me a brush. Some paint. A ply-board. I will paint.
I will paint *"Desolation"*
I will paint *"If there is a God, He ain't here."*
I will paint *"No One Home."*

Be still, and let the dark come upon you [31]
Be still, and let the dark come upon you
Confront God. Confront Him. Confront Him now.
Be still, and let the dark come upon you

Whether dark had come upon me or not, I could not tell. I was only sure of one thing, and one thing only: I was here in *Christ Cathedral* for one reason and one reason only – *to confront God.*

As I took my first defiant step down the center aisle my despair created an uncontrollable inward outburst of tears. Yet I could not cry. The hand of blessing was above me – but there was no blessing upon me – no blessing for me.

As I took the second step I wondered, yet again, *where is my blessing?* My gaze gradually shifted from the large fresco above me to the crucifix at the front of the sanctuary. Worthlessness. Feelings of worthlessness washed over me, followed by feelings of despair, depression and dread. I felt angry, yet fragile, vulnerable, very weak and confused – *yet angry, very angry.*

Was there no hope for me? Was there no help for me? With the third and final uncertain step toward the large crucifix I wasn't sure if I was walking toward something, or walking away from someone – *God.*

Psychosis, they say, involves hearing voices, seeing visions, feelings of paranoia, feelings of being pursued. I heard nothing. I saw nothing. I had no vision. All I saw was a cold, stone-faced Jesus. As I stood there looking at His hard, cold chiseled face, I felt myself nervously shaking, rocking back and forth, filled with at inward trembling and a chill. Was I abandoned by God? Or, was I abandoning God?

As I stood there staring at the dying figure of Christ, carved in stone, my mind was once again filled with troubling thoughts.

Be still, and let the dark come upon you[32]
Be still, and let the dark come upon you
    Confront God. Confront Him. Confront Him now.
Be still, and let the dark come upon you

I was shaken, shaken from my inner world of turbulent, raging thought by the sounds of people in panic. People, filled with fright, were hastily rushing out of the sanctuary. I heard the shuffle of feet, the sound of frightened people running. I heard their voices but could not understand what they were saying. Then, I heard a loud sound – *'gbaam'* – the small boy carrying the golden vessel filled with incense dropped it to the cold, stone floor as he too ran from the sanctuary. A hush of horror lay upon the stunned monks as they quietly cowered behind several pews near the rear of the sanctuary.

I could hear an angry voice shouting, angrily, loudly, above all the other voices, above all the other frightful sounds; but, it seemed far away, yet dangerously near. It was a hostile demanding voice. It was the voice of a man – a man shouting angrily. The terror of his voice, it created a lump in my chest. In fear, people were running from the church. It seemed they couldn't run fast enouch. I was stunned. I was shaken. The yelling and shouting voice -- *was mine.*

> *"Come down from that cross. If you are the Son of God,*
> *come down from that cross."*

My eyes were wild and wide with uncontrollable rage. I stared, disorientated, half-crazed, shouting angrily at the dead figure of Christ carved in stone.

> *"Come down from that cross."*

This was delusional behavior, psychotic behavior, bizarre behavior, but I was powerless to stop it.

> *"Come down from that cross. If you are the Son of God,*
> *come down from that cross."*

I raised one of my fists defiantly into the air, then lowered it to point an accusing finger to the crucifix, screaming like a madman at the stone figure of Jesus.

> *"Come down from that cross. Come down from that cross.*
> *You said, 'Ask and it shall be given.'*[33]
> *Did I not ask? Yet, what was I given? Blank pages.*
> *And silence.*
> *You said, 'Seek, and ye shall find.'*[34]
> *Did I not seek? Yet what did I find? Nothing.*
> *You said, 'Knock and it shall be opened unto you.'*[35]
> *Did I not knock? What was opened to me?*
> *Nothing. Blank pages and silence.*
> *Come down from that cross. Come down from that cross."*

Faint and trembling, a nervous Jesuit priest wearing a long black robe came into the sanctuary from behind the altar. Slowly and carefully he walked toward me. It was Father Paneloux. As Paneloux heard the anguish and the hurt of my cry, his face turned soft and his voice became gentle. Hearing my strangled sobs he calmly lowered my raised hand. Then, he put both of his hands, gently on each side of my face, gently holding my face in his hands.

"Monsieur, please, Monsieur. Look carefully. This Christ is but stone. He cannot hear you. He cannot come down. Monsieur, He is not real."

As Paneloux spoke my eyes once again met the eyes of the young boy dressed in a plain white robe. He stood motionless beneath the sanctuary lamp by his rack of candles. When Paneloux said "He is not real" the boy looked at me and nodded his head, then a single tear slowly crawled down his cheek. Behind that tear was a hidden language whose meaning I did not then understand. Only later would I see the tear – *hear the language -- and understand.*

Suddenly, I once again heard the voice of Emma…

> *"These people do not exist. These are not flesh and blood real people. Each one of them, as you well know, are actually fictitious characters in a novel written by the existentialist writer Albert Camus."*
>
> *"Monsieur, He is not real."*

I had come to the place where nothing mattered anymore, *nothing but hearing from God.* The blank pages. The silence of God. As I stood there I kept hearing the words of Father Paneloux, over and over again….

> *"Monsieur, He is not real."*
> *"Monsieur, He is not real."*
> *"Monsieur, He is not real."*

Suddenly I realized that *I had misunderstood.*

None of what I had experienced signaled God's absence. Everything signaled His presence. The blank pages were His way of speaking to me. Suddenly, my eyes were opened. I could see what earlier was not seen. Hidden pictures were suddenly seen; and, I could not deny the reality of what I was now seeing. *This place, these people – none of this is real.* Yes, Father, this stone Christ, He is not real. Yes, Emma, *these people do not exist.*

Father Paneloux would not understand. Neither would Dr. Rieux. They would both think that I was crazy or that I am insane. However, in a world of insanity the insane are often sane and vice versa. In reality, I was slowly losing my mind – and simultaneously gaining a new mind, a new understanding, a new way of seeing. Gradually, I was dying to an old way of thinking – *and gaining a new previously unknown way of thinking.*

As I walked away a shabbily dressed, legless man sitting on a board that had little wheels mounted on the bottom, rolled toward me then reached out to me. He reached into his tin can and handed me two pencils. "These are for both of you. No charge. My gift to each of you."

Both of you? Each of you? I placed the two pencils in my shirt pocket and said, "Thank you" as the legless man quickly rolled away. With the echoing sound of his squeaking wheels bouncing off of the high walls of the church vestibule I suddenly realized that I had come there for one reason and one reason only – to confront God. God was there too, for one reason and one reason only – to comfort me. Choices have consequences. I had made my choice. God made His.

"These are for both of you. No charge. My gift to each of you."

RESTORE POINT 11:

BEING AND NON-BEING

When Dr. Rieux and Father Paneloux came later that afternoon to check on me they stood for a moment in silence at the doorway to my bedroom. Both men were dressed in black, Rieux in his drab heavy black coat and Paneloux in the traditional Jesuit black trousers and black shirt, with the open white collar. Both men looked tired and worn. And now, because of my bizarre, delusional behavior in the sanctuary they felt it necessary to visit me.

Neither of the men knew that I knew where they had been. Nor were they aware that I was aware of the agonizing death of a child, an innocent child entrusted to their care. The local Police Magistrate, a Monsieur Othon, had a son who had contracted a plague caused by diseased rats. When the boy was first diagnosed, Dr. Rieux impulsively asked the Magistrate and his wife, who were being separated from their son and quarantined in an isolation camp, if there was anything that he could do for them.

As Dr. Rieux stood in my doorway, his stomach was sickened as he remembered the magistrate averting his eyes away from Rieux. "No," he said, then swallowed hard. "But—save my son."[36]

But, Rieux could not save his son, nor could Father Paneloux; and both men were visibly disturbed, despairing the insensible death of the child.

After the child was diagnosed Dr. Rieux consulted with his colleagues, Dr. Castel and with Dr. Richard, former chairman of the medical association in Oran, Algeria. They decided that an untested experimental anti-plague serum would be tried for the first time on the child. After the serum was administered Dr. Rieux would make daily follow-up visits to examine the child. He would habitually position himself at the foot of the child's bed, read the medical record entries then examine the child, always looking for and documenting any signs of progress, remission or regression. Paneloux would come each day too, at the same time as Rieux. Each day he would lean against the wall near the head of the bed and fix his eyes on the child's small plague afflicted body. Each day he would smear a small swipe of holy oil on the child's forehead and pray a silent prayer for healing. But, healing did not come.

Instead, Paneloux and Dr. Rieux watched with fright as tiny, half-formed, painful puss-filled lymph nodes clogged the joints of the child's thin limbs. As the plague tortured and ravaged the child's body each day he would toss about convulsively, his eyes shut, his teeth clenched, his features frozen in an agonized grimace, as he deliriously rolled his head from side to side.

On this, the last day of the child's life, with both men present, the deliriums ceased. The boy's small body tightened, stiffened and stretched, then twisted and contorted. He trembled with each twist, and turn, as his small body was racked with unrelenting pain and spasms. At the end, at the very end, the child's teeth chattered rapidly. Simultaneously, the sound of a death rattle gurgled deep within his throat. Then, there was a final gasp for air as he uttered a long, shrill wail, a wail that caused both men to shudder. A single tear slowly crawled down his cheek as he cried out, "Papaaaa. Papaaaa. Papaaaa." The child then exhaled, breathed a long final breath, his very last, as his small body jerked and twitched, then finally relaxed, firmly held by the grip of death. After checking for any lingering signs of life Dr. Rieux pronounced the child dead. He then closed the child's half open eyes with his thumb and forefinger, placing a small copper penny over each eye to keep them closed.

Paneloux then administered *the sacrament of extreme unction,* anointing the child's forehead with one final smear of oil. Rieux then covered the child's frail naked body and face with an army blanket, then signed the death certificate. He then readjusted the blanket one final time to better cover the pale curves of the child's exposed ribs. The two men, disheartened and in despair, then left the clinic.

The wind, like a tired lament, mourned through the cool night air as a Doctor of Medicine and a Doctor of Theology stepped into what felt like an uninhabited wilderness. Defeated and dejected the two dazed men walked beneath a leafless tree overcome with grief. Such is the plight of suffering love. It sighs and sings of man's grim struggle, an ambiguous harmony of two, no, an absurd symphony of all, an alienated doxology. With the horribly tragic, senseless death of this child justice had taken a wrong turn.

Through their many years of experience with the horror of the plague both Dr. Rieux and Father Paneloux had seen many adults and many children die. Death was no respecter of persons. It killed the elderly. It killed the young. Neither Rieux nor Paneloux, however, had ever watched the agonizing day by day, minute by minute painful death-throes of an innocent child.

Dr. Rieux had placed his faith in a serum. Paneloux had placed his faith in a sacrament. Both men were disappointed, visibly shaken and in despair. Yet, they must continue on, each man attempting to fulfill his mission; Rieux, the things of medical necessity; Paneloux, the things of God.

Paneloux stepped into my room first, and, with a somewhat weak, toneless voice, said, "You look different, Monsieur. Better. Much better. Refreshed."

Dr. Rieux followed Paneloux into my room, wearied over the senseless death of the young child.

"Thank you, Father, for your kind words. I am better. Please have a seat, Father, Dr. Rieux. Please."

I pointed to two empty chairs near a small mahogany table in the room where they could be comfortably seated. The two chairs were to the right of a fireplace. The fire and its flames, wrapped around the logs in the fireplace, cast an array of dancing shadows across the room. An ivory chess set, a plain vase with brownish flowers, and a small candle were crammed atop the small table. I remained standing, momentarily, then began pacing the floor as they sat down. Before I spoke I heard a little voice inside of me whisper, *Be gentle as a dove, yet wise as a serpent.* [37]

Paneloux was seated with his body positioned so that he was partially hidden in the darkness of the shadows. Though his face was somewhat hidden in the darkness, I could see that he was holding a handkerchief to his mouth. His eyes followed each of my steps as I walked back and forth across the room. I could see that his face was drawn, troubled with grief and the accumulated weariness of witnessing the child's horrid death. I must be gentle, gentle as a dove – *yet wise.*

Both men were sick at heart over the death of the child; but, Paneloux, doubly so. As they left the scene of the tragic death of the child Dr. Rieux rebuked the priest for the shallowness of Paneloux's faith.

"In your very first sermon dealing with pain, human suffering, death and this horrid plague, you said 'We deserved this. We were guilty before God and we deserved this.' [38] What say you now? What say you about the brutal, senseless death of this innocent child? We, yes, perhaps we stand guilty before God, if there is a God; but, what of this innocent child? Innocence bears no guilt yet is afflicted nonetheless – and by God…by a just God. No. No. No. I'll have none of it. Never. Never. None of it."

Both men were silent from that point forward; and here they sat in my little guest bedroom, with Paneloux, worried, nauseated, doubly sick at his stomach, holding his handkerchief, telling me how well I looked.

Be gentle as a dove, yet wise as a serpent. [39]

"I've been thinking... and thinking… and thinking, gentlemen... trying to sort things out, trying to figure out how to say what needs to be said in a way that makes sense. In my head I hear the right words, words that seem to make sense out of that which is insensible, but when I try to speak the words, nothing comes out; and, when the words do finally come out they don't make sense, they don't make sense at all."

Dr. Rieux sat in his chair with his arms folded, wearing a seemingly grim poker face. I do not know if I was seeing the doctor's dour bedside manner caused by the death of the child or if I was seeing a man intentionally hiding behind a grim, solemn expression, so as to shield his thoughts and feelings from both me and Father Paneloux. He just sat there, saying nothing, listening intently, studying me, tracking me with his eyes as I spoke and as I paced the floor.

"Forgive me, even now I am having a hard time choosing the right words... There is something I need to say, something that will seem completely illogical, something that, once I speak it, will not make sense to either of you. But to me, in my head, all of that which did not make sense to me – now does… And I now understand… Not everything, mind you, not everything…but enough."

Long ago I discovered that God gives us the gift of intuition and the capacity to think, deductively, logically, so as to develop conclusions. These are mysterious gifts, yet sacred, subtle – inexplicable – God's gift of discernment. Through intuition God gives us the ability to sense and feel that which is beyond us. We suddenly see what previously could not be seen. Through thought God gives us the ability to verify and validate the veracity of that which would otherwise be unknown. Intuition and the capacity to think enable the rational mind to see the order lying behind the appearance. For many, the order behind the appearance is God. When everything seems like it's falling apart, that's when God is putting things together, bringing order out of disorder. Intuition and the ability to think enable us to see this.

From under the fringe of the quilted mattress coverings that hung from the bedding of the mahogany four-poster bed, a cockroach suddenly scurried across the room. Instinctively, I stepped on it, killing it. Just like the cockroach, one of the two men before me would soon experience a similar fate. My seemingly illogical words, like my irrational shoe, would deliver a mortal blow – just as I had with the cockroach.

"South Louisiana," I said, shaking my head as my foot instinctively pushed the dead cockroach toward the fire place.

"Say what needs to be said," said Paneloux, with a weakened voice. "No need to struggle with words. Just say what you have to say."

"Oh, I will, Father. I will. Originally, Father, I was afraid. I had stumbled upon a secret, a surprise; and because of fear, fear of what I had discovered, I became silent. I was afraid, Father, afraid that you and Dr. Rieux might think me insane, or that I was crazy, or delusional, or perhaps the victim of some type of psychotic break. As I wrestled with what I had discovered I doubted the reality of the discovery. I doubted myself. I doubted my God. I doubted my very existence. I even doubted my sanity. But, I am not insane, Father, nor am I an irrational madman. Fear created doubt; but, I will doubt no longer. Fear built false walls of denial; but, I can no longer hide behind denial's illusionary walls. Fear has kept me silent; and I cannot be silent any longer."

"And once again I urge you. Say what you need to say," repeated Paneloux. "You have no need to fear. You are a man of faith, as am I. So, please, Monsieur, say what needs to be said. Anyway, you should know, I hate secrets and I don't like surprises either… And, I detest, I simply detest fear."

I stopped pacing and, pausing for just a moment, I stared into the shadows, searching for the face of Father Paneloux. As our eyes met, I spoke directly to Paneloux.

"Father Paneloux, I have feared fear for most of my life. Even now I fear that what I am about to say will sound insane, but, what is, is; and, what is not, is not. And -- *you are not, and neither is Dr. Rieux.*"

Paneloux contorted his face in such a way that it was obvious that he did not understand what I was saying. He shook his head back and forth quickly, as if he was trying to clear his head before speaking.

"Monsieur, you are correct. I do not understand. What do you mean when you say that I am not, or that Dr. Rieux is not? I do not understand these words, or what they mean."

"What I mean, Father, is that you do not exist; nor does Dr. Rieux, at least not in a literal sense. I know this sounds ridiculous. Nevertheless, neither of you are real flesh and blood people. You are imaginary, imaginary figments of human imagination."

Paneloux felt a deepening of the sick feeling in his stomach. He was sickened, first and foremost, by the death of the innocent child. And sickened yet a second time by harsh words of rebuke spoken by Dr. Rieux denying the existence of God in the aftermath of the child's death; and, now, he was both appalled by and sickened by the seemingly illogical things that I was saying concerning his existence and the existence of Dr. Rieux.

There was silence. No one spoke. No one said anything. All three of us just drank in the silence, hearing only our own thoughts. Eventually, Paneloux calmly drew a long breath, then spoke, breaking the silence.

"Well, Monsieur," he said, "the Bible says that there is a time to remain silent and a time to speak. [40] I am not sure which time this is. Like you I too am having difficulty choosing words. I am not sure what I should say or if I should say anything. Perhaps it would be best if I were to simply ask a question."

Paneloux rose to his feet and walked toward the fireplace. With a brisk movement he swiped his shoe across the floor, kicking the dead cockroach into the flames. He then returned to his chair, and once again sat in the shadows.

"Monsieur, I must say, this is very confusing. If I do not exist then I must ask: who am I? And…" He quickly raised his arm and extended it, with his hand pointing toward Dr. Rieux. "And, who is this man seated here? Who is this man that I know as Dr. Rieux?"

The force of his question required an immediate response. I took a deep breath, gathered my thoughts, and chose my words carefully, very carefully.

"You and Dr. Rieux do not exist, Father, at least not in a literal sense, not objectively. You are, Father, both of you, imaginary characters in a book, fictitious characters in a novel written by a man named Camus, Albert Camus. Like it or not, understand it or not, Camus is your creator."

Paneloux quickly rose to his feet, loudly clapping his hands together as he spoke.

"Monsieur. Wake up from this madness. This is ridiculous. My Creator is God."

"I'm sorry, Father. I understand why you must say that God is your Creator, but, He is not. Your creator is the atheistic novelist and philosopher, Albert Camus."

"Ah. Yes. Now I see. My creator is an atheist. Dr. Rieux does not exist. I do not exist. God does not exist. Of course, Monsieur, you exist and this Camus, fellow – he exists. Rubbish. Sheer rubbish."

"Oh, no, Father. God does exist. He is not, however, your creator. Albert Camus, an atheistic existentialist author, playwright and philosopher, he is your creator. He wrote and published a novel about the Algerian city of Oran afflicted by a horrible plague."

"Oran? Yes I am quite familiar with Oran. Oran is a real place, Monsieur, a real place inhabited by real people. In early 1940, I, the non-existent Father Paneloux, and this man, the non-existent Dr. Rieux, met in Oran when Oran was quarantined for several years during a plague. And, now we are here, dealing with pain, suffering and death in the region surrounding *Christ Cathedral*."

"Father, there never was a plague in Oran during the 1940s. Camus' based his novel on a cholera epidemic that killed a large percentage of Oran's population ninety years earlier, in 1849. The setting for the novel written by Camus, however, was indeed in Oran during the 1940s; but, there was no actual plague in Oran in the 1940s. And, I must stress that you and Dr. Rieux were never actually in the Algerian city of Oran, other than in the novel. Both of you were in Oran only as lead characters in the novel written by Camus. Oran, a real place, was the fictional setting and the 1940s was the fictional time-frame for the novel."

Paneloux sat once again, ran his hand through his hair, then shifted his position in his chair so as to remain hidden in the shadows. Calmly and quietly he used his handkerchief to wipe away great drops of sweat that had formed on his forehead.

"A moment ago, Father, you expressed faith in the one true God as your Creator. You did this, however, because Camus created you to represent a man of faith who affirms the existence of God; and, represent Him and affirm Him you must. Dr. Rieux is not a man of faith. He does not believe in God. He is not agnostic, but atheist – because Camus created him to represent a man of unbelief who denies and cannot affirm the existence of God. Dr. Rieux has no liberty; he has no freedom, to be or do otherwise. And, neither do you."

I paused for a moment to allow Paneloux to briefly contemplate the fact that he had no freedom, that his liberty was limited, constricted and restricted in ways that he could not imagine. He was surrounded by a *determinism* that was greater than he had ever imagined. Any notions of freedom and liberty that he formerly embraced suddenly vanished. His was a narrow, closed universe – and he was boxed in the narrow *ontological* and *epistemological* boundaries of that narrowly defined universe.

"What would it take? What would it take, Father, to convince you that what I am saying about you and Dr. Rieux is true?"

Paneloux stood to his feet, once again moving out of the security of the shadows. With his big hands raised high, he pointed toward me. I could now clearly see his face, his two rosy cheeks overhung by steel-rimmed spectacles. Like an evangelical preacher he spoke powerfully, and emotionally.

"Nothing. Nothing could cause me to deny my own existence. Nothing. The mere notion of such foolishness is implausible. Simply implausible. This is rubbish. Sheer rubbish. Should I, a man of faith, allow you, a man such as yourself, a delusional man, should I allow you to lead me to doubt my existence, to deny my faith, or to disbelieve my God? No. No. Nothing. Nothing could cause me to believe such nonsense. Nothing."

Still standing, Paneloux once again wiped the handkerchief across his forehead and the back of his neck before he continued to speak.

"You are well aware, sir, that the philosopher Descartes dealt with the illogical nature of this type of thinking long ago. He said *'I think, therefore I am.'* [41] Well, I think, therefore I am. And Dr. Rieux, he thinks, therefore he is. *'Cogito, ergo sum.'* [42] Let Descartes put an end to such nonsensical thinking."

It's one thing to be told that you don't exist, at least, in a rhetorical sense. It's quite another thing to be told that you really don't exist at all, at least not in an objective sense. Who among us could believe such a thing about ourselves? Is it not impossible to think of ourselves in such a way? No one can believe such a thing about themselves, no one, unless they were presented with irrefutable proof.

We have a body, a mind, a memory. We think, feel, and we make choices, volitional choices, as we relate to the environment around us. These are but a few of the simpler realities that confirm and affirm the reality of our existence.

Then, unbelievably, someone intrudes, and says, with great seriousness, something completely illogical: "You do not exist." We, in response to such a statement, pause. We think. We feel; and, finally, as we develop conclusions, we exercise volition; we choose our course of action. We make a choice, a choice to respond, and suddenly we hear ourselves speaking: "What you are saying does not make sense. This is craziness. Insanity. Rubbish."

We heard what was spoken to us. We thought upon what was said. We felt the emotional impact of what was said. Then, we choose a natural response and speak it. It is this whole deliberative process, thinking, feeling and choosing, that confirms our existence. Yet the message we hear is illogical, understandably illogical -- *"You do not exist."*

"Please, I understand, Father, I understand how challenging this is. Let me clarify what I am saying. Father, I am not saying that you and Dr. Rieux do not have existence. You do, but not in an objective sense. Your existence is confined to the pages of a novel written by Camus. That is where you exist. That is the primary domain of your existence.

"You also exist in a secondary domain, in the mind of Camus, your creator, and beyond that, in the minds of others who read his novel about you and Dr. Rieux and the plague.

"You also have existence in other areas, for instance, in the critiques and writings of others who evaluate Camus' novel or incorporate you into their writings, books or novels. I know this sounds ridiculous. Nevertheless, it is true. Neither of you are real flesh and blood people. You are imaginary characters, figments of human imagination, the imagination of Camus."

Paneloux simply sat in his chair, once again holding his handkerchief to his mouth, stunned into silence. Not knowing what to think, he could not think at all. He simply did not know what to make of what he considered a delusional conversation nor did he know what to say beyond what he had already said. That he or Dr. Rieux did not exist was preposterous, ludicrous, incomprehensible. Only a buffoon would believe such a thing.

I thought about Descartes. Descartes was the thinker, the doubter, who doubted everything, including his own existence. What crisis of faith preceded the development of his *Cartesian cognito?* Was his doubt spontaneous? Methodical? Or a combination of both? His oft quoted "I think; therefore, I am" is really "I am consciously aware, consciously thinking about my thinking; therefore, I am, therefore I exist." His conscious awareness, or thinking about his thinking verified his existence.

I wondered further: What strange world is this? Strange for Dr. Rieux. Strange for Paneloux. Strange for me. What strange world is this where fundamental philosophical principles are turned on their head – and no longer apply. What of Zhuangzi? What of his dreams? What of his butterfly?

"Well, I do not know what I can say to you about this, other than what I have already said. Nothing, absolutely nothing could cause me to deny my own existence. Nothing. The mere notion of such foolishness is implausible. Simply implausible. *Solipsism,* I recall from my seminary studies, is an epistemological position which holds that knowledge of anything outside one's own mind is an unresolvable question. But, I do not believe that you embrace solipsism. You have resolved your questions. You simply believe that I do not exist. Dr. Rieux does not exist."

"There is a way, Father, that I can prove that what I am saying is true. It will require integrity, emotional strength and honesty on your part; but, I can prove that what I am saying is true."

"Existence? Emotional strength? Integrity? Honesty? Is my character on trial too? And, yet, as I sit here I wonder, Rieux, why do you remain silent? You are a man of impeccable character; an educated man, and a logical thinker. Have you no part in this conversation? Is not your existence being challenged too?"

"To be quite honest, Paneloux," said Dr. Rieux, "I find this whole conversation rather curious. I've heard you preach sermons seeking to prove the existence of God. You've waxed eloquent with the *cosmological argument, the arguments from design*, and other theological strategies in an attempt to prove the existence of God. And, now, you're, well, what strange quirk of fate is this? You're being challenged to prove your own existence in the face of this man's claims. This is most curious, Paneloux, most curious. In my way of thinking if you cannot prove your own existence then how can you prove the existence of God? Your high sounding theological rhetoric and flailing of the hands will not win this battle. No. I think I'll remain silent just a tad longer."

Paneloux was becoming frustrated, feeling like a caged animal. For him this whole conversation was absurd – and that he felt caged made everything even more absurd.

"Father, do you recall your first sermon concerning the outbreak of the plague in Oran? Do you remember the weather on the day prior to the delivery of that sermon? Do you remember the weather the day that you actually delivered the sermon? I remember, Father. I remember, yet I was not there; and, you know that I was not there. I remember because I've read and studied the novel written by Camus about that incident."

Paneloux opened his mouth to say something, without quite knowing what he was going to say; then, chose to say nothing.

"On the day prior to your preaching that first sermon, on Saturday, the sky had clouded up. On Sunday, the day the sermon was delivered it was raining, raining heavily. The image of people walking beneath unfurled umbrellas through the rain to church filled you with anticipation. And, the air inside the Cathedral, Camus said that it was 'heavy with fumes of incense and the smell of wet clothes'[43] as you confidently stepped to the pulpit.

"According to Camus you had a 'powerful, rather emotional delivery.[44] The opening phrase of your message was launched, according to Camus, in clear, emphatic tones: 'Calamity has come on you, my brethren, and, my brethren, you deserved it." [45]

Paneloux angrily snapped in reply.

"Anyone could know the opening line of that sermon. That you know the opening line of the message proves nothing."

"After launching your sermon you quoted a text from Exodus relating to the plague of Egypt, and said: 'The first time this scourge appears in history, it was wielded to strike down the enemies of God. Pharaoh set himself up against the divine will, and the plague beat him to his knees. Thus from the dawn of recorded history the scourge of God has humbled the proud of heart and laid low those who hardened themselves against Him. Ponder this well, my friends, and fall on your knees."'[46]

The priest sat in tortured silence, wondering how I could know more about the content of a sermon he had preached than he did.

"You later described the plague as 'the flail of God'[47] and described the world as 'His threshing-floor.'[48] I am a man of Scripture, Father, and have a fondness for the preaching of the Word. I can still hear your rousing challenge to your congregation: 'See him there,' you said, 'See that angel of the pestilence, comely as Lucifer, shining like Evil's very self. He is hovering above your roofs with his great spear in his right hand, poised to strike, while his left hand is stretched toward one or other of your houses. Maybe at this very moment his finger is pointing to your door, the red spear crashing on its panels, and even now the plague is entering your home and settling down in your bedroom to await your return.' Powerful stuff, Father, powerful stuff, powerfully stated."

Paneloux shivered slightly. He knew that he was over-matched when it came to knowing the content of his first sermon dealing with the plague. He couldn't figure out how but he knew he was over-matched.

"Of course, Father, you had a few more words to say that day; but, you made it very clear that this plague came from God as a just punishment for the sin of the people. 'Calamity has come on you, my brethren, and, my brethren, you deserved it.'"[49]

Father Paneloux sat there, expressionless.

"I don't know whether I am angry, amused, flattered, sad or shocked. While I do find it strange that you would be so knowledgeable about that particular message, this does not prove that I don't exist or that I exist only as a character in a book."

"I agree, Father. I agree. But it does prove that I have an unusual awareness about this sermon, and, even you must wonder how I gained this awareness."

"I already know your reply," said Paneloux. "You will say that you read it in a book written by this fellow Camus."

"You are correct in that assumption, Father. The knowledge that I have was gained from reading Camus' book. If there is no such book, then, you must develop a reasonable, logical explanation to shed light on how I might have gained this detailed information about your first sermon dealing with the plague."

His expressionless stare was still fixed, tightly fixed. He had a clouded, defenseless look that could be seen, even though his face was still somewhat hidden by the shadows.

"With so many people present when that sermon was preached there would probably be many reasonable sources to provide you such information. Printed copies of that message, for instance, may still be available from the church office. So, that you know what you know proves nothing about my existence or non-existence."

He pursed his lips and spoke firmly for added emphasis, "Nothing could ever cause me to deny the reality of my own existence."

"What would it take? What would it take, Father, to convince you that what I am saying about you and Dr. Rieux is true?"

"As I have already said, several times over, nothing. Nothing could ever cause me to deny the reality of my own existence. Nothing could cause me to believe such nonsense. Nothing."

"Then hear me, Father, hear me further. I agree that my knowledge of that particular sermon dealing with the plague does not prove your non-existence. But, it does establish one thing: I have knowledge, an undeniable knowledge of certain facts and events, concerning you and Dr. Rieux. That I have this knowledge raises questions about the origin of my knowledge. By this I mean, how did I gain this knowledge? What is the explanation? Now, if I have only knowledge about a sermon, a particular sermon that you preached, then indeed, that knowledge proves nothing. But, if I have additional knowledge about other aspects concerning you, your life, or Dr. Rieux, his life, and his actions; well, this becomes more and more problematic – unless my position regarding your non-existence is correct."

"Again, as I have already said, several times over, nothing. Nothing could ever cause me to deny the reality of my own existence."

"Let me pose a different situation then. I am familiar, quite familiar with the horrid details of the death of the son of the local Police Magistrate, Monsieur Othon. I know that after the child was diagnosed Dr. Rieux consulted with his colleagues, Dr. Castel, and Dr. Richard and they decided that an untested experimental anti-plague serum would be tried for the first time on the child. How could I possibly know this, Father, how?"

A tiny cheek muscle on Paneloux face twitched, an involuntary, subconscious effort to hide his clenched teeth – and the anxiety that produced that twitching.

"Othon's last words to Dr. Rieux before he and his wife were quarantined were: 'Save my son.' After Dr. Rieux pronounced the child dead earlier today, you and he decided to come here. As you walked together Dr. Rieux rebuked you for the shallowness of your faith. Here, now, let me speak back to you the exact words that Dr. Rieux said to you as you walked here tonight. Rieux said, 'In your sermon you said 'We deserved this. We were guilty before God and we deserved this.' What say you now? What say you about the death of this innocent child?'"

Paneloux's could not escape the pain of his earlier conversation with Dr. Rieux. The priest was at a loss for words. He began to wonder and worry about how I could know these things; private things, private conversations, even private thoughts that had occurred less than an hour ago, privately, between he and Dr. Rieux. These were things that only he and Dr. Rieux would know.

"Tonight, Father, as you walked up the spiral staircase to my room, tonight, just a few brief moments ago, you purposed in your heart to answer Dr. Rieux's question through a special sermon you plan to preach this Sunday. And, one of your goals is to have Dr. Rieux attend church this Sunday. Is this not correct? You have not yet invited Dr. Rieux yet I know your intention. How could I possibly know this, Father, how?"

Everything seemed to be coming at Paneloux – fast, so fast that he hardly had time to think. Seated in the opposite chair, Dr. Rieux sat in silence. He looked disinterested, yet not really surprised as the conversation unfolded. In fact, he looked somewhat sympathetic toward Paneloux, indicating that he somehow understood Paneloux's dilemma.

"Here, Father, is why earlier I said that it will require integrity and honesty on your part. You see, Father, I can prove that what I am saying is true."

I handed him a sealed envelope. "Here is irrefutable proof."

"And, what is this? What is this irrefutable proof?"

"This envelop contains a word-for-word transcript of a sermon you have not yet developed -- *the sermon you will preach this Sunday.*

"As one man of faith to another, I trust your integrity and believe that you are an honest man. As a matter of integrity, you must not read this sermon manuscript until after you have delivered your sermon this Sunday. That's where your honesty and integrity come into play. At this juncture, neither you, nor Dr. Rieux, have read this sermon manuscript. After you preach your sermon, you will find that my manuscript will match, word for word, the sermon that you will have preached. The manuscript is a word for word record of your sermon based on what was recorded in the novel written by Camus."

RESTORE POINT 12:

WHEN NEEDLESS SUFFERING IS NEEDFUL

A chilly, brisk wind was blowing in from the north on the day Father Paneloux delivered his second sermon dealing with the plague. Rieux noted that the attendance was sparse, much sparser, than on the occasion of his first message that focused on pain, suffering and death.

I sat next to Dr. Rieux, on the same church pew, and with him I watched as Paneloux climbed into the richly carved mahogany pulpit. As the priest began to speak, he stumbled over his opening words. Rieux turned toward me and, as he cupped one of his hands over his mouth, he whispered: "He seems unsure of himself. We know why." I gave Dr. Rieux one of my blank looks, a dull stare, without moving any facial muscles. The priest had hardly begun to speak and Rieux was already mocking him.

After struggling through his opening remarks, Paneloux paused, intentionally. As the pause lengthened I could actually feel the congregation being drawn into his hesitation. It was a deliberate, intentional, indirect method of using silence, a lack of language, as a ploy – to garner congregational attention and involvement.

With a sudden loud clap of his hands, a simultaneous stomp of one foot and an accompanying shout, the pulpit and church walls shook as all three sounds converged, echoing loudly through the vaulted high ceilings of the sanctuary. The congregation was jolted to attention – with all eyes fastened on Paneloux.

"Hear me, O people of God." He thundered. "Hear me."

His words were filled with power and passion. He spoke with authority, forcefully, enunciating words and syllables of words with perfect elocution and emphasis. It was as if his every movement was synchronized, linked to each word, each syllable, and each phrase. The effect was powerful, mesmerizing, electric.

"For many long months this plague, this dreadful plague, this horrid affliction of body, and mind and spirit, has been in our midst. And, what an unwelcome companion, what an unwelcome companion this plague has been. What say we now about this plague? We know you, O Plague. We know you far better now than when you first came. 'We have seen you, O Plague. Seen you seated at our tables. Seen you seated in our homes. Seen you seated at the bedsides of those we love. You have walked with us. Waited for our coming. Waited for our leaving.'[50] Waiting. Waiting. Always waiting."

He paused again, staring again at the congregation in silence. It was as if he were a man, one single mighty man of God, staring down at this monstrous plague. He didn't bat an eyelid. He had an aura that asserted his command as speaker, as man of God and as an under-shepherd of God's sheep.

"What is it that you, O Plague, what is it that you want? What, O Plague, is your demand? And, what is it that you, O People of God, what is it that you want? What is your expectation? Your anticipation? Your demand?"

As a preacher I long ago realized that pulpit questions usually give the congregation, not only answers to the pulpit questions, but answers about the questioner, the pulpiteer himself. Through questions and answers we hear what the pulpiteer believes. We see where he stands. Then we decide what we believe. Then we decide where we will stand. We choose. We decide. We stand – either with him, or against him. We agree or disagree.

Thus far it appeared that Paneloux was mobilizing an army, God's army, the congregation entrusted to his care. He urged them to stand together as one with one another and with him to *fight the good fight of faith* [51] and thereby *wage a good warfare* [52] against the plague.

"What is it, O People of God that you want? What is it that you want to know? Hear me. Are our ears stopped that we cannot hear? This plague shouts in the street. It lifts its voice in the square. It whispers in our fears. Shouts through our tears. Can we not, People of God, can we not hear its voice? This wretched voice, this wretched voice of the plague, does it not cry out, cry out to all, cry out for all? Day after day, night after night, the voice of this plague has sounded, louder and louder. Its message is clear. Yet, we have not heard. The Lord saith, 'Let him who hath an ear hear.' [53] But, we have not heard. Let us hear, brethren, and let us stand steadfast, undaunted, unmovable." [54]

The place was electric and Paneloux was about to increase the surging power. He paused again, momentarily, then lifted his right hand high above his head. He suddenly slammed his hand onto the top of the pulpit. Once again the congregation bounced to attention. His right hand quickly rose again, revealing that his fingers were loosely clenched, with one long finger symbolically pointed toward the congregation.

"Calamity has come on you, my brethren, and, my brethren, you deserved it." [55]

In his first sermon, Paneloux preached that the plague was divine in origin and punitive in its intention. He jabbed and pointed his finger again, a second time.

"Calamity has come on you, my brethren, and, my brethren, you deserved it." [56]

He jabbed his finger forward a third time, then drew his hand back, toward his chest, and lightly struck his breast, a sign of repentance.

"Calamity has come on *us,* my brethren, and, my brethren, *we* deserved it."[57]

Father Paneloux was making one point very clear to his congregation: what he had said in his first sermon about the plague -- still held fast. The plague was divine in origin and punitive. For Paneloux God's truth was God's truth, always. It was God's truth then. It is God's truth now. For Paneloux the immutability of truth -- was essential.

During this, his second sermon, a change was seen, not in truth, but in Father Paneloux's understanding of that truth. In this second sermon he intentionally used and emphasized the plural pronoun "we" and "us" instead of the singular "you."

"Calamity has come on *us,* my brethren, and, my brethren, *we* deserved it." [58]

Father Paneloux's initial belief that there were no innocent victims was shaken as he witnessed the agonizing death of Monsieur Othon's son. Paneloux could not deny that the child was an innocent victim. The whole horrid event forced him to rethink his beliefs. Even as he preached this second sermon he could hear the tormenting accusations of Dr. Rieux as they raced across the back of his mind....

"In your first sermon dealing with this horrid plague, you said 'We deserved this. We were guilty before God and we deserved this.' What say you now? What say you about the death of this innocent child? We, yes, perhaps we stand guilty before God, if there is a God; but, what of this innocent child? Innocence bears no guilt yet is afflicted nonetheless – and by God...by a just God. No. I'll have none of it. Never. Never. None of it."

"There are some things we can grasp, brethren, as touching God, and others that we cannot. Pain, tragedy, human suffering and death, these are some of humanity's most vexing problems. It has often been noted that bad things happen to good people. Innocent people suffer, sometimes, from our perspective, needlessly. What can I say about this?

"Hear me. As to pain, there is needed pain and there is needless pain. That pain is needed is sometimes difficult for us to believe, especially when the innocent, such as a child, are unjustly afflicted. Nevertheless, we must believe this. We must believe that sometimes, somehow, needless pain is needful – even when this is difficult to grasp, we must believe. We must believe everything, brethren, or deny everything. And who among us would dare to deny everything?"

There was a low murmuring among the people, heard by the people, but evidently not by Father Paneloux, as he turned his head toward Dr. Rieux and spoke almost directly to Dr. Rieux...

"Who among us would dare to deny everything?"

Father Paneloux was wrestling with heresy in speaking this way, though he was evidently not aware of it. Believe Everything or Deny Everything?[59] Agree with Father Paneloux and believe everything; or, agree with Dr. Rieux and believe nothing. The choice, in reality, was not Dr. Rieux or Paneloux. The choice was Christ or nothing – nothing at all. Here was corrupt reason contending with Revelation. Here was flawed works trying to earn what only grace could give. And, the blood of Christ, the precious blood of Christ, was in danger of being trampled underfoot by a man. By all intents and purposes it appeared that Christ once again would be wounded in the house of His friends. Rieux and I, several monks and priests, and perhaps a few others were aware of the precarious theological ground upon which Paneloux was attempting to stand. He would find no theological balance, not on this heretical sand. He was standing on sinking ground, yet he knew it not – at least not yet.

As Paneloux limped to the close of his message, it was apparent that the power was gone. As he closed his sermon Paneloux paid a passing tribute to the providence of God as presented in the twenty-eighth verse of the eighth chapter of Romans, then ended his sermon with his now familiar statement....

"Calamity has come on *us*, my brethren, and, my brethren, *we* deserved it." [60]

As Dr. Rieux and I walked together among the people exiting the sanctuary at the end of the church service, Rieux once again turned his head toward me and spoke in hushed tones, "Paneloux said his choice was to believe everything, a noble choice...but, in his heart, you and I know that his faith is really no better than mine. His faith is wavering and soon, very soon, he will believe nothing."

A harsh, angry old priest and a young deacon who were walking near us were certainly not as discrete in their conversation about Paneloux's sermon. The elder of the two said that the sermon was eloquent and powerful at the first, but failed at the finish; filled with uneasiness, uncertainty, bordering on heresy.

The old priest harshly denounced Father Paneloux, saying that Paneloux's sermon would create greater insecurity among the people and a greater division between the medical community and the clergy. His last words on the subject were spoken with a loud voice. He sharply, vehemently, and loudly protested in a way that all could hear: "A priest his age has no business feeling so uneasy. And he certainly has no call to preach such theological rot. Shame on him. Shame on him."

Paneloux sat on the edge of his bed. Next to him was a large envelope. As he looked at the envelope he thought about our conversation....

> *"This envelop contains a word-for-word transcript of a sermon you have not yet developed -- the sermon you will preach this Sunday. As one man of faith to another, I trust your integrity and believe that you are an honest man. As a matter of integrity, you must not read this sermon manuscript until after you have delivered your sermon this Sunday."*

He had maintained his integrity. The envelop was still sealed, just as it was when he received it from me several days earlier.

The moment of truth, he thought to himself. *The moment of truth.*

"The moment of truth," he heard himself say out loud to no one. "The moment of truth."

The contents of this envelope had the potential to rip apart everything he ever believed about life, about faith, about himself, about God. He knew that; and he feared it. As he anxiously contemplated that thought even more frightening thoughts surfaced: There are some things in life that, once taken apart, can never be put back together again. Shattered people become fragmented, fall apart, becoming a mere shadow of what they once were. They try to pick up the pieces only to discover that they cannot. Then, they literally fall to pieces. They never recover.

He opened the envelope, pulled out the typed manuscript and laid it on his bed. As his eyes looked downward at the first page he read....

> *"Hear me, O people of God. Hear me. For many a long month this plague, this dreadful plague, this horrid affliction of body, and mind and spirit, has been in our midst. And, what an unwelcome companion, what an unwelcome dark companion this plague has been. What say we now about this plague? We know you, O Plague. We know you far better now than when you first came. We have seen you, O Plague. Seen you seated at our*

> *tables. Seen you seated in our homes. Seen you seated at the bedsides of those we love. You have walked with us. Waited for our coming. Waited for our leaving.* [61] *Waiting. Waiting. Waiting. Always waiting."*

He paused again, stared again in silence. He didn't bat an eyelid. In the back of his mind he heard the oft quoted words of the ancient philosopher Socrates, noticing for the very first time the last four words of his famous statement: "The unexamined life is not worth living *for a human being."*[62]

RESTORE POINT 13:

WONDERLAND

For as far back as he could remember Paneloux seemed to always have the right answers to his own questions. At least, he thought the answers were right; and he thought the questions were his own. But now, well, he wasn't so sure. Now he was filled with doubt and uncertainty, questioning everything, believing nothing.

He no longer had any answers. In fact, he was not sure if he really ever had any answers at all. And he was filled with even greater ambiguity and uncertainty about his questions. What was the origin or source of his questions? How were his questions shaped? And by whom? And, to what intent? To what purpose? He knew from study and experience that questions could be shaped to elicit a predetermined answer. Did the questions he had asked through the years originate with him? Did they originate within his own head? Were they prompted by the Spirit of God? Or, were they – both questions and answers – planted in his mind and mouth by this Albert Camus fellow?

He wondered, *How does a person validate the validity of thought? The authenticity of thought? The veracity of thought?* This was something that he hadn't studied while in seminary. These were questions he had never asked and now that he was asking he wondered: *Could he find answers? Could he find his own answers? Could he find right answers?*

And, now he stood, before me and Dr. Rieux – confused, bewildered, filled with uncertainty, asking questions he had never asked before – and not knowing where to go for answers.

"I don't get it. I don't understand. Sunday after Sunday I stood as a man of God in the house of God, beneath the cross, above the altar, in the Sanctuary of the Lord. I have stood, week after week, year after year, in God's pulpit, the Chariot of God, as I rhetorically called it, proclaiming God's Word to His people. Now, I fear that I was speaking, not for the one true Creator God – but for this atheist, my literary creator Camus. Just thinking this way is enough to make me vomit. My stomach is churning; my head is light; my spirit is trembling. This is too heavy a burden, I tell you, far too heavy a burden for anyone to bear. I am as an orphan, cut off from time, with tomorrow denied. Where then, tell me, where then is my legitimacy?"

Dr. Rieux cocked his head to one side then zeroed in on me with a sort of all too-knowing eye. He turned his head to cast a sardonic glance at Paneloux then diverted his attention back to me. He shook his head, then coughed politely so as to clear his throat, an indication that he intended to speak.

"Sorry about that, excuse. Please."

Dr. Rieux then revealed that he had known about all of this – about their non-existence, in a real sense, and their actual existence, in a literary sense -- he had known about all of this for quite some time. Initially he felt disturbed as he realized that his life was initiated by the author Albert Camus. He began life as an adult. He had no childhood. These and other factors facilitated his gradual understanding of the literary world – and his role in it.

"While the thought was initially uncomfortable for me it did not really bother me a great deal since I was an atheist. The world of literature, where we exist, is a *parallel universe* to the physical world. We are a mirror, a reflection of that world, yet, in a very real sense we are not that world. Through literature we inhabit that world, but it is not our habitation."

Paneloux opened his mouth to say something then quickly realized that he had nothing to say. He walked toward the open bedroom window and silently looked out towards the horizon. The image of the darkening horizon was to him a metaphor – a metaphor of this dreadful moment where so much of his former self was disappearing into the darkness. Calmly, with a sorrowful, broken voice, he spoke again.

"I have done everything that I thought God wanted me to do; everything that I believed God asked of me. And, now, I don't know what to do. I don't know who I am. I don't know who God is. All my beliefs and all my assumptions about myself, my life and my God are now challenged. I see myself as a man who has been standing in a dead world yet not knowing where I have been standing – and now all I see is darkness – I don't know where I stand or where I need to stand. Who is wise enough for such a moment as this?"

There was another moment of tortured silence. His face was expressionless. In the midst of the silence I recalled the words of *Alice In Wonderland.*

> *"How puzzling all these changes are. I'm never sure what I'm going to be, from one minute to another."*[63]

Then Paneloux spoke yet again....

"This is so confusing – so very confusing. What I thought I once was, I am not. By some strange twist of fate I am, yet I am not. I live, yet I am not alive. I have existence, yet I do not exist. Someday I will experience death, yet I will not die. I am a man, yet the essence of what man really is, is denied to me. In my blindness I have seen the illusion of *existence* but not its *essence.*"

Paneloux was confused about everything. His once clearly defined identity and his once clear path for life were now muddied and muddled. Clarity was most needful if Paneloux was to survive and succeed as a man of faith. Once again the words of Alice came to mind....

> *"I can't go back to yesterday because I was a different person then."*[64]

In many ways, Paneloux was like a person born blind who suddenly gained sight. When a person who has been blind from birth or childhood has their sight restored something unexpected and unusual happens. When that person looks out at the world for the first time, they don't see human faces, trees, houses, clouds or objects. In reality, they have sight but they do not yet see. What the person experiences instead is a buzzing confusion as their mind is flooded with meaningless patches of color, light, shade and shapes. Their first experience of sight makes no sense, no sense at all.

This is how it was for Paneloux.

Slowly, however, patterns begin to emerge for the newly seeing person, patterns that eventually become recognizable objects. But for a period of time even these objects make no sense. The once blind person must be painstakingly guided by professionally trained personnel to identify each object correctly and to correctly associate each object with information received from the other senses (hearing, touch, taste, and smell). Through this process the newly seeing person gradually constructs meaningful patterns of thinking that enable him to see, and to understand, what he is seeing.

This is the process that Paneloux must pass through. Just as the once blind newly seeing person learns to distinguish the color "blue" from the color "red," or a "circle" from a "triangle," so too must Paneloux develop patterns of thinking that distinguish the difference between actual physical reality and reality in the context of a literary environment. Just as these patterns of thinking become mental maps for the newly seeing person to enable him to interpret, understand and safely navigate his way through the physical, visible world that he had never seen; so too must Paneloux develop new mental maps to interpret and understand what he called his *strange new world.*

What are these mental maps? They are thinking patterns. Like *Alice In Wonderland*, Paneloux was puzzled by and struggling with his new mental maps.

> *"Who in the world am I?" said Alice, "Ah, that's the great puzzle."*[65]

Mental maps are thinking patterns, some conscious, many unconscious, that we use to evaluate experiences and interpret life. Each mental map is like a lens on a camera. They color, clarify, classify and interpret everything that we experience and encounter in life. These mental maps enable us to make sense out of our world. They enable us to understand ourselves, others, God, and everything else in life.

Miscalculation and confusion suddenly replaced Paneloux's interpretation and passion for life. He was not so much cynical as he was bitter; bitterly confused. Life was somehow much more complicated for him now.

> *"Sometimes," said Alice, "Sometimes I've believed as many as six impossible things before breakfast."*[66]

I suddenly stood to my feet in an effort to begin the arduous journey of enabling Paneloux to see and to understand his new reality, his new life, within the context of this new literary environment. He must learn to read between the unwritten lines of life in this strange new world.

Then, with a loud accusatory tone, in an effort to shake him, awaken him, I began shouting, shouting the name of Camus.

"Camus. Camus. Camus did this. He did this to you, Paneloux. And, whether it bothers you or not, he did this to you, Dr. Rieux. This Camus, this Albert Camus, he took you and he shaped you, he shaped each of you, using words and language, syntax and linguistic liberty, shaping you into fictitious characters. For what intent? -- To persuade men. I say, to persuade foolish men to deny the existence of God.

"And now, you have begun to see behind the literary veil; and, what do you see? See him there, in the shadows, standing behind and speaking through both of you. See, there he is. And, see. There you are, both of you. Both of you have been shaped, one as a man of faith, a man of belief, and the other, as a man of unbelief. Camus. Camus. Camus did this. Both of you are helpless, powerless to change this. But why, why were you shaped thus? To what end? To what purpose? Again I say, hear me, again I say -- to persuade men, real men -- to persuade foolish flesh and blood men to deny the existence of their true Creator -- *God.*"

As I continued pacing, walking back and forth, Paneloux's mind was suddenly filled with questions, alarming questions, distressful questions, heretical questions, philosophical questions. Was he caught in some kind of mind-bending dream? Must he now destroy everything he had worked so hard to build? Questions, burning questions, were throbbing inside his head.

"Tell me. What is faith? Is it a deposit in my memory by this fellow Camus? I thought it was a force in my life. Now I wonder, do I even have life? Do I have faith? I don't want to think about this? I don't want to talk about this. Yet, I cannot not think about this. I cannot not talk about this. I am compelled, compelled to talk and compelled to think."

There are many verbal and non-verbal clues, as well as behavioral clues a person may give to indicate they are in shock. Paneloux was on the edge.

"Is it my fate to die as a fictional being? Is this my destiny? And, if so, how many deaths must I die? Since there is no resurrection for fictional beings, must I recur again and again and again, and then die again and again and again? Shakespeare is oft quoted as saying that 'All the world's a stage, And all the men and women merely players: They have their exits and their entrances.' [67] What, pray tell, what am I? Who, pray tell, who am I? How many entrances must I make? How many exists?"

Paneloux frantically threw his hands upward, he stood, stared at me then spoke with a frenzied voice as he joined me in pacing. There was an unnatural note to his voice as he suddenly stopped pacing to speak.

"But where is our freedom, our liberty? Can we not exercise choice? Do we have volitional options? Do we not have control over any of these matters? Must determinism by this fellow Camus be our eternal fate? What of self-determinism? And, human responsibility? Are these simply abstract concepts that have no meaning? Are they simply mental constructs formulated by the philosophers? Is the examined life, as Socrates said, restricted to physical *human beings?* What of literary beings, literary characters?"

As Paneloux resumed his pacing his facial expression was tight, with his lips and cheeks drawn downward, signaling doubt and disbelief, anxiety and fear – and anger.

"Father, I can see that you are frightened."

"Yes. – You better believe I am. But, frightened is the wrong word. I'm more than frightened. I'm terrified – Terrified out of my wits."

His fear had expanded into terror. Left unchecked, his terror would soon expand into panic. I paused, then shifted awkwardly, surprising myself at the steadiness of my voice as I spoke.

"Liberty? Free will? Freedom? Choice? Volitional options? The answers to your questions are 'yes' and 'no.' You have a theological bent, a persuasion, that was originally predetermined by Camus. You, Father Paneloux, are bent towards belief; and you, Dr. Rieux, are bent toward unbelief. All of your individual acts, choices, and volitional options must conform to your particular theological bent. You have freedom and liberty to exercise choice and free will within the context of these parameters – belief for one, unbelief for the other."

"Yes. Yes. On one level I understand," said Paneloux, "I understand exactly what you are saying. On another level, however, though I understand, I cannot accept what you are saying."

Unconsciously, unintentionally, Paneloux spoke a line from *Alice In Wonderland....*

> *"I'm afraid I can't explain myself, sir. Because I am not myself, you see?"*[68]

He paused, stared at me for a fraction of a second, then resumed his pacing. I then paused, grabbed a couple of pencils and handed both Paneloux and Dr. Rieux a pencil and a blank sheet of paper.

"Please, Father, please be seated. Here is a simple exercise that illustrates your particular theological bent. On this paper that I have in my hand I am writing a series of letters and bunching them together tightly. Look closely and you will see that the letters make a statement, a simple statement about God. The statement that you see reveals something about your ability to see or not see God. Look carefully at these bunched letters, separate the letters then write the sentence that you see within the bunched letters on your paper. Quickly now, write what you see as you look at these letters.

GODISNOWHERE

"Paneloux, what have you written?" He looked at his paper and thought speculatively for a second or two. "I have written what is plainly seen, 'God Is Now Here'"

"And, Dr. Rieux, what have you written?" Dr. Rieux didn't respond immediately either, but not for speculative reasons. "I too have written what is plainly seen," he said with a strained voice. "God Is No Where."

I commandeered the conversation immediately before either of them could speak.

"Strange, is it not? Two men see the same thing, yet what they see they see differently. One sees God as present; the other sees God as absent. Those perspectives are the direct consequence of your theological bent, a bent created and shaped by Camus."

I took a quick side-glance look at Dr. Rieux. He simply sat there, paper and pencil in hand, with a solemn look on his face. He was irritated; yet, he attempted to disguise his irritability, doing nothing and saying nothing; beyond what was required when I asked a question.

"Do either of you know, really know, what you've actually been doing? I mean, as opposed to what you thought you were doing? All of your actions and behaviors have been guided by your beliefs, beliefs shaped by Camus. Belief always determines behavior. Camus knows this. That's why he shaped you with a particular theological bent. Camus did this. But why, why were you shaped thus? To what end? To what purpose? Again I say, hear me, again I say -- To persuade men. To persuade foolish men through his novels that God does not exist."

Dr. Rieux gave me an angry-looking raised eyebrow and a cold, silent stare. His stare was cynical, conveying an air of arrogance and suspicion. Father Paneloux gave a different look as all the doubts and thoughts about the realities and unrealities of his life taunted him.

"If you want to help me," Paneloux said, "then tell me what you think I need to know."

"Let's do one other exercise, first. On your paper I'd like to ask each of you to draw a triangle or a circle. The size doesn't matter. Just draw a simple triangle or a circle."

Dr. Rieux half glanced at Paneloux. He was slowly screwing up his face in a futile attempt to distract Paneloux who was diligently using his pencil to draw the outline of a triangle.

"When we draw a triangle or a circle on a piece of paper, according to the philosopher Plato, our circle or triangle is a representation of what a real triangle or a real circle actually is. The triangles and circles that we draw are not exact, nor are they perfect."

Dr. Rieux smiled a sarcastic smile that revealed rather than disguised his pessimism and cynicism.

"Long ago Plato realized that all of our earthly representations of triangles and circles were imperfect; but, somewhere there was a perfect triangle or a perfect circle that served as a perfect model for our imperfect representations. Plato felt that these ideal perfect models, whether of triangles or circles, were located in the mind, in the realm of ideas. We have an idea that enables us to know, for instance, what a triangle is, so, when we are asked to draw a triangle we don't draw a square. What we do draw is our idea of a trianble."

For just a brief moment I caught Dr. Rieux's attempt to control a facial twitch. He had drawn his triangle, put his paper down, then experienced a facial twitch, just for a second.

"This is ridiculous," Dr. Rieux snorted.

"No so, Dr. Rieux. Not so. You see, Plato really wasn't a mathematician and he wasn't especially interested in triangles or circles or squares. He thought higher and he thought deeper than that. You see, he applied his analogy of circles and triangles to more important life issues, focusing on concepts like justice, love, beauty, truth and so forth. For Plato every imperfect representation that we see on earth – every representation of justice, of love, of beauty – he reasoned there must be an ideal, a perfect eternal unchanging ideal, that was somewhere behind all of our earthly imperfect representations."

Dr. Rieux at first appeared to consider Plato's propositions seriously, at least for a moment, but he wasn't smiling. Instead he slowly and silently shook his head from side to side seeming to silently say, *No. No way. Not so.*

Paneloux, however, was just the opposite. He nodded his head in agreement. Evidently he had been exposed to Plato's philosophy through his seminary education and his ongoing theological studies. And if not, then he was at least connecting the dots, gaining understanding.

"For Plato," I continued, "there must be perfect eternal love from which all our imperfect earthly expressions of love descend. Plato's understanding eventually became known as *idealism.* He further deduced that since God, and God alone is perfect, the eternal ideal for love, justice, and beauty, indeed the eternal ideal behind all reality is in God, and within Him alone."

Paneloux cocked his head to one side and narrowed his eyes. He appeared to be thinking, allowing what I had thus far shared to help him gain a new understanding, a new understanding of who he really was. For a brief moment he recalled what he had said just a few minutes earlier: *I have existence, yet I do not exist. I am a man, yet the essence of what man really is, is denied to me.*

It was apparent to me that Dr. Rieux was becoming frustrated, irritated and resistant to the content of this little exercise and the conversation that flowed from it. His face twitched again, so much so that he discreetly attempted to rub and lightly massage his cheek in an effort to gain better control of his facial muscles.

"Think with me, Paneloux. When Moses was atop Mount Sinai God showed him the pattern of the heavenly Tabernacle that Moses was to build on earth in the wilderness. God also showed Moses a pattern for all the furniture in the heavenly Tabernacle that was to be used in the earthly Tabernacle once it was built. Moses was instructed to make the earthly Tabernacle and the furniture that was to be used in it exactly as God indicated – *based on the heavenly Tabernacle* – according to the heavenly pattern. The Hebrew word for pattern is *tabniyth.* It is also translated in other places in the Old Testament as *likeness, form, similitude* and *figure.* The idea conveyed is simply this: In heaven there is a perfect Tabernacle. The earthly Tabernacle was to be a representation of and made in the *likeness* or *image* of that perfect heavenly Tabernacle."

"I understand," said Paneloux, "I understand the basic concepts set forth by Plato; and, I am familiar with the biblical teaching concerning the heavenly Tabernacle and its pattern. In fact, if I remember correctly, David passed on the same pattern of the heavenly Tabernacle to Solomon to guide him as he built the first Temple. But, I do not see what this has to do with me or Dr. Rieux or our existence."

"It can serve, father, as a significant starting point to provide a deeper understanding of who you really are. Earlier you said: *'I have existence, yet I do not exist. I am a man, yet the essence of what man really is, is denied to me.'* I understand those sentiments – and *existence* and the *essence* of what man really is, is where we must begin. 'Who am I?' is the first basic philosophical question. Thus it is here that we must begin."

Unable to control his nervous facial twitching Dr. Rieux suddenly stood up and released his anger and frustration. Paneloux was caught off guard, unprepared. He had never seen Dr. Rieux behave like this; and quite frankly, neither had I. Shaking his finger toward me, Dr. Rieux began to speak, harshly and impatiently.

"What's next? A card trick? A slight of hand? Or more mental gymnastics? Are we supposed to be impressed? Or, perhaps amused? What strange logic is this that you employ? Circles? Triangles? Patterns. Representations. Likenesses. Things in heaven. Things on earth. I'll tell you what I think. Life is a mystery. The focus of the mystery for me is not human existence. I have never wondered or worried about why man exists. The mystery for me is me, my existence. Why do I exist? It seems to me that we're all vague something's – whether we exist in the physical world or in the literary world. I don't need a circle or a triangle to tell me that I exist. As one of you said earlier, 'I think therefore I am.' [69] Well, here I am, Bernard Rieux. I, Bernard Rieux, think, therefore I, Bernard Rieux, exist. Period. That I exist is resolved. Why I exist is not. What is my essence? I do not know. I don't really care. I am what I am. That's what I am. That's it – that's my essence…that's my existence. Beyond that, who cares? There is no reason why I exist. I just do."

"How wrong, Dr. Rieux. How terribly wrong. Thinking men and women through the ages have wrestled with these two issues: *essence and existence.* And, now, Paneloux, as a thinker, is wrestling with the same deeper realities of life; the deeper reality of his life, because he cares."

I turned toward Paneloux and directed my words to him.

"Hear me, Father Paneloux. Hear me. Who you are and why you are, are significant questions. I intentionally began with Plato more for the sake of Dr. Rieux because he rejects the Bible and the God of the Bible. Now, for your sake, Father, let us move from Plato to the Bible. As you are aware, the Bible reveals that in the beginning God said, 'Let us make man in our image, after our *likeness*…' Because man is a creation of God, made in the image of God, it may be deduced that man's *essence* precedes his *existence.* Before Moses could build the earthly Tabernacle he must first have a plan or a blueprint or a pattern that revealed the *essence* of that Tabernacle, that is, what it was to be like when it came into *existence.* When Moses built that Tabernacle, the Tabernacle then came into *existence,* but its *essence* preceded its existence.

"In like manner God knew what man would be like before He created man, *before man had existence.* God knew man's *essence,* before He created man, before man had *existence.* The *likeness* of what man would be is man's *essence.* When the Bible says that God said "Let us make man in our *image,* after our *likeness...'* it is indicating that the *essence* of who man is came into *existence* when God said, *'Let us...'* It is this *essence* that gives man's *existence* meaning and purpose. *A man is not simply bare existence.* He is not just here and that's it. The fact that man is here, that he has *existence* and that he has *essence, the image and likeness of God,* indicates he and his life have meaning, purpose and value."

Paneloux stared at me intently as I spoke. He was thinking, thinking carefully. Dr. Rieux was staring too – and still struggling with his facial twitching. No matter how hard he tried Dr. Rieux's internal theological bent was being externalized and the message of that externalization could be summarized in two words – anxious denial.

"You say, Dr. Rieux, *There is no reason why I exist. I just do.* The opposite is true. Life has meaning and purpose, Dr. Rieux, because man is made in the *image* of God. By way of creation God imparts His *essence* to man. God's *essence* and man's *essence* are inseparably linked because man is made in the *image* of God. Man is not God; never has been, never will be. Man does, because of his *essence,* bear the *likeness* of God. Because of man's *essence,* life has meaning and purpose. Life has meaning and purpose because God does exist and God gives not only *existence,* but His *essence* to man. This is why I say, you and your theological bent are wrong, Dr. Rieux, there is a reason why you exist. You will never discover that reason, Dr. Rieux, until you discover God and His redemptive love."

Dr. Rieux closed his eyes for a second. His voice, when he eventually spoke, had the beginning of outrage within it.

"Monsieur, I do not want to argue or fight with you. For me, life, real life, life as you know it in the physical universe is simple, yet complicated. Usually, I try to avoid these types of conversations. For me, your kind of real physical life is too difficult and too complicated to explain. As I said earlier, I exist. You exist. You are alive. I am alive. However, you must be honest, Monsieur. I did not ask to be born; neither did you. You did not cry out for existence. You just suddenly came to be. You came into existence. You were born. Then, you grew. You became physically stronger and your ability to think increased. And, here is what I think. You did not ask to be born; and yet, here you are. You cannot change this. You are powerless to change this. At some point you will die. You cannot change this either. You are powerless to change this. I do not say that your explanation for your existence is absurd. I say your existence itself is absurd. For me, your life has no meaning. You live. You suffer. You die."

Paneloux sat, silent and still. He knew that more was at stake than that which met the eye. This was more than a debate about philosophical perspectives.

"Remember, Monsieur, as I shared earlier. I have been aware of my existence in a literary sense for quite some time. I used to lie awake striving and struggling to understand all of this. I drew one immediate conclusion: I did not choose this life. This life was chosen for me. Another conclusion: a character in a novel, such as myself, or Father Paneloux, cannot die. Even if we are 'killed off' by Albert Camus in the novel – *we cannot die.* Because we are literary characters and not flesh and blood men, we suddenly become alive again when the novel is read again by another reader. Granted, our existence is limited – but it is recurring. The fact that this occurs in literature illustrates that it cannot occur in real life. Therefore, there is no recurrence of life in your realm; and, death, in your realm, is both inevitable and irreversible – and that's what makes your existence in a physical sense so absurd."

"Spoken like a true *atheistic existentialist,* Dr. Rieux, and consistent with your theological bent which was shaped by Camus, indeed, one of philosophy's greatest atheistic existentialist."

My thoughts traveled to the work of art at *Paw Paw's Plaza.* That painting, like the writings of Camus, contained many, if not all, of the elements of existentialism. On one level both Camus and the unknown artist portrayed the emotional components of existentialism in their works: frenzied feelings of desolation, disorientation, displacement, alienation, estrangement, futility, desperation and despair. On another level they both conveyed the rational, or should I say the irrational, conclusions of existentialism:

cynicism, pessimism, nihilism, atheism and the conclusion that life is absurd because it is always terminated by death. On the volitional level they both represented man as lacking freedom, with options for liberty denied, with meaning obliterated, morals negated, and meaningless choices with tragic conclusions about life. These were the very thoughts and feelings expressed by Dr. Rieux and Father Paneloux, evidence, according to my way of thinking, that they were created and shaped by Albert Camus.

I paused speaking for what I thought would be for just a few seconds. All of a sudden, however, I was overwhelmed with dizziness. My head was spinning. My sight began to blur. I was having difficulty focusing. I felt like my brain was throbbing. There was pain, severe pain inside the back of my head; and my jaw was suddenly throbbing – throbbing with pain.

I placed my hand on the back of a chair for balance. I became so dizzy and weak that I had to sit down. I was scared and afraid. I remember silently asking God to help me. Nausea. My head was spinning, faster and faster. Then, I can't explain why, for some unknown reason I tried to get up from the chair, but I couldn't seem to get my balance and collapsed to the floor.

"Father, please pray for me. Something's wrong. Dr. Rieux, something's wrong, something's terribly wrong inside my head."

Dr. Rieux quickly came to my side and started pressing two fingers to the side of my neck trying to find a pulse. As everything became darkness I heard Dr. Rieux, "For some reason he is bleeding, bleeding uncontrollably, hemorrhaging from the back of his head."

Rieux once again pressed his two fingers to the side of my neck. My eyes and my thoughts became blurred.

"I can't find a pulse. I think he's dying."

Dr. Rieux started pounding on my chest, trying to get a heartbeat. My chest began bouncing up and down, up and down. A bridge between what was and what was yet to be was collapsing. Modulations of various timescales raced through my brain. The past overstepped its boundaries. In the distance, beneath the shadow of a dark rolling cloud, I saw a tilted dry gray tombstone and heard the sound of weeping. There was a flutter, a single flutter of my heart, a soft single flutter. I could feel it, just for a second.

Darkness. Confusion. A Distant Flash of Light.
"He's Light. He's Moving. Regaining Consciousness."

Paneloux spoke in an anxious voice…
"He's as white as a ghost."

Rieux spoke with finality….
"He's dead."

Confusion. Disorientation.
The Fading Face. The Fading Bernard Rieux.
The Fading Voice.
"He's Dead."
"He's Dead."
"He's Dead."

RESTORE POINT 14:

DEFRAGMENT-DISSOLVE

Confusion. Disorientation.
The Fading Face. The Fading Bernard Rieux. The Fading Voice.
"He's Dead."
"He's Dead."
"He's Dead."

A Distant Flash of Light.
A Sudden Darkness.

Voices. Frantic Voices. Panic. Pandemonium.

"POWER FAILURE. POWER FAILURE."
The Overhead Procedure Lights Flickered Then Went Out.
Medical Equipment – Beeping. Beeping. Beeping. -- Sounding Alarms.
Nurses. Doctors. – Shouting. Shouting. Shouting. – Nurses. Doctors.

"Code Blue. Code Blue. Code Blue."
"GET THE CODE CART. GET THE CODE CART. "

"Anesthesia Machine Malfunction."
"Compurecord Failure."

"Bernard, the backup generators are not working."
"Are you kidding me?"

"Oxygenation Depletion." "Ventilation Malfunction."
"Anesthesia Levels Falling."
"Great. The radial arterial line to monitor blood pressure
has crapped out."
"This is Dr. Castel. This is Castel. Emergency Power Needed
IMMEDIATELY."

"Dr. Richard here. Will Someone Please Activate
The Backup Generators."
"Communications are down, sir."
"Cyber down. Cellular down. Infrared down. Nothing's Working,
Sir. Nothing's Working."

"This is Dr. Rieux speaking, will someone please activate the Backup
Power System - NOW."
"Nurse. See if you can locate any flashlights."

A Sudden Flash of Light.
Electrical Power On. The Sound of Applause.

"POWER FAILURE. POWER FAILURE."
Power Off Again. Lights Off Again.
Then Darkness. Darkness. A Return To Darkness.

"Where am I? Where am I?"

Straps. Straps. Surgical Chair. Straps. Straps.
I Was Strapped in a Surgical Chair.
Rotating. A Large Circular Glass Room. Rotating.
A Sudden Flash of Light.

Total Darkness.
A Flash of Light. A Flashlight. A Flash of Light.
A Single Beam of Light. A Flashlight. A Single Beam of Light.
Tubes. Wires. People. Running Everywhere. Tubes. Wires. People.

Voices. Frantic Voices. Panic. Pandemonium.

A Slit Across My Scalp. From Ear to Ear. A Slit Across My Scalp.
Skin. Peeled Away. Peeled Away from the Skull. Peeled Away. Skin.
A Flap of Skin. Peeled Down to the Eye Sockets. A Flap of Skin.
The Top of the Skull. Sawed Off. Sawed Off. The Top of the Skull.

A Shrill Screaming Voice. Filled with Fear. Filled with Fear. A Shrill Screaming Voice.

"WHAT ARE YOU DOING TO ME?"
"WHAT ARE YOU DOING TO ME?"

"Calm Down, John, Calm Down."
"Please. Stop Screaming, John, Stop Screaming. Please."

"Can anyone tell me how much Sevo does he have on board?"
"Get me more anesthesia technicians. NOW."

"He's Hemorrhaging. Dr. Rieux. Cranial Hemorrhaging."
"Significant post-operative blood loss."
"Abnormal surgical swelling."

A Shrill Screaming Voice.
My Voice. My Voice. Oh. God. It's My Voice.

"WHAT ARE YOU DOING TO ME?"
"WHAT ARE YOU DOING TO ME?"

"Shut Up. Shut Up, John. Shut Up."

"Propofol. Fentanyl. Midazolam."
"Use Peripheral Intravenous Lines Manually."

"Add Nitrous Oxide. Add Isoflurane. Add Vecuronium."
"Supplement an infusion of Remifentanil."

"Stand-by to use the manual bag-valve resuscitation device."
"Get him deeper. Give him more Versed so that he won't remember any of this."
"Where are the extra anesthetists? I shouldn't have to make these calls."

"WHAT ARE You Doing to me… Doing to me… Doing to me…
"Where am I? What are you…are you…you…yoooo doing to me?"
"Row, row, row your boat, gently down the stream. Merrily, Merrily, Merrily, life is but a dream."

Look. Look. A Butterfly.
It's Beautiful.
Look. On God's Finger. Look.
A Butterfly.

"I See You. I See You."
"Merrily, merrily, merrily, life is but a dream."

"Shut Up, John. Shut Up."
"Nurse. In the top drawer of my surgical desk is a staple gun. Get it. Get it NOW."
"What about those flashlights?"

"Got another one. Got another flashlight."
"Hold it steady. Shine it on his chin."
"Hand me that staple gun."
"Hold His Mouth Open. Hold It Wide."
"What are you doing, Bernard? What in the world are you doing?"

"Shut up. I'm nailing his tongue to his chin. He won't shut up so I'll make him shut up."

ack-ack-urkkk-yackkk
Gaging. Choking. Gaging.
Rotating. A Large Circular Glass Room. Rotating.
Spinning. Glass Room. Spinning.

ack-ack-urkkk-yackkk
Tongue Throbbing. Heart Pounding. Throbbing. Pounding.
Pounding. Pounding. Pounding.
A Distant Flash of Light.
Echoes. Loud Echoes.

Nurses. Doctors. – Shouting. Shouting. Shouting. – Nurses. Doctors.

HE'S TACHYCARDIC. HE'S TACHYCARDIC.
HIS BP IS DROPPING RAPIDLY. HIS SATS ARE LOW –
TOO LOW. GOING LOWER.

Shouting. Shouting. Shouting.

GET SOME MORE HELP IN HERE... ANESTHESIA...

"Brain Embolism. Brain Embolism."
"He's thrown a blood clot. Blockage. Hemorrhaging."
"He's Flatlined. He's Flatlined."
Flatlined.

"HE'S DEAD."
"What? What did you say? What?"
"HE'S DEAD."

"This is Albert. This is Albert. May I have your attention? This is Albert."
Everyone was silent. Everyone was still.

"We have exactly ten minutes to transport him through time. Ten minutes."

"Ten minutes for him to be restored."

"Ten minutes."

"Count Down Activated."

Defragment-Dissolve 10:00... Defragment-Dissolve 09:59... Defragment-Dissolve 09:58...

Defragment-Dissolve 09:57... Defragment-Dissolve 09:56... Defragment-Dissolve 09:55...

The Electrical Power Suddenly Came On.

"In ten minutes everything and everyone in our world will begin to dissolve."

"Dissolve. Defragment. Disappear."

"We have ten minutes."

Nurses. Doctors. – Shouting. Shouting. Shouting. – Nurses. Doctors.

"D. Rieux, this is Albert. Do something Rieux, Do something."

Defragment-Dissolve 09:07... Defragment-Dissolve 09:06... Defragment-Dissolve 09:05...

"We must have that *Apocalyptic Psalm.* This man is the only one who can lead us to it! Do something Rieux. Do something. He must survive this. He must live."

"We stand at the very edge of that abyss. Annihilation. Extinction. Non-existence. Oblivion. Nothingness."

"Defrag-Dissolve Continuing"

"Thanks, We're on target."

Defragment-Dissolve 09:04... Defragment-Dissolve 09:03... Defragment-Dissolve 09:02...

"We must have the *Apocalyptic Psalm*, Dr. Rieux. We must have the *Apocalyptic Psalm.*
Nurses. Doctors. – Shouting. Shouting. Shouting. – Nurses. Doctors.

"Mr. Grand. Paging Mr. Grand. This is Dr. Bernard Rieux. Grand, what is the Restore Point?"
Defragment-Dissolve 08:57… Defragment-Dissolve 08:56… Defragment-Dissolve 08:55…

"Tricky Coordinates, Dr. Rieux. Tricky Coordinates."
"Get him back to Esplanade Avenue, New Orleans."
"Seated in the car. In the rain. He can be fully restored there."
"This is Grand speaking: Once he's in the car I'll keep him talking till restoration is complete."

Defragment-Dissolve 07:20… Defragment-Dissolve 07:19… Defragment-Dissolve 07:18…
Defragment-Dissolve 07:17… Defragment-Dissolve 07:16… Defragment-Dissolve 07:15…

"Bernard. Dr. Richard. This is Albert. Activate Your Crew."
"Bernard. Richard. This is Joseph Grand. The Restore Point is Saturday, October 20, 2012, 1:11 p.m."

"Dr. Castel? Dr. Rieux here. Initiate the Restore Point for Saturday, October 20, 2012, 1:11 p.m."
"Dr. Castel. Dr. Rieux. Fifteen minutes later, at exactly 1:26 p.m. bring him back to *Christ Cathedral.*"
At exactly 1:26 p.m. place him where he left off in the conversation with Paneloux."
"It's tricky but it must be done."

Defragment-Dissolve 05:02… Defragment-Dissolve 05:01… Defragment-Dissolve 05:00…

Defragment-Dissolve 04:59… Defragment-Dissolve 04:58…
Defragment-Dissolve 04:57…

Darkness. Confusion.
A Distant Flash of Light.
Echoes Of A Fading Past.
Spinning Sounds. Rectangles. Squares. Spinning Sounds.

Confusion. Disorientation.
The Fading Face – The Fading Bernard Rieux -- The Fading Voice

"He's Dead."
"He's Dead."
"He's Dead."

"Saturday, October 20, 2012, 1:11 p.m."
"Saturday, October 20, 2012, 1:11 p.m."

Echoing. Echoing. Echoing Inside My Head.
"He's Dead."
"He's Dead."
"He's Dead."

Defragment-Dissolve 00:09… Defragment-Dissolve 00:08…
Defragment-Dissolve 00:07…
"Saturday, October 20, 2012, 1:11 p.m."

A clap of thunder.
Defragment-Dissolve 00:00

RESTORE POINT 15:

RESTORATION

There was a loud clap of thunder as Emma parked the car on Esplanade Avenue. The threatening rain shower suddenly began to fall. It looked like chaos on the Esplanade as people ran in different directions trying to avoid the sudden downpour. Thin sheer sheets of plastic suddenly covered everything and everyone. People huddled under these makeshift plastic tarps while others stood under the overhanging canvas awnings in an effort to avoid the rain.

I don't know if it was a reaction to the rain or not but my head ached, my jaw was throbbing, and it felt like I had bitten my tongue. Perhaps it was the humidity. I really wasn't sure. Hopefully, like the rain, these pains would eventually pass.

We sat in the car and waited for the rain to pass. Emma and I shared some of our thoughts about art, artistic images and their relationship to *metaphorical thinking* with Mr. Grand. Then I began to share with Grand the strange, melancholic story of a New Orleans artist, an unusually gifted painter named Bill, Bill Hemmerling.

"Yes. Yes. I've heard of this Hemmerling fellow," said Mr. Grand. "A remarkable man. A simply remarkable man. Some say he has a connection with that controversial piece of art in the infamous *Paw Paw's Plaza.*"

"Oh. I was not aware that you were familiar with Bill Hemmerling or the controversy that surrounds *Paw Paw's Plaza.*"

"Oh. Yes. Yes. I'm not an expert, of course, but I am familiar with Hemmerling and the controversy about *Paw Paw's Plaza.*"

Mr. Grand looked through the rain toward the neutral ground on Esplanade Avenue, just for an instant, then looked at his watch, then looked at me with a peculiar intentness. It was as if he were observing me, making mental observations, not only of what I was saying, but of how I was saying what I was saying. It was uncomfortable, sensing that I was being so closely observed this way.

"Let's get back to focusing on *metaphorical thinking*. I really need to understand it better. *Metaphorical thinking*, as I understand it" said Mr. Grand, "is a rather simplistic, yet profound way of thinking, a biblically therapeutic way of thinking, utilized by many, many people to safety navigate the complexities of life."

The soft rains continued falling as the massive oaks swirled back and forth with an almost mystical cadence.

"As I shared earlier, one of my primary goals is to better understand the deeper implications of the theological, therapeutic strategies of *metaphorics*. Is there perhaps a nuts-and-bolts, simplified understanding of how *metaphorics* works. You've talked about mental images, visual cartoons, symbols and metaphors; but, how does *metaphorical thinking* actually work."

"A nuts-and-bolts understanding? There is, Mr. Grand. Yes, I believe there is. While it is true that everything seemed to come together at *Christ Cathedral*, the pieces that came together were already present – long before I had the *Christ Cathedral* experience."

"I'd like to hear your simple explanation."

"One primary key was something that happened to me before the hurricane and before the *Christ Cathedral* experience. I was driving home one day when something happened that triggered a deeper understanding of *metaphorical thinking.*"

Mr. Grand spoke again without blinking.

"I'd like to hear about that."

I shifted myself so as to look directly into the eyes of Mr. Grand. The soft rain continued to fall.

"Well, I was driving home one evening, Mr. Grand, down Jean Lafitte Avenue in Chalmette. Unfortunately, I hate to say this, but, I was driving just a little bit too fast. Suddenly, as I rounded a curve on Jean Lafitte Drive I was greeted by flashing lights. No, it wasn't a policeman. It was a Traffic

Control kiosk strategically located on the Jean Lafitte neutral ground. The kiosk was actually a LED sign activated by a radar sensor device. The sensor system provided a digital readout that flashed the words 'YOUR SPEED' in large blinking lights. Below the flashing 'YOUR SPEED' sign was another sign that flashed the words, 'SPEED LIMIT' which quite naturally led me to frantically put my foot to the brakes. I quickly slowed down and reduced my speed below the posted speed limit."

"I've had that happen to me," related Grand.

I paused just for a second to allow Mr. Grand to create a mental image of the Traffic Control kiosk. Truth is voiceless, yet speaks many languages. I was confident that God's truth would speak to Mr. Grand even if it was filtered through the analogy and image of a Traffic Control kiosk.

"Later that night, Mr. Grand, during my Bible study quiet time, I reflected on the whole of that experience. I linked several different elements of the experience with the traditional understandings of how God uses the Bible to change us -- *revelation, inspiration, illumination and interpretation.*

"As I thought about the kiosk experience I began to realize that the Traffic Control kiosk sign didn't actually tell me anything that I didn't already know. I knew the speed limit and I had a speedometer in my car that indicated my speed. I knew I was driving a bit too fast. And, if I wanted to confirm my speed a simple glance at the speedometer would have sufficed. But I didn't look at the speedometer and I doubt that I would have slowed down if I had. No new knowledge was gained through the kiosk, yet I reduced my speed, my behavior changed. Again, no new knowledge was gained – *but my interpretation of the knowledge that I had changed."*

I paused momentarily, distracted by the sound of the tires of a *Big Easy* double-decker tour bus as they hissed on the steaming asphalt of Esplanade Avenue. Light mists and fine sprays of rain water leaped over the azalea plants on the neutral ground as the bus came to a stop. Like the tour bus the rain had also stopped. My headache eased, somewhat; but, my tongue was still strangely sore.

"As I continued thinking about the 'YOUR SPEED' incident, Mr. Grand, I recalled that though I was startled by the flashing lights I quickly realized that there would be no punitive action, no negative consequences, and no legal penalty because of my speeding. There was no policeman to give me a speeding ticket. Nevertheless, I slowed down. Somehow, the kiosk had encouraged me to do the right thing – and, I immediately did the right thing. My behavior changed – I slowed down. Again, no new knowledge was gained – *but my interpretation changed* – and I wanted to know why. "

Emma, Mr. Grand and I were simultaneously startled as a young man, seemingly coming from nowhere began kicking his legs high in the air like a prancing horse as he ran across the neutral ground on Esplanade Avenue toward the tour group as they exited the bus. He stopped running, rather abruptly as he reached the very edge of the neutral ground. Like a proud stallion marching in place, he continued moving his legs up and down, prancing, without any forward movement.

"Strange people, eh, Mr. Grand. Strange people."

The young man's shouts grew louder and louder – and more and more obscene. I turned my eyes quickly from the young man to continue talking with Grand, hoping that somehow my words would drown out the foul language.

"In the months that followed I discovered that the 'YOUR SPEED' signs utilized a technology called a *feedback loop* to elicit changed behavior among speeding drivers. Somehow, the *feedback loop* created a mental image of a cop with a radar gun that resulted in my behavioral change – slowing down, reducing speed. Research indicated that the mental image of a traffic cop with a radar gun was actually more effective in changing human behavior than a real cop with a radar gun. Somehow, the mental image was greater than the reality. The *possibilities* of what could happen had greater influence than the *actuality,* greater influence than the *actuality* of what would *actually* happen – in this case *nothing.* In essence, the kiosk was utilizing the power of a metaphor – the mental image of a cop with a radar gun – to create behavioral change – to lead people to do the right thing."

Just as the young man's shouting reached a fever pitch, the lights of a nearby police car came on and began flashing. In an instant, the young man's voice was silenced. He literally stopped, mid-sentence, and turned and started walking, calmly and nonchalantly, toward *Paw Paw's Plaza.* My eyes turned back toward Mr. Grand as I continued talking.

An old man with a walker, who evidently had a hearing problem, spoke rather loudly to no one in particular as he walked by our car, heading towards *Paw Paw's Plaza.* Other people walking in the same direction joined a small, yet growing crowd admiring the large Hemmerling style painting on discarded ply-board. A few people from the tour bus group sat in the folding chairs on one end of the plaza, while others stood behind the chairs stretching their legs.

Mr. Grand appeared to be searching the small crowd, just for a moment. If I hadn't known better I would have thought that he was looking for someone. Between his quick glances at the crowd he also started looking back and forth at his watch. This back and forth process, crowd then watch, crowd then watch, was very distracting.

"Should I continue, Mr. Grand. Or, would you prefer that we pause to take a look at the painting."

"No. Definitely, no. I have been taking notes on everything you have shared. I do apologize. For a moment I thought I saw someone that I knew; but, this cannot be so. I am far too far away from home. Please do continue."

"Well, Mr. Grand, though the language was often quite technical I was eventually able to develop four stages or steps to use biblical metaphors to facilitate behavioral change. I must stress, however, that change always begins with a personal relationship with Christ. That personal relationship with Jesus is the true starting point. Jesus said, 'Without me ye can do nothing.' Anyone, Mr. Grand, anyone who attempts to modify or change behavior without Christ will ultimately fail and either fall back into their old behaviors or develop cross addictions or other inappropriate behaviors which will create recurring, endless cycles of negative life-dominating problems."

"Now, you say there are four stages or steps that form the nuts-and-bolts of *metaphorical thinking?* That's it? Only four?"

"That's it, Mr. Grand. Four simple steps; but, don't lose sight of the starting point, Mr. Grand. John, in the book of Revelation, uses the image of Jesus standing at a door and knocking. That image is symbolic of Jesus knocking at the door of our hearts, at the door of our lives. This same John told us in the Gospel that bears his name that we cannot do anything without Jesus. Never lose sight of the starting point for it is there that we begin again, empowered by Christ for radical change."

"Yes. Yes. We can talk about that later. At this point I must be true to my assignment and focus on *metaphorical thinking*. If you don't mind I'll record our conversation from this point forward. Sometimes I struggle with language in its written form. The recording will help me explain *metaphorical thinking* more accurately."

"A recorder? That's fine with me, Mr. Grand, especially if recording our conversation will enhance the accuracy of our conversations. But, remember the starting point, Mr. Grand. Remember Christ – *He is the starting point. He is where we begin. Without Him we can do nothing."*

I did not realize it as we sat talking in the car but there were competing values at work between us. One of my primary concerns in developing *metaphorics* focused on the potential value to others by attaining and acquiring those intangible things that give life value. Grand, however, embraced a different value. He valued *metaphorics* and *metaphorical thinking* primarily because of its potential value to him, the potential financial value. I should also add at this point that neither of us realized that Grand's misutilization of *metaphorics* and its use of *images* would be linked to the long ago prophesized *image of the beast* spoken of in the book of Revelation.

I should also add at this point that while Grand suffered a lifelong intense anxiety with written language, through the advent and advancement of computer technologies he surprisingly discovered that he had no difficulty with the complex *binary language* of computer programming. He discovered that he had the uncanny ability to create complex programs and solve technological problems that were beyond the abilities of even the most advanced, upper echelon binary technicians.

It was here, in this technological arena, that Grand identified the potential financial value of *metaphorical thinking* and its potential to create massive wealth and power.

The big secret that had the potential to create wealth and accrue power for Grand was a special genetic software that he had secretly developed while working in his lab with plague infected rats, poisonous caterpillars, chrysalis and butterfly's and the DNA of *metamorphosis.*

Utilizing a complex *binary code* and its language of zeros and ones, Grand somehow created long strings of *binary code* that he intertwined and fused with equally long DNA strings of genetic material containing the *genetic code* of the DNA of *metamorphosis.* As the *genetic codes* and the strings of *binary codes* and the DNA of *metamorphosis* codes intermingled, swapped material and subsequent qualities, they were then merged, fused into one new set of codes. These codes gave birth to a new genetic mutation that was far superior to the original individual strings. The codes of the new mutated, string would then have an extremely powerful influence over the entire organism's genetic software through electronic and biological connectivity created by Grand.

Grand reasoned that adding an additional string, a long string of metaphoric codes, would enhance the value of *metaphorical thinking* and speed up the process of behavioral modification in humans. His ability to do this depended upon his capacity to thoroughly understand *metaphorical thinking,* inside and out....hence, his fraudulent assignment from Templeton which Grand concocted to gain this deeper understanding.

He would later discover that there were unintended consequences that he hadn't considered that would unfold as he merged *metaphorics* into his genetic software. He was blinded by what he saw at the end of the long string of new mutated genetic codes – himself, pulling the string for massive financial gain, the accumulation of wealth and global power. Needless to say, I did not share Grand's values nor did he respect my convictions – or my earlier cautions about the danger of such an endeavor in relation to population control.

Traditionally, biblical conviction is the insight or perception of something a person should do, or should not do. Conviction is the overwhelming awareness of right or wrong, primarily in the area of character, conversation and conduct as expressed in the context of a person's life.

The brutalization of humanity by greedy men in their mad quest for wealth and power is one of the sad realities of human history. In a world where truth is denied and hearts are filled with greed and darkness that threatens to overwhelm, here is a man – Joseph Grand -- hearing about *metaphorical thinking* and the conviction it produces -- *yet feeling none.* Greed, covetousness, lust for power – these emotions were dominating Grand's dark heart, yet his conscience was seared. He felt no conviction. He felt nothing except lust for power and avarice.

The recorder kept recording and Grand kept poking at keys as he typed. I continued speaking ignorant of the dark forces of spiritual warfare working within him.

The Holy Spirit was working to quicken Mr. Grand. Mr. Grand quickly quenched the work of the Holy Spirit. He wanted the reward irrespective of the risks. The impulse to be a risk-avoider had dominated Grand for as long as he would remember. He was determined to overcome that impulse and become a risk-taker. The stakes were high. For Grand it was all or nothing. Grand wanted it all.

"Biblical metaphors, Mr. Grand, are Holy Spirit produced images. They deal with *actualities* and *possibilities.* They enable a person to see the temporal and eternal consequences of avoiding biblical Confrontation and resisting biblical Conviction. The mental image of the Consequence leads to Choice. And there, Mr. Grand, in a simple format, are the four stages of *metaphorical thinking – Confrontation, Conviction, Consequence and Choice.*

"Choice," said Grand. "Before you address the subject of choice I must ask a question. I am quite sure that there are literally thousands of metaphors in the Bible. "How do you know which to choose?"

"You are correct, Mr. Grand. There are hundreds of thousands of colorful metaphors in the Bible and there are tens of thousands of beautiful and meaningful figures of speech in the Bible that enhance the value of *metaphorical thinking*. Years ago I was fortunate to purchase a copy of an old, out-of-print book, very difficult to find. It was published in the 1800s and titled *A Concordance of Biblical Metaphors.* It is an alphabetical listing of all of the metaphors used in both the Old and New Testaments, with an extensive Hebrew-Greek cross-reference of every metaphor. Because it is a concordance it does not provide content or commentary about the metaphors. Instead, it serves as an index that allows the researcher to find metaphors where they appear in the Bible. This enables the researcher to see where, how and when the metaphor was utilized and applied.

"Because of the time, difficulty and expense involved in creating a concordance that could be linked to *metaphorical thinking*, Emma and I, utilized the *Concordance of Biblical Metaphors* to identify metaphors in the Bible. We researched and identified the principal biblical metaphors and published a biblical reference work titled *Biblical Metaphors And Their*

Transformative Power In Biblical Counseling And Therapy. Using standard biblical research tools Emma and I identified 777 biblical metaphors that we associated with transformative power. Of course, we only touched the tip of the iceberg. There are 788,258 words in the Bible. Most of them are nouns. Many of them are metaphors."

An older couple wearing yellow Missouri Volunteer t-shirts with matching yellow baseball caps briefly distracted us. They were evidently amused by the antics of the young man. Laughing and shaking their heads, they quietly walked across the neutral ground toward *Paw Paw's Plaza.*

Mr. Grand punched a final few notes then quickly looked at his watch.

"It's 1:22 p.m., Mr. Grand. Do you have another appointment?"

"No. No. But I would like to see the painting at *Paw Paw's Plaza.* Perhaps while we are at the *Plaza* you can share some thoughts about the relationship of art, metaphor and mental images.

As we walked toward *Paw Paw's Plaza* the man in the Missouri Volunteer t-shirt stood up, shook my hand, then, looking directly at me he asked a question.

"Aren't you that preacher that was on FOX News Network a few weeks ago? I'd be willing to bet you are, and if you're not, you're a dead ringer or have a twin brother."

"No. No," interrupted the woman, who was evidently his wife, "It was PBS, not FOX. I definitely remember -- it was *PBS Religion And Ethics."*

As Emma, Grand and I exchanged pleasantries with the couple from Missouri, the old man we saw earlier walked towards *Paw Paw's Plaza.* He held tightly onto his lightweight walker as he slowly and carefully placed one foot in front of the other, slightly dragging his left foot.

"Are you going to give a speech or preach or something?" asked the lady from Missouri.

"Well, I was going to share about *Paw Paw's Plaza* and about the hurricane with Mr. Grand," I said pointing toward Grand. "He's visiting our city, seeking to gather information for a series of articles he's writing. If it doesn't matter to Mr. Grand it's OK with me for you to stay and hear some thoughts that I'll be sharing."

Before Grand could say anything the old man with the walker, who evidently had a hearing problem, spoke rather loudly to no one in particular.

"What'd he say? Is he going to give a speech or something? Tell him I said to please speak loud."

As I nodded my head in the old man's direction to indicate that I would speak loudly, other people joined our small, yet growing crowd. Some sat on folding chairs, while others chose to stand. I cleared my throat then, just as I began to speak I simultaneously began to sense that strange things were about to happen. The first indication was the quiet gathering of swirling black clouds above us. They had a mysterious, grey glow as they tumbled and turned.

"Here, my friends, is art born of sorrow. Here we see, not only what the artist saw, but, on a deeper level; we see the artist himself. Like Christ, our artist is a man of sorrows. Like the Old Testament prophet Jeremiah, our artist is one who weeps – not through….

Suddenly there was the crashing, clapping sound of thunder, several flashes of lightening, and a hard downpour of rain. People again were running in different directions. I don't know exactly how it happened but someone bumped against a cross that was part of a memorial display at *Paw Paw's Plaza,* causing the cross to fall toward me. Even though I grabbed at the cross in an attempt to protect myself, my attempt was unsuccessful. The cross fell, hitting me on the head. I somehow managed to hold onto the cross as I tumbled to the ground. My head was spinning. In my dizziness I saw a swirling blurry image of a motionless spray-painted Silver Statue man. Someone, a man dressed in black, helped me to stand. As we walked away, my legs were wobbly. I was dizzy, totally disoriented. I collapsed, stumbled, then fell...

I tried to get up again but I began to stagger. Then I heard a different sound, voices, familiar voices. It was the voice of Dr. Rieux and Father Paneloux.

RESTORE POINT 16:

THE AD NAUSEAM OF MAN

I was scared and afraid. I remember silently asking God to help me as I stumbled and fell. *Nausea.* My head was spinning, faster and faster. Evidently I had collapsed, falling to the floor.

Dr. Rieux quickly came to my side.

"Are you OK, Monsieur? Are you OK?"

"Yes. Yes. How clumsy of me. I must have tripped or something."

"It looks like you hit your head," I heard Dr. Rieux say. "Are you sure you're OK?"

"Yes. I'm fine. I feel fully restored."

There was an irony in my innocent choice of the word "restored," an irony that caused a slight smirk to come upon the face of Dr. Rieux.

"Now where were we? I believe we were talking about *atheistic existentialism* and your perspective, Dr. Rieux, that life is absurd."

I could feel physical power returning to my body, I spoke with a strong firm voice and increased mental clarity.

"And what, may I ask is the root cause of this feeling that life is absurd, Dr. Rieux? The answer, Dr. Rieux is the fallacious belief that there is no God."

"This is not a fallacious belief, Monsieur," said Dr. Rieux. *"There is no God.* As I shared earlier, *God is nowhere."*

"Dr. Rieux. Hear me. You have been seduced by the prose and theological bent of Albert Camus. That which you deny – the existence of God -- is the very cause of that which you denounce – the absurdity of life. The dark seed of Camus has blossomed into a black flower, casting a dark shadow of despair and absurdity over everything you see."

As Dr. Rieux walked across the room I recalled a small portion of *A Psalm Of The Apocalypse.* I did not know it just then, but *the three shaped by the pen* were *Camus' foul sons – Joseph Grand, Dr. Rieux and – Father Paneloux.*

Fictional characters always represent something greater than themselves. Joseph Grand represented the philosophy of *materialism.* Rieux represented *atheistic existentialism.* Paneloux represented man's proclivity to *religiosity.* Thus they are described as *Philosophers Three – All Agree*

A Dark Seed Blossoms
Flowers, Black, Three In Number, Stand Tall
Shadows, Bleak, A Terrible Fall.
Kyrie Boethei. Lord Help.
Lord Help Us All.

Three. Three. Shaped by the Pen.
Recurrence. Recurring, Again and Again.
Philosophers Three – All Agree
What Ill Hath Befallen Thee
Camus' Foul Sons, Foul Sons Thou Art
Who are, will be, yet are not --
A Devious Plot.
He Who Has Eyes, See.
Unholy Trinity. – Unholy Three.

Dr. Rieux walked across the room, turned toward me as if to say something, but did not speak. That was his choice. My choice was clear. I could not remain silent.

"In this you are correct, Dr. Rieux: if there is no God then life is absurd. But, there is a God, sir, and His very existence abolishes the absurdity of life. His existence lifts the darkness of despair and replaces it with the light of hope."

I could feel strength welling up inside of me as I continued speaking.

"Look. Dr. Rieux. Look there and you will see, if you will but open your eyes, you will see that God's lively hope is always before us. Is there pain in life? Yes. Human suffering? Yes. Dread and Despair? Yes. Death? Yes. In the dark shadows of life you will find all of the ingredients necessary to produce mankind's greatest nightmares. But look carefully, Dr. Rieux, look. God's lively hope is there too. It is the light that shines in the darkness. It is the sweet dream in the midst of the nightmare."

As I turned and sat in my chair I began to think about how very difficult it is to convince a person that their understanding of life – what it is and what it is not – is wrong, especially when their interpretation is the only one they've ever known. Tragically, in the case of Dr. Rieux his interpretation was not his own; it was a shadow, a dark projection of the mind of Albert Camus. And, up to this point, Rieux and I had exchanged verbal punches; but our exchange was nothing more than shadow boxing.

"Well, I disagree." said Dr. Rieux, "Your religion and your philosophies are feeble attempts to convince yourself and others that life is not absurd, that life is not the bad joke that it really is. You are a coward, sir, and you run from despair, run from dread, and you run from death – and even your running is absurd. Death will catch you. Strangle you. Choke the life out of you. You are helpless and you are hopeless. And why? Because of the seed, the dark seed of despair, sown, not by Camus, but by the cursed Nazarene. And what is the blossoming black flower that cast a dark shadow over mankind? It is the Gospel that bears the Nazarene's name. And the nightmare? The nightmare is Christianity, the dark faith that deceives and denies man freedom and autonomy and supremacy in the universe.

Dr. Rieux angrily and bitterly interpreted life, not merely as a man of unbelief, but as an angry, hostile, atheistic man of unbelief – and there is a difference. Some men are simply men of unbelief; ordinary men who go about their ordinary everyday chores with an absence of faith. They bother no one, argue with no one – they simply live and die in unbelief. Other men, however, like Dr. Rieux, are not ordinary men of unbelief. They are ornery, hostile, angry. They are antagonistic and aggressive against anyone who professes faith. Dr. Rieux, with his atheistic bent shaped by Camus, was slowly revealing himself to be more of the latter and less of the former – ornery, not ordinary.

Walking in the dimness of reason and logic, life held no real mystery for Dr. Rieux. Nor was there, in his estimation, any inherent or deeper meaning to life. Through the unfocused mental lens of his *atheistic existentialism* he deduced that any meaning or sense of mission that a person might embrace was subjective, purely subjective. For Rieux the supposed meaning of life was nothing more than an assigned meaning, an assigned meaning brought into existence and projected onto one's life by the subjective experiences of the individual. As for a man's life mission, Rieux was an *atheistic existentialist.* A man's life mission was self-created, having no transcendent or higher value. The thing to do, according to Dr. Rieux, was to choose your life vision and your life projects then strive to fulfill that vision and complete your projects to the best of your ability.

Here. Before me. Here stands Dr. Rieux. A lost man, a cognitive wanderer, an *atheistic existentialist* -- anchored in *existential despair* -- with his ornery mind steeled against truth and hope. Yes. Here was Dr. Rieux, angrily wandering in a desert of doubt and disbelief and abandoned faith. Unbelief had become his illusionary oasis, his escape. At the heart of his illusion, he had accepted the idea that man is nothing but an absurd, grotesque dream, a cosmic orphan wandering alone, solitarily walking across the infinite nothingness of space – alone, without God because there was no God.

It would be easy to mistake Dr. Rieux for a self-made man. He is not, however. He is anything but. Rieux is man made in the flawed image of man. A grandiose reinvented man. A make-believe man. A fictitious man. Terribly twisted. Terribly distorted. Concocted and Contrived.

No. Rieux is not a self-made man. He is a Camus-made man. Nothing more. Nothing less. Rieux is a vanity mirror – a vain reflection of Albert Camus projecting himself and his atheistic philosophy onto the world. A thing reflecting a thing. A flawed image reflecting a flawed image.

Rieux was articulate, a deep thinker and could perform just about any task that was consistent with his highly complex, highly defined atheistic character, but only if he were prompted by Albert Camus. The personality that animated Rieux was Albert Camus – though Rieux was not always consciously aware of this.

The relationship between Camus and the fictitious characters he created is complex – and best illustrated using the analogy of a computer.

Just as a computer is unaware of the existence of its programmer, so too were Dr. Rieux and Father Paneloux and all of the characters in *The Plague* unaware of the tremendous influence that Camus was exerting on them and through them. A computer does not know that it is a computer even though it can think and perform assigned tasks. But, think with me for a moment, what are the assigned tasks that a computer performs. It only performs those tasks originally created by the programmer and only those prompted or requested by the user – and Albert Camus was both. He programmed the assigned tasks for all of his literary characters, shaped their personalities, formed their theological and philosophical bents and used them to promote his atheistic philosophy -- atheistic existentialism – on his unsuspecting readers.

Father Paneloux, on the other hand, even though a creation of Camus, saw life through the eyes of faith, albeit a miniaturized faith. Because he was created by Camus, his faith eventually constricted, withered and died. And therein lies the tragedy of Father Paneloux, his faith never did flourish. There were parameters or limits placed on the faith of Father Paneloux, parameters and limits that were predetermined by Albert Camus.

In the end, the faith of Father Paneloux collapsed as even he surrendered to existential despair. In his surrender he had fulfilled the purpose of Camus, who used Paneloux to project faith as a fallacy to a worldwide audience. In the end Camus would lead Father Paneloux like a confused child to embrace the *ad nauseam of man* rather than the *ad gloriam of Christ.* In the end Paneloux, led by Camus, would turn away from the *Holy of Holies* and embrace the *vanity of vanities.*

Nevertheless, the end for Father Paneloux was not yet. And because his end was not yet it was to him, to Paneloux, that I must turn to continue the conversation. He still had the reasoning powers of a man of faith, reasoning powers placed there by Camus so that he might adequately reflect belief – a necessity if Paneloux was to be a credible character. I had made as much headway as possible with Dr. Rieux. I must go further with Paneloux; and so to him I turned. And, through him and our conversation perhaps others would turn to faith in Christ. And so, I turned to Paneloux.

"Rieux calls Christ the cursed Nazarene. He speaks of the Gospel as a blossoming black flower and of Christianity as a dark nightmare. And, he says there is no God. But, there is a God. There is a God, Father. You know this. And I know this too. There is a deep flaw in human nature that produces unbelief. The Bible calls this flaw sin. But, what say you, Father, do we not both know that sin, this flaw, does not negate the existence of God? No. The flaw, our sin, actually confirms God's existence; and drives even the most ardent unbeliever and the vilest of sinners to seek God. Our deep prayer is that all men would seek God and find Him through faith in the Son, Jesus Christ."

"Yes. Yes. I know." said Paneloux. "I do indeed know that there is a God. And, I too know that sin, this fatal flaw is imbedded in human nature. I've done battle with it often. Sin, in and of itself, indeed, just as you say, vilifies and thereby verifies that there is a God."

Sin, in its simplest form, is rejection of God. It is that rejection that confirms, rather than negates, His existence.

"Yes, Father, there is indeed a God. I know this and you know this too. And, because God exists life has meaning, a transdent, higher meaning and mission for every life. And, there is a fixed, firm, righteous standard, an absolute morality because of the moral rightness of God's holiness – and, there is hope, an abundance of hope in the midst of even the darkest despair – because God exists. Is there mystery? Of course. Yes, of course. But mystery does not create despair. Mystery promises hope. Mystery engenders even greater hope.

"Indeed, Father, all of these mingle together, one with another – mystery, meaning, mission, morality – they mingle and merge thereby creating what the Bible calls *a lively hope.*"

All at once Paneloux suddenly sprang to his feet. I feared he was having a nervous breakdown a he struggled for composure. He began to move his hands as if he were preparing to punch it out with a punching bag. In the midst of his movements he raised his right fist high in the air, triumphantly thrusting it upward, as he lifted his voice simultaneously crying and shouting...

"Oh. Despair. Why come you here to mock me. You indeed are an unwise counselor. Indeed, I will entertain you no longer. Death to despair. Death to despair. Hope is my portion. Hope is ever more my portion."

Paneloux was desperate. He was a broken man, horribly broken.

In the midst of Paneloux's anxious, weeping tirade, the sickly looking old woman with tired, yellowed eyes who had earlier brought me a cup of warm milk entered the room. Once again she slowly and carefully placed one foot in front of another as she walked toward Dr. Rieux. I nodded to her, smiled and said "Hello, Mademoiselle. Hello." She jerked her head toward me, then smiled a half smile, and winked.

"Hello, Monsieur. I old woman, Monsieur, foolish old woman. My eyes dim and so my mind."

She carefully bent her head forward to the ear of Dr. Rieux and whispered something that only Rieux could hear. A look of surprise came upon his face as his eye brows raised high, a look that was followed by a churlish smile.

She then turned and walked across the room toward me and whispered in my ear.

"Monsieur, Dr. Rieux share his secret to you. I cannot. I share to you secret I not share to him. John the Younger, who is boy he meet you later tonight. This your secret – to you and you alone."

"Thank you, Mademoiselle. Thank you."

She laughed a low, disturbing kind of laugh, raised her hand to bid farewell, then turned and winked at me as she left to return to the kitchen.

"I old woman." she repeated, several times, as she walked away from us. "I old woman. I old woman, foolish old woman."

"Indeed, she is," said Dr. Rieux with a chuckle. "Always has a secret to tell, that one, always has a secret to tell. I guess she told you, Monsieur, about our secret visitor, eh? Who did she tell you was coming?"

"It was difficult to hear as she spoke, Dr. Rieux."

"Well, it will not be a secret for much longer, Monsieur. We do indeed have a special visitor who is coming, coming to visit all three of us."

"And who might that be?" asked Paneloux with a trembly voice, still wrestling with terror, doubt and disbelief.

Dr. Rieux stood confidently, then looked directly into my eyes as he spoke.

"Tonight, Father, all three of us will meet in the dining room of *Christ Cathedral* with the old woman's secret guest.... Albert Camus."

RESTORE POINT 17:

THE MYSTERY OF OBLIVION

Applause. Loud Applause. Cheers. More Applause.
The Sound, the Echoing Sound of Applause.
A Distant Flash of Light.

"Ladies and Gentlemen. May We Have Your Attention.
Ladies and Gentlemen."

Straps. Straps. Surgical Straps.
I Was Strapped, Still Strapped, in a Circulating Surgical Chair.

"Ladies and Gentlemen. Please Welcome Mr. Albert Camus IV."

Slowly Rotating. Clockwise. A Large 18,000-square-foot Circular Glass Room. Slowly Rotating.
My Circulating Surgical Chair. Slowly Rotating. Counter-Clockwise.
Everything was swirling. Images. Time. Space.
Swirling like a whirlpool with currents and cross-currents.
Applause. Loud Applause. Cheers. More Applause.
The Sound, the Echoing Sound of Applause.
A Sudden Flash of Light.

"Ladies and Gentlemen. Please Welcome Mr. Albert Camus IV. Ladies and Gentlemen. Mr. Camus."

"Thank you. Thank you."

Applause. Loud Applause. Cheers. More Applause.

"Thank you. Thank you."

The Sound, the Echoing Sound of Applause.

"Thank you. Thank you. Please be seated. Please be seated."

From my vantage point I could see the circulating observation rooms on the second and third levels of the tall circular building. Each room was filled with shadowy figures and faces, many faces. Their observation rooms were linked, one to another, yet separated and segregated by large trapezoids of curved plate glass. Floor to ceiling glass inner walls provided each observation team panoramic views with multiple sight lines to the lower level rotating surgical area. High above there was an elegant vaulted ceiling with a glass dome at the center surrounded by bright stage lights pointed downward, focusing on the surgical area and my rotating surgical chair.

I could see large computer and video monitors, mounted on the curved walls of each observation room on the second and third levels. These screens, with rapidly flashing numbers, words, pictures, equations, and other symbols that represented facts, concepts, and ideas, were projecting and processing data, encoding, decoding, encrypting and preserving information. Additional large screen video and computer monitors lined the entire upper circle of the lower level surgical room where my rotating surgical chair was located. They too were part of the encryption protocol, processing large batches of digitalized encrypted information.

On ground level, seated within two curved glass circular connecting cubicles, I could see four small, white haired men in white lab coats, white shirts and white ties. They were silently hunched over their computer keyboards which were attached to several thin, flat-screen computer monitors. Each of them had matching faces which were dour in appearance, drawn, and lined with many wrinkles. They looked somewhat absent. Their colorless eyes made them look like holograms. It was as if they did not exist. It seemed that they were from a different dimension. They were somehow here, yet not here, at the same time. They were focusing only on the encoding, decoding, encrypting tasks designated to them. Their necks were rigid, in an almost tortured position, as they dutifully continued typing with their heads bent forward close to their dimly flashing screens. Their cold skeleton-like hands with long slender fingers moved magically across their keypads, typing, documenting everything said and everything done as Mr. Camus IV spoke to the people in the upper level observation rooms. A network of multiple surveillance cameras, ultraviolet x-ray security devices, fingerprint identification systems and high-tech eye-scanners provided tight security.

"Thank you. Thank you, distinguished members and colleagues of the medical and scientific communities; thank you. Thank you, administration, faculty and trustees from various institutions of higher education, including special guests from Israel's prestigious Hebrew University and my highly esteemed alma mater the University of Paris....Thank you."

Applause. Cheers.

"Thank you....esteemed physicists, astronomers, and astrophysicists; welcome all. We send special greetings to the newly-elected pontiff, the Holy See, and his Vatican City representatives. We also welcome the ambassadorial contingent from the United Nations, and express appreciation to the dedicated staff, talented and energetic members of the *United States Defense Advanced Research Projects Agency,* here in Blacksburg, Virginia. I am deeply honored to speak to such an esteemed, diverse group of world class researchers, scientists and acclaimed global citizens and recognize how privileged we all are to have several of the world's most prominent classical and contemporary philosophers and theologians present for such an historic occasion as this."

Applause. Cheers. More Applause.

"Thank you. Thank you."

The Sound, the Echoing Sound of Applause.

"Thank you. Thank you. Let me begin by saying that it is my great honor to speak to such a diverse and distinguished group of colleagues on this historic occasion – though my initial remarks will be less formal and more personal that this symposium may imply."

Applause. Cheers.

"Let me begin first by sharing that while some of my colleagues call me by my given name, Albert, and others by my surname, Camus, I am more widely known and addressed as AC4. Let me continue by acknowledging my deep indebtedness to my great-ancestor, Albert Camus. In 1957, my namesake, Albert Camus, made history when he received the Nobel Prize for Literature. He was the first African-born writer to receive the award and the second-youngest recipient of the Nobel Prize in Literature, after Rudyard Kipling. My great-ancestor also had the unfortunate distinction of being the shortest-lived of any Nobel literature laureate to date. He died in an automobile accident approximately two years after receiving the award. He was a great man and his greatness lives on through the overwhelming influence of his philosophical view of reality so eloquently expressed through his writings."

A Sudden Flash of Light. As the flash faded I caught a brief glimpse of a frail elderly man, AC4, standing behind a microphone. He too, like the four white-haired men, had the appearance of a hologram. His voice, however, was strong, powerful, and commanded attention as he spoke. His demeanor seemingly conveyed character, conviction, dignity and authority. Yet, he looked old, very old. He stood on the rotating platform not far from my surgical chair, with the aid of a walker, constantly keeping his left leg bent at the knee so as to keep his left foot from touching the ground.

As AC4 continued speaking about his great-ancestor, Albert Camus, I heard another voice, a now familiar voice, speaking in low tones. It was Dr. Rieux. I wondered, *How did he get here? What's he doing here?* Dr. Rieux was also standing beside my surgical chair, speaking in whispers, "How much Sevo does he have on board?"

"He's Light," came a whispered reply. It was Dr. Castel. I felt a sense of dread, a flush of anxiety and worry. Dr. Castel, like Dr. Rieux, originally lived in the Algerian city of Oran. They were both fictional characters created by Albert Camus in his novel *The Plague.* I originally met them at *Christ Cathedral* in lower St. Bernard, Louisiana, and then again on a different occasion at *Paw Paw's Plaza* in New Orleans. Now they were here, in Blacksburg, Virginia, in this facility. But, *why were they here?* And, more importantly, *Why was I here? Why was I strapped in this surgical chair? Why? Why?*

"He's moving, Rieux, he's moving, regaining consciousness."

"Sevoflurane. Increase his Sevo. Keep his mouth shut. Keep his tongue nailed to his chin. Deaden the pain and muffle the memories, but don't eradicate them. Keep him light, but conscious, aware and awake. I want him to remember *this time."*

This time?

My heart began to race as a medicinal hot flush rushed through my veins. My face was flush. It felt hot. The muscles on my neck began to tighten. There was a pressure, an indefinable pressure, working its way through my body.

"This time? This time?" What did he mean, I want him to remember this time?

My underarms began to perspire profusely. Even now, as I write, my memory of the event is more like a dream then reality. It was that singular word – *reality* – that drew me back into what was being said by AC4 as he spoke.

"Indeed, understanding the nature of reality," said AC4, "was an ongoing passion for my grand-ancestor as it is for each of us, irrespective of our diverse professional disciplines."

He hesitated, just for a moment, creating anticipation, then spoke forcefully, symbolically raising one hand to point a thin finger upward, toward some unseen imaginary place high above his head.

"In philosophy, reality usually refers to the state of things as they are, as they *actually* exist, rather than how they might *possibly* exist or appear to exist. *Actualities. Possibilities.* Historically, these two polar positions seem to have always been in conflict. They have constantly confronted, challenged and, yes, sometimes confused our finest and brightest critical thinkers. Someone answers a philosophical question by positing a philosophical answer and immediately that philosophical answer becomes the next philosophical question, creating an endless cycle of philosophical inquiry. New *possibilities* arise, then are discarded as we reach for a single *actuality.*

"Reality, according to the definition of terms established for this symposium, is a term which describes that which encompasses everything that has *actually* existed, exists now, and will exist in the future. Thus, there is a distinction between reality, the *actuality,* and the mind's apprehension of that reality with its many theoretical *possibilities.* The mind's apprehension of reality, according to this view, is subjective, imaginary and quite often illusionary, because the mind's apprehension of reality is inextricably rooted, subjectively -- in the mind."

AC4 paused briefly, allowing his eyes, which were large and somewhat set widely apart, to scan the upper level observation rooms.

"The tension between the two, between *actuality* and *possibility,* between *objectivity* and *subjectivity,* is as old as Aristotle and Plato. Plato pointed to the heavens, to the *universals,* to the *ideal.* Aristotle pointed to the earth, to the *particulars,* to what Plato called the *representations* of the ideal. These two competing views have produced irresolvable, irreconcilable philosophical and metaphysical schools of thought – irresolvable and irreconcilable, that is, *until now.*

Loud Applause. Cheers. More Applause. The Sound, the Echoing Sound of Applause.

"Until now, *epistemological uncertainty, ontological ambiguity* and *teleological questions* have clouded some of our finest philosophical understandings. As cognitive wanderers we have often searched for answers where there were none. Our dialectic has been one of despair. We are the self-inflicted victims of philosophical history, walking in the dimness of our cherished ideologies, proclaiming light where there was none. In spite of all our boastings we can neither explain ourselves, nor our universe -- much less reality – *until now.*"

I caught a brief glimpse of the frail AC4, still standing behind a microphone as another wave of applause filled the building. He quietly pulled a soft, white handkerchief from his back pocket, patted his forehead, then, in a manner reminiscent of Father Paneloux, raised his hand high into the air, pointed heavenward, and shouted....

"Until now. Until now. Until now."

Applause. Loud Applause. Cheers. More Applause.

"Until now. Until now. Until now."

The Sound, the Echoing Sound of Applause. The shadowy figures in the observation rooms on the second and third levels of the circular building suddenly stood, filling the building with cheers and applause.

"Thank you. Thank you. Please be seated. Please be seated."

AC4 once again patted his forehead with his handkerchief before he resumed speaking.

"My esteemed colleagues, you have been eye-witnesses to history. Here, in the underground facilities of the *United States Defense Advanced Research Projects Agency,* utilizing the latest, state-of-the-art technologies, we have begun an exploration of the deeper nature of reality that has and will exceed anything ever attempted by our predecessors. Thus far we have taken several brief excursions into *alternative realities* as our research team travelled in two primary directions, the past and the future. We have also taken brief explorations of other realities, *self-generated parallel realities* created by the conscious mind as well as *self-existing parallel realities* inhabited by beings as real as any of us."

As AC4 continued speaking he simultaneously pointed toward two men, Dr. Rieux and Dr. Castel, who were seated in a special ground level observation chamber. A small contingent of military personnel, some enlisted, some officers wearing full dress uniforms, sat behind Rieux and Castel. Sitting behind them was an even larger group of scientists wearing white lab coats. Behind them, also seated, was a smaller group of civilians and educators, dressed in suit and tie.

"Prior to your participation in this symposium we, and by we I mean the personnel of the *United States Defense Advanced Research Projects Agency,* together with my colleagues from the Algerian city of Oran, and physicists from the University of Wisconsin-Madison, we devised and perfected an approach that helped us to first, unlock the hidden shapes of *alternate dimensions* and second, to actually gain access into multiple *parallel universes."*

Loud applause once again echoed throughout the building as Rieux, Castel, and the military, scientific and educational groups stood in response to AC4's speech.

"Together we have explored *the quantum nature of existence,* stretching our *rationalism* to *the breaking point.* We have confronted our intellectual inconsistencies, exorcised our scientific prejudices and evicted the elevated conceptual incoherence produced by our various competing philosophical ideologies. Together, we set out on an uncharted philosophical journey, moving beyond the familiar metaphysical landmarks, venturing forth into what can only be described as unknown realms and unexplored regions of existence. Using experimental data provided by the University of Wisconsin-Madison we were able to verify the existence of more cutting edge, elusive dimensions of reality. The verification of these aspects of existence validated the veracity of *string theory,* the essential component of the unified *'theory of everything.'* These series of verifications and validations enabled us to evict many of the previous monstrous irrationalities that we once embraced, those monstrous irrationalities spawned by our own illogical thinking.

"One of the most astounding discoveries that we made is that there are subatomic particles that converge and commingle to form the essential building blocks of reality or existence. You might say that we have uncovered the hidden, unexplored and elusive DNA of existence. Some have called these subatomic particles *dark matter.* Others have likened these particles to *gravity.* Irrespective of how it is labeled these subatomic particles of this DNA of existence are curled up in tiny geometric shapes at every point in our universe and all other *alternate realities* or *parallel universes.* These subatomic particles, the hidden dimensions of reality that form the basis of all reality, are just that, particles, material in quality and yet simultaneously immaterial, invisible, unseen, yet discernable and decipherable, encoded with meaning, images, symbols, metaphors, and more."

As a speaker I learned long ago that there is power in a pause. Wisdom pauses after introducing a key fact, a thought-provoking concept or a complex, new idea. AC4 wisely paused; then, clapping his hands together, he quickly resumed speaking.

"Our preliminary explorations have also revealed some of the intricate and interwoven complexities of existence and reality. Thus far you have been but partial observers. Our team, however, has travelled far longer and deeper than we could have ever imagined when our journey began. We have travelled across the breadth, length, depth and height of reality, all realities, astounded by what we have seen, heard and learned."

AC4 paused for a moment as Dr. Castel handed him a glass of water. The heat from the overhead lights combined with the energy of public speaking caused the back of AC4's shirt to be drenched with sweat. Nevertheless, after carefully drinking the cooling glass of water, AC4 resumed speaking.

"For instance, one fundamental aspect of reality that we almost immediately encountered was that there are several primary strands or cords of reality, seven to be exact, that run parallel, each one beside the other, sometimes within one another. These seven strands form the underlying structure of all *realities, alternative dimensions,* or *parallel universes* -- seven, no more, no less."

Everyone was silent as AC4 paused, reaching once again for his glass of water.

Discussion and debate concerning the actual existence of *alternative dimensions,* or *parallel universes* has a long history, especially in science fiction and the field of physics. For several decades physicists have bantered about the possibility of their existence. That the global community's upper echelon was involved in such high level discussions concerning, not their *possibility,* but their *actuality,* was inconceivable – but it was happening.

"Everything within each of these seven strands or cords of reality is linked together by tiny vibrating strings of energy. Each of the seven strands stand alone as an independent reality, yet each are woven together much like small cords are woven together to form a large rope. While there is diversity and autonomy among the seven strands, there is also an underlying cohesiveness that creates existential unity, balance and harmony as existence within each strand unfolds. The strands or cords exist, using the language of science fiction, as *'parallel universes'* that run, independent, one from the other, yet side by side, again, in a sense, sometimes within each other. In essence, there is no real spatial differentiation between the strands. Though independent, nevertheless, they are tightly woven together, working together, in unity, forming the sum total of all reality. What occurs within one strand of reality seems to affect events within each of the other individual strands of reality. There is form, a rigid form, yet freedom, freedom expressed through some type of metaphysical interrelatedness, a cohesion, a correlation of events and experiences between each of the strands of reality as existence unfolds. Again, these strands of reality are hidden and unseen by the natural eye, until one actually enters into one of the *alternative realities.*

It is then that one discovers that these *alternative realities* and *parallel universes* are no less real that the reality which we inhabit and experience in what we narrowly define as our three-dimensional universe.

"Historically, many have rejected the notion of *alternate realities* and *parallel universes* and the idea or notion that such a unity between the physical and metaphysical might actually exist. For many, to acquiesce at this point would imply that the universe is an outward physical expression of an unseen omniscient, omnipotent metaphysical reality. However, according to the definition of terms established for this symposium the term *'metaphysical'* refers to that which is above, outside of or beyond the physical; beyond the range of imagination. There is no religious sentiment implied in our definition. For some there are theological implications that stir the religious imagination when the term "metaphysical" is used. For this symposium, there are no theological implications implied. None whatsoever."

The immediate outburst of applause revealed an antagonism toward religious belief or faith in the existence of God. As their applause ended a thought ran through my mind: *Anyone can deny the existence of God but no one can deny God existence.* While science and physics could not prove the existence of God they also could not refute God's existence – because refutation was *not a viable scientific possibility.* Both the affirmation and the denial of God's existence, are faith positions – positions taken by each individual as an act of volitional choice; a choice with consequences, *eternal consequences.*

"Among the seven strands of reality, one strand is an overwhelmingly dominant strand and appears to our physicists to be the controlling strand. All of the multiple strands of reality are under the aegis and authority of this central strand. This dominant central strand was before there was time, space, material or existence, or reality as we know it and it will exist when time, space, motion, existence, and reality as we know it ends. This dominant strand, we have called it the *Alpha/Omega*, was present prior to and at the beginning, at the point of what the physicists call *'singularity'* -- it was present at *'singularity'* as the *Alpha/Omega*. Some view this *'singularity'* as the point of the beginning of time, space and existence, the genesis of all that is, the point of origins, or what some call *the big bang* or what others would view as *the act of creation.* From the *Alpha/Omega*, from this overwhelmingly dominant strand of reality proceed all other strands of reality. Further explorations reveal that from each of the individual seven strands there proceeds another seven strands, from which proceed additional strands of seven, *ad infinitum."*

The Big Bang. Singularity. Here is a theory deduced from simple astronomical observation. The expansion of the universe with galaxies, stars, planets and everything in between expanding, racing away from one another gave birth to the Big Bang theory. The theory postulates that if the expansion could be reversed the universe and all that is within it would contract to a single point. This single point from which everything expands and towards which everything will eventually contract is *the point of singularity.*

From a time perspective singularity is the point from which time, space, motion and matter emerged. From an ontological perspective the stuff of creation emerged from nothing and/or nothingness.

I recalled my earlier conversation with Mr. Grand concerning the universe and its coming into existence by chance. I distinctly remember sharing with Grand that his...."atheistic view of creation – *Nothing (chance) creating something from nothing* requires a greater miracle and greater faith that the theistic view – *Someone creating something from nothing."*

AC4 was providing his audience a glimpse of something majestic, something wonderfully majestic, other-worldly and breathtakingly beautiful – a view of self-generating, self-multiplying, *parallel universes* filled with imaginative beauty – but, he was hiding an ugly truth.

Physics is based on mathematics. Without the tools provided by mathematics physics would be dead on arrival. Physics is based on mathematics because mathematics is so precise, so exact, fixed. There is no variableness, neither shadow of turning in mathematics – it is firm, fixed, absolute and immutable. This immutability of mathematics is the foundation of physics, the scientific method and empirical research. 2 + 2 = 4, always. This is an absolute, immutable fact. 2 + 2 never equals 3, or 5, or any number other than 4. This mathematical precision is essential, absolutely essential to physics. Water freezes at 32 degrees.

When a physicist or someone who is familiar with physics, like AC4, discusses reality, he doesn't hold up a photograph and say, "See. Here is reality." No. What he presents is not a photograph but an equation, an equation that is dependent on mathematical precision. It is important to realize that the equation is not reality but a mathematical description of reality based upon mathematical precision. This mathematical description may or may not actually correspond to reality. The key is the ability to recognize which equations correspond to reality and which do not.

The ugly truth is simply this – even though physics is based on the precision of mathematics – the leading physicists, utilizing the precision of mathematics, have arrived at completely different, wildly differing conclusions concerning reality.

One leading physicists, utilizing the precision of mathematics has concluded that there is no reality. Another, utilizing mathematical equations, deduces that reality consists of a steadily increasing number of *parallel universes.* Still another, with the precision of mathematical equations "proves" that reality is created by observation. Another physicist equates and deduces that consciousness creates reality.

The ability to recognize which equation does and which equation does not correspond to reality is essential. That little phrase – *the ability to recognize* – reveals the ugly truth about physics. Physics is not as absolute as the physicist would have us believe.

The imaginative beauty set forth by AC4 may indeed be filled with other-worldly, breathtakingly beautiful imagery – but, if it does not correspond to reality then it is deceptive and that, in an of itself, is ugly.

Yet, according to AC4, this breathtaking view of reality was something that was not only real but something that has been there all along as a hidden gem obscured by the ordinary events and experiences of physical life and human history. Since the creation of the world this *Alpha/Omega* has been ever-present in all realities, *alternate realities* and *parallel universes.* The power and nature of the *Alpha/Omega* has consistently and constantly been present in and beyond our universe. It was present at and prior to the beginning as the *Alpha/Omega*, and it will be present and continue to exist as the *Alpha/Omega* beyond what we intuitively know as the end. Yet one would have never guessed it was so, said AC4, unless one looked deeply, very deeply into the underlying nature or DNA of reality.

But, I wondered, is this view of reality correct? Was it *actuality?* Or, was this *ad infinitum* subdividing of strands into additional strands simply another theoretical *possibility* that would dissolve and disappear under intense investigation and scientific scrutiny? Would its meaning, whatever that might be, prove to be meaningless – another metaphysical mirage? Or would it be verified?

The Bible presents *the act of creation* in a way that speaks to both the common, salt-of-the-earth man and to scientific-minded physicists. The physicists began focusing on time, space, and material roughly two hundred years ago. The Bible, from the very beginning, has always stressed that time, space and material were all created simultaneously at the moment of creation (or the moment of *singularity,* as the physicists call it.) *In the beginning (a reference to time) God created the heavens (a reference to space) and the earth (a reference to material).*

Once the vocabulary, language and illusionary descriptions were striped away from AC4's depictions of *alternative realities,* it appeared that he was promoting some modern day type of metaphysical *'Gnosticism.'* The second century *'Gnostics,'* who were ruled heretics by the early church, believed that God was the central, ultimate reality, the source of all that is. God, being a Spirit, is holy and every reality outside of God is physical, material, and evil. Consequently, all *alternative realities,* even though they proceed from God, proceed as progressive emanations with a gradual distancing by each successive emanation, further and further away from God. No matter how colorful the language employed by AC4, his descriptions were theologically heretical and in conflict with and inconsistent with both the biblical revelation and historical scientific conclusions.

"The reality of something we thought couldn't possibly exist has now been detected and confirmed," continued AC4. *"Parallel universes, alternate realities,* and more are no longer the stuff of science fiction. A critical step must now be taken, not only by the scientific community but by all humanity.

"The average mind is accustomed to only three spatial dimensions and lacks an adequate frame of reference for a *multi-dimensional universe.* Using different types of mathematical geometries, physicists have been able to, for several decades, discern and verify the existence of 6-dimensional and 10-dimensional *parallel universes.* This *ad infinitum* subdividing of each individual strand into seven additional strands will offer new challenges for even our finest physicists and will require the ongoing development of an ever-expanding frame of reference as we study and ponder *multi-dimensional universes, ad infinitum.* In a sense, reality stretches and stretches like a rubber band and just when you think it's going to break it suddenly doubles in length and continues to stretch.

"In one sense, a metaphysical sense, this *ad infinitum* is linked to what the philosopher Paul Tillich called the *'eternal now.'* Again, all of the strands are tightly woven together, working together, in unity, forming the *'eternal now'* or sum total of all reality – yet each strand is separate, independent, autonomous, existing as a segregated expression of all reality – *past, present and future."*

There was an antagonistic stirring among the audience at the mention of Tillich. Science charged Tillich with faith and faith charged him with science. AC4 was either ignorant of this dual antagonism or didn't care that it existed.

"I want to stress that we have travelled backward to *the point of singularity* and discovered that the overwhelmingly dominant strand of reality, *the Alpha/Omega,* was present prior to the moment when all that is came into existence. All things, all realities, all *parallel universes,* proceeded from and continue to proceed from and consist and subsist within the *Alpha/Omega.* Without the *Alpha/Omega* nothing – neither space, nor time, nor material, nor existence, nor any of the realities that proceed from the *Alpha/Omega* -- would exist. There would be nothing, -- nothing – without the *Alpha/Omega.*"

The contingent from the Vatican, understanding the biblical and theological implications of the phrase *Alpha/Omega*, offered a brief, somewhat muted applause. A conspiracy of silence was the meager offering of the more empirically-minded, cynical secularists.

"Know this, my friends, there is an undeniable confluence between all of the strands, cords or substratums of reality and the dominant *Alpha/Omega.* Sometimes the autonomous strands become entangled, producing instability, creating metaphysical disruptions. When this occurs the tangled threads are untangled by the intervention of the *Alpha/Omega*, the controlling strand. Accessing the *Alpha/Omega*, in which we and our realm are embedded, forced us to go beyond our intuitions, beyond our physics to metaphysics, necessitating deeper explorations of the metaphysical underpinnings of existence. Using new techniques and experimental protocols we have already begun unraveling the mystery of the mechanics of the DNA of existence. Studying the elasticity and expansion of the universe exposed us to curious behaviors and amazing phenomenon. To our surprise, the *Alpha/Omega* actually facilitates the dramatic extension of such concepts as meaning, morals, a sense of mission and purpose and more of the aesthetic values and aspects of existence into all of the various strands of reality.

"We were also surprised to discover that another strand of reality was populated by a complex system of numbers, metaphors, images, symbols, equations and elegant mathematical ideas. These all worked together by utilizing and developing mathematical calculations to construct a system of absolute, rather than relative, moral conclusions. These moral conclusions are not based on feelings or intuitions, but on immutable, mathematical-based moral absolutes. This particular *parallel universe,* which is neither metrical nor mechanical, is filled with moral structure and overflowing moral meaning, overflowing in the sense that it influences all other strands of reality. It appears to function as a type of moral model, influencing all of the strands, utilizing mathematics; not old math, nor new math, but a higher type of math that employs and applies numerical values to clarify moral considerations, choices and consequences. It also appears that the *Alpha/Omega* is the actual author of this moral system. Though we searched diligently for a statistical-physics-based model to decipher this system, none could be found. The *Alpha/Omega* somehow worked all of the consequences of multiple moral choices together for some higher, absolute, moral good. It is this ultimate higher moral good that somehow obliterates evil and removes moral incoherence from the equation.

"Immanuel Kant, when he developed his philosophical concept often referred to as *the moral imperative,* was moving in this direction. Unfortunately, he was diverted to other projects and he never returned to more fully develop his thoughts concerning *the moral imperative.*"

I found it absolutely amazing that those who embrace and espouse *moral relativism* are seeking to create an *absolute moral standard* based on mathematics, which is, in their estimation, absolute. The reputation of absolute moral truth is being brought to task. Its value and relevance are being challenged by a veiled counterfeit that parodies itself in a discolored form of relativism.

> *Where is the philosopher? Where is the scholar? Where is the debater of this age? Hasn't God made the world's wisdom foolish?* [70]

The philosopher Friedrich Nietzsche criticized the ethics of Christianity and sought to replace its moral standard with a secular ideology.[71] Now, it appears, that AC4 and his secular colleagues were intent on fulfilling Nietzsche's efforts through higher mathematics.

"Again, we have travelled backward to *the point of singularity* and discovered that the dominant strand of reality, the *Alpha/Omega*, was present. We also travelled laterally, to other realities such as the moral universe. The *Alpha/Omega*, once again, was there. We have also traveled forward into the future in an attempt to unravel the riddle of the end, the end of existence, that baffling mystery of oblivion, the enigma of non-existence and non-being – and the *Alpha/Omega* was there. In this *Alpha/Omega* we live, we move, and we have our being, our existence. The *Alpha/Omega* is the absolute ground of our being, the ultimate actuality, the ultimate reality."

A low rumble of thunder. A faint flash of light. Unseen, yet it was heard in the distance as Dr. Rieux rolled a high-backed chair onto the platform for AC4. AC4 carefully lifted one leg as he sat down, keeping the weight off of his afflicted left foot.

"Thank you, Dr. Rieux. Even though we understand the term *'non-existence'* when we hear it spoken or read it in print, it is a term that we will never be able to adequately define nor fully understand. The term simply refuses to fit within the conceptual limits of our rational understanding. Nevertheless, we have documented that at some point in the future, reality as we know it will collapse. Whether we call this collapse *'the eschatos'* or *'the terminis'* or *'the apocalypse'* or simply *'the end'* is not important. When *'the terminis'* will occur, we do not know; but, we would like to know. What is important at this point is that we have been able to verify that there is a cataclysmic, momentous and violent concluding event at some point in the future, the near future, when all that is, all that exists, all realities, shall cease to be – except the *Alpha/Omega*.

"For those of us who have worked together thus far on this project and in preparation for this symposium, there has been and continues to be an escalating tension, a tension between what is and what is certain to be. The end of existence, that baffling mystery of oblivion that I mentioned earlier, the enigma of non-existence and non-being, is closer than we first believed. Therefore, on behalf of humanity, on behalf of the global community, we have quietly called and assembled this top secret symposium, and extended, under a cloak of secrecy, private, unpublicized invitations to each of you. Elusive, fleeting, and baffling as it is, the abyss of nothingness, the mystery of mysteries, lies before us. We stand at the very edge of extinction, of annihilation, of non- existence -- that mystery of oblivion. A cataclysmic, momentous and violent conclusion looms on the horizon. Who among us is wise enough for this hour?"

A very small red light began blinking. A tiny blinking red light. On the second level. Bold. Bright, then a voice, a challenging voice....

"Monsieur. Monsieur. I am Jean Tarrou, Chancellor and Chairman of the Mathematical, Science and Physics Division, National Academy of Science, University of Paris, Paris, France. Monsieur. I object, I vehemently object, I vigorously object to this metaphysical madness. This concept of 'nothing,' of 'the void,' of 'oblivion' – is sheer metaphysical madness."

RESTORE POINT 18:

MYSTICS AND MADMEN

Curiosity about the universe, its origin and its ultimate destiny has stirred religious imagination, fueled scientific inquiry and spawned philosophic thought. Where did the universe come from? Is there evidence for an intelligent Designer? Or, is God a suspicious delusion, an illusion, a creation of the mind? Does God actually exist as Creator? Or, is the universe an eternal, self-generating machine, a vast self-creating organism eternally emanating from infinity? If God does exist, does He interject Himself into human history – and the affairs of everyday life? Do other realities, *alternate realities,* other *parallel universes* exist? Or, are we alone? History offers many *possibilities* in response to these questions; yet, instinctively, we know that there is only one *actuality -- only one right answer to each question.* And, that's what made the opening questions posed by Chancellor Tarrou so puzzling. His focus was on the character of the man, AC4, rather than on the content of his message.

"Monsieur. I object, I vehemently object, I vigorously object to this metaphysical madness. This concept of *'nothing,'* of *'the void,'* of *'oblivion'* – this negation of reality is sheer metaphysical madness. Yet, neither of my questions have anything to do with science, physics, or metaphysics. There is something that I find troubling, deeply troubling, specifically *about you Monsieur AC4 -- specifically about you."*

The French take great pride in their language. Frenchmen from Paris, however, though equally prideful, speak *"Parisian French,"* a slightly different, highly animated form of French that involves the unconscious use of forearms, hands and fingers when talking. Chancellor Jean Tarrou was true to his Parisian culture when he spoke.

"Monsieur, you make frequent reference to Albert Camus as your namesake and grand-ancestor. Tragically, roughly fifty years ago, in 1960, Albert Camus died, as you shared, in an untimely automobile accident. He left behind a son and a daughter, twins, Catherine and Jean. They were born in 1945 which means, by my calculation, the twins are now approximately 60 years of age. Here is what troubles me, Monsieur AC4. Even if Albert's son, Jean, was named Albert, which he is not, thereby making him Albert, Jr., there still would be insufficient time between then and now for the Albert Camus family line to have produced an Albert Jr., then an Albert II, followed by an Albert III, then finally, an Albert IV.

"Pardonner, Monsieur. Pardonner, Monsieur."

Chancellor Tarrou sarcastically cocked his head to one side and simultaneously raised his eyebrows and his hands upward, making slow circular motions with his hands, pointing towards the upper level observation areas, as he spoke.

"Pardonner, Monsieur. Pardon my reference to age, Monsieur, but you are significantly older than the children of Albert Camus, so much so that for you to be Albert Camus IV is a chronological, biological impossibility. I believe an explanation is in order, Monsieur Albert Camus IV, or Mr. AC4, or whoever you are. This is my first issue, *an integrity issue,* Monsieur. This is my first issue."

A muffled sound of mumbling voices, coupled with dull, muted conversations and soft, murmuring whispers rushed across and through each of the observation rooms on the upper levels of the building. It proved to be the first stirring of the proverbial hornet's nest.

Chancellor Tarrou stood, cold and motionless as a statue, breathless, caught in a pause of silence, just for a moment. Scanning the upper level observation rooms, he nodded to his colleagues, as the ruffling voices gradually died down. Tarrou was a short man whose somewhat wrinkled face was surrounded by silver hair and a bright silver beard. He was, however, youthful in appearance. He was a world renown physicist, a man of letters, cosmopolitan in appearance, well-educated and distinguished. He spoke with grace, dignity, culture – and force. Beneath those noble qualities, however, was a simmering, seething, indignant kind of controlled anger. He did not like nor did he trust AC4.

Oddly, Tarrou never blinked as he spoke, nor did he blink when he paused. He simply stood, seething, like a coiled angry snake ready to strike, staring at AC4, his prey. Suddenly and swiftly, Chancellor Tarrou's hand came up and out, quickly pointing downward, vigorously shaking an accusing finger at AC4. Chancellor Tarrou's voice took on a harder edge, becoming cold, calculating and sarcastic in tone. He carefully enunciated every syllable with slanderous emphasis. The tone of his voice would rise, then fall, becoming a series of rhythmic sounding hostile accusations.

"MON-SIE-UR. Monsieur A-C-4, concerning THIS MAT-TER of IN-TEG-RI-TY, the REG-IS-TRAR of the Univer-SITY of Paris sent our delegation the following classified, encrypted telegram:

> *'Albert Camus IV did not attend the University of Paris. There are no transcripts, no public records, and no documentation to indicate that any Albert Camus was ever a student at our University. The Nobel Prize Albert Camus received an undergraduate and a postgraduate degree from the University of Algiers'*

AGAIN, MON-SIE-UR, I BE-lieve an EX-PLA-NA-TION is in OR-DER, MON-SIE-UR A-C-4, concerning these issues of *IN-TEG-RI-TY."*

AC4 was looking downward, staring intently at the floor. Once again, ever so quietly AC4 pulled a soft, white handkerchief from his back pocket and patted his forehead. He then raised his head to respond to Chancellor Tarrou. Tarrou's fist and palm collided yet again, stressing the strength of Jean Tarrou's convictions. Before AC4 could respond, however, Tarrou's hand and fist collided yet again as he resumed speaking, or should I say, *resumed shouting.*

"MY SE-COND ISSUE CON-CERNS THIS PI-TI-ABLE MAN strapped in the rotating surgical chair. At this juncture we know him only as Dr. John. Who is this Dr. John? Does anyone here know this man? What are his credentials? Can anyone vouch for his credibility? What is

his area of expertise? What is his field of study? Theology? Biblical revelation? Physics? Science?

"Science, which we represent, my friends, is based on reason and the empirical method while Christianity, which this man represents, is based on revelation and intuition. We are told that he is a pastor. Can a pastor, can any pastor, can this particular pastor, add an ounce of credibility to science? Or, in our case, what can he possibly add to this scientific symposium? So once again I ask, Monsieur, Why is he here?"

With clarity and power Chancellor Tarrou spoke eloquently and forcefully, waxing strong against AC4. I could not tell if AC4 was shaken. Nor could I tell if those on the upper levels were swayed. In his writings, Aristotle outlined three elements of persuasion; logic, emotion and character. [72] With this largely secularized crowd, Tarrou seemed to satisfy Aristotle's criteria.

"It really gets my blood boiling," Tarrou said in a high-pitched voice, "that we have not learned anything from the past. Nearly two thousand years ago Quintus Septimius Florens Tertullianus, better known as Tertullian, and a recognized early Christian patriarch, asked a critical question: *'What has Athens to do with Jerusalem, or the Academy with the church?'* [73] His answer? *Nothing. Nothing. Nothing.* Today I ask: *What has reason to do with revelation? What has science to do with religion? And, what does this man of religion have to do with we men of science?*

"My answer to each question? *Nothing. Nothing. Nothing. What has reason to do with revelation? Nothing."*

Chancellor Tarrou repeatedly brought his right fist down into the palm of his left hand each time he said *Nothing* to suggest his determination and conviction.

"What has science to do with religion? Nothing. What has this man to do with us? Nothing. Nothing. Nothing."

The fist and palm collided again and again and again, loudly.

Silently, AC4 shook his head to express his disagreement. Ironically, neither AC4 nor Chancellor Tarrou believed in God, revelation or religion. AC4 felt as strongly about segregating faith from science as did Tarrou. The mere possibility of faith being interjected into the symposium, however, created adversarial contention.

"God, my friends," shouted Tarrou, "God is an imaginary thing."

Tarrou once again slammed his fist into the palm of his hand.

"God, my friends, is a figment of human imagination."

The sound of the fist hitting the palm a second time reverberated through the building. Spontaneous bursts of applause broke out

"God, my friends, is the byproduct of a misguided, collective religious consciousness that lingers from mankind's unenlightened, historic past."

The fist and palm collided yet again, with equal force.

"We are beyond that, my friends, beyond intuition, beyond suspicious delusion, beyond self-inflicted illusion. Through science we have progressed beyond the primitive darkness of ancient myth into the full light of reason.

"So I ask again, who is this man and why is he here? What has this man to do with us? There is something very unsettling, something disingenuous about his presence and about his participation in this scientific symposium. What role or function does he play in this symposium? Does he enhance or devalue the credibility of this symposium? What can this man of delusional faith possibly contribute to we men of science? *Nothing. I say, Nothing. Nothing. Nothing.*

"Please address these two issues, Monsieur MC4. Please address them. *Your Integrity. And, this man's Credibility.* Monsieur, I question both. Think these questions through *MON-SIEUR, THINK THESE QUES-TIONS THROUGH CARE-FULLY. CARE-FULLY. CARE-FULLY.*"

Chancellor Jean Tarrou, Albert Camus IV, Dr. Rieux, and others like them tragically believe there is no God. Wandering in a desert of abandoned faith, unfaith and unbelief has become *their* illusionary oasis. At the heart of *their* illusion they have accepted the lies of *atheistic existentia;* first, that there is no God because God is imaginary, non-existent, a non-entity, an illusion; second, that life is an absurd, grotesque dream, filled with despair and dread, and; third, that man is but living dust lost in the vast expanse of the universe, alone, terribly alone, wandering solitarily across everlasting nothingness.

The thin, frail AC4 rose to stand on one foot behind his microphone. In the glare of the overhead lighting he looked almost saintly, carrying himself with and conveying a certain air of holiness and a sanctified dignity. There was, however, nothing holy, sanctified or saintly about AC4. To his credit as a speaker, there was no hesitancy in his voice as he spoke. His voice was neither contentious, nor belligerent, nor argumentative as he looked intently and spoke directly – firmly, yet gently -- to Chancellor Jean Tarrou.

"My dear, dear, Monsieur Jean Tarrou. Hear me, Monsieur. Hear me. The line of demarcation – the line separating the past, the present and the future -- that line, Monsieur, is thin – very thin. So too is the line that separates *alternate realities, parallel universes, different dimensions and multiple modes of existence.*

"Chancellor Tarrou , you and each of your colleagues," said AC4 as he waved his hand in a circular motion toward the upper level observation rooms, "through participation in this symposium we have traveled backward and forward and laterally in time, through time, and across time to different destinations at various points in history."

Spontaneous bursts of applause broke out, slowly echoing throughout the building. These people had not only been witnesses to these travels but participants. They were in a sense eye witnesses to and could testify to the validity to these travels as we have passed through many *alternate realities, parallel universes and multiple modes of existence.*

AC4 held his hands wide apart to visually suggest the experience and the expanse of their epoch-making travels. As he continued speaking AC4 used the fingers of one hand to help his audience follow his brief mention of a series of places that they had visited as they traveled backward, forward and across time. At the mention of each particular place AC4 poked an imaginary hole in the air, creating an imaginary map.

"Each of you have observed and enjoyed several brief excursions as you traveled with us and with this man, this man of faith, to the Algerian city of Oran, to the *French Quarter* of New Orleans, Louisiana, and, to *Christ Cathedral: The Church of the Final Judgment* in lower St. Bernard, Louisiana. And now, as colleagues, we are assembled together at this critical historic moment in the top secret underground *Defense Advanced Research Projects Agency's* facility in Blacksburg, Virginia."

Everyone was listening intently as AC4 spoke. Spontaneous bursts of applause once again came from the crowd as AC4 continued to speak. He spoke of time as directional, using his hand to draw a horizontal line from left to right.

"Time appears to have a starting point and appears to be moving onward, moving forward toward its final destination, and end point. Through this symposium, however, you have discovered that time is also vertical, creating and providing access to differing *alternative dimensions,* some distant, some nearby, or relatively close in the grand scheme of things.

"We visited several of these nearby places at different times. Our journey together began on August 29, 2005 in Chalmette, Louisiana, as a strong hurricane raged in the Gulf of Mexico. At that time, because of the hurricane, we relocated to this very facility in Blacksburg, Virginia. From there we traveled to the Algerian city of Orange together then forward through time to the present."

As he paused momentarily, AC4 raised his hands upward to suggest a symbolic unity between himself and those in the upper level observation areas. Spontaneous bursts of applause broke out once again. This indicated a strong show of support for AC4. The symposium participants were eye witnesses to these things.

"This *we* have done *together* as participants in this symposium. Upon our safe arrival at each of these destinations or at the time of our departure from each of these places, you, Chancellor Tarrou , and you, my colleagues, applauded our success as we traveled through time -- time past and time future -- *together."*

Raising his hands high over his head AC4 balled each hand into a fist, then, shaking them, he called to the crowd, *"Time Past. Time Future. Together. Together."*

The applause rose to thunderous heights as more and more people stood, cheering as AC4 repeatedly emphasized the word *together.* That which we have seen, that which we have heard, that which we have handled – we have done *together.*

> *"Time Past. Time Future. Together. Together."*
> *"Time Past. Time Future. Together. Together."*

After a brief period of applause, AC4 lowered his hands then raised them yet again. With open palms he waved his hands in repetitive motions, up and down, asking the crowd for silence

"Hear me, men of science. Hear me. Prior to your participation in this symposium we, and by we I mean the personnel of the *United States Defense Advanced Research Projects Agency*, together with my colleagues from the Algerian city of Oran, and physicists from the University of Wisconsin-Madison, we made additional journeys prior to your participation in this symposium. We have traveled extensively backward, forward, and laterally through time.

"Men of science. We actually traveled backward in time to *'singularity,'* that mysterious point of origin, that place of beginnings, where time, space, material and existence began."

No sound came from the crowd at the mention of *'singularity'* – everyone simply sat in stunned silence, astonished. Powerful telescopes and new technologies had enabled astrophysics to see *'singularity'* from great distances; but no one had peered into or beyond the *'event horizon.'* Trying to get that kind of direct look was like seeing the unseeable. *Taiwan's Academia Sinica Institute of Astronomy and Astrophysics* had come close, providing visual images within a nanosecond of *'singularity'* – but no one ever saw into or beyond that point -- *until now.*

AC4 described in outline form what was beyond that point, touching lightly on three things: First, the underlying cosmic *processes* that govern the behavior of *'singularities,' 'event horizons,'* and *'naked singularities'.* He then, secondly, provided additional insight by describing the *mental processes* that underlie human *perception* of these astronomical phenomena. His third focus was on relationship of *physics* with a focus on *atmospheric resistance, gravitational attractions, and the curvature of the event horizon.*

"We also gained access to multiple *parallel universes,* some existing in the past, some in the future, and others that co-exist simultaneously parallel to our own universe.

"These movements, backward, forward, and laterally through time are one of the primary reasons for this symposium. Know this: What lies before us will require more from us than did that which lies behind us. Before us? *Great Danger. Great Danger.*"

The people on the second and third levels became silent again, intently focusing on AC4, becoming hushed, as silent and still as a deserted church house on a Monday morning. The initial reaction to the mention of *Great Danger? Numbness.*

As they glanced back and forth at one another and recognized the prestigious people attending this particular symposium they began to sense the seriousness and the gravity of what was before them.

"Chancellor Tarrou , I say to you, Monsieur, your premise is correct, there is insufficient time for the Albert Camus family line to have produced an Albert Camus IV within the context of the fifty year time-frame you have described. Your conclusion is incorrect, however, because you incorrectly assume that I am of this generation -- *which I am not* -- and that my existence is confined within your fifty-year time span – *which it is not.*"

AC4 shrugged his shoulders then clutched his temples with both hands, suggesting frustration. His Parisian instinct was using a full compliment of body language, mannerisms and gestures to express his passion, sincerity – and frustration. Nothing about his non-verbal communication appeared to be forced, rehearsed, or in any way unnatural. Speaking slowly, AC4 looked directly at Chancellor Tarrou.

"I say to you, Monsieur, and to any others who are skeptical and cynical about this that just as you traveled with us backward in time , so too have I traveled backward in time from my generation -- to this particular point in time – *your generation.*"

The low sound of murmuring could be heard racing through the crowd then, just as quickly, everyone grew quiet and the murmuring subsided.

"Furthermore, there are no transcripts, no public records, and no documentation to indicate that I attended the University of Paris because I have not yet attended the University of Paris. My time has not yet come."

Bits of muted conversation rushing across and around the observation rooms could barely be heard; but, this much was certain -- *they were talking.* It was difficult, if not impossible, to understand the muffled sound of competing voices. Many people were speaking at the same time, but one loud defiant voice was easily identifiable -- *Chancellor Jean Tarrou.*

The skin on Chancellor Tarrou's forehead wrinkled, becoming uneven as his bushy white eyebrows hooded over his eyes, eyes that blazed with anger, hot anger. His lips tightened, turning down at the ends. As he rose to his feet he raised one clenched fist high in the air.

"This is preposterous. Completely contrary to our understanding of the nature of reality, reason, scientific inquiry and, I might add, simple common sense. Such talk is ridiculous, absurd. You are, Monsieur, a charlatan, a fraud -- and you are inviting derision and mockery. Derision and mockery, not only for yourself – but for the esteemed members of this symposium.

"It is imprudent, ludicrous, irrational, thoughtless and nonsensical for any man of science to embrace the radical metaphysical and philosophical ideas thus far proposed. You seek to capitalize on imaginary ancient primordial fears of invasion by hostile entities inhabiting far-away realms and *alternative realities*. And you seek to capitalize on modern aspirations of time travel, *multiverses* and *parallel universes,* yet, your currency is worthless, without value because it is counterfeit, scientifically non-negotiable and untenable under the gaze of empirical scrutiny."

Rubbing the back of his neck, AC4 appeared to be troubled, stressed, worried. It would soon become apparent, however, that appearances are deceiving. AC4 looked up again as he spoke, directly at Chancellor Tarrou.

"Chancellor Tarrou, Monsieur, a few moments ago I shared that we traveled backward, forward, and laterally through time. Do know that I and our team fully understand the difficulty that you and others may experience in apprehending and validating the veracity of our claims. New ideas, new paradigms, new ways of understanding, new cosmologies, all are challenging, difficult and carry with them dramatic risks and vulnerabilities. There are very real differences between this new paradigm and the more traditional, older existing narratives. Like Columbus, we have traveled across an ocean, an ocean of time, an ocean of space, to discover new territory *-- a strange new world."*

"Extraordinary claims require extraordinary evidence," shouted Tarrou, "and you, Monsieur AC4, are making extraordinary claims."

"Extraordinary evidence? Science makes no such demand, Monsieur. Science only demands an empirical verification; nothing more, nothing less."

If body language could be heard instead of seen and if facial gestures were given voice, it would be apparent, very apparent, that Chancellor Tarrou was about to explode. Another outburst was apparent, one filled with sarcasm, anger and contempt for AC4.

AC4, however, remained composed, softly and calmly pinching the bridge of his nose. His eyes were closed, tightly closed. They opened quickly, however, at the angry sound of Chancellor Tarrou's voice.

"Monsieur AC4, I find it incredulous, simply incredulous that…'

"Silence. Be silent, Tarrou. Be silent."

As he raised his voice AC4 simultaneously raised his hand, forcefully, with determination, in a strange, mesmerizing way – pointing directly at Chancellor Tarrou. Mysterious, radiant gentle wisps of color, very fine, very thin, very faint, barely perceptible, flowed from AC4's hand toward Chancellor Tarrou.

"Be silent, Monsieur. Be silent. You, Monsieur Tarrou, seem to think you have power over me – and over this symposium. Hear me well, Monsieur. Hear me well. You have no such power – none whatsoever. It is I, Monsieur, it is I who has power, power beyond your ability to comprehend – and, now you force me to use it."

The fine linear shadows, the pale wisps of color that continued flowing and swirling from AC4's hand, had a sedative effect on Tarrou.

"You, Monsieur Tarrou, you, sir, will now be silent. *You WILL be SILENT.* You will sit down. And, you *WILL be silent!* Do you understand, Monsieur? *Do you understand?"*

RESTORE POINT 19:

PROTOCOL

Chancellor Tarrou was standing defiantly with his arms folded across his chest. Then, suddenly, without warning his defensive posture softened. His hostility, anger and his defensiveness vanished, completely. He said nothing. He simply turned toward his chair, sat down, crossed his legs, then began kicking one foot slightly, back and forth, back and forth. As he sat there he began looking around, simultaneously tugging at his ear with one hand, while he nodded his head, offering friendly smiles to anyone who would look his way. He appeared to be stunned, confused and befuddled.

A light murmur was quickly silenced as AC4 resumed speaking.

"It is regrettable that we must tolerate such drama. Too little time is available for unprofitable digressions."

AC4 carefully backed up to sit once again on his high-backed chair. He slowly lifted his leg as he sat down, keeping the weight off of his afflicted left foot. Whatever it was that he had done with his hand seemed to sap him of strength. He briefly rubbed the top of his good leg. Then, once seated, he continued speaking.

"Listen carefully. We have been in this room before, together, all of us, several times. Most of you already inwardly sense this. The great majority of you have felt the tug of those strange intuitive feelings called *Déjà vu.* Inwardly, you sense and feel familiarity. You know that you have been here before. There is a reason for that – *you have been here before.* Each of you, individually and as a group, have been here before -- several times. By *'here'* I mean you *have been* in this *exact moment* in this *exact place – several times."*

Another light murmur raced across the observation area, then became subdued as AC4 once again continued speaking.

"This is actually our seventh meeting -- *together* -- in this room, at this *exact moment* in time. I understand that this is confusing; but, bear with me. Hear me out. Our team knows who will speak next. Our team knows what will be said next and who will say what will be said. Our team also knows how each of you and how each of your larger groups will respond. Neither I, nor any of our team, however, are omniscient – but, we do know what we know because we have been here with each of you before – *six times."*

"Again. This is actually our seventh meeting -- *together* -- in this room, at this *exact moment* in time; and, this will be our final meeting – the *eschatos* is nearer than we first believed.

Now, please, listen carefully. We have a wealth of detailed information that must be shared. Your ability to mentally recall prior narratives, conversations and discussions will return as we work our way forward. Cognitive compression and storage, closely associated with mental retention, is part of the *Déjà vu* process we have utilized to facilitate recall.

"Do note that in the <u>first section</u> of your syllabus you will find transcripts and narratives of each of our prior meetings – including your questions and answers to your questions during each of the sessions."

AC4 got up from his seat and stood confidently on one foot, with his hands on his hips. His strength evidently had returned. He looked to the upper levels, making eye contact with many before continuing to speak. He sat down quickly on his high-backed chair and began speaking again, with a dull sounding professionalism of a university professor.

"Located in the <u>second section</u> of your syllabus is a detailed narrative of the thoughts and travels of this man, Dr. John. He has functioned primarily as a *human drone.* We have seen with him, through him and within him, utilizing his consciousness to travel backward, forward and laterally through and across the universal, unified field of consciousness that forms the cosmic grid of space and time. We will explain his role as well as the role of consciousness in the development of this syllabus as we work our way through the printed material."

"Do note that at specific points in the narrative we have inserted *'restore points'* similar to those on your computers. This will enable you to return and restart the journey at the *'restore point,'* if you sense that need."

As my surgical chair continued its rotations I would occasionally get a fleeting glimpse of Chancellor Tarrou. He was still sitting in his chair, still nodding his head, offering friendly smiles; only pausing occasionally to bite his nails. He appeared to be quite nervous and insecure.

"The contents of the third section of your syllabus are devoted to actual position papers developed by each of you and/or by your group pertaining to vital issues generated through our journeys together and through each of our progressive meetings. We view the inclusion of your position papers in this syllabus as a vital contribution to this project.

"Please take forty-five minutes to review your syllabus. Please note the entry title, the page, paragraph and line numbers of the specific entries that you wish to explore during the syllabus review and share time. Use the *Restore Function* when and as often as you choose. No matter which direction you travel whether backward or forward in time, and no matter how much time is actually expended to complete your journey, your actual time will be calibrated and compressed so that you will return to this *exact place* in exactly forty-five minutes. You will discover as you *'restore,'* read and research your syllabus that the feeling of *Déjà vu* will disappear and you will remember and recall, vividly, the content, conversations and, yes, even the conflicts of each prior meeting."

The people in the observations areas were suddenly very much involved and thoroughly engrossed with the printed material in the syllabus. The room was filled with the sound of turning pages. People were writing entry titles, page, paragraph and line numbers where they had made what they believed to be significant contributions. What a creative way for AC4 to insure the involvement of the participants. Their attention was focused, totally focused, on the printed material of the syllabus. Subconsciously, however, they were searching for their own contributions.

As they continued to work their way through the syllabus their faces took on a different appearance, an appearance of conscious awareness, that sense of certainty. The *Metaphoric MC Tracer Device,* with its built in cognitive compression and storage system, was working. It was secretly, unknowingly and without permission installed in back of the jaw bone of all participants in the symposium. And, now the *Metaphoric MC Tracer Device* was mentally compressing and storing vast amounts of data as mental imprints were indelibly etched onto each person's memory storage banks. They were not only comprehending the material – *they were retaining it.*

The Déjà vu was disappearing. It was being replaced by certitude. They were remembering. They were retaining.

As a soft tone sounded, signaling the conclusion of the first review period, it was apparent that the *Déjà vu* feeling had totally disappeared. Cognitive compression, retention and total recall capabilities had replaced the *Déjà vu.* The people in the observation rooms were now aware, fully aware, of all of the previous meetings. The narratives, transcripts, documentations, and position papers were somehow recalled, reviewed and retained, imprinted on memory. They were conscious, aware and knowledgeable of all that had transpired, everything. Even so, some still had questions. The first to stand was -- *Chancellor Jean Tarrou.*

"Chancellor Tarrou." said AC4 with a firm voice, "Again, Monsieur, again I must stress that this symposium has no time available for unprofitable, non-productive conflict."

With a wary eye on AC4, Tarrou, speaking with a conciliatory voice, attempted to explain to his colleagues his earlier loss of coherence – caused by AC4's mysterious hand.

"The experience made me feel as if I were locked inside a dream. Whether or not it was a dream I do not know. If it was a dream, well, it was definitely not a typical dream. Know this. The experience, whatever it was, does not and did not change who I am: I am a skeptical, cynical atheist -- *by choice.* I do not, nor will I ever, embrace that which is mythological, illogical or empirically unverifiable."

He had regained his confidence and spoke as a man driven by strong conviction. A long tense silence followed his deliberate pause. Then, with slight tears moistening his eyes he continued speaking.

"Men of science. I do not apologize for my skepticism. Nor for my cynicism. Nor for the issues that I raised earlier. Let me say again, I am a skeptical, cynical atheist -- *by choice.* I am a simple man, yet born with the capacity to reason, and the courage to ask *uncomfortable questions."*

He let the words *"uncomfortable questions"* linger, hanging in the air before he continued speaking. As he stood there, I wondered about Chancellor Jean Tarrou. Something brought him to atheism. Some experience gave birth to doubt, cynicism and a skeptical approach to God and life. There was some experience that was fueling his atheism with its spiritually-neutered, totally secularized belief system as its shield.

In his novel, *The Plague,* Albert Camus traced the root and origin of Tarrou's fierce opposition to *capital punishment.* According to Camus, when Tarrou was a child his lawyer-father, a prominent prosecutor, took young Jean to work with him one day. As that day's court proceedings unfolded, Tarrou's father was successful in procuring a *death sentence* for a guilty criminal. Jean was appalled that his father had done such a thing. Young Tarrou felt empathy and an affinity toward the criminal -- and rebelled against and rejected his father.

Camus correctly saw this event as the root of Jean Tarrou's opposition to *capital punishment.*

Hidden beneath that opposition to capital punishment, however, was the deeper root of Tarrou's atheism. Jean transferred his rebellion against and hatred toward his earthly father to a deeper, more hideous rebellion against the heavenly Father. He identified with the criminal who violated the law, because he, Jean Tarrou, in a more profound way, had violated God's law; and, just as the criminal was under a sentence of death for violating man's law so too was Jean Tarrou condemned, under a sentence of death for violating God's law – *the wages of sin is death.* Young Tarrou rebelled against and rejected both the sentence and the Judge – *God* – thus his atheism.

Tarrou proudly proclaimed that he had made a choice for atheism. He was blind, however, to the childhood circumstance that gave birth to that choice.

"I will not digress to the prior issues I raised earlier. I say what I say at this point to assure my colleagues, the participants in this symposium, that they should present their questions to Monsieur AC4 without hesitation. No harm came to me. No harm shall come to you. Do not be silent, my friends. Do not be silent. Do not let my temporary incoherence – my temporary dream-state – cause any hesitation. I see now what I did not see earlier. My mind, once clouded, is now clear."

"Thank you, Chancellor Jean Tarrou. Our intent, earlier, was not to harm you – nor is it our intent to harm anyone."

Chancellor Jean Tarrou nodded his head in deference to AC4. It was a symbolic sign of acquiescence toward AC4, a silent acknowledgment that he now understood more fully the challenge before the participants in the symposium.

"As I shared earlier, we know who will speak next, what will be said and how the larger group will respond. We have heard you, Tarrou, seven times now, and appreciate your thoughts. Dr. Rieux will introduce our next questioner."

Chancellor Tarrou, still standing, placed his hands in his pockets; with his shoulders slightly hunched, he sat down again.

The next man, a very tall man, was an American psychiatrist. He was nervous, very nervous as he moved rather awkwardly, clumsily, toward the microphone in his third level observation room. His face was pale, ashen. As he continued walking toward his microphone he paused momentarily, then, without warning he stopped walking, stood still and blew his nose loudly into a soft tissue. His colleagues patted him on the back, encouraging him, seeking to chase away his anxiety, as he resumed walking to his microphone. His hand was shaking as he tapped on the microphone in an effort to determine if its volume was working. After stating his name he read from a paper that had several hand-written questions scribbled on it.

"Greetings from the Department of Psy, Psy, Psychiatry and Behavioral Sciences, Johns Hopkins Hospital, Baltimore, MD. Out institution has occupied a di, di, distinguished place in the field of psychiatry since 1913. Today, we continue our long tradition of excellence in psssy, psychiatric care, teaching and research through our participation in this symposium."

He paused for a moment to catch his breath. He was not a stutterer. He was more of a stammerer, an extremely anxious stammerer.

"Mr. AC4 and his team have provv, provided each of us with an excellent, comprehensive syllabus to guide us during this symposium. One pri, pri, primary concern, Monsieur, has to do with reality – *possibilities* and *actualities*. In our field of study, psychiatry, many of our clients have difficulty di, disst, distinguishing reality from psychotic distortions of reality.

"In the psychiatric discipline the word *'anomaly'* is used rather loo, loos, loosely to describe the content of an unusual experience, usually one that is not explained in conventional terms. Consequently, because of a lack of conventionality, a formal de, def, definition of *'anomaly'* has not yet been finalized. This lack of a formal definition creates divergent opinions, much debate, and di, dif, differing descriptions and therapeutic approaches. With this said, the questions that our staff and my colleagues raise fall under that broad psychiatric umbrella called *'anomaly.'* This is our....excuse me...."

Suddenly, he stopped speaking. He paused momentarily, swallowed hard, then coughed a nervous cough. He appeared to tremble, just briefly. He wiped a thick bead of sweat from his forehead as his free hand clutched his note paper with quivering fingers. His voice trembled as he attempted to continue speaking. He once again moved anxiously from side to side, dancing back and forth, from foot to foot, as he resumed speaking.

"Excuse me, colleagues. Anxiety with pu, pub, public speaking has been my nemesis since childhood."

He paused again as one of his associates handed him a glass of water and some pills. He quickly popped his head backward, so as to take his medication, then resumed speaking.

"As I started to share, friends, our psy, psy, psychiatric team at Johns Hopkins has one primary concern -- Dr. John, the human drone. Our concern is that of *psychosis,* extreme psychosis. Dr. John, *the drone* as you called him, is actually a surrogate through whom we travel, hear and see. He projects back to us that which he hears and sees as we travel through him across the unified field of consciousness into these *alternate realities* and *parallel universes.* Monsieur, a question: does he project actual verifiable reality or is he projecting a psychotic distortion of reality?

"A psychosis is a mental disorder characterized by a loss of contact with reality as it is normally defined. Persons suffering from psychosis often report delusions, unrealistic interpretations of reality, hallucinations, false perceptions and their behavior can be unpredictable and incomprehensible. Their grasp of reality is distorted by psychosis. The most common and most widely known type of psychosis is, of course, schizophrenia. Schizophrenics often pro, pro, project a magical world view, an animated universe, populated with powerful intelligences."

His voice began trembling again, so he paused, just momentarily. Then still moving and dancing anxiously back and forth, from foot to foot, he asked a simple, final question.

"Can you address this concern, Monsieur AC4?"

Almost immediately, one of the four small, white haired men seated behind the curved glass cubicle, began punching keys on his key pad. Several rapidly flashing video projections raced across the large screens. The *first set* of video projections focused on psychiatric nomenclature, terminologies, words, phrases and definitions dealing with psychosis. Fast moving gestalt images and accompanying sketches, pictures and photographs of genetic space forms then raced across the giant screens. These were followed by *a second set* of projections, genetic time forms and DNA sequences, coupled with brain chemical fluctuations and an accompanying molecular analysis of synaptic fluids. The *third set* of projections focused on psychiatric statements, criteria and conclusions drawn from the *Diagnostic and Statistical Manual of Mental Disorders.* All three projections -- the terminologies, the images and the professional statements -- were merged, then rapidly converted into algebraic forms, geometric symbols and simple basal equations.

In ways that I cannot explain these algebraic forms, geometric symbols and basal equations were projected as a *fourth set* of progressions across the giant video screens. A mathematical process utilizing differential equations rapidly studied the data from several different perspectives. The differential equations, which were beyond my ability to comprehend, translated the algebraic forms, geometric symbols and basal equations into long lines of numerical values which were then resolved into roots, with the roots replaced with higher numerical values. Inexplicable, fast moving numerical additions and subtractions followed. As numerical values and totals were recalculated and reprojected they were subjected to a triangular division by prime numbers then the transcendental number, *pi.*

All of the final totals, the *fifth set* of projections, were then encoding and encrypted, translated into English, the global language of science, and projected onto the large screens, with additional lower case sub-titles written in the ethnic language of each nationality represented.

Applause. Loud Applause. Cheers. Everyone was amazed by what they had just seen. Never, in the history of science, had such massive amounts of data been analyzed so efficiently and effectively.

Dr. Rieux stood as the applause subsided. He then pointed upward, toward the tall psychiatrist from Johns Hopkins Hospital. Rieux then explained the question and answer process they had just witnessed.

"All future questions will be processed and projected in the same manner as this first question. Each of you is becoming aware of the capabilities of our information processing system. You have also probably noticed that you have increased intellectual capabilities to mentally comprehend, retain and store knowledge and information. As a prerequisite for participation in this symposium the institution, government, or governmental agency or organization that you represent pre-authorized the installation of a *Metaphoric MC Tracer Device* to enable you to mentally comprehend and compress, retain and retrieve vast amounts of knowledge, information and data as mental imprints are indelibly etched onto your memory storage banks."

Loud Applause. Cheers. As the cheers and applause continued Dr. Rieux walked toward Dr. Castel. Rieux then leaned over and whispered something. He simultaneously pointed to the upper level toward the Vatican City representatives, who were standing in defiance. For them there was some prophetic connection between the *Metaphoric MC Tracer Device* and end time prophecies. I did not quite understand why but at the front of the papal contingent was a man that I knew – *Father Paneloux.*

I would later discover that Father Paneloux was now serving as Dean of the College of Cardinals in Rome. It was widely reported that Paneloux was secretly summoned to Rome, called before a clandestine ecclesiastical tribunal and immediately excommunicated. He was then reinstated by papal decree then ordered to appear before the College of Cardinals who determined that he met the canonical qualifications to lead the College of Cardinals. Father Paneloux was affirmed to this prestigious position by the Roman pontiff following his election by his peers in the College of Cardinals.

Paneloux's presence in this new capacity had obviously raised concern. The integrity of the papacy was publically called into question. The

Pope, when questioned about Paneloux's election became defensive. An international newspaper had photographs of Paneloux and the Pope seated with seven mysterious black robed monks, who, according to the newspaper article, represented the seven deadly sins. Above the photographs and accompanying article was an ominous headline – *Something's Amis.* It triggered memories of the dinner meeting where Paneloux denounced simony plus some recollections that I had from *A Psalm of The Apocalypse…*

Seven Cities Rise, Seven Cities Fall
One, On Seven Hills -- The Leader of All
Like A Rope Stretched O'er the Abyss
Unholy Pope, Something Amis
Secular City, Once Sacred, Sterile, Stained Within
Antiochus. That Swine.

In biblical prophecy, Rome is widely recognized as the city seated on seven hills destined for an apocalyptic fall. Thus one of history's most recognized religious centers -- *The Leader of All* – has become a *Secular City, Once Sacred, Sterile, Stained Within.* When secular needs take precedence over spiritual needs; when money takes precedence over ministry – the church becomes -- *Like A Rope Stretched O'er the Abyss.*

As Dr. Castel left our rotating platform Dr. Rieux continued to explain the process and procedures of the symposium and the information processing system. Meanwhile, I was curiously wondering – how did Paneloux get here? Why was Paneloux here?

A final bit of information was projected on the large video screens. I was unable to read everything that was projected but the first notation that I read began with the statement….

Final Analysis
Entry Title: A Molecular Analysis of Psychosis and Psychotic Disorders
Symposium Section 3: Page 1204 Line Number: 17 and following

Johns Hopkins Hospital, Psychiatry and Behavioral Sciences, Baltimore, Maryland

Sequential Information Processing Conclusion
The Sequential Information Processing System recognizes a large number of psychotic disorders, including but not limited to, general psychosis, disorganized psychosis, catatonic psychosis, paranoid psychosis (schizophrenic), residual schizoaffective disorder, undifferentiated, and other non-specified forms of psychosis…
According to current diagnostic criteria and molecular analysis of synaptic fluids, DNA sequences and brain tissue analysis, the candidate – Dr. John – does not warrant any type of psychotic designation nor does he meet the criteria for a diagnosis of psychosis.

As my surgical chair continued to rotate I caught a fleeting glimpse of someone in a room, a rectangular shaped room with a curved glass front, high above both the second and third level observation rooms. The light in this room was bright, but not as bright as the others. Whoever it was had the appearance of a dull whitish shadow, dissolving in and out of the light. He would walk toward the curved glass front, momentarily look down at the flow of data on the screens, briefly study what was being projected, then pace back into the shadows, only to repeat the process, over and over again. His back and forth movements made him appear to be worried, very worried. He looked lonely, standing in solitude, in the half-light that fell through the small circular windows that dotted the back wall of his room. Then I saw him full face – *it was Joseph Grand.*

RESTORE POINT 20:

CHAOS AND CONFLICT

Joseph Grand was now a man of great wealth and great power – *but he had no principles. None whatsoever.* How strong the powerful. How selfish. How alone. I found it strange and sad. In this place filled and flush with light, there was a darkness, a deep darkness, a dark presence, working in the insanely dangerous heart of Grand as he paced back and forth in the shadows – *totally absorbed by the beckoning call of darkness.*

Suddenly, just as that thought raced through my brain, Grand walked to the edge of his room's curved glass front wall, and stopped – and looked down -- *directly at me.*

Staring intently at me Grand raised both of his hands high in the air just as AC4 had earlier. The same type of mysterious, radiant wisps of color, very faint, barely perceptible, flowed from Grand's hands, blanketing everyone in the entire building.

I can't explain it but it felt as if I was suddenly trapped inside a dull, slow-moving dream. It was as if time was distorted, twisted and twisting, then suddenly standing still. All of the voices that had so loudly filled the large room with sound were silenced – in an instant. The whole building and every one in it – silent, totally silent -- with a monastic-like hush. All movement ceased, instantaneously. It was if a dream-like paralysis swooped over everyone and everything. *Suspended animation.* Dr. Rieux, Dr. Castel, even AC4 were motionless, rigid, inanimate, unable to move.

Then, with his body rigid and fixed, the head atop the shoulders of AC4 slowly turned toward me. Rigidity kept me from moving any part of my body but I could see and I could hear. We looked at each other. His eyes met mine. He spoke – *yet his lips did not move.*

"I want what is mine and I want it now."

"He means what he says, Dr. John" shouted Grand, "and he will get it."

Even though I was strapped in the surgical chair, I could feel my legs weakening under me. A flush of fear rushed over me. My heart was pounding, my breathing, constricted. A tingly feeling began to race through my entire body, creating a mysterious pain in my chest, like tiny stabs of electricity. I felt as if I was in my body, yet outside of my body -- watching my body from a distance.

The face of AC4 was gray with dark hollows draining the color from his already pale eyes. With a strained movement he slowly tilted his head forward.

"I said I want what is mine -- and I want it now."

Suddenly, the silence was shattered. The room once again filled with sound and movement. Grand's hands and his shadow were gone, dissolved before my eyes. It was as if he was nothing more than a cloud of dust, blown away by unseen wind. The radiant wisps of color that once filled the building grew faint, then disappeared completely.

The noise of the computers calculating and recalculating surged, seeming twice as loud as before Grand's intrusion. Their sound served as a static technological backdrop as questions were hurled from the upper levels to the lower level circulating platform. Dr. Rieux, Dr. Castel and AC4 fielded question after question as small red lights on the upper levels flashed on, then off, then on again as the mad rush of questions escalated.

The four small, white haired men seated behind the curved glass cubicle, were rapidly punching keys on their key pads. *'Back everything up. Back everything up. Export to the cloud. Export to the cloud.'* Rapidly flashing video projections raced across the large and small screens while the words of AC4 echoed in my head…

"I want what is mine."

As AC4 turned away from me I was shocked, surprised and mesmerized by what I was now seeing. I had never seen anything like the escalating pandemonium generated by this symposium. The moment-to-moment intensity of rapid-fire questions and answers; a forest of outstretched arms waving like trees blowing in wind; the quick movements of the white haired men; all of this caused a whirling inside my head. The rapidity of the question-answer pace was nearly unbearable and, unbelievably, more nerve-wracking than anything I had ever encountered. Yet in a strange, inexplicable way the whole scene, the ambiance and the environment it created was riveting, fascinating. It seemed as if I could watch everyone and everything that was unfolding for hours, continuously, and never lose interest. The men and women on the upper levels, with raised voices were shouting back and forth, hollering and hurling questions to the unholy triad of Dr. Rieux, Dr. Castel and AC4, demanding verbal replies, engaging in loud back-and-forth shouting conversations, even debating finer points -- with enormous lightning-fast calculations constantly projected onto the screens.

Sometimes, the people in the upper levels would violently push and shout at their colleagues as they fought for the button that controlled their respective red lights. It was unimaginable chaos, filled with a sea of harried faces, and hundreds of people rushing about, shouting and gesturing to one another, watching monitors, and entering data into terminals. It was absolute chaos, sheer chaos. Everything was chaotic.

I felt as if I was trapped in a strange dream, a chaotic, confused dream.

"I want what is mine -- and I want it now."

I did not know it as the flurry of questions were bantered back and forth but this technological dream or whatever it was would become an apocalyptic nightmare – *and I would be in the middle of it.*

As AC4's words echoed inside my brain again and again I cannot adequately describe what was transpiring inside the *Defense Advanced Research Projects Agency* in Blacksburg, Virginia. It was an untranslatable experience.

Dr. Rieux's voice could be heard above the others as he replied to a question concerning protocol posed by a physicist associated with the United States Aeronautical Services Agency in Belvoir, Virginia.

"In this symposium we utilize three types of statements," shouted Rieux, "*Analytical Statements, Synthetic Statements,* and *Scientific Statements.*[74] *Metaphysical Statements* are disregarded. As a category of thought they are nonsensical, viewed as a dark blemish on the face of reason and as such are not open to empirical testing. Since metaphysical statements are outside of the realm of sense verification the symposium regards such statements as *"non-sense."*

The robust applause echoing throughout the building in response to Dr. Rieux's remarks further revealed the open hostility of this largely secularized crowd toward matters of faith. Chancellor Tarrou further confirmed this as he impulsively stood, enthusiastically shouting praise to Dr. Rieux for the benefit of the crowd.

Strangely, Dr. Castel was silent. He stood on the podium with his head bowed as the crowd continued to applaud and cheer. If I hadn't known better I would have said that he appeared to be praying.

"Faith, revelation, theology, metaphysics or whatever it is called" shouted the fiery Chancellor. "These are nothing more than unwelcome ideological intrusions. In and of itself revelation is nothing more than presuppositional madness, is it not? Sheer chicanery. What can we say, men of science? Revelation is nothing more than a romantic premise without evidence and a hindrance to mankind's *upward evolutionary progress.* Thank you, Dr. Rieux, for saying *'No.'* to *Metaphysical Statements* and Thank you for calling revelation what it is -- *nonsense.* I commend you, Dr. Rieux. I commend you."

Applause and loud cheers broke out again. The aversion to faith and revelation was never more apparent than in the crowd's response to Chancellor Tarrou's words.

Upward evolutionary progress? Such is the dark genius of the desecrated mind. *Upward evolutionary progress?* Utopian wishfulness would be more descriptive. Evolution is not an upward progressive path, but a downward regressive spiral, a regressive spiral filled with not only intellectual inconsistencies but a problematic and painful devolution of civilization's real progress.

At its inception the fallacious notion of mankind's *upward evolutionary progress* initially produced a moderately optimistic view of man, his world and progress. This optimism, however, was eventually shattered when the attacks of serious thinkers against the false notions of societal progress was followed by a great global depression and two of history's most destructive wars -- wars that painted many human beings as violent, irrational animals. Early optimism quickly soured, turning into bitter illusions. Ensuing, ongoing economic, political, and social disruptions, the continuous rise of harsh dictatorships and other incidents of barbarism, terrorism and suicide bombers sealed any belief in the notion of mankind's *upward evolutionary progress.*

Oh. If only I could speak to this crowd, but, I can not. My tongue is nailed to my chin. My voice is silenced. *BUT, MY THOUGHTS ARE NOT.*

As the applause subsided I was shaken from my thoughts as the escalating flurry of questions started again. Dr. Rieux addressed several questions pertaining to time travel and the philosophical dilemma known as the *grandfather paradox.* If a time traveler travels backward in time and murders his grandfather before his grandfather had wed, so the paradox goes, then the time traveler would not have been born. Consequently, since the time traveler would not have been born he would not exist. Therefore, there would be no opportunity for the time traveler to travel backward through time. His non-existence denied him that opportunity. Consequently, the grandfather would not have been murdered, would wed, have children and grandchildren, among whom would be the time traveler who then would have the opportunity to travel backward in time to murder the grandfather, thus creating a never-ending circular philosophical nightmare – *the grandfather paradox.*

There was murmuring in the upper levels, sounds of discontent and disbelief as the implications of the *grandfather paradox* dawned on those who were just now becoming familiar with this particular philosophical paradox.

"How can this be?" shouted a representative of the United Nations from the upper level. "Are not time and history immutable? Unchangeable? The past may sometimes be long forgotten, Monsieur, but does it not still have immutable, unchangeable boundaries?"

"Yes. Yes, Monsieur. Both time and history are immutable," shouted Dr. Rieux as he looked upward to the questioner, "yet, expand your vision, Monsieur, and know this: history, though immutable, can be changed, creating alternate histories. When this occurs new realities come into existence, realities that run parallel to our own, *parallel universes.* You should know, however, that the impact of these newly created alternate histories affects all other realities – except the *Alpha/Omega* reality."

The immediate impact of this statement reverberated through all of the upper levels. Many people were becoming agitated. Others were frustrated. The great majority were disturbed, deeply disturbed, fearful that some unseen tenets of Christian revelation would find its way into the symposium.

"What you speak, Monsieur," shouted Dr. Rieux, "is historically an unchallenged philosophical assumption. This unchallenged assumption is based upon prior conceptions that are conditional and transient because of time-based cognitive limitations. One fundamental component of science, Monsieur, can be summarized in one word: *Verify.* Our scientific inquiry has verified that there is a more viable, expansive interpretation that fosters a new paradigm concerning history."

"Again, I ask, how can *this* be?" shouted the representative of the United Nations. "If that which is immutable is simultaneously mutable and if that which is unchangeable is somehow simultaneously changeable – is this not a philosophical madness that is greater than the *grandfather paradox*? Does not this illogical thinking create yet another, even greater paradox? If what you say is correct does not historical certainty then mutate, becoming mere improbable coincidence that is somehow probable? Does this not create a strange, new world, a strange new world that is uninterpretable, impossible to explain or understand?"

"What you speak is an unchallenged philosophical assumption," interjected AC4, "an unchallenged assumption that affirms both epistemological and ontological intolerance – and negates the primacy of rationalist science. What we are attempting to do, Monsieur, is to move above and beyond the ceiling of limiting paradigms. Our intention is to distinguish and differentiate differences so as to create philosophical transitions – a unity among diversity, if you will. We can no longer afford to think in either figments or fragments. The best answer to any philosophical question, Monsieur, is *both/and* rather than *either/or.*"

Spoken like a true secularist, AC4, spoken like a true secularist. Oh. How I wish I could speak. Relativity. It sees black as white and white as black. Unity is diversity and diversity is unity. Something is negated; everything is affirmed – philosophical fluff. *The emperor has no clothes.*

"Monsieur, the key philosophical concept to assist in resolving this dilemma is called *antinomy*," shouted Dr. Rieux. "The philosopher Immanuel Kant utilized this term [75] in discussing *logic* and *epistemology* to contrast the actual incompatibility of two equally true laws that nevertheless simultaneously coexist, yet whose very existence negates the existence of the other."

"Then history, Monsieur Rieux, then history has no shape or form," shouted the representative from the United Nations. "It is not fixed. Freedom runs rampart, destroying form, obliterating structure – negating rather than affirming historical content and historical context. And, we, we children of time who populate history, we become victims of history rather than victors – slain by self-infliction. Listen, Dr. Rieux. Hear me. Take heed, colleagues. I mean no disrespect, but I seem to hear the sorrowful sound of *Invictus* on bended knee -- *weeping.* We are no longer *masters of our own fate."*[76]

Hear, I thought, is a scientist with the mind of a philosopher, the heart of a poet and the tongue of a preacher. He seems to intuitively sense that if Dr. Rieux's resolution of the *immutability-mutability* issue is correct -- then historical meaning becomes a mirage. Man and mankind are then thrust into darkness, the darkness of a long narrow street, a street that we call *time – a street that has no light.*

I salute you, sir, whoever you are. I salute you for your mind, your heart, your tongue. Yet I wonder, were your words an expression of freedom? Or determinism? If, as AC4 asserted earlier, each of us have been in this exact moment and this exact place – many times – where then, sir, is your freedom? Yet, I wonder further, what do these words – Freedom and Determinism – what do they mean if Dr. Rieux is correct in his analysis concerning *antinomy?*

Freedom. Determinism. If Dr. Rieux is correct then these become empty concepts – explaining nothing. History becomes a masquerade with a face that constantly changes. Order becomes disorder. Control becomes chaos. Ancient utopian visions evolve into catastrophic dystopias. Rieux would have history, like a door attached to loose hinges; repeatedly swing back and forth – creating historical incoherence. History would then move whenever and wherever the winds of change and time would blow, leading nowhere.

With a sense of exasperation I must confess I did not understand everything that was being shouted back and forth regarding history, immutability-mutability, or this term *antinomy*. Nor could I untangle the tangled theological thoughts and philosophical barbarism that *antinomy* seemingly created. But I do recall that the reformer Martin Luther wrote a little booklet titled *Against the Antinomians.* If Luther was opposed or *Against the Antinomians*, I was fairly confident that I would stand in opposition as well. However, without my Bible commentaries or access to my pastoral library, I could not be sure if Dr. Rieux and Luther were addressing the same issues.

The discussion of *antinomy* led to fierce, fruitless verbal battles over other philosophical paradoxes related to *causality*, *circular causation* and the *predestination paradox.* Human beings, it seems to me, simply cannot tolerate an explanatory vacuum. We want to know. We want answers. Hopefully, we will ask the right questions. As far as hearing the sorrowful sound of *Invictus* on bended knee – *weeping* – weeping because we are no longer *masters of our own fate – I say "Foolishness. We never were and we never will be."*

AC4 interjected himself back into the conversation with a booming voice. Yet, he looked old, very old, and tired. He stood once again on the rotating platform not far from my surgical chair, tightly griping his aluminum walker, constantly keeping his left leg bent at the knee so as to keep his left foot from touching the ground.

"We must all understand and face some hard facts. There is little time to waste. Immutability. Mutability. Hear me, some things are irreversible. Some things are unavoidable. Some things are inevitable. Let us come to order. Let us come to order. Hear me. Hear me. There is an unavoidable eventuality confronting history and those who populate history. This inevitability may be unstoppable. It may be irrevocable. And, this is why this symposium has been assembled. Please heed my call for a return to order."

No one heeded AC4's call for a return to order. The conversation suddenly shifted into the fascinating field of astrophysics with heated debate over issues pertaining to *time warps, time-space continuums, time travel* and the bending, folding or warping of time.

An astrophysicist from the University of Wisconsin-Madison spoke from the second level in an effort to assist Dr. Rieux, Dr. Castel and AC4 in explaining matters pertaining to astrophysics.

"Hear me, colleagues. I and my colleagues from the University of Wisconsin-Madison have thoroughly reviewed the astrophysical and astronomical material presented in the symposium's syllabus. So much, so very much has been accomplished through this symposium. The historic conflict in describing motion, for instance, a conflict that has existed between Newton's laws of mechanics and Maxwell's theory of electromagnetism, that conflict is now resolved through this symposium. There is a new confluence of ideas within the syllabus, ideas that create new theoretical schemes that alter the geometry and topology of the space-time continuum. Everything in physics, according to the syllabus, is now defined in terms of everything else. *Quantum mechanics, quantum physics, particle physics, quark theory,* these and a host of other concepts have been reduced to numerological relationships that make the traditional understanding of time, space and matter obsolete.

"Augustine of Hippo, who died in AD 430, wrote: `If nobody asks me, I know what time is, but if I am asked then I am at a loss what to say.' [77] One of the primary problems with *time* is that, like Augustine, we know what it is but have difficulty talking intelligently about it. Because this is so we have invited Dr. Raymond Rambert, Professor of Philosophy, from the prestigious University of Oxford, in the United Kingdom to assist us in this portion of our discussion. Dr. Rambert."

Raymond Rambert was a journalist, a very good journalist from Paris. He matured through his experience with the plague at Oran and, as a consequence, abandoned journalism to pursue a post-graduate degree in philosophy from the University of Oxford. Rambert, a deep thinker, developed his analytical skills at Oxford and was added to their faculty upon completion of his degree.

"Here me, Men of Science. Let us speak and let us consider *time.* Is time absolute? Some say, 'Yes.' Others say, 'No.' Is time relative? Some say, 'Yes.' Others say, 'No.' What say you concerning time? Is time infinite, as some believe? Or, is time finite? Some, and you may be in that number, believe that time is an illusion. Others believe that time is real, so real that it predated the universe before the universe came into existence. What say you? What say you about time? Some believe that time has many dimensions. Others believe that time is one-dimensional. What you believe about time is important, very important, vitally important, to the work of this symposium."

Rambert closed his eyes momentarily, then opened them and continued speaking.

"This man, AC4, and the leadership of this symposium, have indicated that time as we know it, time which sprang from the abyss of *nothingness,* is about to return to *nothingness.* Time, as we know it, is about to come to its end."

Dr. Rambert continued delving deeper and deeper into the dissolution of and disappearance of time, touching on the latent qualities of *nothingness.* His was a strange conversation that was more complex than any could imagine. At a certain point he returned to the subject of *time travel.*

"As time and space bend, ladies and gentlemen, they lose uniformity, taking irregular shapes. Nevertheless, it is this bending that enables a *warp bubble* to travel millions and millions of light years across time *without any consumption of time*, because with the bending of time and space, *time vanishes*. During this process, the *warp bubble* moves, yet without movement -- at *time-warp speed* -- across the universe, across *multi-universes,* into and through *alternate realities* and *parallel universes.*"

The astrophysicist who stood beside Rambert was very patient in answering questions as the discussion turned toward *sub-atomic particles, anti-matter, fractal dimension measurement, inversion, tachyons* and *variable light speeds.*

In some inexplicable way while the astrophysicist explored and explained time, its compression and its cessation, I recalled the words of a poem I had memorized in college, words written by the poet T. S. Elliot in *The Four Quartets: Burnt Norton…*

Time present and time past
Are both perhaps present in time future

And time future contained in time past.
If all time is eternally present[78]

Questions one again moved back into the frightening realm of medical disorders and the possibility of me as their drone being mentally ill. The whole tone of the symposium changed with that shift away from astrophysis.

"Please, please, colleagues. We have dismissed psychosis earlier during this symposium. These are, however, additional psychiatric, psychological issues and medical considerations that must be addressed."

The sound of murmuring once again began rumbling among the participants. The people were obviously disenchanted with the shift of focus going back to possible mental illness.

"No. No. Hear me, please. I must ask: Are we exploring the unknown world of this man's illusionary subconscious or are we perhaps charting the movements of his unconscious mind? Are these subconscious memories a type of psychological projection? Has anyone explored the possibility of *delusion? Dissociative disorder? Folie a deux?*"

Tempers flared. Arguments ensued with the shift to mental illness. This was not what the majority wanted but the minority prevailed.

"What about *organic disorders?* Have we explored organic disorders? Organic disorders can interfere with both the neural functioning and stability of the nervous system producing extraordinary experiences. *Deliriums? Epilepsy? Neurological disorders? Have we explored these possibilities?*

Anger among the majority increased as the focus on medical disorders and mental illness issues continued. Some, in their impatience, became aggressive. A harsh stain of hostility colored the mood of the crowd as a man on the third level began yelling, screaming and banging the button that controlled his red light.

"I know it may sound far fetched but we must leave no stone unturned. Have we explored the possibility of *astral projection?* What about *bilocation?*"

People from disciplines outside of the field of psychiatry, psychology, mental health and medicine were beginning to feel harassed by the recurring medicinal and mental health issues. Some of the mental health specialists, who stood to ask questions, were shouted down by impatient colleagues.

Somehow, the content of the symposium began to gradually shift – but not the mood of the participants.

What followed was a question and answer period of unusual intensity fueled by a clash of fundamental philosophical assumptions. People continued to loudly express their philosophical opinions and ideological positions. The tension of the *immutability-mutability* conflict gave birth to a contentious conflict concerning *unity-diversity* and the issue of *universals-particulars.*

"There are no *universals* and no *final unities. Unified field theory* is *just that – a theory,"* shouted a philosopher from Israel's Hebrew University. *"The diversity of the particulars* is too great, far too great, to have proceeded from a singular *universal.* Oneism? A dream, a figment of a fragmented mind. The unseen ideal? A philosophical bogy-man hiding in the dark. The cosmic tree of life? Man's desperate cry for life beyond the grave. All linked together. Foolishness. These words about *parallel universes, alternate realities,* and different dimensions – philosophical poppycock. I don't buy it. Not at all. We are alone in the universe. We are alone. And, like our ancestor's, we wonder why. That's what this symposium is really about."

With the professors defiant shout -- *We are alone in the universe. We are alone.* -- something strange happened. I recognized him. He was the young man who was kicking his legs high in the air like a prancing horse as he ran across the neutral ground at *Paw Paw's Plaza.*

"You know what this painting really means? It means we're on our own. That's what it means, dude. That's what it means.... We are alone in the universe. We are alone. And, like our ancestor's, we wonder why. That's what this symposium is really about."

"Not so." shouted Dr. Rieux. "Not so. That *is not* what this symposium is about – not at all."

A rowdy chorus of cheers and jeers erupted but no one knew what was aimed at Rieux and what was aimed at the Hebrew scholar.

Whoever he was, the disagreeable philosopher from Israel's Hebrew University spoke like a despairing atheistic existentialist. Amazing people, these atheistic existentialists, amazing people. They create their own alienation and then protest their alienation. Go figure.

The crowd eventually shouted down both Dr. Rieux and the Hebrew scholar. Loud voices again rose from the crowd, asserting various ideological positions. The discussions became heated again as opinions and positions became lines drawn in the sand, adversarial lines, hostile lines of demarcation. Participants began to see their own stubbornness reflected in the stubbornness of their peers – and they didn't like what they saw. Each person became as it were a kind of mirror, a mirror that reflected the philosophical face of the other. Yet, in some strange way the stubborn face of the other mirrored their own. And so, here they were, colleagues, sharing similar secular values, yet in almost constant conflict – because of stubbornness.

On the other hand, each person had a different history. Many had different languages. Most had different politics. Some had different religious beliefs; many, the majority, had none at all. None of this, however, was the source of their conflict and division. The meeting was becoming unruly, even hostile, not because of differences, but because of similarities -- and stubbornness.

Consequently, scores of participants were behaving badly, rudely asserting themselves by banging the buttons that controlled their red lights and constantly electronically queuing for authorization to speak. Others simply started shouting their concerns and questions. Instead of forbidding inquiry AC4, Dr. Rieux and Dr. Castel encouraged continual questioning.

The computer-generated multimedia displays continued rapidly flashing numbers, words, pictures, equations, and other symbols, constantly calculating and projecting conclusions. Facts, concepts, and ideas, related to the questions posed were rapidly projected then processed, with the final data, encoded, decoded, encrypted and preserved.

As the questions continued a different kind of thought crossed my mind: By my calculations I have been strapped in this surgical chair for two months and four days and I had no clear idea concerning my location. *Wherever I am, I've got to get out of here.*

The loud, booming voice of Chancellor Tarrou once again took me away from my thoughts. As he stood he cocked his head to one side, raised his eyebrows then his hands. Pointing his hands downward he once again spoke directly to AC4.

"Pardonner, Monsieur. Earlier in the symposium you made reference to the concept of 'nothing,' of 'the void,' of 'oblivion' – of the negation of reality.

"Then, a few moments ago you spoke *of little time* and of our need to face *hard facts*. I listened carefully, Monsieur, as you mentioned *things irreversible, things unavoidable, things inevitable.* Forgive us, Monsieur, for our failure to heed your call to order. Forgive us and please share with us, Monsieur.

AC4 took what seemed a long time before answering Chancellor Tarrou's questions about *things irreversible, things unavoidable, things inevitable.* He started to speak, then paused. An unplanned hesitation. For just a brief second he glanced once again at me. His words, without sound, echoed once again, like a whisper – in my mind.

"I want what is mine."

I did have what AC4 wanted. He knew it; and, I knew it -- A *Psalm of the Apocalypse* written by John the Younger, Son of Cosmas, Son of John from the Isle of Greece

"I want what is mine.

RESTORE POINT 21:

A MEANINGLESS NOTHING

Things Irreversible. Things Unavoidable. Things Inevitable. A Psalm of the Apocalypse.

The apocalyptic nightmare. Possibilities. Actualities. Determinism. Freedom.

Words, defined by their context, have meanings, meanings that are shaped as much by our internal passions as by our external perceptions. Our perceptions and passions work together, however, to help us discover the relationship between words, which are symbols, and their meanings, which are interpretative. Words, therefore, are interpretative tools of thought that not only reflect our perceptions and passions – but have the power to actually change them.

AC4 had a doubly daunting task. The first horn of his dual dilemma was to negotiate *his way* through the interpretive process with scientific integrity. The second horn of this dilemma was for AC4 to safely lead the *symposium participants* through the same interpretative process – again, with integrity. Carefully chosen words that were strategically spoken through the course of the symposium – stated above, stated below -- raced through his mind as he stood once again to speak.

"Things Irreversible. Things Unavoidable. Things Inevitable. A Psalm of the Apocalypse.

The apocalyptic nightmare. Possibilities. Actualities. Determinism. Freedom."

AC4 knew that these words and the vocabulary that he would employ to clarify their contextual meanings would represent different things to different people. To the theologically-minded these words would likely be linked to *Christ, the second coming of Christ* and *the eschatological consummation of all things.* For the philosophically-minded the same words would more easily be married to philosophical concepts such as *being, non-being and nothingness, oblivion, and the negation of reality.* For AC4, however, his understanding traveled between these two polar positions. His interpretative focus? The destination, not the journey. His ultimate concern? A final, end time catastrophic event. The destination? A cosmic collapse that would eliminate, dissolve and annihilate all strands of reality, with the exception of the *Alpha/Omega.*

With that burden placed squarely on his shoulders AC4 struggled to stand on one foot. The crowd, though calm for the moment, had the potential to become more threatening and chaotic as AC4 spoke – *and he knew it.*

"As a scientist," (He especially emphasized the word *scientist), "As a scientist,* I affirm the fundamental tenets of science, naturalism, and secularism."

He paused for a moment to allow his opening words find their mark, then, for emphasis, he repeated the first three words emphatically yet again as he resumed speaking.

"As a scientist, I am adamantly committed to epistemological rubrics, the scientific method and empirical observation."

He paused yet again. Words, like arrows, must hit their target.

"As a scientist, I acknowledge that within the discipline of science, it is not uncommon for differing conclusions to be drawn utilizing the same data and the same scientific methodologies. *Triangulation, conclusion validity* and *conclusion reliability* are but a few of the terms utilized by the scientific community to describe this conflicted phenomena."

He paused yet again before beginning the difficult task of leading his colleagues to the point of entertaining and eventually embracing a *paradigm shift.*

As he resumed speaking his right hand slowly raised then descended, gracefully slicing through the air with movements like those of a conductor leading an orchestra. His melody was soft, solicitous, reflective. His right hand moved in concert with his now familiar three word phrase, over and over again, three times.

"As a scientist... As a scientist... As a scientist... Hmmm."

He mimicked thinking out loud, carefully coordinating his words with the movements of his hands. Then again, perhaps instead of thinking aloud, he was talking to himself, allowing the symposium participants to overhear his conversation. Whatever it was that he was doing it was effective and it was certainly drawing everyone more deeply into his presentation.

He then became silent, pausing again, just for a few seconds, then looking directly at the people in the upper observation rooms before he began speaking directly to them, once again using his hands for added emphasis.

"As a scientist... As a scientist... As a scientist...

"As a scientist I must deduce that if differing conclusions are sometimes drawn from applying the scientific method to the same data then how much more, I ask, will conclusions differ when the same data is handled by those of other disciplines who do not utilize epistemological rubrics, the scientific method or empirical observation?"

He ran his fingers through his hair several times, then once again resumed speaking spontaneously, directly to the crowd. He had no written notes, nor printed outlines. Nor did he use a teleprompter. He did, however, know when and how to conceal and when and how to reveal his emotions and body language to sway his audience.

"History reveals that people, many people, both inside and outside of the scientific discipline, have predicted some type of end to humanity, human history, even the universe itself. This end – or *eschatos* – is usually seen as a cataclysmic consummation of all things."

True to his Parisian heritage AC4 waved his hands, slapped his thighs, utilized humor, simulated terror, whined, and occasionally bowed or shook his head -- all of these and a host of other non-verbal communications were utilized to persuade, to make points, or to gain advantage in creating a sense of urgency for the *paradigm shift.*

"The popular story of the elephant and the six blind men illustrates how people form their understandings of reality, belief systems and paradigms. In the story six blind men touch then describe an elephant. One touches the tail while another touches a leg. Another touches an ear while still another touches the trunk, so on and so forth. Although each man touched the same elephant each description was different. The descriptions differed, of course, because each man had actually touched a different part of the elephant."

There was mild laughter as AC4 concluded the story. Most of the participants were familiar with the elephant story. Nevertheless, he capitalized on that laughter, using it to disarm the crowd by getting them to lower their defenses.

"Hear me, Men of Science. The elephant story has a primary warning: fallacious, preconceived notions, unchallenged assumptions and limited perceptions produce misinterpretation."

AC4 then mimicked their laugher as he simultaneously impersonated a blind man feeling the head and the trunk of an elephant, humorously raising his hand up into air then downward.

"Men of Science. All six blind men did agree on one thing – *there was an elephant in the room."*

AC4 then smiled a wide smile as laughter once again filled the room. Although the laughter represented only a slight mood change AC4 was now ready to begin the heavy work of effecting a *paradigm shift.*

"Men of Science. Hear this man of science. We have an elephant in the room."

There was more laughter, but this time, just as the laughter subsided AC4 slowly tuned to face the Vatican City contingent. They were seated on the second level. Raising his hand AC4 pointed in their direction.

I wondered, was AC4 implying that Rome or religion represented blindness? Or, was he implying, in some metaphorical way, that the church was like the elephant in the room? Secularism was his religion, no doubt, and science was his bible with the scientific method serving as his ritual. Surely, however, the representatives from the Vatican City were not invited to the symposium so as to be objects of derision. Fortunately, irrespective of what AC4 felt about religion or the church, that was not the case.

"My old friend, Cardinal Paneloux, whom I worked with during the plague in the Algerian city of Oran, is with us. The Cardinal and I also worked together at *Christ Cathedral – The Church of the Last Judgment* in lower St. Bernard, Louisiana. Please stand, Cardinal. Let us honor you."

The applause was sparse. Then it became slightly stronger, signaling either mild approval or perhaps simple courtesy. Undaunted, AC4 continued to speak as the Cardinal stood momentarily then returned to sit with the papal contingent.

Something was amiss. This type of promotion does not happen without Papal intervention.

The mere thought of *Papal intervention* once again brought to memory a portion of *A Psalm of the Apocalypse....*

Seven Cities Rise, Seven Cities Fall
One, On Seven Hills -- The Leader of All
Like A Rope Stretched O'er the Abyss
Unholy Pope, Something Amis
Secular City, Once Sacred, Sterile, Stained Within
Antiochus. That Swine.
Flee Babylon, the Harlot, the Whore
The Closed Door.
Avel.

I wondered, what is the connection between this *Papal intervention* and *A Psalm of the Apocalypse? Could something Papal be amiss?* The city on Seven Hills -- The Leader of All was a sure reference to Rome. Could this promotion indicate that this Pope was indeed an *Unholy Pope?* Since the Pope's election many mourned that Rome had become a *Secular City, Once Sacred, Sterile, Stained Within.*

"When Cardinal Paneloux, who was recently affirmed as Dean of the College of Cardinals in Rome, when he thinks about *the end*, the *eschatos,* he thinks in terms of the return of Christ, the apocalypse, Armageddon, the Last Days or perhaps the end of the world."

From my vantage point all I could see was leering faces, glaring at each other, glaring at AC4, glaring at Cardinal Paneloux, glaring at the papal contingent, glaring at anyone and everyone. *Unbelief never smiles.*

AC4 then pointed in the opposite direction to a different observation room.

"Dr. Adolf Westergaard, over here, is the lead professor of Viking and Medieval Norse Studies at the University of Iceland. Dr. Westergaard is seated in the Scandinavian observation room across from Cardinal Paneloux. Please stand, Dr. Westergaard. Please stand."

Perfunctory applause once again sporadically spread across the building. It was mingled with sneers, sarcastic murmurings, jeers and more glaring looks.

"Dr. Westergaard would perhaps be more familiar with the teachings of *Ragnarok,* which deals with similar end time catastrophes yet differing cosmologies, eschatological concepts and conclusions."

Chancellor Tarrou was not pleased with this ever so slight metaphysical shift. He was frustrated, fidgety and agitated as he listened intently, measuring AC4's every movement and every word. He hated and had little tolerance for the insertion of what he considered religious figments and metaphysical fragments.

"Since the beginning of time people have been thinking about the end of time. Many have made predictions about how and when the end would happen. Most of us are familiar with *Nostradamus, Bishop Ussher, the Mayans* or others who predicted the end. Even now the Muslims expect the Mahdi to appear. The Christians are looking for the Christ. Orthodox Jews are looking for their Messiah. Others look for the incarnation of Krishna and still others look for the reappearance of Mohammed. Each of these messianic types are associated with the end of the world."

Chancellor Tarrou looked to his right, then to his left, carefully studying the expressions on the faces of his colleagues. *Nostradamus? Bishop Ussher? The Mayans? The scientific method? Empirical observation? Epistemological Rubrics?* For Tarrou there was no rational scientific connection between these terms – *none whatsoever.* Tarrou once again looked to his right, then to his left. He was comforted but not calmed to see that some were becoming as agitated as he.

"Most major religions have developed their own cosmologies and eschatological schemes. Christianity, Judaism, Hinduism, Buddhism, Islam, all have their own view of the end. When members of any of these religious groups hear words like *Things Irreversible. Things Unavoidable. Things Inevitable.* linked with a phrase like *A Psalm of the Apocalypse.* Or, when they hear a phrase like *The apocalyptic nightmare.* linked with words like *Possibilities. Actualities. Determinism. Freedom.* – they interpret these words differently than do those outside of their ecclesiastical discipline."

Tarrou was about to explode. He stood and walked quickly to the front of his observation booth and began repeatedly pushing his red button. It was deactivated. AC4 gave a knowing smile; as did Grand. AC4 continued speaking as Tarrou frantically continued pushing on his red button.

"In similar manner when dealing with these words and phrases a Poet might sense romance. A Philosopher might deduce reason. A Politician might respond with rhetoric. A Psychologist might discern regression and repression. And a Preacher might experience revelation. Each has differing perspectives, differing perceptions, differing passions, differing disciplines – that lead them to see things differently.

"Therein lies the great challenge of this portion of our symposium. The challenge is that of dealing with prejudicial biases and perceived notions, each generated by our differing disciplines and differing life experiences. Each of you must continually deal with this as we proceed...and, I confess, this is an ongoing challenge that I too, as symposium moderator and *as a man of science* must deal with as well."

AC4 paused for a moment as Dr. Castel once again handed him a glass of water. After drinking the cooling glass of water, as AC4 resumed speaking, I could hear Chancellor Tarrou cussing and shouting blasphemies as two uniformed military officers roughly pushed him back into his cubicle and down into his chair. Suddenly, a soldier's arm was raised high. His hand held a glass syringe. I was shocked as the long, sharp needle at end of the glass syringe was slammed into Tarrou's neck.

"Paraldehyde. 10ccs each carotid artery. Stay still, old man. Stay still." The soldier's arm was raised high again. The glass syringe was slammed into the other side of Tarrou's neck. "Hypnotic. Watch it. Keep it away from air. It'll turn to vinegar. And, don't break the glass syringe. That stuff eats plastic."

The chancellor quickly became silent. He just sat there, flopped in his chair, dazed, like a man caught in the grip of some sort of weird medicinally induced hypnotic trance. AC4 ignored the whole incident and simply continued speaking.

"Hear me carefully, I and the personnel of the *United States Defense Advanced Research Projects Agency* and my colleagues from the Algerian city of Oran, along with the physicists from the University of Wisconsin-Madison, as best as we are able, have confronted and exorcised our scientific prejudices and evicted the conceptual incoherence they produced. This was not an easy task.

"We discovered that many of our long cherished philosophical and scientific ideologies were like old clothing that still hangs in our closets. They were stylish and trendy once, but no longer. They must be discarded. There must be space for new clothing. There also comes a time when well-worn philosophical and scientific ideologies, like old clothing, must be discarded. As someone long ago said, *'you cannot put new wine in old wineskins.'*[79]

"With these images in place, conceptual images of an *elephant* and *old clothing* still hanging in our intellectual closets, let us pause to hear briefly from some of your colleagues, associates and contemporaries who have cleaned their intellectual closets through their participation in this symposium. We have prearranged for some special people to introduce themselves at this juncture in the symposium. General? May we begin with you, sir?"

"I am General Robert Bellamy, Commander, National Security Agency, Ft. George Meade, Maryland. Honored to be here. I would like to make one thing clear: *the elephant is indeed in the room."* A cartoonish image of an elephant suddenly flashed on the large screen, causing simultaneous laughter and applause.

The general was followed by a tall, dark-complexioned man whose white clothing was of a Middle East style -- a classic white *galabiyya* and a tall, tightly wrapped white turban. "Identity protected, sir, top secret classification, presently in training, covert operations, CIA, Headquarters, Langley, Virginia." After briefly sharing his cathartic experience through his participation in the symposium there was another round of applause.

Another military man, tall and slender, in full dress uniform immediately came forward. "Intelligence Officer, sir, Kanoehe Air Force Base, Oahu, Hawaii. I worked intently with many of the distinguished theorist, physicists and scientist involved in this symposium. Our work involved the utilization of very complicated numerological relationships. We developed square roots of negative numbers, created imaginary numbers and applied them to a newly emerging geometry and topology of the space-time continuum. We discovered that everything was mathematically defined and linked in terms of corresponding numerical schemes equated within everything else. These linkages or underlying codes are empirically verifiable. They reveal an underlying unified code that is greater than the sum of its parts; so much so that exact predictions could be made about future phenomena. As we probed further…."

As the Intelligence Officer concluded his remarks two people came forward to speak. One, a short, heavy set translator stood beside a silver-haired female physicist who spoke in Swedish.

"I am Dr. Agda Håkansson, Soder Aeronautics Agency, Stockholm, Sweden. Working with my colleagues from the Karolinska Institute, in Stockholm, this symposium enabled us to utilize particle physics to explore the ability of *tachyonic propulsion systems* to move objects faster than light. Applying the *philosophy of reductionism* to astrophysics provided new avenues of thought that enabled us to develop a simple process of reducing theories of everything to simpler common denominators. This in turn facilitated the development of…"

Dr. Håkansson was followed by a representative from the Nuclear Subterranean Weaponry Development Department, in Vancouver, British Columbia who in turn was followed by a host of political leaders and military officers representing several NATO nations.

Then, AC4 brought out the big gun, the crowd pleaser – Sidney Eisler.

"Ladies and gentlemen, may I introduce the honorable Sidney Eisler, Secretary of State, the United States of America."

There was loud applause and a standing ovation. The symposium participants were not aware that Mr. Eisler was in attendance. The ever-popular Eisler had recently made an unsuccessful bid for the U.S. presidency. He and several incoming U.S. Cabinet members were attending the symposium.

"Ladies and gentlemen, both the president and the president elect of the United States of America send greetings and encouragement. You have been entrusted with sacred responsibility. History, holding its breath, looks upon you, and your deeds, and this hour, your hour, with wonder and with worry. In the past, man has always prevailed. May it be so yet again."

After Secretary of State Eisler returned to the U.S. Cabinet observation room the introductions continued for several minutes longer with a host of astrophysicists, scientist, representative's from the U.N. and governmental leaders, both domestic and abroad. One by one, they stood and they spoke, all endorsing and confirming the veracity of the content of the symposium, briefly explained some finer points of the syllabus and concluded by praising AC4 for his ceaseless labor in this enterprise.

AC4 stood tall on one foot, greatly encouraged through the words spoken by such distinguished world leaders, scientists and colleagues from such a wide range of disciplines.

"Come with me, come now, come with me, as we carefully step into a most delicate philosophical and scientific arena. It is an unknown, unexplored, and as yet unexplainable arena where no one, no thing and nothing exists – no time, no space, no material, nothing -- the arena of *nothingness.* "

As AC4 continued speaking I heard the soft sound of voices, whispering, in different corners of the building, in different languages. *Whispers.* Sometimes, for a public speaker, not a good sign. *Whispers.* Sometimes, a sign of suspicion, a bad omen. AC4, however, interpreted the whispering as a good sign – as a sign of courtesy. Courtesy was much needed at this juncture. Suspicion was not.

"As shared earlier during this symposium, we have documented that at some point in the near future reality as we know it will collapse, cease to exist, and dissolve into *nothingness.* Whether we call this collapse *'the eschatos' 'the terminis' 'the apocalypse'* or simply *'the end'* is not important. What is important is that we have verified that *the elephant* is in the room."

The whispering ceased. Silence. AC4 captured the moment. The *paradigm shift* was almost, almost complete.

"Men of Science. You have the *freedom* to describe this elephant – this *nothingness* -- in the language of your choice, in the language of your discipline, or in the language of another discipline. Know this, however, irrespective of how you describe it a cataclysmic, momentous concluding event will occur in the near future. Whether you reject or whether you receive this conclusion is immaterial. This eschatological concluding event is *unavoidable, inevitable -- an irreversible actuality*. This has already been empirically verified, several times over."

Once again, AC4 paused, surveying his audience. He had a deadly serious, stern look on his face as his eyes looked upward, intently surveying and staring at as many people as possible before repeating his last sentence for emphasis.

"Let me, ladies and gentlemen, let me repeat: a cataclysmic, momentous concluding event will happen in the near future. This has already been empirically verified."

His face was still stern – then a more serious, deeper, darker expression surfaced. His face became grave, very grave in appearance, almost ashen, as he delivered his unique, compelling brand of cosmic commentary.

"Men of Science. When this final cosmic event happens, listen now, *when* this final cosmic event happens -- *not if, but when it happens* -- all that is, all that exists, all realities, all things visible, all things invisible, everything, will suddenly, swiftly and speedily merge, become one, then cease to exist – *except the Alpha/Omega. This is an unavoidable, inevitable, irreversible actuality.*

"Space will evaporate. Time, merging with the *Alpha/Omega,* will fold in on itself, then cease to exist. Time will be no more. If there were to be time beyond this point -- and know this: there will be no time -- nevertheless, if time did exist beyond this point, then it would be a timeless time, a time that is no time, a meaningless nothing. There will be no tick of the clock. There will be no clock. There will be no tick. Men of Science. Hear me. Beyond this point there is no space, nor time *-- even eternity withdraws.*

"The Alpha/Omega existed before there was a beginning and will continue to exist beyond the end, beyond the concluding event – not beyond space, but without space; not beyond time, but without time; not beyond eternity, but without eternity. *Such is nothingness."*

AC4's voice was filled with power and passion, yet perceptive, very perceptive. He spoke fervently, with authority, forcefully and firmly, persuasively. His gestures, his hand movements, his language -- everything about him was being used to accomplish the *paradigm shift.*

"Time's temperature is nearing its boiling point. History is heating up. Just as water reaches a boiling point, then evaporates, so too is time and history becoming more and more volatile. The volcano is about to blow. The cosmic landscape will soon be obliterated. *Not rearranged. Obliterated.* With a fervent heat all that is shall be dissolved with nothing remaining – *nothingness.* All biologies will end. All biographies will end. With a great noise, the elements, both seen and unseen, and all *parallel universes,* all multiverses, all realities, shall melt, disappear and dissolve. *Nothingness.*

"*Nothingness. Nothingness. Nothingness.* Indefinable. Inconceivable. Incomprehensible. We can presume to know what this *nothingness* is; but, we cannot penetrate it.

"Nevertheless, inscrutable as this *nothingness* is we presume to name it. We have chosen to call this climatic eschatological event, this final collapse, this dissolution of all things -- *the Omega Point.*"

RESTORE POINT 22:

OMEGA POINT: MECHANISM OF THE UNIVERSE

We have chosen to call this climatic eschatological event, this final collapse, this dissolution of all things -- *the Omega Point."*

He paused again, staring at the people in the upper levels in silence. The only thing that was heard was whispers – *"Omega Point." "Omega Point." "Omega Point."*

"Hear me. This Omega Point. It is Unavoidable. Hear me. This Omega Point. It is Inevitable. Hear me. This Omega Point. It is eminent. Even now, the Omega Point is knocking at the door."

The Omega Point. Yes. Yes. I remember learning about the *Omega Point* while a student attending seminary. *The Omega Point.* It was applied to an *evolutionary, pantheistic heresy* devised by the French Jesuit Pierre Teilhard de Chardin. He viewed the *Omega Point* as the highest level, as the very pinnacle, of evolutionary progress. Teilhard was convinced that when the *Omega Point* was achieved creation would become one with the Creator, with Christ. The individuality, the uniqueness and the diversity of man would cease to be through some type of unifying pantheistic absorption into the godhead – *the Omega Point.*

Many thinkers immediately rejected Pierre Teilhard de Chardin's theory, viewing it as a sort of *pantheistic nirvana* baptized with the language of Christendom. Others looked at the *Omega Point* with a jaundiced eye, eventually expressing strong disapproval. Their critique? Pierre Teilhard de Chardin seemed to set forth a fatalistically suspicious view of history. A suspicious view because it made one singular moment the culmination of the evolutionary process. Fatalistic because man in his diversity, in his unique individuality, would be swallowed up, absorbed in a modern day version of the ancient fallacy of *Oneism.* With no additional progress to be gained, and with backward devolution an impossibility, these thinkers reasoned that only one viable option remained – *annihilation, cessation of being, existential nihilism. – Nothingness.*

Because of his overreliance on *mystical pantheism* in discerning the experience of faith, Pierre Teilhard de Chardin, at least in my estimation, sawed off the very branch on which he was sitting. Abandoning Christian truth he twisted and distorted Christian language, unwittingly constructing a hollow, empty, Faustian *nihilism.* Pity the poor Pierre Teilhard de Chardin – he drowned in the murky waters where mystics swim.

"Elusive, fleeting, and baffling as it is, the abyss of *nothingness* lies beyond the *Omega Point.* And we, tonight we stand at the very edge of that abyss. We stand at the edge of extinction and we stare at annihilation, at non-existence. And what looks back at us? *Oblivion. Nothingness.*

"A cataclysmic, violent conclusion dances on our horizon. The future seems dark, dark with a darkness so deep, so very deep. *We see nothing. The Omega Point. Nothingness.*"

I was shaken from my thoughts about de Chardin by the sight of AC4 raising his right hand as he pointed toward the large and small screens.

"On the graphic that is being projected on the large and small screens you see seven vector lines," said AC4, "one for each of the seven primary *alternative realities.* In the center, the thicker, red vector line represents the dominant *Alpha/Omega* strand of reality. Each of the seven primary vector lines appears to be moving parallel, one with each other and with the *Alpha/Omega.* However, though they are moving in the same linear direction, toward the future, they are not actually moving with perfect parallelism.

"What appears to be a perfectly parallel path is optically deceiving. The actual paths that these seven primary *alternative realities* travel will lead them to eventually converge, becoming one with the dominant *Alpha/Omega.* Some of these *alternative realities* are moving toward the point of convergence faster than others. Some are moving slower. Neither spatial distance nor chronological time has any relevance or importance for the slower moving realities. When the first of these seven primary *alternative realities* merges with the *Alpha/Omega*, all other realities will instantaneously converge and simultaneously merge – becoming one – absorbed by the *Alpha/Omega – the Omega Point.*"

The mood of the crowd grew more and more ominous. During this portion of AC4's presentation the four small, white haired men were silently projecting visual evidence, documentation, charts and graphs onto the large and small screens.

"Men of Science, colleagues, we are no longer dealing with theory. Nor are we postulating the hypothetical. The *Omega Point* is not one *possibility* among many. It is *actuality, the only actuality.*"

He paused, just briefly, then continued speaking. Sometimes, silence speaks louder than words, and more effectively.

"Your second syllabus, which is now being distributed, is titled *'Omega Point.'* This syllabus contains conceptual discussions about the *Omega Point,* sources documenting concepts, parameters and purposes of each study, their overlaps and disparities with other applicable concepts and how the concepts have been empirically verified. Research questions, methodologies, variables, results, including magnitude, statistical significance, extent of cross-verification, conclusions, and implications are also in the syllabus."

At this point Chancellor Tarrou interjected himself back into the conversation. He spoke slowly, with a slurred voice. Though he had trouble enunciating his words clearly as he attempted to speak, everyone could understand what he was saying. He was clearly still under the influence of the paraldehyde injections.

"Vectors? Vectors, Monsieur?" he said. "Your vectors are meaningless… meaningless lines that form a cage, a cage that traps you in an intellectual prison of your own making. *Apocalyptic nightmare? Alpha/Omega? Omega Point.* I said it before, Monsieur, and now I say it again – *this is Metaphysical Madness. Sheer Metaphysical Madness.*"

With a wave of the hand that symbolically dismissed Tarrou, AC4 resumed speaking.

"I apologize, colleagues. There is something in human nature that causes resistant to change. We hesitate, cling to our *old clothes* -- our irrational fears and our inconsistent ideologies. We embrace incoherence and existential anxieties as we shrink back, retreat and withdraw into the old, into the comfortable, into the familiar. We like familiar landmarks. *We like old clothes.*

"Tarrou is blind, blind to this singular fact: something extraordinary is happening. Like Tarrou, we can close our eyes -- *and lament our blindness.*

"Know this: reality has not changed. It is our understanding of reality that has changed. And today, today, in this present moment we are not bigger men because of our new understanding, nor are we bigger because of our new knowledge. We are smaller, smaller than we have ever been.

"Look around you. Weep. Our wisest statesmen, our most learned educators, our most accomplished scientists, and our most astute philosophers, the world's best and the world's brightest, all assembled here in this building. And, what do we see? We see the darkness. Stunned by what we have seen, stunned by what we have heard -- *we stand mute* – smaller, yes smaller, smaller than we have ever been."

A loud, booming voice from above suddenly shouted, startling everyone.

"There is one who can help us."

The noise of shuffling feet moving as heads simultaneously turned upward, toward the loud sounding voice that filled the building.

It was Grand. It was Joseph Grand who spoke so loudly.

"Monsieur Camus," said Grand. "You say you see *darkness.* I say at the moment of darkness *light* is near. You speak of *smaller.* I see *larger.* Let us not be as small men standing on a whale, fishing for minnows. We have already caught the big fish.

"There is one who can help us. And, Monsieur. He is near, very near. He has taken the bait. We have caught the fish. He is near. He is here."

"Here? Who is here that can help us?" cried a voice from the second level. Once again, the noise of shuffling feet filled the room as all heads turned at the same time in the opposite direction toward the voice on the second level. "Who is it?" he cried, "Who is it?"

Once again heads whipped back toward Grand, rapidly, as his loud voice shouted his reply.

"He is the one who can help us. He is the one."

Joseph Grand, like a dull whitish shadow dissolving in and out of the light of his upper room, stood with his arm extended over his railing. At the end of that arm was his hand, pointing a long finger downward -- *at me.*

"He is the one. He is the one."

Every head now turned at the same time toward me. Hundreds of eyes stared at me. I was still strapped in my circulating surgical chair, rotating on the platform. Eventually, AC4's eyes met mine. Somehow, he spoke words that no one other than me could hear.

"I told you. I warned you. I want what is mine. The Psalm. A Psalm of the Apocalypse."

A very small red light began blinking. A tiny blinking red light. From the second level a voice, a now familiar challenging voice was heard – Jean Tarrou. Two of Tarrou's colleagues stood beside the Chancellor, one on either side, holding him up so that he could be seen as he spoke. His mind was clear yet his body was still weak from the *paraldehyde* injections.

"He is the one. He is the one." mocked Jean Tarrou. "He is the one. He is the one. You, Monsieur Grand, and you, Monsieur AC4, seem to imply that which we feared. Our fear? That there is an underlying belief held by the leaders of this symposium, a underlying belief that the universe is an outward physical expression of an unseen omniscient, omnipotent, metaphysical transcendent reality – *God.*

"'He is the one. He is the one,' you declare concerning this pastor, this man of faith. What does this declaration – *He is the one.* – what does this declaration mean?

"I will tell you what it means, Monsieur." continued Tarrou. "It means this, hear me, Men of Science, if indeed this man of faith is the one, then once again science must turn to something above science for redemption. Once again science must turn to something outside science for salvation. Once again science must turn to something beyond science for deliverance. You speak of *old clothes,* Monsieur. Your kind of thinking is a detour, a detour that will lead science to embrace that which is the byproduct of a misguided, collective religious consciousness that lingers from mankind's unenlightened, historic past. I'll have none of it, none of it."

The two uniformed military officers appeared again. Pushing Tarrou's colleagues aside they began reaching for Tarrou in order to force him back into his chair.

Someone yelled out from one of the observation rooms, "Let him speak." Another small group of people from the opposite side of the building then started shouting, in unison, "Let him speak. Let him speak. Let him speak."

As the shouting subsided AC4 resumed speaking, directly to the Chancellor, with the symposium participants overhearing the conversation.

"Monsieur Tarrou," shouted AC4, "Like you, I affirm the fundamental tenets of science, naturalism, and secularism. What is your problem, Monsieur? What is your problem? You have repeatedly disrupted and hindered the progress of this symposium. What is your problem?"

Tarrou seized the moment, the momentum and the microphone, a strategic mistake on the part of AC4. Open-ended, undefined questions place the control of the content in the hands of your opponent, and Chancellor Tarrou had become AC4's primary component.

"My problem? My problem?" shouted Tarrou into the microphone, "My problem is the same problem that I posed earlier, Monsieur. What has science to do with religion? And, what does this man of religion have to do with we men of science? I object, I vehemently object, I vigorously object and I will continuously object to this metaphysical madness."

"Monsieur Tarrou," shouted AC4 in response, "Like you, I too am a man of science. I too am committed to the scientific method and empirical observation. There is no metaphysical madness here, Monsieur – only this empirically verifiable scientific fact: an eschatological concluding event is near, very near. *It is unavoidable and inevitable. It is an irreversible actuality.*"

Before Chancellor Tarrou could reply a fierce argument and a scuffle broke out in one of the upper observation rooms. Some participants were strongly committed to the rubric of AC4; others were swayed by Tarrou. Military police wearing blue uniforms rushed into the upper decks in an attempt to quell the scuffle and restore order.

A handcuffed physicist from the University of Wisconsin-Madison, whose nose was bleeding, was accompanied by two security guards away from the symposium to a medical aide center. He was in a frenzied state, kicking wildly while shouting…

"What does this man of religion have to do with we men of science?"

The hostile tone and loudness of his voice would rise, then fall.

"What does this man of religion have to do with we men of science?"

Hisses and shouts were directed by rowdy participants in some of the upper observation rooms. Some were directed toward the handcuffed physicist. Others were directed toward the security police. Still others, toward AC4.

"What does this man of religion have to do with we men of science? What does this man of religion have…."

As the sound of the physicist's shouting grew dimmer, fading more and more into the distance, others stood in his stead. They shouted, one louder than the other, competing one with another in an effort to be heard. It was sheer pandemonium as one person after another shouted, louder and louder, competing for center stage. Small red lights were blinking and continued blinking, feverously, as the echoing voices yelled back and forth.

"A Psalm of the Apocalypse. We must have it."

"He is the one who can help us. He is the one."

"What does this man of religion have to do with we men of science?"

"Metaphysical madness." "Metaphysical madness."

"We must have it. A Psalm of the Apocalypse."

"He is the one. He is the one. He is the one."

"I told you. I warned you. I want what is mine."

"Metaphysical madness." "Metaphysical madness."

"I want what is mine." "I want what is mine."

"A Psalm of the Apocalypse. We must have it."

"He is the one who can help us. He is the one."

"Metaphysical madness."

"I want what is mine."

Someone, a tall, slender man, jumped from a second level observation room into the surgical arena. He was running towards the platform where

AC4, Dr. Rieux, Dr. Castel and I were located. Military police captured then removed him from the building after a brief scuffle. It was the tall man, the nervous, American psychiatrist from Johns Hopkins Hospital. Evidently he had overcome his fears and social anxieties.

Many of the arguments became physical, sordid brawls. Sordid. It was sordid, undeniably sordid. Some cussed. Others shouted with uncontrollable rage.

Two scientists began wildly attacking each other as a circle of their colleagues edged them on -- shouting blasphemies. Some pushed. Some shoved. Some punched. This contemptible behavior was beneath the dignity of such high caliber global citizens. Nevertheless, it was happening. Men of science, men of intellect, were being ruled by their passion – and their proclivities. It was a horrid display of degrading human behavior.

More military police arrived to restore order. The increased presence of military police increased the level of fear, sparking more angry outbursts. One woman angrily shouted to no one in particular, "Metaphysical Madness? What justifies this madness?" She repeated her questions over and over again as she repeatedly moved her hand back and forth across the face of the crowd. "What justifies this madness?"

Swinging and punching wildly, and shoving each other into one another, I felt like I was witnessing a street fight. It was hard to believe that this was the world's best, the world's brightest. But, it was.

All of a sudden the entire building shook, then shuddered with a long drawn out shaking. The shuddering and shaking was accompanied by a sound, a thunderous sound like that of a loud explosion. A protracted continuation of that first massive, explosive sound rumbled throughout the entire building. The substructure and walls creaked, several times, rhythmically, as the building swayed. Then the initial shaking and swaying gradually slowed, then stopped completely, just for a few seconds, only to be followed by another explosion. Its force and sound shook the entire building with even greater force. A loud roar, like that of heavy, thick thunder, continued to reverberate and vibrate through the building. *Something was happening. But, I did not know what was happening.* Whatever it was it certainly couldn't be ignored. Everyone else in the building, however, was unaware that something was transpiring. Something terrible was happening, yet, no one was aware of it except me.

The low repetitious sound of rumbling continued, but no one could feel or sense the rumbling – *but me.* There was a flash, a bright flash of light flickering, but no one was aware of this – *but me.*

I could hear the muffled voices of AC4 and Grand as they continued shouting, attempting to dialogue with the disgruntled crowd. I could see the violent madness of the symposium as it continued to unfold. As Grand and AC4 continued their efforts to end the chaos and confusion the four small, white haired men aggressively continued their visual projections. They were completely unaware of the shuddering, of the shaking, of the swaying of the building, and of the explosions. And there, to my left, was Rieux and beside him, Castel. They were busily engaged in efforts to restore calmness. I could see the military police. I could hear them shouting commands as they continued their attempts to restore order. They gave no indications that they were aware of the explosions or anything connected with the explosions. Yet, as the shaking and rattling of the building continued, and as the flickering of the lights happened over and over, again and again, it became more and more apparent that I was the only one aware of any of this.

RESTORE POINT 23:

METAPHYSICAL DISRUPTIONS

Suddenly, the entire front of the Defense Advanced Research Projects building collapsed, turning in upon itself; or, I should say that it appeared to collapse. I say appeared because what made this collapse most unusual is that the Defense Advanced Research Projects facility was an underground facility. Nevertheless, I know what I heard and I know what I saw.

I heard a terrible noise, a shuddering, shaking explosive sound, the harrowing sound of a building collapsing, and then I saw debris and dust rising and rolling, blanketing everything, like a heavy thick rolling dust cloud. The front of the building, underground or not, crumbled, then totally collapsed. Even so, I could still vaguely see and hear the symposium as it continued – as if nothing had happened. Again, no one attending the symposium was aware of what was happening – *except me.*

As the dust and debris gradually settled I could see a pale orange-streaked darkness slowly spreading across an even darker evening sky. The front and top of the building were completely destroyed – gone. A great dull, flat light, the moon, began to show its familiar face as it slowly rose higher into the night sky. In a strange, fascinating way, the moon cast long haunting shadows that created an eerie glow as twilight mingled with night. The long shadows produced a dreamlike ambiance, with contrasting shades and rolling streaks of colors, deep blacks, bright whites, and bluish-grays.

In the distance I began to hear a chorus of voices singing, singing in Italian the words *"Te Deum. Te Deum. Te Deum. Thee, O God, we praise. Te Deum. Te Deum. Te Deum. Thee, O God, we praise."* It had the nostalgic feel of a memory, or of a dream, with the sound of sweet music heard long ago.

As the singing continued I began to think about something AC4 had said during an earlier portion of the symposium: *"These strands of reality are hidden and unseen by the natural eye until one actually enters into the alternative reality."*

I wondered, Was this some strange no-man's land between parallel realms? Had I in some mysterious way entered into an *alternative reality?* Had I somehow crossed into a *parallel universe*?

I also remembered AC4 saying that *"Sometimes the autonomous strands become entangled, producing instability, creating metaphysical disruptions."* AC4 also said that *"When this occurs the tangled threads are untangled by the intervention of the Alpha/Omega, the controlling strand."*

Could I anticipate some type of intervention? Should I? Was I caught in some type of time warp? Was this AC4's *metaphysical disruption?*

> *"Te Deum. Te Deum. Te Deum. Thee, O God, we praise."*
> *"Te Deum. Te Deum. Te Deum. Thee, O God, we praise."*

The singing gradually faded, diminishing into the distance. It was as if some invisible conductor leading an off-stage choir and orchestra had slowly brought his hand down signaling a *diminuendo.* The rumbling of the building ceased. In the distance I could hear the retreating, dull roll of thunder. Lightning once again flashed, a bluish-white stretching across the darkening night sky, from the east like long fingers reaching toward the west. As it flashed I saw an imposing very tall, square tower. The Christian cross, the symbol of the eternal, ever-present Christ, stood resiliently atop a steeple. The tower, like a strong, silent sentinel, was shrouded in stone. A slender beam of light, a singular light, pierced the darkness, shining downward.

A clap, a powerful startling clap of thunder rumbled again. It was immediately followed by another brilliant burst of lightning. The lightning flash enabled me to see two massive, wooden doors at the base of the old stone tower. Strange sounds, sounds of iron grating and screeching behind the large wooden doors leaked to the outside. The noise of gigantic gears turning, straining to draw back the large iron bolts that locked the doors, screeched and squealed, piercing the night air. This unbolting of the massive doors was immediately followed by a jangling sound as heavy rusted chains strained and creaked, each pulling in its own direction, prying open the massive doors.

As the great doors were slowly opened, I heard the stomping of horses, three large white Friesian horses. Behind them I saw heaven standing open and there, behind the first three horses, was a fourth, even larger, white Arabian-like horse. Beside him, holding the reigns of the horse tightly, was a man, silent, tall, dressed in a silvery-white cloak and hood. He simply stood there. He did nothing. He said nothing. He simply stood and stared intently at me.

The first three horses continued walking, slowly walking toward me. As they lifted their legs high, their bodies, half in darkness, half in light, and their gait, took on an aristocratic like air. Their heavy hooves thudded and clopped along a shiny, rain-soaked black cobblestones street. The solid, hard sound of their hooves caused the platform and my surgical chair to rattle, vibrate and shake. The wisps of swirling light hovered around each of the horses, playing over their chiseled muscular bodies. Around them, light and darkness -- and lifeless waste.

Three tall men, wearing cloaks and hoods, walked in silence beside each of the Friesian horses. Their cloaks and hoods were silvery-white. They were sharp-featured men, with a defining look of distinction, dignity and character. They resembled the spray-painted Silver Statue men in the *French Quarters* of New Orleans. As they slowly walked toward me they held the reins of the horses tightly, occasionally yanking the biteless bridles to keep the horses walking in unison. I could see the body heat and vapor of the horses as they methodically continued their slow, relentless march toward me. I could hear and I could see their breath escaping through their terribly large nostrils.

Each of the first three men, with his other hand, clutched and held high a crooked stick. Fixed atop their sticks were torches, orange flamed torches of dancing fire. The flames threw long orange shadows everywhere as the fire flickered in the draught created by the open doors.

As lightning flashed yet again I could see that each of the first three horses was hitched to what appeared to be large old wooden-wheeled wagons, funeral carriages. Atop each carriage was a plain wooden casket. They suddenly stopped, the men and the horses stopped. The men gazed at me in silence.

The man in the middle said something to the other two men, then slowly started walking toward me. He hesitated as he neared the rotating platform. The glare of swirling white dust, the wisps of light and rolling fog mingled and rolled around him, blinding me, hindering me from seeing his face.

The sense of mystery deepened as an exceptional play of light and shadow danced around him as he stepped onto the rotating platform. He then knelt down in front of me. His silvery-white cloak had an insignia across the chest; an insignia that featured an eagle, a winged man, an ox and a lion, symbols of the *four evangelists.* [80] As he knelt before me I heard his firm voice speak, directly to me.

"The Noble Army of the Martyrs Salute Thee. TE DEUM"

There was a familiarity there, in what I saw, his face, and in what I heard, his voice. I tried to speak, but could not.

"No worry," I heard him say. "I can hear what you wish to say."

My voice was silent, yet I heard myself speaking to him. I heard my voice. Speaking, inside my head -- and *somehow he heard me.*

"Are you one of the souls from under the altar? I saw the Souls of the Martyrs under the Altar. White Robes. White Robes were given unto every one of them. White Robes."

"You reached the Fifth Seal, John, you reached the Fifth Seal."

"I saw the Souls of the Martyrs under the Altar. White Robes. White Robes were given unto every one of them."

"You must go back, John. You must go back."

"Is that man, that man in the back by that big white horse, is he a soul from under the altar?"

"He is the *Angel of the Apocalypse,* John. *The Angel of the Apocalypse.* The white horse is for the One who is called *Faithful and True.*[81] He will come forth following the death of the last martyr. You must go back, John. You must go back, back to the Fifth Seal."

"Go back? Why must I go back?"

"An old man is dying, John. He, the last martyr of the New Testament age, is dying. Two, after him, will taste death – they, the first among many.

See -- The Just Man –
Struggling For Breath

Running to Certain Death
He, a Martyr, the Last, Runs, Yet Not Alone
Nor for sin does he Atone -- But for Fear
It crawls down his cheek, a tear
At his Death, Two Olive Trees, They Appear.
End Time Prophets. Slain. The Second Woe.
The first shall be last and the last first
Shiv`a.

"The last martyr?"

"Of this dispensation, yes. He is the last martyr of the New Testament age. The other men, the two standing beside the horse drawn caskets, are the two witnesses, God's end time prophets who, like olive trees, will stand and prophesy for twelve hundred and sixty days, clothed in sackcloth.[82] They will be killed, martyred, during the time of Jacob's trouble. They are the first martyrs who suffer martyrdom during the time of Jacob's trouble."

"Are you one of the souls from under the altar? I saw the Souls of the Martyrs under the Altar. White Robes. White Robes were given unto every one of them. White Robes."

"No, John, I am not. I am *Leitourgós.* We first met in your church sanctuary, long ago. It was then that your journey began, John. It all began then. It began there. You reached the Fifth Seal, John, you reached the Fifth Seal – six times. Fear held you back."

"Leitourgós? Leitourgós, I saw the Souls of the Martyrs under the Altar. White Robes. White Robes were given unto every one of them."

"You must go back, John. You must go back. This is the seventh and final time."

"Go back? Why must I go?"

"You must set fire to the seventh, final copy of *A Psalm of the Apocalypse* by casting it into fire in the *Candle.* The flames and smoke from its burning will trigger the *eschatos.* The seventh, final parchment is with the boy, John the Younger. You must go back, John. You must go back. Even now the evil one is plotting to gain possession of the final copy."

"I will go back. I will go back."

"The Noble Army of the Martyrs Salute Thee. TE DEUM."

"I will. I will go back."

"In thh, thh, the Candle – in the dar, darkness
A slen, slender flame leaps – in soll, soll, solitude.

One, becomes many, bu, bu, burning bright.
A lab, labyrinth leads the way, but not in the light of day."

Everything suddenly disappeared. *Leitourgós,* the horses, the caskets, the white cloaked, hooded men, the large wooden gates, the tower -- everything connected to the experience was gone -- except the sound of my voice echoing in my head....

"I will. I will go back."

"The Noble Army of the Martyrs Salute Thee. TE DEUM."

"I will go back."

"I will. I will go back."

I was shocked as I heard the words of AC4 and the symposium participants. Someone in the crowd was yelling, "We must have *A Psalm of the Apocalypse.* We must have *A Psalm of the Apocalypse.* We must have...."

It was then that I heard AC4's words matching mine.

AC4 shouted, "I will. I will go back."

Inside my head I was shouting....

"I will. I will go back."

"I will. I will go back."

"I will. I will go back."

Applause. Loud Applause. Cheers. More Applause.
The Sound, the Echoing Sound, of Fading Distant Applause.
A Distant Flash of Light.

RESTORE POINT 24:

BUTTERFLY EFFECT

Physicists, scientists, and others have discussed and written about the so-called *butterfly effect,* a philosophical premise closely associated with *chaos theory.* The *butterfly effect* hypothesizes that in a sufficiently complex system, like a weather system, for instance, a small cause -- the flapping of butterfly wings on the African coast – could conceivably have a disproportionately larger effect than any could anticipate -- the creation of a hurricane in the Gulf of Mexico.

In relation to history the *butterfly effect* postulates that an insignificant person or a minor event can conceivably have a great, far-reaching ripple effect beyond that which anyone could possibly imagine. These ripples have the potential to create subsequent, unforeseen effects and events of great historical consequence.

In popular culture the *butterfly effect* has become a *metaphor* to illustrate how obscure moments shape history and how insignificant people of little or no consequence can actually alter, affect or afflict the future. In practice the *butterfly effect* creates hidden threads of cause and effect that only appear obvious in retrospect as the consequential effects ripple forward through time and circumstance.

Someone, a preacher friend, once said that the hinges of history swing on the insignificant. The focus of that statement was not on history, nor on the hinges of history, nor on the swing of history – *but on the insignificant.* God often uses insignificant people in insignificant corners of the world to accomplish great things of historical significance. Imagine that. The hinges of history swing on the *insignificant.*

Butterflies are certainly insignificant. And so are small boys. Which brings me to John the Younger. Was he, metaphorically speaking, a *butterfly?*

Was John the Younger simply an insignificant boy in an insignificant corner of the world? And if so, did something of great historical significance swing on this insignificant boy? When I first came to *Christ Cathedral* the sickly old woman from the kitchen who had given me a cup of coffee and a biscuit told me that John the Younger was a boy, a small, insignificant boy of no consequence.

But, was she making a correct assessment? Just who is this boy – this John the Younger – who is he? He evidently likes to write poems. When I was a boy I used to write poems too, especially religious poems. Whoever this John the Younger is, I must confess, at this point I knew very little about him. I do know that he is only a boy. I also know he is destined to live a long life. *Leitourgós* shared while we were at the *Defense Advanced Research Projects Building* in Virginia that John the Younger had grown old and was at that point -- *dying.*

My first goal was to locate this boy, John the Younger. He was evidently more significant than the old woman realized. At least one of his poems – *A Psalm of the Apocalypse* – has great value, gained modest notoriety, and increased in significance because of its linkage to apocalyptic events -- AC4, realizing this, was desperate to have the seventh, last, final copy. *Leitourgós* stressed that I must destroy that seventh, final copy by setting it on fire. He said that the flames and smoke from its burning would trigger the *eschatos,* and, it appeared that *A Psalm of The Apocalypse* was saying the same thing.

In *the Candle* – in the darkness
A slender flame leaps – in solitude.
Its flame. Its flame.
With fiery mouth thunders.
Eschatos. Eschatos.
It Hungers. Hungers.
Its tongue, a flame, hungers.
Eschatos. Eschatos.
Shiv`a

Leitourgós said that the location of the seventh, final parchment, was known only to the boy, John the Younger.

The logical, safe place to begin my search for John the Younger to gain access to the seventh parchment was the old woman. When she and I finally met she shared shocking news -- Father Paneloux had died while I was absent.

It saddened me that I was unable to be here for Paneloux while he was in such emotional pain as he approached death. When we were together last Paneloux was in despair. Our conversation about the reality of his existence led him to doubt everything that gave his life meaning and purpose. He doubted himself. He doubted his existence. He doubted his faith. He doubted his God. He doubted life and simply chose to die. Because he died of inexplicable cause and not the plague Rieux diagnosed and recorded on his death certificate that Father Paneloux was a *"doubtful case"*. Angry, alone, depressed, in despair, he chose to die -- it must have been a terribly horrible experience. He was a shattered, broken man – caught in a life and death struggle with doubt and existential despair.

When I was last here, at *Christ Cathedral*, Dr. Rieux announced that he, Father Paneloux and I would be dining with a special guest later that evening – Albert Camus.

Needless to say, Albert Camus did not keep that dinner engagement. Neither did I. Dr. Rieux and Father Paneloux dined that evening, with Albert Camus, but not *the* Albert Camus. They dined with AC4, Albert Camus IV. According to the old woman Joseph Grand, Raymond Rambert, and elderly Dr. Castel also attended the dinner.

"I was shocked by what I was hearing at the dinner meeting," shared Castel, "and so too was Father Paneloux."

Dr. Castel and I met at *Christ Cathedral* at the insistence of the old woman. She felt that Castel would be helpful to me in locating John the Younger. Castel and I sat in a stuffy, small alcove, a recessed room with pillars and draperies on one side that separated the recessed area from an even smaller room filled with choir robes. The alcove was on the second floor, near the narrow spiral staircase that led into a vestibule at the rear of the sanctuary of *Christ Cathedral.* The old woman served us hot tea as we talked.

"The thrust of the dinner conversation that evening," shared Castel, "focused on geopolitical control, global economic redistribution of wealth and population management – on a scale surpassing anything I could have imagined."

I felt my eyes narrowing as I looked at Dr. Castel. As he continued speaking I wondered -- *Could this man be trusted?*

"The command center to implement this globalized plan is located in something called the *Defense Advanced Research Projects Building,* an underground facility located somewhere in the United States."

My eyes widened when he mentioned the *Defense Advanced Research Projects Building.* Dr. Castel had been there. I had been there. In that very facility he stood with Rieux and AC4 on the circulating platform near my surgical chair. He administered anesthesia, hypnotic and other psychotropic drugs to me. Yet, he talked as if I knew nothing about that facility.

Drawing on God's leadership, trusting your gut and using the wisdom of experience are important for crisis resolution. *Choices have consequences.* Ignoring God's leadership, stifling His inward promptings, resisting His nudges and intuitions create ambiguity, produce indecisiveness and facilitate hesitation. Encouraged by these three forces working within me I spoke very pointedly to Dr. Castel, without hesitation.

"Dr. Castel, why should I trust you?"

Castel shifted his position in his chair. The chair appeared to be uncomfortable – and so did he. He delicately wiped his forehead with his handkerchief. It was hot in the small alcove and the conversation was beginning to heat up. The muscles of his face were strained, tightly contorted. He appeared startled at my lack of hesitation in confronting the trust issue so early in our conversation.

"Monsieur," said the elderly Dr. Castel, "I have lived a long life. As a physician I have dealt with crisis, intense pressure, and with issues that were literally life or death. Like others I discovered that when life is dark, faith is bright, visible. In the darkness it is seen, like a star shining in the night. Like you, Monsieur, I too am a man of faith. Unlike you, my faith is not always as visible, at least not as visible as I would like. This lack of visibility leads you, no doubt, to ask this question of me."

He closed his eyes and suddenly grew silent, just for a moment.

"*So, why should you trust me?* Monsieur, let me begin first by saying that without risk-taking, there can be no trust. Trust is risk dressed as choice.

You either give or withhold trust. The choice and the risks are yours as to whether you give or withhold."

I learned long ago that trust and risk, indeed, are always imbedded in choice. People who fear risk usually have difficulties with trust and as a consequence avoid choice. Nevertheless, risk is a frontier that one must choose to cross on the way to the Promised Land of trust. I looked directly into the elderly man's eyes as I carefully chose to take yet another step toward trust.

"Trust, as you say, Monsieur Castel, is often given – and often withheld. I would also add that trust is also something that is built. You say you are a man of faith. Why should I believe such a thing. Is it not said that men of faith are known by their fruit – their deeds of goodness."

"Yes. Yes. I agree, Monsieur. Let me respond by sharing that there was a time in the life of the apostle Paul when he was not recognized as a man of faith. Yet, he did not hesitate to defend himself and give proof to verify the validity of his faith. Do know that I am not comparing myself to Paul. Like Paul, however, I will not hesitate to defend myself in this matter of faith."

Castel was suddenly speaking with the fervor of a new convert. His voice was filled with what appeared to be genuine spiritual enthusiasm.

"Look carefully, Monsieur, in the narrative of the plague that afflicted the Algerian city of Oran. The narrative, as you know, was written by Albert Camus and is recorded in the novel titled *The Plague.* Look carefully and you will see that I, Castel, was always busy doing good. In a time of great crisis I, Castel brought forth good fruit, Monsieur. *I brought forth good fruit.*

"The development of the anti-plague serum was my *mission,* my personal *ministry* project, my call from God. Camus would not describe my efforts as *ministry*, nor use ecclesial language in his narrative for atheistic reasons that are obvious to you.

"When Monsieur Othon's son died, look carefully, Monsieur. Read Camus' narrative. I too was there. You do not mention my presence in your narrative of the child's death at *Christ Cathedral* – but, I was there – bringing with me the peace of Christ. Camus, in *The Plague,* described my presence at Oran in this way, and these are his words, Monsieur. These are the words of Albert Camus: *'Castel was seated, reading, with every appearance of calm, an old leather-bound book.'* [83] Camus saw that I had an *appearance of calmness.* Camus, Monsieur, used secular descriptions – *appearance of calm* -- to describe *biblical peace*, an outward expression of the fruit of the Spirit. And what was that *leather-bound book,* Monsieur? It was a veiled reference to my Bible. Camus, as narrator of *The Plague,* with his atheistic leanings, would not, could not, make direct reference to the Bible, or my Bible reading or the *calmness* that the Spirit produced within me. For Camus to mention such things would conflict with the existential purpose of his written narrative and he would have none of that."

Castel continued speaking with a firm, enthusiastic voice, asserting himself, exuding confidence. His command of language, his expressions and his gestures made his ability to speak and testify seem effortless. He was calm and confident, speaking with authority.

"Look again, carefully, Monsieur. You have been writing a narrative account of what transpired at *Christ Cathedral* and at the *Defense Advanced Research Projects Building.* Reflect and recall my deeds, deeds of compassion -- a glass of water given, several times over, and protection for you and your dignity in your time of affliction at the defense facility."

Sometimes people have hidden skills, assets that they do not readily utilize, for whatever reason. Dr. Castel was apparently gifted with the ability to think logically and persuasively communicate what he was thinking. Up to this point this was a hidden asset.

"You say, Monsieur, that trust is something that is built. Again, I agree. Words, Monsieur, all I have at this time are words, words that bear true testimony to the fruit of my deeds. Words are my bricks. My testimony is my mortar. Perhaps my words of testimony – my brick and mortar -- can build trust. I have nothing else to offer. You see, your trust, as I said earlier, can either be given or withheld, Monsieur. That choice, and the consequential risks of that choice, is yours."

Experience is the best teacher. How many times have I heard that? How many times have I said that? *Experience is the best teacher.* No one, however, can gain experience without choice and risk. I can act as tough as nails, exude masculinity, even mask and hide my fears, but experience has not shaped me into that false image. That self-created macho image is not who I am. No.

Whatever I do in life and wherever I go in life, circumstance, experience and choice reveal who I am. Once I know who I am, I must be true to myself and not be misled by some illusionary false image of myself. This gives me faith in myself, the kind of faith that enables me to place faith and trust in others. Experience, therefore, is not what happens to a man but what a man does with what happens to him – *grow in faith and trust.* Dr. Castel used what had happened to him to build a testimony, a testimony that was now building trust.

"Perhaps, perhaps trust between us can yet be built, Monsieur, let us continue our conversation with that as our goal. Continue speaking, Dr. Castel. Continue speaking. Tell me more about this dinner."

"Let me then continue, Monsieur, by adding that ever since that dinner meeting I have been rather subversive, working undercover. This is not in my nature, Monsieur. I'm not normally a 'snoopish' person. Nevertheless, my long term effectiveness in this endeavor depends on my not being recognized as subversive. Quiet assessment has been an integral part of what I have been and continue to do. I do my best to avoid looking suspicious. I try to be inconspicuous while keeping my eyes and ears open, constantly attentive, always attempting to decipher developments. Quiet assessment, Monsieur, quiet assessment."

As Dr. Castel spoke I remembered a man of faith in the Old Testament portion of the Bible who was placed by God in a position of power in the palace of the rebellious King Ahab and his wicked wife, Jezebel. Obadiah, who had oversight of the palace, was a subversive, working undercover for God. When Elijah raised Jezebel's ire by defeating the prophets of Baal at Mt. Carmel, Jezebel decided to kill Elijah and the prophets of God. Obadiah, even though he worked in a highly visible position, managed to hide fifty prophets of God in a cave and fed them until he could smuggle them to safety. Once the first group of fifty was saved, he did it again with another fifty.

Obadiah was one of God's secret agents. He was careful to protect his identity and avoided arousing suspicion. He was able to remain calm when under duress while he worked in the midst of constant danger. He made a choice, a choice filled with great risk, embracing the consequences, for one reason and one reason only -- *He trusted God.* I wondered, *Could it be that Dr. Castel is one of God's secret agents – an Obadiah.* I began to think that he was – with his words and his testimony, his bricks and mortar – *he was building and gaining my trust.*

"Well, Monsieur, as the dinner discussion continued, Father Paneloux was appalled, and became increasingly more and more indignant. His mood was nasty, as nasty as any I'd ever seen. As he stood, preparing to leave, he threw his napkin on the dining table. Then he spoke, angrily.

'This whole scheme has a godless, apocalyptic slant to it' said Paneloux. He was visibly upset with what he had heard about global population control and threatened to notify the authorities."

I've often heard it said that anger lies at the base of depression and that depression is actually destructive, toxic anger, turned inward. Father Paneloux was already angry and depressed from our earlier conversation. Perhaps his explosive anger was an outward expression of the inward accumulation of smoldering emotion that he could contain no longer, a depression so deep, so dark, that it led to his own death.

"Paneloux became like an angry madman, a stranger that none of us knew," added Dr. Castel. "None of us had ever seen him behave this way – he was overflowing with anger, filled with hostility, even shouting foul blasphemies. As he turned to leave the dinner meeting he threatened a second time to notify the authorities.

AC4, in an act of desperation, attempted to barter for Paneloux's silence by promising him a promotion to an upper echelon position among the Catholic hierarchy in Rome. Paneloux became even angrier at AC4's suggestion, shouting belligerently as he walked away."

"I will not stand before God stained with the sin of *simony.* I will not."

"With that he walked out. Everyone was stunned to silence, startled by this uncharacteristic outburst by Paneloux. As he was leaving the old woman returned and refilled our wine gasses. We sipped our wine silently for a period of time and then the conversation continued."

As Dr. Castel resumed talking about the dinner conversation it became apparent that whoever or whatever forces were behind the global control plot were, at least at this point, unknown. Whoever was leading this scheme had their identity shrouded in secrecy – and silence.

"No one said anything or gave any indication concerning who or what was driving this globalization plan," related Castel. "I did not know who was leading this movement. I don't think any of the others knew either."

"I was under the impression that AC4 was the ring leader. Evidently you feel differently."

"I do. I do feel differently. AC4 has too many questions and too few answers to be the point man for this endeavor. Too many questions that he often refers to others. Too few answers in that he depends on others for answers that a leader would normally provide. No. Ultimately, leadership at the very top doesn't work that way."

He stretched his arms above his head momentarily, then as he placed his hands on his lap, he chewed on the inside of his lip for a long second, before speaking again.

"AC4 is, in a sense, the voice of the movement, Monsieur, he is the public mouthpiece. He is rather adept at public speaking, very persuasive, and seems ideally equipped to lead the symposium and coordinate public relations. He also has a comprehensive knowledge of science, physics and cutting-edge technologies."

Castel scratched the back of his head as he thought about and talked about his experience with AC4. He really wanted to be as accurate as possible in drawing conclusions. AC4 was involved in a scheme that had the potential to alter the course of world history. That involvement and its potential required a correct, accurate assessment of AC4's strengths and weaknesses as a leader and his assets and liabilities as a leader.

"AC4 lacks the organizational skills," said Castel. "He lacks the organizational skills to pull off something of this magnitude. Drawing on the technological strengths of Grand, AC4 demonstrated an ability to organize a syllabus, and, coordinate a symposium. But when I consider the massiveness of this global initiative I just can't convince myself that AC4 has the organizational ability necessary to be at the helm. He's near the top of the leadership structure but he's not leading the inner core, if there is one – and I believe there is."

We both agreed that the whole affair was also far too sophisticated for Rambert. Raymond Rambert was not the mastermind. He has a brilliant mind – *but is not the mastermind.*

"Raymond Rambert is a journalist," shared Dr. Castel, "a darn good journalist from Paris. He's the kind of guy who matured through his experience at Oran. That maturity led him to further his education. His exposure to philosophy helped him to mature further. Through philosophy he has honed his skill to think things through and develop conclusions – and philosophy has helped him develop a social conscience. He now feels that a societal problem is everyone's problem, in general, and, his problem, in particular. He did not, of course, always feel that way. He was selfish, self-centered and concerned only about himself when we first met in Oran. Now he's more other-oriented.

"Even though he's maturing, he's still a follower, not yet a leader. In the early stages of the quarantine at Oran, Rambert appeared to be a man who wanted to do the right thing; but, he seldom did the right thing. Everything was about him. For a long period of time, while we were quarantined, he would do flip-flops, up one day, down the next. Consequently, his level of commitment vacillated. He talked often about love and his love for a girl in Paris, but love, or perhaps I should say, the idea of love, was in his head, not in his heart. Genuine love, Monsieur, generates unwavering passion for what is right.

"When I first met Raymond Rambert at Oran he was a passionless man. His only passion was for the girl in Paris. As I stated earlier he was inclined to do the right thing only because it was the right thing. He has, of course, changed since Oran. The plague had that maturing effect on many of us. But his growth and maturity is yet too recent to qualify him for ultimate leadership. He was passive, as I said, and lacked passion when we first met. Because his change is so recent I'm convinced that he does not yet have the emotional strength or stamina to persevere at the helm of such a massive project as this. I find that he has limited expertise in many of the fields necessary to provide ultimate leadership. Like Dr. Rieux, Raymond Rambert interprets his participation in this globalization scheme as his duty to mankind. For him it just feels like the right thing to do."

Dr. Castel shrugged one shoulder. He seemed pensive, and somewhat apprehensive as he began to think about Dr. Rieux. He and Dr. Rieux were colleagues in Oran. As medical practitioners, they had developed a mutual respect. Castel had known Rieux for many, many years and held him in high esteem, until this latest episode at the defense facility.

"Rieux, as I just shared, sees what is transpiring as, not so much his duty, but as his mission, at least at this moment in time. Rieux usually finishes what he begins -- his *'projects'* as he calls them. For Dr. Rieux these *'projects'* give his life meaning. That's why he became a physician. That's why the plague in Oran became his mission. Rieux is a man who looks for projects that demand something of him. It is his reaction to challenge that led him to *Christ Cathedral* and to the defense facility in Virginia."

Atheistic existentialism had convinced Rieux that life ultimately has no inherent meaning and that there was no such thing as absolute moral right or wrong. Man, according to Rieux, rather than search for inherent meaning has to create his own meaning. And, rather than discover and conform to some external absolute moral code, each man has to determine and develop his own moral consensus. Once those two aspirations are accomplished they merge and find expression through social projects, doing good, helping others. These man-created special projects consolidate and constitute man's mission, at least according to Dr. Rieux. This man-centered mission satisfies the conscience as man's aspirations reach for something higher than himself – *the glory of man.*

"Rieux is an excellent leader, Monsieur, but not here. In this project he is a participant, a key participant, but not the ultimate leader. He simply is not the type to build something like this. However, I will say this about Rieux. He is an avowed atheist. In Oran he was what I would call an *ordinary atheist.* For some reason while at *Christ Cathedral* Dr. Rieux became an *ornery atheist.* He absolutely detests theism and has even greater distain for Christianity. I'm not sure about the inward motivation that fostered this increased hostility. But, nevertheless, Rieux is definitely not at the top either."

"Which leaves Grand."

"As the dinner conversation continued it became obvious to me," related Dr. Castel, "that Grand is in over his head. Grand, as you are aware, is notoriously corrupt. He seems to always find a way to make a profit off of the sufferings and misfortunes of others. His filthy fingerprints are all over everything, every aspect of this globalization plan. His technological skills and abilities provided Grand an opportunity to ascend to the upper echelon of this global change hierarchy – and ascend he did. But, again, Grand is not the head. His *Metaphoric MC* device has awesome, yet terrible potential. The *MC* stands for *Mind Control.* It also functions as a *Mind*

Copier. And, it can also be used to enhance *Mental Cognition*. It is the quality of his *MC device* that has propelled him to the top of the organization's infrastructure – but again not to the very top."

Deeply rooted anxieties and fears seemed to surface as Dr. Castel talked about the unbelievable capabilities of Grand's technology. Heroes are recognized by their deeds, by the things they do. Sometimes, however, it takes courage to simply be. The two, being and doing are inseparably linked. Both require courage. So here was the elderly Dr. Castel, troubled as anxieties and fears surfaced. Within him he heard the whisper of a voice, the voice of God -- *Be thou courageous, o man of God. Fear not.*

Castel cleared his throat then sat tall in his chair as he continued speaking.

"Nevertheless, we have nothing to fear in Grand. Grand is not the head. I fear, however, that he is dominated by invisible forces that have power over him. Whatever or wherever or whoever these powers are, Grand has certainly culled their favor as well as the favor of large segments of the population. The global community will eagerly follow Grand because of the blessings he has already provided and because of the benefits he promises to provide. Even now millions in Europe and in the North American continent are manipulated through his *MC device?*

"The underlying appeal of the *MC device,* Monsieur, is behavioral modification that uses a therapeutic technology you developed. I believe you called it *metaphorics* or *metaphorical thinking.* Grand amplified the power of this therapeutic behavior modification system to create rapid behavioral change. Using his technological talents and abilities Joseph Grand corrupted and converted metaphorical imagery, creating greater mind control capacities. He utilized the combined efforts of the psychological and psychiatric communities then merged them with the collaborative efforts of modern information processing technologies. This enhanced *metaphorics* effectiveness by accomplishing behavioral change, mind control and more."

I was struggling to contain my anger as Dr. Castel shared how Grand had misused *metaphorics*. Deep inside I began to feel some of the same feelings that afflicted Paneloux. No. I didn't want to die. Paneloux did, but I didn't. But, there was a part of me that wished Grand was dead.

I remember warning him, I distinctively remember warning Grand about the danger of this very thing, I told Grand that *there are many who see what you evidently do not yet see and they fear what you do not yet fear.'*

I remember warning Grand, as strongly as possible that *'this kind of unholy merger of mankind with technology - computerization, mechanization, automation, cybernation and other technologies - in an effort to achieve behavioral modification and change will have an unintended consequence, the mutation of man. And with mankind's mutation will come the loss of meaning and the abolition of morality.'*

Obviously, Grand chose not to heed my warning. In my absence after the incident at *Paw Paw's Plaza,* Grand actually stole and intentionally manipulated *metaphorics* – choosing greed and power -- to the detriment of all. My last words of warning to Grand when we discussed these wretched possibilities were that *'humanity can never, could never and must never bear such a burden."*

And now, the corrupt little mind of Joseph Grand has developed a scheme that will impose that burden upon the weary shoulders of humanity.

Who was it that was imposing this burden? Joseph Grand utilized technology to develop *MC devices* – but he was not the driving force behind this movement. Dr. Castel and I eliminated AC4, Joseph Grand, Raymond Rambert, and Dr. Rieux as the ultimate leader. Nevertheless, someone, some yet unknown leader was behind-the-scenes pulling the strings. Someone was at the helm. But who.

Perhaps it was a *Freudian slip*, perhaps not, but in my brain I heard the voice of AC4 mimicking a line from the *Wizard of Oz....*

"Pay no attention to that man behind the curtain." shouted AC4 inside my brain. "Pay no attention to that man."[84]

Whether this was a *Freudian slip* or not, it seemed to be some type of internal confirmation that we were on the right track – someone was behind the scenes – *behind the curtain – and that man, whoever he was, would eventually be seen.*

Someone, some yet unknown leader was behind-the-scenes pulling the strings. Someone was at the helm. But who?

The participants at the symposium appeared to be just that, participants. They were world leaders, global leaders, but none of them gave evidence of being the anonymous leader of this global takeover.

"Well, someone is in charge, Dr. Castel. Someone is leading this movement, that much is sure," I said.

"What we do know at this point is that a loosely connected, but enthusiastic, well-coordinated network of world leaders is united in a quiet conspiracy to create a global empire that places all nations of the world under one maniacal leader."

But, who is that leader?

"I do remember someone *whispering* a name, Monsieur. It struck me as odd when I heard this name because it is the name of the lead character in a philosophical novel written by the German philosopher Friedrich Nietzsche."

One of Friedrich Nietzsche's lead characters?

"Who was it?" I heard myself ask.

"Someone called -- *Zarathustra.*"

"Zarathustra?"

The air grew think and humid as a heavy presence, a sense of evil, seemed to fill the room. "I do not know if that is someone's real name, Monsieur, or if it is an allegorical signification."

I became silent as eerie sounding whispers echoed that name over and over in my head.

Zarathustra.
Zarathustra.
Zarathustra.
Allegorical Signification.
Zarathustra.

"I must find the boy, Dr. Castel. I must find the boy."

The whispering voices then began reciting a small portion of John the Younger's *A Psalm of the Apocalypse.*

Six, Imperfection, the Number of Man
Six thrice, Woe unto the Earth, the Beast
In the Latter Day, his Feast –
Six, Imperfection, the Number of Man
War Man at the End of Time
Zarathustra
An Image – A Symbol -- Who will understand?
Six thrice, the Number, the Beast, a Man
Shiv`a.

RESTORE POINT 25:

TWO PENCILS

The old woman from the kitchen returned once again, at just the right time. She smiled another tired smile as she slowly walked across the room to refresh our cups with more hot tea. As she served tea she began to repeat her now familiar refrain, "I old woman, foolish old woman. My eyes dim and is my mind too...... I old woman."

As she continued her mumbling I remembered something Dr. Rieux had said about her, "Always has a secret to tell, that one, always has a secret to tell."

Secrets to tell. People with secrets quite often know things that others do not. If anyone knows where the boy is, it would be this old woman. I had already concluded that the logical, safe place to begin my search for John the Younger was this old woman. My intuitions were now in high gear, nudging me, nudging me, urging me, to approach the old woman now.

"Mademoiselle, can you tell me, where is the boy, this John the Younger?"

"Shhh. Quiet, Monsieur, quiet. I old woman, foolish old woman."

She walked slowly, with deliberate, yet faltering steps, one careful step at a time, crossing the room, until she stood before me. Slowly, she bent down, drawing her face close to my ear to whisper, what I thought would be another secret. Her whisper, however, was spoken loud enough for Castel, who was seated across the room, to hear her. Her secrets were seldom silent.

"Why, Monsieur, he still be in *Christ Cathedral,* where you last time see him."

I turned my head quickly, looking first at the old lady, then at Dr. Castel, then back again to question the woman. "Where I saw him last? Have I met John the Younger, Mademoiselle? Have I met him?"

"I old woman, foolish old woman."

"Dr. Castel, have I met John the Younger? Have I met him?"

"That I do not know, Monsieur. I do not know John the Younger and would not recognize him if we were to meet. I have heard his name, however, usually whispered secretively by AC4 and Grand. Other than their occasional whispers I know nothing of this John the Younger."

The old woman turned toward Dr. Castel.

"You here stay, Monsieur. Please here stay."

After instructing Castel she once again turned to face me. Raising one of her hands upward to her face she put one long thin finger across her mouth to indicate that we should be silent. She then waved with her other hand for me to follow.

"Shhh. Quiet, Monsieur. Shhh. Shhh. Shhh. I old woman. I foolish old woman."

With her free hand she gently pushed open the door, led me out of the alcove then pointed to the narrow spiral staircase that led to the vestibule at the rear of the sanctuary of *Christ Cathedral.* .

"Shhh. Quiet, Monsieur. Shhh. Shhh. Shhh. John, Younger, he in sanctuary. He there, where you last time see him."

She laughed a low, disturbing kind of laugh as she returned to the alcove. Just before she entered the alcove she turned, looked at me -- *and winked.*

I looked at her and then – *I winked.*

"I old woman. I foolish old woman. I old woman. I foolish old woman."

Slowly and quietly I walked down the narrow spiral staircase into the vestibule at the rear of the sanctuary of *Christ Cathedral.* I was there for one reason and one reason only – *to meet John the Younger.*

I paused at the rear of the sanctuary, drew a deep breath – and stood motionless. Before me was beauty, stunning beauty in every direction. A large, stained glass circular dome at the far end of the sanctuary was positioned high above the main altar. Beneath the dome, above the altar, was a very large work of art, a fresco depicting a weeping angel, with huge white feather wings, towering high in the heavens, holding an open book, the *Lamb's book of Life*.

A second, massive, ancient fresco, a monumental composition of the *Judgment Seat of Christ* ran the full length of the sanctuary of *Christ Cathedral.* Jesus is seated on a Throne surrounded by a large circular rainbow. An upward gesture of blessing, made by his right hand, has two fingers pointed upward. I found myself staring intently at the soft rays of light as they danced across the two-fingered symbol of blessing. *Bless the Lord, O my soul. Whatever may lie before me, Let me praise Thy name.*

It was a moment of sacred silence, reverent silence, a silence that was suddenly undergirded by a chorus of voices singing, singing in Italian -- *"Te Deum. Te Deum. Te Deum. Thee, O God, we praise. Te Deum. Te Deum. Te Deum. Thee, O God, we praise."*

It was the *choeur de cathedral* beginning their weekly rehearsal. Interspersed between the notes and stanzas of their anthem I could hear the *chef de choeur,* the *Choir Master*, shouting commands in two languages, French and Italian. In French he shouted to the choir, *"Admirateur. Admirateur. Admirateur."* which translates into English as *"Sing Worshipful. Sing Worshipful. Sing Worshipful."* In Italian he shouted *"Tremolo. Tremolo. Tremolo."* to the musicians playing stringed instruments. The voices and violins combined, creating a nostalgic mood, a calming ambiance , a feel of memories and dreams, a rich mystical blend of sweet music.

As the music flooded the building and my spirit I continued surveying the beauty of the sanctuary. I was overwhelmed, caught up in the sheer ecstasy of the moment when I was suddenly startled by a rickety, squeaking sound, a sound that I did not anticipate hearing in the vestibule of the church. As I turned toward the sound I saw that it was the legless man. With loudly squeaking wheels he was rolling across the marbled floor of the vestibule toward me. Then, just as he had done when I last visited *Christ Cathedral,* he reached into his tin can and handed me two pencils. "These are for both of you. No charge. My gift to both of you."

Both of you?

I think I'm beginning to understand.

I placed the two pencils in my shirt pocket and said, "Thank you" as the legless man turned and quickly rolled away. The echoing sound of his squeaking wheels bouncing off the high walls of the church vestibule triggered early childhood memories.

In the neighborhood where I lived as a child there also lived a legless man. He too sat on a little board that had wheels mounted on the bottom. He always had an old tin can stuffed with yellow pencils in front of him and beside it, an empty cigar box where people would toss a few coins or a couple of dollars in return for a pencil. In my mind I could hear the voice of the legless man as he called out…

"Pencils. Ten cents. Pencils. Two nickels. Ten cents.
Pencils. Pencils."

The neighborhood rumor was that once a year the legless man would go to a church and give away two miracle pencils. Whoever received these two pencils would have to give one of the pencils to someone else. This simple act of generosity would then trigger a miracle for two people, rather than just one. So, yes, this legless man and his two yellow pencils brought back a memory, a life-dominating, life-changing childhood experience.

One day, when I was a boy helping at church the legless man gave two pencils to a stranger. I did not know this stranger. He was an older man who was either visiting the church or just passing through the area. I remember the priest talked with him briefly. The stranger seemed upset, either with the priest, or with God, or about something else. I'm not sure. After they talked the stranger left the church.

Later, I don't remember why, but the stranger returned to the church. He talked with me for a little while and noticed that I had a speech impediment. Reaching into his pocket he gave me one of his two pencils and told me to place it crosswise in my mouth. He then told me to bite the pencil as hard as I could until the pencil broke. I did and it shattered splinters inside my mouth. As I spit out the wood splinters, my speech disorder, which caused me to repeat sentences and speak in rhyme – disappeared. *A Miracle. Sometimes miracles seem rare and curious. But, not always.* This was a miracle. My miracle. Everyone in our neighborhood celebrated my miracle. Everyone knew the legless man. No one knew the stranger. No. Not from that day till this.

"Two pencils. Two pencils. My gift for both of you."

As I stood in the vestibule I became overwhelmed by music, the beauty of the sanctuary and my childhood memories. My childhood memories began with a sound – the squeaking wheels beneath the legless man sitting atop his board, rolling across the hard floor of the vestibule. Now, the memories came to an end, not through sound, but through sight – *the sight of a young boy.*

The boy was dressed in a plain white robe working at rack filled with candles. He was having difficulty lighting the candles and appeared to be frustrated. He lowered his head, tensed his body and clenched his fists, evidently to better control his frustration.

For reasons unknown to me the boy suddenly and slowly turned toward me. It was as if he intuitively sensed my presence. He looked at me, directly at me. Our eyes met. We both stood still, not moving an inch, nor blinking an eye, saying nothing. We just stood there staring at one another. It was as if there was some indefinable connection, a kinship between us. I wondered, *Was this boy John the Younger?*

He calmly turned away from me to resume working with his rack of candles. I looked briefly at the large, elevated, crucifix. A larger than life stone body of Christ was fastened to two large wooden beams, portraying His death for the sins of the world. My eyes then glanced at the *eternal flame* as its fire continued to flicker inside the sanctuary lamp. Then I looked at the back of the boy's head as he worked with the candles. He suddenly stopped, as if he could feel my stare, then turned to face me a second time. Our eyes met again. We both stood motionless, silently staring, once again, staring intently and directly at one another.

"My name is John. And your name is?"

"My na-na-name is is Ja, Jon, Johnny."

The soft voices of the choir and the stringed instruments of the musicians gradually decreased in volume as the *chef de choeur* slowly brought his hand down signaling a *diminuendo.* The *diminuendo* gradually became a subtle silence, a momentary pause, creating yet another moment of sacred silence. In that moment I remembered when I made my first visit to the sanctuary of *Christ Cathedral.* I had come for one reason and one reason only -- to *confront God.*

Paneloux, the priest, was there. He tried to calm me. It was then, during that first visit to the sanctuary, as Paneloux consoled me, that the boy, this very boy, looked toward me. I remember, he looked directly at me, nodding his head as a single tear slowly crawled down his cheek. Behind that tear was a hidden language, a language whose meaning I did not then understand. Now, as our eyes met yet again that tear, that very same tear, once again crawled down his cheek – *and I heard -- and I understood.*

Eschatos was near.
Grace would soon end.
Judgment would begin.
A single tear crawled down my cheek.

This boy, indeed, is John the Younger.

When I was a boy I was often confused and sometimes troubled by a recurring dream. In my dream I would see myself in a church talking to an older man. As I grew older the dream continued, yet changed in one subtle way. I would see myself in the same dream, not as a boy, but as a man standing in the same church talking to a boy. As I looked at the boy I could not help but wonder: *Was this that dream being dreamt again? And, if so, was I the man? Or the boy? Or both?*

"I know you, Johnny. I know you here."

I softly tapped my hand to my chest, near my heart.

"And we have been here before, both of us, many times."

"Yes, an-an-and I kn-kn-know you too."

His small hand gently tapped his chest. This whole conversation, our being here in this place, everything about everything that was happening, felt *strange, unreal, even untrue – so much like a dream.* I wondered again. *Was that dream being dreamt again? Déjà vu.*

Memories rushed to the surface of my mind. In my head I heard three words repeated over and over again, followed by the words of Emma.

"*Strange. Unreal. Untrue.*" "*Strange. Unreal. Untrue.*"

"Truth is sometimes stranger than fiction. Sometimes, what actually happens is more bizarre than anything imagined."

"Strange. Unreal. Untrue."

"Truth is sometimes stranger…."

"These people do not exist. These are not flesh and blood real people."

As we continued talking the boy stuttered and stammered, straining to put sentences together. He spoke in *rhyme* and *riddle,* using *repetition, similes,* and *lyric,* with meaning sometimes hidden in *symbols;* sometimes in *metaphors;* sometimes in *pity sayings* For some reason I heard Emma speaking in my head, repeating, yet again, the words she had spoken at *Café' Du Monde.*

"These people do not exist. These are not flesh and blood real people."

"Strange. Unreal. Untrue." "Strange. Unreal. Untrue."

"Truth is sometimes stranger…."

"We met here," I said to the boy, "half a life ago. Sometimes, I try to remember. Sometimes, I try to forget. Yet, in my dreams I have seen this moment recurring again and again."

"I-I-I am you; and, you are me. Op-Op-Open your eyes; and, you will see. A ri-riddle—A mystery. I-I-I am you; and, you are me."

"These people do not exist. These are not flesh and blood real people."

"I wro-wro-wrote a poem – a poem I wrote. It speaks of te-te-terrors and troubles remote. Troubles and terrors, re-re-remote, remote, written in the poem I-I-I wrote."

"These people do not exist. These are not flesh and blood real people."

I stood, confused, bewildered.

I was standing, not in the shadow of, but in the light of – *yesterday, my yesterday – today.* In this *yesterday,* in this old timeline, I stood with memories still fresh of timelines yet to come. I did not, I could not, understand. Circular reasoning, contrasts and conflicts, competing theologies, philosophies, and ideologies tripped me up at every turn – *Such is the injury of time. Such is the injury of thought.*

"I thought of a thought that was never thought," I said to the boy, "and wondered, *What could it be?* And now you stand before me; yet, I still cannot see."

In the choir loft musicians in the string section, playing violins and cellos suddenly stood, joined by a haunting choral accompaniment, a chorus of voices, very smooth, very soft – tenors. I thought of the final copy of *A*

Psalm the Apocalypse as they eloquently shifted from singing the *Te Deum* in Italian to a combined Latin arrangement of the sacred *Trisagion – Holy, Holy, Holy -- Thrice Holy -- Agios O Theos – Tersanctus.*

Kyrie Boethei. Lord Help.
Lord Help Us All.
Trisagion – Holy, Holy, Holy
Thrice Holy -- Agios O Theos – Tersanctus.
TE DEUM.

"I have come for the parchment."

"I know."

"Can you tell me where it is?"

"Yes."

"Where is it? Where is it, Johnny?"

In *th-th-the Candle* – in the da-da-darkness
A slen-slen-slender flame leaps – in so-so-solitude.

One, be-be-becomes many, bu-bu-burning bright.
A lab-lab-labyrinth leads th-th-the way,
But not in the light of day.

Be-Be-Beware. The man with one sh-sh-shoe.
Even now he sear-searches for you.

I knelt down on one knee, looked up at the cross, then at the boy. Reaching in my top pocket I pulled out a yellow pencil.

The fl-fl-flame. The fl-fl-flame. With fi-fi-fiery mo-mouth thunders.
Eschatos. Eschatos.
Its fi-fi-fiery mo-mouth hungers.

The tone of his voice indicated fright.

"Be-Beware. The man with one sh-sh-shoe is-is-is sear-searching for you."

I saw Castel standing by a little door, slightly behind, yet beside the main altar. He was quietly signaling me to come to him quickly. I hurriedly reached for the boy's hand then looked directly into his frightened eyes.

"Take my hand, Johnny, and knot your fingers through mine."

"Be-Beware. The man with one sh-sh-shoe is-is-is sear-searching for you."

"Everything is going to be OK. Everything is going to be OK. Bite this pencil. Bite it hard."

I let go of Johnny's hand as he began spitting splinters on the sanctuary floor.

Everything is going to be OK. Everything is going to be OK.

Dr. Castel quickly pulled me through the small door into a small room, the *sacristy,* located off the Epistle side of the main altar. The little room was filled with priestly vestments, golden chalices, missals, unconsecrated communion hosts and other items used in the Catholic mass.,

"AC4 is here. He is on the second floor," said Castel, "He is on the second floor searching for you. You must go now."

"But, I don't have the parchment."

"Listen carefully. Time is of essence. AC4 is here. He is searching for you. We have been in this room before, together, you and I, several times. You already inwardly sense this. You have felt the tug of those strange intuitive feelings called *Déjà vu.* Inwardly, you sense and feel familiarity. You know that you have been here before. There is a reason for that – *you have been here before.* You and I have been here before, John -- several times. By *'here'* I mean we *have been* in this *exact moment* in this *exact place – six times, to be exact."*

In ways that I could not explain I knew that Dr. Castel was speaking truth. So much of this conversation – not only what he is saying but how he is saying what he is saying – has that ring of familiarity. Indeed, I had been here before, in this *exact moment* in this *exact place – several times.*

Rapid thoughts, racing thoughts and repeated murmurings raced through my mind then became subdued and finally became silent as Dr. Castel resumed speaking.

"This is actually our seventh meeting -- *together* -- in this room, at this *exact moment* in time. I understand that this is confusing; but, bear with me. Hear me out. I already know what will be said next. I know what will be said. I know what you will say. I know what I will say. I also know how you will respond. I am not omniscient -- but, I do know what I know because I have been here with you before – *seven times.*

"Listen carefully. I have a wealth of detailed information that must be shared with you. Your ability to mentally recall our prior meetings and conversations will return as we talk. Time, however, is of essence. AC4 is here. He is searching for you."

"But, I don't have the parchment."

"Think. Think. What did the boy say? Where did he say the parchment was?"

In my head I once again heard the stammering voice of the boy….

In *th-th-the Candle* – in the da-da-darkness
A slen-slen-slender flame leaps – in so-so-solitude.

One, be-be-becomes many, bu-bu-burning bright.
A lab-lab-labyrinth leads th-th-the way,
But not in the light of day.

Be-Be-Beware. The man with one sh-sh-shoe.
Even now he sear-searches for you.

He said that the parchment was in *the candle.* But, how can a parchment be in a candle?"

"The Candle is an abbreviated name for the *Chapel of the Candle,* which is located behind the *labyrinth* at the rear of *Christ Cathedral. The Chapel* is called *the Candle* because at midnight semi-reflective glass and mirrors reflect the light of a single candle – *the Christ Candle.* The light of that single candle is multiplied by the reflective glass and mirrors, giving the illusion of many candles – flooding the entire building with light. It utilizes a lighting concept similar to that of the holocaust museum in Israel."

"That's what the boy meant when he said that *'In the Candle – in the darkness -- a slender flame leaps – in solitude. One, becomes many, burning bright.'*

And, evidently there is a *labyrinth,"* I said, "between the two buildings, between *Christ Cathedral* and the *Chapel of the Candle,* because he added that *'A labyrinth leads the way, but not in the light of day."*

"Yes. Yes. And when he said *'but not in the light of day"* he means that the light of *the Christ Candle* can only be seen from the *labyrinth* at midnight. At midnight it will project a single narrow beam of light that shines down into the *labyrinth.* "

"What shall I do then? It is not yet night."

"Monsieur, you must begin to work your way through the *labyrinth* so that you can be in position at midnight. At midnight all of the reflective glass and mirrors, except those on the upper level, in the *Belfry Tower,* shut down. The upper level light will then form the single narrow beam of light down into the *labyrinth.* This will enable the light of *the Christ Candle* shining into the *labyrinth* to *lead the way."*

As we continued talking Dr. Castel shared that the design of this *labyrinth* is based on the earliest known *labyrinth,* a Roman mosaic *labyrinth* in the *Reparatus basilica* in *Orléansville/El-Asnam* in *Algeria,* not too far from the city of *Oran* where Dr. Castel, Dr. Rieux and others battled the plague.

"At the very center of the *last quadrant of the labyrinth* is a large black marble central stone with an inscription in Greek, *Kyrie Boethei,* which in English means *'Lord Help.'* Hear me. Be at the black marble central stone at midnight. God will answer your cry for help. He will be your refuge. He will be your strength. You will discover that God is indeed *a very present help.* [85]

"Behind the black marble central stone is a large wooden Christian cross. On each of the wooden side beams of the cross are carved the Greek letters *Alpha/Omega.* There is no stone body of Christ fastened to wooden beams. This cross is a plain, bare, wooden old rugged cross. Christ is not on this cross because He is no longer on the cross. He is risen.

"In the Candle – in the darkness -- a slender flame leaps – in solitude."

"At midnight, a single, slender, sliver of light from the high tower of *the Candle* will shine upon the cross. From your position behind the black marble central stone, the light on the cross will enable you to see a *straight and narrow way through the last quardrant of the labyrinth, to the Candle. Follow the light. Everything is going to be OK. Everything is going to be OK.*"

Whether intentional or not, when Castel repeated to me the very words I had spoken to the boy, I knew -- Everything *was going to be OK.*

"Dr. Castel, what did the boy mean when he said, *'The flame. The flame. With fiery mouth thunders. Eschatos. Eschatos. Its fiery mouth hungers.'* It seemed that he was frightened, very frightened and very much wanted me to know about *the mouth, the thunders and hungers* -- whatever that means."

"It means that the parchment must be set on fire using one flame, and one flame only – *the flame of the Christ Candle. The Christ Candle* is the *single slender flame. The Christ Candle* is the only *flame* that *leaps in solitude. The Christ Candle* is the only candle located in the high tower of *Chapel of the Candle.* One flame, and one flame only can set the parchment on fire – *the flame of the Christ Candle.*

"Other flames, other fire, the fire from torches or fire from other sources are regarded as *strange fire. Strange fire* is prohibited, unacceptable and will meet with God's strong disapproval. *Nadab* and *Abihu*, the sons of *Aaron*, offered *strange fire* and there went out fire from the LORD, and devoured them, and they died before the LORD.

"*Listen now.* No other fire will suffice. *'Its fiery mouth thunders (that is, it calls for) and Its fiery mouth hungers for (that is, it desires to be fed) A Psalm of the Apocalypse. Once the flame is fed – Eschatos."*

"Once the flame is fed – Eschatos."

My thoughts took me back to my pastoral office in my church in Chalmette. It seems so long ago. I remember *Leitourgós* instructing me to burn *A Psalm of the Apocalypse.* He indicated that when I did, the flames and smoke from the burning parchment would trigger the start of a series of events, catastrophic, eschatological end-time events.

Back then I made a choice. I was now living in the consequences of that choice. When I made that first choice the stakes were higher, much higher than I realized. And now, another choice, and even higher stakes -- the final *eschatos.*

My heart fluttered as a wave of anxiety rushed over me, then through me. I could only think about something that Castel had said just a moment earlier:

> "At the very center of the *labyrinth* there is a large black marble central stone with an inscription in Greek, *Kyrie Boethei*, which in English means *'Lord Help.'* Hear me. Be at the black marble central stone at midnight. God will answer your cry for help. He will be your *refuge.* He will be your *strength.* You will discover that God is indeed *a very present help.*

"Everything is going to be OK. Everything is going to be OK."

"Come. Follow me. Time is of essence. AC4 will shortly begin searching the sanctuary and the surrounding rooms. I want to take you to the top of the *Christ Cathedral Belfry Tower* to enable you to gain a better feel for and a broader perspective of the *labyrinth.*

At the rear of the *sacristy,* to the right, between two tall pillars, there was an open archway that led to a long, narrow, dark hallway, a passageway. The passageway was attached to the rear of the *Belfry Tower* of *Christ Cathedral.* A monk, wearing a shaved circle on the back of his head, was walking down the hallway toward us carrying some books. When he saw us coming toward him he stopped in place and turned to the side so that his back was pressed against the wall as we walked pass him. I could not help but notice that there was a clump of silver spray paint on the back of his head, on the curls of his hair where his hair met his neck.

"Bonsoir. Comment allez-vous?"

"Bien, et vous?"

"Bien, merci."

As we entered the lower level of the *Belfry Tower* I immediately noticed a strong musty odor, an odor that became stronger as we climbed to the top.

"Unfortunately, Monsieur," said Castel as he wrinkled his nose, "the musty smell has grown quite strong in the *Belfry Tower* since the bells were removed from the bell tower."

"I'm fine, Monsieur. I'm fine."

A long, winding, narrow circular stairwell at the base of the *Belfry Tower* led to the top, to the very top of the *Belfry Tower*. Several bas reliefs were overlain on the stairwell walls. A few old tapestries were draped over the railings that circled upward with the stairs.

On the upper level of the stairwell a pull-down ladder led to a trap-door that provided final access to the *Belfry Tower*, which was flooded with daylight from a skylight at the top. The *Belfry Tower* was framed with rough, raw wood and heavy beams. Two of the original four bells were resting on the floor of the *Belfry Tower*. Even though they were obviously no longer in use, the two old bells held their traditional place of prominence in the *Belfry Tower*. They simply sat there like two old grandfathers who had seen better days. A massive beam, which originally bore the weight of the four bells, was still in place.

"There was an effort to replace the bells with more modern *carillons*. Unfortunately, the church ran out of money before completing the project."

I took in a breath, released it slowly, then took in another as I wiped sweat from my forehead with my handkerchief. A cool gentle breeze rushed across and through the *Belfry Tower* as I stared down at the *labyrinth*. There, in the distance, near the horizon, was the steeple atop the tower of the *Chapel of the Candle*. It too had a *Belfry Tower*. Though the outline of the building was difficult to discern, it greatly resembled the tall, square tower that I saw in a vision while at the defense facility. Somewhere, inside the faraway steeple of *the Candle, in the darkness a slender flame leaps – in solitude -- the Christ Candle.*

A slight wave of vertigo made me dizzy and weak and created momentary nausea. Until the feeling passed I clutched onto one of the rough wooden beams of the *Belfry Tower*. Down below, for just about as far as the eye could see, was the *labyrinth*, a very massive *labyrinth*.

"I had no idea that the *labyrinth* would be so large."

"That's why I felt it important for you to gain this perspective."

Castel explained some of the history and design of the *labyrinth*.

"There are twelve sections laid out in three quadrants, with each having rich symbolic value."

Each of the twelve sections represented the twelve tribes of Israel. The traditional Christian cross is in the design of each of the twelve.

"If you hold your hand this way you can clearly see the Christian cross in each of the twelve sections."

Castel also shared that just as there are six *cities of refuge* [86] listed in the Bible, there are six *resting places* in the *labyrinth*. Each of these *resting places* has a small altar overlaid with bronze, with four horns, one on each corner of the altar.

"The altars look like small dots from this vantage point, but on ground level they are quite imposing. You should have ample time to stop at these places of refuge. Hopefully, you won't have to stop out of necessity."

The altars were originally incorporated into the design of the *labyrinth* to serve as *resting places*, places of *refuge* from the heat for those who walk the *labyrinth*. These places of rest quickly became places of worship. Some report a heightened sense of the presence of God. Still others find comfort and security at these places, a security that represents *sanctuary and safe haven.*

A noise, a noise made small by distance, let Dr. Castel know that AC4 was near. The noise came again. It was the voice of a man, speaking in French – *the monk.*

"We must go now, Monsieur, AC4 is now in the sanctuary and nightfall will soon be upon us. You must now work your way through the *labyrinth*. I must go to AC4. I will divert him away from the *labyrinth* for as long as I possibly can. He does not know I am subversive.

"One final thing, Monsieur….

Follow God. Follow your intuitions."

RESTORE POINT 26:

THE LABYRINTH

A pale orange-streaked darkness slowly spread across the evening sky. A great gray ball, a dull, flat light, the moon, began to show its familiar face as it slowly rose higher into the night sky. In a strange, fascinating way, the moon cast long haunting shadows that created an eerie glow as twilight mingled with night. In a mysterious way as dusk became night it produced a dreamlike ambiance, filled with contrasting shades and rolling streaks of colors, deep blacks, purples, fading dull yellows and bluish-grays.

As night set in the *labyrinth* took on a sacred, solemn appearance, majestic, yet full of shadows and mystery. The height of the prickly hedges, their thickness plus the surrounding foliage that fringed the stone pathways weaved their way through the maze. Each quadrant was segregated from the others by flaring orange-yellow flames that sat atop several torches. Everything about this place, everything about the *labyrinth,* felt *"Strange. Unreal. Untrue."*

This is where old myths and legends are born.

As I began my journey through the *labyrinth* I prayed the inscription that Dr. Castel said was inscribed on the black marble central stone, making it my personal prayer -- *"Kyrie Boethei, Lord Help."*

> *"Kyrie Boethei, Lord Help."*
> *Follow God. Follow your intuitions.*
> *Everything is going to be OK. Everything is going to be OK.*

I knew very little about *labyrinths,* other than what I had read in theological and archaeological journals. They are, of course, universally recognized as a *life metaphor* or as a *life symbol.* Like a *labyrinth,* life's pathway has obstacles, complications, difficulties and challenges. Life, like a *labyrinth,* is filled with the unknown, filled with the unexplored and filled with unexpected twists and turns – *and choices.*

"Kyrie Boethei, Lord Help."
"Kyrie Boethei, Lord Help."
Follow God. Follow your intuitions.
Everything is going to be OK. Everything is going to be OK.
"Kyrie Boethei, Lord Help."

As I entered the first quadrant of the *labyrinth* I walked right then left and then back toward the right, searching for a pathway to the second quadrant. Somehow, I turned back on myself and reached a dead end. Goodness. I was only in the first quadrant and I was already having difficulties. As I paused to mentally retrace my steps, I thought about Moses and the people of God as they left Egypt. The wilderness, with its unexpected twists, turns and dead ends, must have seemed like a giant *labyrinth* to them. They were in unfamiliar territory, travelling unknown terrain – and so was I.

Ye have not passed this way before. [87]

Even though the children of Israel were in unfamiliar territory, traveling through strange, foreign terrain, God led them, each step of the way, safely, through every unexpected twist, just as He promised. They faced great obstacles, dealt with complications, overcame difficulties and advanced in adversity. God led them safely through the *labyrinth* of life – *God, lead me.*

"Kyrie Boethei, Lord Help."

But, as I continued walking I wondered, "*How did they know which way to go?"* Differing choices lead to divergent paths and different destinations. In life, as in a *labyrinth,* a wrong choice can lead to a dead end. How did they know which way to go? I was only in the first quadrant and I had already reached a dead end – and I didn't know which way to go.

> *How did they know which way to go?*
> *"Kyrie Boethei, Lord Help."*

I felt myself spinning, looking every which way for the pathway to the second quadrant. I turned to the left, another dead end. I turned back to the right, another dead end. The prickly hedge was not my friend. My arms were red and scratched. The back of my shirt was wet with sweat. A wave of anxiety ran through me, washing over me, filling me. I was flush with the onset of fear and anxiety. A tremble, just a small tremble, raced through me. Small, but I felt it.

How did they know which way to go? How can I know which way to go? I began to pray with greater urgency

> *"Kyrie Boethei, Lord Help."*
> *"Kyrie Boethei, Lord Help."*

> *God led by night in a pillar of fire.*

Suddenly, the orange-yellow flame that sat atop one of the torches flared up. The flame became large, much larger than any of the other torches – *obviously so.*

"Monsieur, Je vous aiderai. Tout droit."

High above, in the *Belfry Tower of Christ Cathedral,* I could see, barely see, the image of a man waving his arm, trying to get my attention.

"Monsieur, Je vous aiderai. Tout droit."

"Monsieur." – Sir. "Je vous aiderai." – I will help you. " Tout droit." – Straight ahead.

It was the monk, the one with the shaved circle on the back of his head. Earlier he greeted Dr. Castel and me as we walked the hallway to the *belfry.*

"Monsieur, Je vous aiderai. Tout droit."

"Merci. Merci." Thank You. Thank You.

I waved my hand toward the monk as I moved straight ahead into the second quadrant. In the second quadrant the hedges abruptly turned back again to the right, then again to the right, then back again to the right, so often that I lost all sense of direction. Suddenly, the orange-yellow flame flared up. This one, however, was not showing the passageway to the third quadrant. It was giving light to one of the six *resting places* in the *labyrinth*. If anyone needed a refuge – *I did* -- and my journey through the *labyrinth* had just begun.

I heard the words of Dr. Castel echoing in my brain.

"Each of the six *resting places* has a small altar overlaid with bronze, with four horns on each corner of the altars. The altars are intended to be places of worship for those who walk the *labyrinth.*"

Instinctively, *intuitively*, I reached for the *horns of the altar.* [88]

Lightning flashed, a bluish-white lightning stretching across the darkening night sky, as I grabbed the horns. As it flashed I saw my hands tightly gripping two of the four the horns. My hands were trembling. The horns were shaking. It was electric. Everything, every muscle and every bone in my body, was vibrating, trembling, shaking.

Your young men will see visions. Your old men will dream dreams. [89]

I felt a soar, an indescribable soar, a soar of spirit. Isaiah, the prophet, spoke of soaring, *"of mounting with the wings of an eagle."* [90] This felt like that kind of soaring. Yet, it was not so much a feeling as a change of awareness, with external awareness shadowed by a heightened spiritual awareness. There was a shift of perception, a purifying of perception. The soar, that sheer ecstasy of the moment enabled me to know the unknowable, see the invisible, think the unthinkable, hear the inaudible. It was as if I was plumbing the depths. The psalmist described it as *deep calleth unto deep.* [91] I felt a burning pain in my chest, a pain that was almost unbearable. I felt like *a living sacrifice* on the altar of God. I think, but I'm not entirely sure, but I think this experience is what the mystics call *ecstasy.*

"Kyrie Boethei, Lord Help."

"Kyrie Boethei, Lord Help."

A clap, a powerful startling clap of thunder rumbled again. It was immediately followed by another brilliant burst of lightning. The lightning flash enabled me to see a man, a man holding a torch. This man was receiving a vision in the night. I watched as the man with the torch peered, peered into a dream, peered into another man's dream. The focus of the dream was a great towering statue. The head of the statue was gold, the chest and arms, silver, the belly and thighs, of bronze, the legs of iron, and the feet of iron and clay.[92] This diminished quality of the elements reflects the diminished quality of the governments through the passage of time.

A Voice. A whispery, cadenced voice spoke a couple of lines from *A Psalm of the Apocalypse.*

> *Four, Four Monarchies. Kingdoms, Kingdoms, Four.*
> *No Less. No More.*

The towering statue represented four successive monarchies, four kingdoms. The vision closed with their inferior governments being shattered by Christ as He established the government of God's Kingdom on earth.

As my vision of the man with the torch peering into the dream of another man as his dream closed, I heard the final instructions the man received....

"Seal the vision, even to the time of the end. Seal the vision."[93]

The man with the torch? Daniel, the prophet of God. It is related in Scripture that he had five apocalyptic visions that pointed towards Messiah's first and second coming. At each of the altars in the *labyrinth* I had the same ecstatic experience – and a vision of Daniel receiving one of his five apocalyptic visions.

Suddenly, my thoughts tumbled –

> *"This place, these people – none of this is real."*
> *"These people do not exist. These are not flesh and blood real people."*

With the sound of Emma's words suddenly racing through my brain, my spiritual high tumbled downward, quickly. I was troubled, confused

– confused by an inward tension, a tug-of-war that spiraled downward, leading me into darkness and terror. It was a strange, tight tension, a consequence of light battling darkness, of flesh waging war against the spirit. I had experienced this confusion, this tension, this battle before. What was most troubling is that I was dealing with this again. I thought I had resolved this. Which made this tumbling downward all the more troubling.

Dr. Castel once said *faith is like a star. It shines brightest in the dark, At* times my faith did indeed shine bright, like a star. At other times, the light of my star, my faith, grew dim. When faith vacillates, when it wavers, when it surrenders to doubt and fear, it becomes like *a wave in the sea, driven and tossed.* [94]

> *"Kyrie Boethei, Lord Help."*
> *"Kyrie Boethei, Lord Help."*

I wondered, "*What is wrong with me? Am I dealing with a faith deficit? Is this a constriction of faith? A miniaturization of faith?*"

> *"Kyrie Boethei, Lord Help."*
> *"Kyrie Boethei, Lord Help."*

I must confess, I am not sure why this *wavering of faith* would surface now, when I most need a strong, dependable, unwavering faith. What I do know is that this strange inward tension made it feel as if there were two of me, fighting within me, vehemently opposed, each one against the other. A part of me was dominated by fear, the other part, by faith. Someone once said, *"Where there is faith there is fear. Where there is fear there is faith."* [95] And, I might add, these two opposing forces were waging war, an unrelenting war, each one against the other – *within me.*

I learned long ago an important truth that I have had to learn, over and over again: the inner tension, the inner war, is the spirit's hunger for light, for greater faith, being challenged by the darkness, the darkness of fear – and doubt. It is there, in the tension, in the tautness of this tug-a-war that fear is overcome as faith grows stronger. Without this tension, without this inner battle, faith will fail, leaving one disillusioned, alone and alienated, dominated by the darkness of fearful, duplicitous thoughts. This tension is a troublesome thing – but necessary.

"Kyrie Boethei, Lord Help."
"Make a Faith Choice. John, Make a Faith Choice.
Fear held you back."
"Kyrie Boethei, Lord Help."

The pathway created by the maze of hedges led me forward, then left and then right and then back again so often that it was impossible to determine if I was making any real progress. Faith and fear continued their inward battle as I sought to follow God, my intuitions, and the flaring torches. Each step was a simple, basic truth: trust God.

"For we walk by faith, not by sight."[96]
"Kyrie Boethei, Lord Help."

Gentle winds, like soft whispers, began to rustle and blow across the *labyrinth* as I entered into and passed through the third, fourth and fifth quadrants. Images, voices and troublesome, terrifying memories flashed across my mind. Fear drew me backward into the past, or perhaps, forward into the future, or perhaps, in both directions, simultaneously. In ways inexplicable faith had its pull too.

"Where there is faith there is fear. Where there is fear there is faith."

"I saw the Souls of the Martyrs under the Altar."
"White Robes."

"Make a Faith Choice. John, Make a Faith Choice. Fear held you back."

Darkness. Confusion.
A Distant Flash of Light.

The winds began to rustle with greater velocity, racing through the hedges, passing over and winding their way through the quadrants. A faint echo of thunder softly rumbled in the distance. The pale moon, with a frightful face, was once again peering through the dark clouds. The orange-yellow flames atop the torches were beginning to move and gyrate faster and faster.

"Kyrie Boethei, Lord Help."
"Kyrie Boethei, Lord Help."

My hands trembled yet again as they gripped the horns of the fifth altar. Once again I saw Daniel holding a torch, receiving another apocalyptic vision, a vision in the night. *Four Beasts, Rise Out Of The Sea and One, Like The Son Of Man.* [97] The four beasts are four monarchies, four kingdoms, the same four portrayed by the large statue in the first vision.

Four, Four Monarchies. Kingdoms, Kingdoms, Four.
No Less. No More.

In the distance I began to hear a faint chorus of voices singing, singing in Italian *"Te Deum. Te Deum. Te Deum. Thee, O God, we praise. Te Deum. Te Deum. Te Deum. Thee, O God, we praise."* The whole place took on an air of nostalgia, a feel of memory, mingled with a frightful feel of a dark dream, with mysterious sounds of music, stringed instruments and voices heard long ago. The hedges and the foliage continued rustling in the twisting winds as I worked my way through the *labyrinth.*

It was four minutes until midnight.
"Follow God. Follow your intuitions."
"Kyrie Boethei, Lord Help."

"Make a Faith Choice. John, Make a Faith Choice. Fear held you back."

I felt that intuitive stirring again, this time compelling me to run rather than walk. Rather than run, however, I quickened my pace to a slow jog, jogging toward the final quadrant that contained the altar with the black marble central stone. My breathing increased as I jogged faster. My heart began beating a tad faster. I could hear the sound of my breath rushing through my nostrils. There was something working within me, something far greater than *intuition -- Something holy.*

Something within me, something strong, something holy, began urging me, urging me, prompting me, pushing me, shouting within me.

Hurry. Hurry. Run faster. Hurry. Run faster. Run faster.

As I began to run faster I heard a sound in the distance behind me. It was that sound that triggered my inner alarm and urged me to run faster. A quick glance behind me let me see who or what created that sound. There, in the distance, behind me, I saw -- *the dark figure of a man – AC4.*

"Kyrie Boethei, Lord Help."
"Kyrie Boethei, Lord Help."

I could hear the dull groan of AC4 behind me. He wasn't running very fast, but he was definitely running as fast as he could – toward me.

"I want what is mine and I want it now."

Behind AC4, much farther behind, was old Dr. Castel. He was too old, far too old, to run or keep pace with me or AC4. Nevertheless, he walked then jogged then walked as fast as he could, attempting to keep pace.

As I ran across the final maze of stone pathways that weaved through the quadrants, the inward compulsion to run faster became stronger, more demanding, more urgent.

Hurry. Hurry. Run faster. Hurry. Run faster. Run faster.

My heart began beating faster and faster. I don't know if it was from fear or fatigue or the quickening pace of my running. I could feel a painful thumping in my chest. I was gasping for air, struggling for breath. Fear and anxiety pushed me. Like dark companions I could hear their mocking voices whining within me.

Hurry. Hurry. Run faster. Hurry. Run faster. Run faster.

As I quickened my pace a low lying hedge suddenly appeared. My body instinctively reacted. Jerking my right leg high, I hurdled the low lying hedge. Lifting both legs high to complete the hurdle, I landed on both feet, then fell hard to the ground. As I struggled to stand, there before me was the final quadrant. In the center of the quadrant was the altar with the black marble central stone. Behind it was the cross. As I stood there first looking up, toward the cross, then downward at the black marble central stone, I read the Greek inscription, *"Kyrie Boethei, Lord Help."*

"Where there is faith there is fear. Where there is fear there is faith."

The threatening rain shower did just that – threatened – then seemed to hold its breath as a soft rumble protested.

> *"Te Deum. Te Deum. Te Deum. Thee, O God, we praise.*
> *Te Deum. Te Deum. Te Deum. Thee, O God, we praise."*
> *"Was this a dream being dreamt again?"*
> *"Kyrie Boethei, Lord Help."*
> *"Kyrie Boethei, Lord Help."*

The black marble stone altar began to vibrate, then shudder and shake. The shuddering and shaking was accompanied by a thunderous sound like that of a loud explosion. A protracted continuation of that first massive, explosive sound rumbled throughout the entire *labyrinth.* The tall hedges swayed, rhythmically swayed several times as rough winds raced across the *labyrinth.* The rain slowly started to fall then stopped. The shaking gradually slowed, then stopped completely, just for a few seconds, only to be followed by another explosion. Its force and sound shook the *labyrinth* with even greater force. A loud roar, like that of heavy, thick thunder, continued to reverberate and vibrate through the *labyrinth.*

The singing gradually faded, diminishing into the distance. In the distance I could also hear the retreating, dull roll of thunder. Lightning once again flashed, a bluish-white lightning stretching across the darkening night sky. As it flashed I saw an imposing very tall, square tower. The Christian cross, the symbol of the ever-present Christ, stood resiliently atop a steeple. This must be the *Chapel of the Candle.* The tower, like a strong, silent sentinel, was shrouded in stone. A slender beam of light, a singular light, pierced the darkness, shining downward toward the black marble altar. *The Christ Candle.*

A clap, a powerful startling clap of thunder rumbled again. It was immediately followed by another brilliant burst of lightning. The thin beam of light from the *Christ Candle* enabled me to see a straight, narrow passageway shouldered by tall hedges on either side. The straight, narrow passageway provided a direct route from the last quadrant of the *labyrinth* to the *Chapel of the Candle.*

Suddenly I was startled by the sound of an angry voice as strong arms violently yanked me backward. It was AC4. He grabbed my right arm and held it tight. His grip was painful, unbelievably painful. Swinging me around, he pulled my face close to his. His jaw was clenched tight. His eyes, wide. His voice was deep and raging…

"I want what is mine and I want it now."

I felt my right leg beginning to buckle. I was beginning to fall. Instinctively, I reached for and grabbed AC4. I was twisting closer toward him, trying to hold onto him to keep from falling.

"I want what is mine and I want it now."

I could not keep us from falling. SLAM. As we fell to the ground, AC4 slapped me then shoved my face into the grit and gravel.

"I want what is mine and I want it now."

SLAM. He slapped me again. As he held me down with the full weight of his body on my back, he slapped me again, a third time. SLAM. He then planted one of his knees in the center of my back to hold me in place. It was amazing the physical strength of AC4.

He was angry, very angry – in a rage. Great beads of sweat ran down his face, his neck and his arms. He had a deep scowl on his face. He grunted, grunted several times, as he struggled to keep me pinned to the ground. SLAM. He slapped me again, across the back of my head. I wiggled as hard as I could to escape – with no success. My body cramped from being in such an awkward position.

"I want what is mine."

"Kyrie Boethei, Lord Help."

"Kyrie Boethei, Lord Help."

As awkward as the situation was, it became even more awkward as old Dr. Castel tumbled over the low lying hedge, landing on top of AC4 and me. Somehow, Castel's fall enabled me to get free. I could hear AC4 shouting, cussing and blaspheming as I ran toward *the straight, narrow way* toward the *Chapel of the Candle.*

"I had him. I had him, Castel. You dumb klutz. I had him and he got away. Castel, you clumsy old fool. Get me to the defense facility. Hurry. Get me to the defense facility now.

As I raced through the narrow hedges, the *Chapel of the Candle* began to come into view. Behind me was the fading shadow of AC4, an angry, shouting blur. Old Dr. Castel walked behind him, at a distance. Inexplicably, Castel turned toward me. Even though we were separated by distance, I smiled when I saw him raise his arm to wave at me.

Before me stood the *Chapel of the Candle*, with two massive, wooden doors at the base of its old stone tower. As I continued to run toward the *Chapel,* the sounds of AC4 shouting faded into the distance.

Strange sounds, sounds of iron grating and screeching behind the large wooden doors leaked to the outside. As the great doors were slowly pried open, I heard the stomping of hooves, horse hooves, as three large white Friesian horses came into view. Behind them I saw heaven standing open and there, behind the first three horses, was a fourth, even larger, white Arabian horse. Beside him, holding the reigns of the horse tightly, was a man, silent, tall, dressed in a silvery-white cloak and hood. He simply stood there. He did nothing. He said nothing. He simply stared intently at me.

Three tall men, wearing cloaks and hoods, stood in silence beside each of the Friesian horses. Their cloaks and hoods were silvery-white. They were sharp-featured men, with a look of distinction. Each of the first three men, with his other hand, held high a crooked stick. Fixed atop their sticks were torches, orange flamed torches of dancing fire. The flames threw long orange shadows everywhere as the fire flickered in the draught created by the open doors.

As lightning flashed yet again, I could see that each of the first three horses was hitched to what appeared to be large old wooden-wheeled wagons, funeral carriages. Atop each carriage was a plain wooden casket.

They suddenly stopped, the men and horses stopped. They stood still. They gazed at me in silence.

The man in the middle said something to the other two men, then slowly started walking toward me. He hesitated as he neared the hedge. The glare of swirling white dust, the wisps of light and rolling fog mingled and rolled around him, blinding me, hindering me from seeing his face.

The sense of mystery deepened as an exceptional play of light and shadow danced around him as he began walking toward me. He then knelt down in front of me, saluting me. His silvery-white cloak had an insignia across the chest; an insignia that featured an eagle, a winged man, an ox and a lion.[98] As he knelt before me I heard his firm voice speak, directly to me.

"The Noble Army of the Martyrs Salute Thee. TE DEUM"

He extended his hand toward me. As he led me into the building he looked at me and said....

"It has begun."

RESTORE POINT 27:

THE CANDLE

As Castel and AC4 faded into the distance I sat in the *Belfry Tower* of the *Chapel of the Candle.* Using the light of the *Christ Candle* I read the last original copy of *A Psalm of the Apocalypse.* As I read the final stanza I recalled the words of the boy when we met last in the sanctuary of *Christ Cathedral* and memory enabled me to see myself seated in my office at the Chalmette church as I translated and read that stanza for the very first time....

> *"In the Candle – in the darkness -- a slender flame leaps – in solitude."*

Sitting *in the darkness,* alone, *in solitude,* I looked at the *slender flame* of the *Christ Candle.* I quietly folded the small parchment scroll, then prayed -- *"Kyrie Boethei, Lord Help."* With trembling hands I held the scroll above the *slender flame* of the *Christ Candle.*

"The flame. The flame.
With fiery mouth thunders. Eschatos. Eschatos.
Its fiery mouth hungers."

As the parchment touched the *slender flame* atop the *Christ Candle* the scroll burst into flames. Jumping backward to avoid the flash of fire I suddenly recalled the interpretive words of Dr. Castel.

"Once the flame (with its hungry, fiery mouth) is fed
– Eschatos."

Then I thought about *Leitourgós* and what he said just a few moments earlier as I entered the *Chapel of the Candle.*

"It has begun..."

As the smoke of the burning parchment rose higher and higher I saw a strange occurrence in the midnight sky. A bizarre pattern of light movements flashed across the dark sky. The sky actually appeared to be broken. I don't know if it was a crack or a rip in the fabric of space, or a hole in the sky or a tear -- but something was wrong.

The first evidence of this was that the sky was suddenly green, not a light benign shade of green, but a brilliant lime green, almost florescent in appearance. A slow, pale brightening began to spread high above the horizon as a cluster of bright white light swirls began circulating, spilling downward out of the center of the break or crack in the green sky. The rotating spirals, first slowly, then rather quickly, changed their movements, making new patterns of light as they rapidly spread across the entire sky.

I heard the rapid, frantic neighing of a horse, a white horse, and saw flashes of his long white mane as he violently kicked his front legs high into the air. He had no rider – but was saddled, and ready to be mounted. Trumpets blared loudly. The long sound of a single *shofar* filled the air, competing with the trumpets. It was a blaring sound, piercing, like a loud sounding warning. Ram horns sounded too, many ram horns, repeatedly. I also heard loud voices, shouting in unison with a poetic cadence....

Seven, the Number of Perfection
And of Weeks
Daniel saw Seventy, of Years
One Disappears, Cut Off – Eternal Tears

One Week Remains, Singular. Alone.
Earth's Final Judgment – The Great White Throne

In *the Candle* – in the darkness
A slender flame leaps – in solitude.

One remains
Only One, One Week of Years
The Lamb, The Lion -- Final Tears
Jacob's Time of Trouble.
It now appears.
A labyrinth leads the way,
But not in the light of day

The light patterns, which dispersed across the sky, were above the clouds, woven into and yet passing through the clouds, connecting with brilliant light patterns beneath the clouds. They took on the appearance of a giant fisherman's net, with squares of different sizes linking together. Some became rectangular in shape, others resembled perfect squares. They appeared to be linked yet simultaneously, appeared separate, one from the other.

Suddenly, without warning, a fast-moving, rotating column of rectangles and squares merged, flowing out of a common center, forming a thin rotating tube, with the appearance of a narrow rapidly circulating funnel. As it rotated it reached from the broken green sky toward the troubled earth. The hedges and the foliage in the *labyrinth* continued rustling and turning in the twisting winds of the rotating funnel. The lower part of the funnel was surrounded by violently rotating translucent clusters of greenish bright white clouds of dust.

As the rotating column danced across the sky it had the look and sound of an approaching tornado illuminated by frequent flashes of lightning -- but this was not a tornado.

At this point, everything happened quickly, very quickly.

There was a loud convergence of sounds, whooshing sounds, overshadowed by sounds like that of a rumbling freight train, or perhaps the loud, rushing rapids of a waterfall, or of a roaring jet engine. It was deafening. There were whistling noises, whining, humming noises, rattling sounds like tens of thousands of buzzing bees mingled with the sound of electricity cracking.

The entire *Chapel of the Candle* vibrated. I could see rectangles and squares of bright green and white light racing rhythmically through the entire building, bouncing off of the walls and ceilings. Their energy created a dark greenish black and white powdery impression on whatever part of the building they touched, an impression like that of an x-ray or a reverse photographic negative. In rapid succession the rectangles and squares were methodically racing across and pressing against the walls, leaving what appeared to be a radioactive residue of greenish white dust.

Strangely, inside the rectangles I could clearly see ancient Hebrew numerals for the number seventy and inside of the squares were the Hebrew numerals for the number seven. Hebrew, the language of God. Seven and Seventy. The key to the prophet *Daniel's vision of seventy weeks.*[99] It appears that *Daniel's seventieth week is drawing near.*

Seven, the Number of Perfection
And of Weeks
Daniel saw Seventy, of Years
One Disappears, Cut Off – Eternal Tears

Daniel, an Old Testament prophet of God, had several visions and revelations from God through the angel Gabriel that focused on the end times. Several of these visions and revelations focused on a seventy weeks of years chronological scheme that were linked to the time when the long-awaited Messiah – Jesus Christ – would appear. The historical record indicates that everything happened in accordance with the chronological sequence that the archangel Gabriel gave Daniel. When Christ was crucified, *Cut Off* at the end of the sixty-nineth week, according to this timescale, one week of the seventy remained on Daniel's chronological calendar. Consequently, even though Daniel saw *Seventy weeks of Years, One Disappears, Cut Off – Eternal Tears.*

As with the squares and rectangles, the Hebrew numerals were stamped rapidly, methodically, leaving the same dark greenish black and white powdery impressions.

Each stamping was accompanied by a chorus of voices, a mournful, nostalgic sounding choir of male and female voices, singing in Italian the words *Te Deum. Te Deum. Te Deum. "Thee, O God, we praise" Te Deum. Te Deum. Te Deum. "Thee, O God, we praise."*

Trumpets continued blaring. The long sound of the *shofar,* a piercing sound, once again cut though the night air. The ram horns increased their volume and intensity.

Each rectangle would swirl, in a circular fashion, with an emblem at its center – a *Jerusalem Cross*. As each rectangle revolved with the *Jerusalem Cross* at its center, the Hebrew numeral for seventy would appear, then the *Jerusalem Cross* would spin and revolve again becoming a square, with the Hebrew number for seven appearing.

One remains
Only One, One Week of Years
The Lamb, The Lion -- Final Tears
Jacob's Time of Trouble.
It now appears.
A labyrinth leads the way,
But not in the light of day

The rapid, frantic neighing of the white horse continued as he violently kicked his front legs high into the air. Still no rider – Still saddled, and ready to be mounted. Trumpets sounded once again. The long sound of a single *shofar* filled the air.

One Week Remains, Singular. Alone.
Earth's Final Judgment – The Great White Throne
In *the Candle* – in the darkness
A slender flame leaps – in solitude.

The long sound of a single *shofar* filled the air. It seemed as if I was moving in slow motion, yet everything around me was moving fast, very fast. A series of loud creaking sounds from above the *Belfry Tower* caused me to turn, look up, and react quickly by bending my body close to the floor of the *Belfry Tower.*

All of a sudden the entire *Belfry Tower* shook, violently, then shuddered with a long drawn out continuous shaking. The shuddering and shaking was accompanied by a sound, a thunderous sound. The protracted continuation of that first massive, explosion rumbled throughout the entire *Chapel of the Candle*. The substructure and walls creaked, repeatedly, rhythmically, as the *Belfry Tower* swayed several times. Then the initial shaking and swaying gradually slowed, then stopped completely, just for a few seconds, only to be followed by another explosion. Its force and sound shook the entire building with even greater force. A loud roar, like that of heavy, thick thunder, continued to reverberate and vibrate through the building.

Inexplicably it appeared that the *Chapel of the Candle* was converging and merging with the defense facility in Virginia. I could see the defense building. I could see AC4, Dr. Rieux, Grand and Dr. Castel – and even hear their voices. The symposium participants were clearly visible too.

Simultaneously, in ways that are beyond explanation, the *Defense Advanced Research Projects building* and the *Chapel of the Candle,* and the *labyrinth* seemed to be occupying the same space. It was as if two massive chunks of reality were colliding, merging, converging, cohabitating, one with the other.

As I sat near the *Christ Candle* in the *Belfry Tower* of the *Chapel of the Candle,* I surveyed the interior of the defense building – I saw myself there, in Virginia – *still strapped into my surgical chair.*

I know this sounds insane. Nevertheless, I know what I saw and I know what I heard. I was seated there still strapped in my surgical chair and I was seated here beside the *slender flame* of the *Christ Candle* in the *Chapel of the Candle.* I began to think about several things AC4 had said during the symposium: *"These strands of reality are hidden and unseen by the natural eye until one actually enters into the alternative reality."*

Was this portion of my journey between *parallel realms?* Had I in some mysterious way entered into an *alternative reality?* Had I somehow crossed into a *parallel universe?* How could two realities simultaneously occupy the same space? This was a definite *time warp. It had to be. Or, did it?*

I also remembered AC4 saying, *"Sometimes the autonomous strands become entangled, producing instability, creating metaphysical disruptions. When this occurs the tangled threads are untangled by the intervention of the Alpha/Omega, the controlling strand."*

Could I anticipate some type of intervention? Should I? Was I really caught in some type of time *warp?* Or, was something else going on here? Was this one of AC4's *metaphysical disruptions?*

AC4 also said during the symposium that *the actual paths that these seven primary alternative realities travel will lead them to eventually converge, becoming one with the dominant Alpha/Omega. When the first of these seven primary alternative realities merges with the Alpha/Omega, all other realities will instantaneously converge and simultaneously merge – becoming one – absorbed by the Alpha/Omega – the Omega Point."*

Was this *the Omega Point* or the beginning of the *Omega Point?* What comes next? *Oblivion. Nothingness. The second coming of Christ?*

"Te Deum. Te Deum. Te Deum. Thee, O God, we praise."
"Te Deum. Te Deum. Te Deum. Thee, O God, we praise."

"It has begun." "It has begun." "It has begun."

The long sound of the *shofar* pierced the night sky yet again; but, this was not *the final trump,* not yet. The trumpets blared once again as shouting resumed. As the trumphets sounded again I once again thought of *A Psalm of The Apocalypse* and its focus on *Daniel's seventy weeks.*

Seven, the Number of Perfection
And of Weeks
Daniel saw Seventy, of Years
One Disappears, Cut Off – Eternal Tears

In Daniel's chronological scheme the *seventy weeks of years* calculated each day of the seventy weeks as one year. Biblical chronologists have determined that a total of 483 years passed from the time the command was given to rebuild the walls of Jerusalem to the crucifixion of Christ.

According to this timescale a seven year period remains to fulfill biblical prophecy. Some call this seven year period *Jacob's Time of Trouble*. Thus, *A Psalm of the Apocalypse* pointed toward the final week of Daniel's prophecy.

One Week Remains, Singular. Alone.
Earth's Final Judgment – The Great White Throne
In *the Candle* – in the darkness
A slender flame leaps – in solitude.

One remains
Only One, One Week of Years
The Lamb, The Lion -- Final Tears
Jacob's Time of Trouble.
It now appears.

The phrase *Jacob's Time of Trouble* [100] was initially used by Jeremiah, an Old Testament prophet. Both Jesus and Paul used the terminology of Jeremiah as a reference to the final seven years of Daniel's timescale, hence, the seven years of tribulation.

During the seven years of tribulation the judgment and wrath of God unfolds, beginning with the seven sealed scrolls, the first four of the seven seals that are open unleash the four horsemen of the apocalypse.

The horsemen. The horsemen.
Four in number.
Apocalypse. Apocalypse.
Do not slumber.
Burning Winds. Twisted Land.
Waters Rise and Rage.
Eschatos. Eschatos.
The Lion. The Lamb. The Cage.

I could hear the muffled voices of AC4 and Grand as they shouted and attempted to talk with the disgruntled crowd. I could see the violent madness of the symposium as it continued to unfold.

The four small, white haired men continued their calculations and their visual projections. They were completely unaware of the shuddering, of the shaking, of the swaying of their building, or of the convergence of the *Chapel of the Candle* with their building. Two realities were violently merging – yet no one other than me seemed to be aware of what was happening.

There, to my left, inside the defense facility was Rieux. I could almost reach out and touch him. And there, beside him, stood Dr. Castel. Both men were busily engaged, attempting to restore order and calmness. They were surrounded by and being aided by the military police. I could hear their shouts and commands as they continued their attempts to restore order. They gave no indication, none whatsoever, that they were aware of the explosions or anything connected with the convergence. Yet, as the shaking, rattling and rumbling of both buildings continued it became more and more apparent that I was the only one aware of any of this.

Suddenly, in the midst of the chaos and confusion AC4 collapsed. His good leg seemed to literally dissolve and disappear beneath him. One minute it was there – the next, it was gone. I would later learn that both of AC4's lower legs had dissolved due to his excessive abuse of the laws of physics as he deployed the thin, yet powerful faint wisps of color from his hand. He had concealed the loss of the first leg for many years; but now, with the loss of the second leg nothing could be hid. I was shocked as two of the small, white haired men seated behind the curved glass cubicle left their post to strap AC4 to a little board that had wheels mounted on the bottom. *AC4 was now a legless man.*

"Hook me up, Grand. Hook me up to the *MC Mind Copier device,*" demanded AC4. "Hook me up. Rieux, help me get this done."

AC4's body was stiff and fixed, strapped to his wooden board. The head atop the shoulders of AC4 slowly turned toward me. I could see the rigidity of my body, tightly fastened to the surgical chair. The straps kept me from moving but I could see and I could hear. We looked at each other. Inexplicably, I was outside of myself, seeing myself see myself as his eyes met mine.

"I want what is mine and I want it now. You may not have it in your hand; but, it is in your head. I want what is mine and I want it now."

AC4 began to angrily shout orders to the medical staff. A team of nurses quickly shaved his head. Several electrodes that were woven into my skull cap were quickly attached with electronic and tubal connections to electrodes and tubal connections on the skull cap secured to the shaved head of AC4. Flat screen computers were in place to monitor the electrical activity of each of our brains. Additional cables were run from a port on my *MC Mind Copier device* to an *MC Mind Copier* port located on the back of AC4's head.

"Grand, listen carefully. I want you to *mind copy* and transfer everything, absolutely everything inside his brain. Copy and transfer it all into my brain – except the data in the religious strata."

"That's not possible," shouted Grand from his upper room.

"Do it." shouted AC4. "Do it. No religious strata. No religious data."

"We do not yet have the capability to subdivide segments, Monsieur. We cannot do that."

"Do it. Just do what I say, Grand. Do it."

Grand shrugged his shoulders, then pushed several buttons and pulled several levers. Under his breath, in a rather snide way, I heard him say, "And how do you want your eggs, Monsieur Camus? Scrambled? Or fried?"

One of the four small, white haired men seated behind the curved glass cubicle, began punching keys on his key pad. Rapidly flashing video projections raced across the large screens. Fast moving gestalt images and accompanying sketches, pictures and photographs of genetic space forms raced across the giant screens. These were followed by projections, genetic time forms and DNA sequences, coupled with brain chemical fluctuations and an accompanying molecular analysis of synaptic fluids. All analytical processes were merged, then rapidly converted into algebraic forms, geometric symbols and simple basal equations.

Lights began to flash. Buzzers and alarms began to sound. Red lights began to rapidly blink. *Warning signals. Warning signals. Warning signals.* Something was wrong. Something was seriously wrong.

People began scurrying back and forth, somehow not bumping into one another. Dr. Rieux walked briskly toward Castel, a tight frown distorting his entire face. He quickly turned and walked in the opposite direction and then began a frenzied pacing, back and forth, back and forth, as the physicians, nurses, technicians, and a host of others dressed in white uniforms moved toward AC4.

AC4 threw his head backward, then pitched it forward violently, as the *Mind Copier* sorted and transferred massive amounts of codified data. The medical staff, startled, momentarily by AC4's violent movements, froze. Some backed away in fear. AC4's arms suddenly flew high above his head, then returned to rest on his lap. His body began to shake, trembling and jerking with a sudden, violent twitching. His teeth chattered as he lowered his chin into his chest. His eyes grew wide, very wide, as he looked at Rieux, Castel and finally toward me. Then, a sheepish little boy look came over AC4's face – and he grinned a silly boyish grin. It was the mischievous smirk, the grin of a little boy who was up to no good. It was *a cat ate the mouse kind of grin;* but, in this case, *the mouse ate the cat.* AC4 evidently *bit off more than he could chew.*

He lifted his hands upward as he began an irrational rant, raising his voice, shouting in an effort to command attention.

"The sum of the square roots of any two sides of an isosceles triangle is equal to the square root of the remaining side." [101]

He looked around – and grinned.

"Oh joy. Rapture. I got a brain. [102] How can I ever thank you enough, Monsieur Grand? How can I ever thank you enough?"

It was as if AC4 had blown a mental fuse. He was talking out of his head, mimicking characters and reciting lines from *The Wizard of Oz.* Grand shrugged his shoulders and raised his hands. It was as if he was saying, "I told you so."

"Back where I come from," announced AC4, "we have universities, seats of great learning, where men go to become great thinkers. And when they come out, they think deep thoughts and with no more brains than I have. But they have one thing I haven't got -- *a diploma.* Therefore, by virtue of the authority vested in me by the *Universitartus Committiartum E Pluribus Unum,*[103] I hereby confer upon me the honorary degree of Th.D. Drum roll, please. Ta-dah."

Grand shrugged his shoulders and raised his hands again.

"Pay no attention to that man behind the curtain." shouted AC4 as he pointed toward Grand. "Pay no attention to that man." [104]

AC4 quickly maneuvered himself around on the squeaking flat board, raised his head toward Grand, and shouted: "I'll fight you, I'll fight you with one paw tied behind my back. I'll fight you standing on one foot. I'll fight you with my eyes closed... ohh, wait a minute, I don't have a foot. I don't have a leg to stand on. Put 'em up, put 'em up. Why, I'll... Ruff... Ruff... Ruff."

The symposium was in total disarray. Dr. Rieux, Dr. Castel, security, the medical staff and a host of others were literally running in circles, attempting to capture AC4. It was an absurdly horrible scene, sheer madness. AC4 was rapidly wheeling his way across the ground level floor, constantly moving in circles, first this way, then that, then back again. Faster and faster, round and round he went. The sound of loudly squeaking wheels filled the defense department building. Then they caught him.

The last that any of us heard of AC4 that day was his insane, irrational shouts as security rolled him out of the defense department building.

"Pencils. Ten cents. Pencils. Two nickels. Ten cents. Pencils. Pencils. Oh joy. Rapture. I got a brain. How can I ever thank you enough? Put 'em up, put 'em up. Why, I'll... Ruff. Ruff. Pencils. Ten cents. Pencils."

RESTORE POINT 28:

ZARATHUSTRA

As the irrational shouts of AC4 faded into the distance I could hear rhythmic whispering voices from inside the defense department building…

Zarathustra. Zarathustra. Zarathustra.

The sound of that name -- *Zarathustra.* -- triggered thoughts of *A Psalm of the Apocalypse.*

Zarathustra
An Image – A Symbol -- Who will understand?
Six thrice, the Number, the Beast, a Man

Six, Imperfection, the Number of Man
Six thrice, Woe unto the Earth, the Beast
In the Latter Day, his Feast –
Six, Imperfection, the Number of Man
War Man at the End of Time

In the upper level a figure, the figure of a man, emerged from the glare of light and the swirling fog that filled his upper level suite. It was Joseph Grand. He began shouting with great enthusiasm into his microphone, seeking to gain the attention of the crowd. His face was full, flushed with excitement.

"Ladies and Gentlemen. Please. Welcome *Secretary General Antiochus Zarathustra.* Ladies and Gentlemen. Please. Please. Please stand. Please, welcome *U. N. Secretary. Antiochus Zarathustra."*

"Secretary General. Speak to us, Monsieur. Speak to us."

"Thank you. Thank you, Monsieur Grand. Thank you colleagues." Applause. Loud Applause.

Zarathustra
A Dark Seed Blossoms

Cheers. More Applause. "Thank you. Thank you." The Sound, the Echoing Sound of Applause. The building was filled with the feel of a global messianic fervor.

Zarathustra was a smooth-tongued, hard-nosed, cold-eyed European politician. On more than one occasion he danced near the edge of political suicide, only to emerge more politically powerful than any could anticipate. Those who knew Zarathustra best saw him as a vile, treacherous, arrogant, self-seeker, a power broker in the strictest sense. The world, however, was astounded with his geopolitical exploits.

Zarathustra
A Dark Seed Blossoms

Zarathustra. Zarathustra.
Overman, Underman, An Unholy Jeer.

God Is Dead. God Is Dead.
Thus Spake Zarathustra –
His scandalous tongue seduces many
The Nations Shout with Glee
An Unholy Harmony
God Is Dead.

Zarathustra single-handedly strengthened the crumbling brotherhood of free Western nations. He consolidated the European Economic Community by creating tax free trade zones that produced economic viability and prosperity among member nations. He calmed middle-Eastern anxieties by establishing a seven year covenant between the Palestinian state and the nation of Israel. The world was even more amazed as the Palestinians were awarded East Jerusalem as its capital to secure their signature on the seven year covenant. The Secretary General had promised peace – and he delivered what he had promised. *At least it appeared to be so.*

His most famous line which seemed to mesmerize the global elite was *"If there is a Voice, the people will hear it. If there is a Vision, the people will see it. I am the Voice. I have the Vision."*

Three dwarfs, tiny little men, on leashes stepped onto the platform with Zarathustra. One of the three, a crippled dwarf, rode on Zarathustra's shoulder. Every so often the Secretary General would jerk one of the leashes to control the behavior of the little men. At other times he would pat their heads, treating them more like pets than human beings. On several occasions Zarathustra would raise one finger upward while looking sternly at the little men. The dwarfs would then squat close to the floor in obedience.

Zarathustra, a social Darwinist, was very open about his belief that life was a struggle for survival, survival of the fittest. The weak, according to Zarathustra, should not exist but be exterminated to facilitate mankind's upward, evolutionary mobility. Sharia's bloody sword had his secret sanction. He often spoke dark proverbs and frequently quoted William Blake's *Proverbs of Hell.* He interpreted Blake's *The cut worm forgives the plow* [105] as humanity (the cut worm) will forgive the plow (ethic cleansing) once the evolutionary leap is completed. Like Adolph Hitler, Zarathustra believed that *"life does not forgive weakness."* [106] Some admired his progressive *thanatopic ideologies* with its open endorsement of *genocide, euthanasia,* and *ethnic cleansing.*

Others felt Zarathustra should not and could not be trusted. They feared that if he were left unchecked, then certain unfettered, sociopathic behaviors on a global scale would be the dire consequence. One religious leader, an internationally known televangelist, proclaimed that he had a dark vision of Zarathustra as the Beast of Revelation towering over humanity against a dark night sky shouting blasphemies and obscenities against the most high God.

This man, this Zarathustra, valued no one, other than himself. For Zarathustra, the proverbial pedestal was for him, and him alone. His entourage guaranteed that center stage was always reserved for Zarathustra. No one was held in high esteem by Zarathustra and of those who were esteemed, none were to be esteemed more than Zarathustra. His distain for the weak was such that he actually suffered feelings of nausea and disgust when he contemplated common people. His attitude toward the little men on the end of his leashes confirmed his ideology and his distain for his fellow human beings.

In European folklore dwarfs were cherished and highly valued. The deeds and exploits of dwarfs were legendary. In many quarters they were valued above other human beings. Early Europeans believed that these tiny men lived in the bowels of the earth where they guarded caches of gold, silver, jewels and other buried treasure.

In a few short years the world would discover the truth about Zarathustra. This hellish maniac, this extreme sociopath, this beast of a man, was indeed from the bowels of the earth -- *but he was no treasure.*

As the applause grew silent, Zarathustra stepped across the platform to the microphone. He casually leaned back, half standing, half sitting on the same high back chair used by AC4. He ran his hand through his hair, then shifted his position as he spoke.

"Hear me well. If there is a Voice, the people will hear it. If there is a Vision, the people will see it. I am the Voice. I have the Vision. These tales of woe, of desolation, of decimation, of devastation -- these are friends, not foes – and should not be feared. Humankind has passed this way before and will pass this way again. *Recurrence. Infinite, eternal recurrence.* The future has already happened and the past has happened, again and again and again, and is happening, yet again, even now. As an illustrious American president once said, '*We have nothing to fear but fear itself.*'"[107]

Calmly and quietly he used his handkerchief to wipe away great drops of sweat that had formed on his forehead.

"Catastrophe. Calamity. Hearts melt. Knees tremble. Every face grows pale. There is no riddle here, Men of Science. What is, has been; what was will be; and, what will be has already been. This then is the riddle, not of catastrophe, but of *the casuistry of events, constant recurrence, eternal recurrence, and its return.* Because the future has already happened and the past is happening, *the riddle of the casuistry of events, of time, of recurrence and its return is resolved.*"

With his hands raised high, Zarathustra pointed toward the crowds in the upper deck. I could now clearly see his face, his thin cheeks, his narrow forehead beneath which hung steel-rimmed spectacles. Like an evangelical preacher he spoke powerfully, and emotionally.

"Wake up, Men of Science. Wake Up. Who hath beguiled you? Who hath bewitched you? And with what? With fabricated tales of woe? Who hath bewitched you with these strange ideas? An insane man selling pencils? A confused time traveler? Or perhaps this man, a metaphysical magncian who believes he is from the magical Land of Oz?

"To whom shall we liken this AC4, this peddler of pencils? I liken him to a man too feeble to lead who scratches an imaginary, make-believe map in the dirt. Then, with mud on his finger he points to his map and shouts, 'This is the way. Go this way.' Who will follow such a man? Is this not sheer folly? Think. Think. Think. O Men of Science. Think. Where is your scientific rationality? Who has created this atmosphere of ambivalence? Why are you tossed about like a wave of the sea? Ambuiguity has become your banner."

Still standing, Zarathustra once again wiped the handkerchief across his forehead and the back of his neck before he continued to speak.

"The *infinite cycle of eternal recurrence* will soon once again emerge, not as some quasi-theological *Omega Point* but as the greatly anticipated upward evolutionary leap. You, my friends, you will soon overcome the restrictions of time, resolve its riddle and embrace *eternal recurrence.* The *return, the infinite, eternal recurrence* -- it calls you to overcome, yet you cower in fear, vasacillating."

Zarathustra's voice was filled with power and passion. He spoke passionately, resolutely, as one with authority. It was as if his every movement was synchronized, linked to each word, each syllable, and each phrase as he spoke. The effect was powerful, mesmerizing, electric.

"Men of Science. Look here. Look unto me. See he who stands before you this day. I have, I Zarathustra, I have overcome. For me, in me, and through me the riddle is resolved. I, yes I, Zarathustra, I have made the leap and climbed the evolutionary scale. I am a brighter flame, a god who dances before you, a new god who will show you the way. I, yes, I, Zarathustra, I am the way. I am Overman. I am Underman."

Zarathustra didn't bat an eyelid as he made his appeal to the symposium participants. He had an aura, an aura that asserted his command as a leader.

"Who is this God? He is dead. We killed him with nails. We killed him with knives. Behold, a new god now stands before you."

Zarathustra. Zarathustra.
Overman, Underman, An Unholy Jeer.
A Divine Funeral,
The Procession Draws Near
The Sound of Weeping
Sharia law(less) Unholy Dread
Who Will Bow The Head
God Is Dead
Shiv`a. Keriah. Avel. Keriah. Shiv`a.

God Is Dead. God Is Dead.
Thus Spake Zarathustra –
His scandalous tongue seduces many
The Nations Shout with Glee
An Unholy Harmony
God Is Dead.
Say The Unholy Three
God Is Dead. God Is Dead.
Templum aedificavit – Build A Temple
TE DEUM.

The place was electric and Zarathustra demonstrated great power, then quickly grew pensive and thoughtful. The ebb and flow of his ability to persuade was carefully moderated as he continued to speak.

"Old myths, friends, old myths built on fear, control and after-death promises and provisions, these old myths, they die agonizingly slow deaths. Then they return and recur, marring mankind's upward evolutionary path. That is their tendency. That is their alarming tendency."

He paused again, momentarily, then lifted his right hand high to point to Chancellor Tarrou.

"One of your number, Chancellor Tarrou, described the resurrection of myth as 'Metaphysical Madness.' Like Herculean sailors of old you must stop up your ears lest you be seduced by the siren song of old myths. Careful, Men of Science. Their song is a call to certain destruction."

He paused speaking as Chancellor Tarrou stood in his upper level observation room, garnering applause from the crowd.

"If, as AC4 proclaimed," continued Zarathustra, "if as AC4 proclaimed, if this old myth should resurrect and return again – be it in the form of some mythological God or in the form of some pseudo *Alpha/Omega* – we shall kill him again. We shall meet him again. We shall defeat him again. We shall kill him again."

He suddenly slammed his right hand into the palm of his left hand for emphasis. Once again the symposium attendants bounced to attention. His right hand quickly rose again, revealing that his fingers were clenched, tightly clenched into a fist. After shaking his fist several times one long finger symbolically pointed toward the symposium participants in the upper level observation rooms.

"I say to you, darkness leads to light -- *Be still, and let the dark come upon you. Yes. Be still, and let the dark come upon you.* [108]

"I say to you that peace does not produce peace. No. War leads to peace. Hear my cry, O Men of Science. Peace. Peace. Glorious Peace. Global Peace. Prepare for war and you prepare for peace. We shall not go silently into the night. We shall stand. We shall fight. We shall make war that we might gain peace. *Confront This Myth. Confront Him. Confront It now. Make War.*"

Applause. Loud Applause. Cheers. More Applause. "Thank you. Thank you." The Sound, the Echoing Sound of Applause.

"Global Hunger? Global Hunger is yesterday's burden," said Zarathustra. "Global Population Control? This is but a phantom fear. Eat. Drink. Be Merry – for tomorrow we make war that we may make peace.

"Let the *Jezreel Valley* widen her jaws. Let *Merj ibn-'Amir,* the *Plain of Megiddo* make way for there shall be a gathering of armies in this valley at the place of *Armageddon* to make war that we may have peace."

Zarathustra hesitated, just for a moment, creating anticipation, then spoke even more forcefully, symbolically raising one hand to point a thin finger upward, toward some unseen imaginary place high above his head.

"Before you is light, the light of a new day, the light of a new way. The light of Zarathustra. Choose this day whom you will follow. A mad man, a seller of pencils, who draws imaginary maps in the dirt? A dead man, a myth, whom we have killed and will kill again? Or, your Secretary General, Zarathustra?

"Hear Robert Blake, a paradoxical poet-philosopher as he declares his eternal Gospel – and choose your way.

"Thou art a man, God is no more.
Thine own Humanity learn to adore."[109]

"How long will you cower, O Men of Science, troubled by anxious thoughts? With weak, tame minds you live in chains, the chains of chaos and confusion. Oh pitiable and foolish men of science, how long will you couch down, fettered by fear? *'Thou art a man, God is no more.'*

"We are standing at the most critical moments in human history. Why do you remain sick? Why do you remain silent? Speak. Behind us, the history of the human race, a history whose origin is hidden in obscurity. Before us, a different type of obscurity. A darkness? Yes. Yet a darkness that is filled with infinite mountains of light. Let us together ascend to new heights."

Applause. Loud Applause. Cheers. More Applause. Zarathustra paused briefly, allowing his eyes, which were narrow, yet set apart, to scan the upper level observation rooms.

"This symposium, under the leadership of AC4 has greatly enhanced our awareness of the hitherto unrecognized dimensions of our world. *Parallel universes, alternate realities,* and a host of other cosmological realities have enabled us to see as we have never seen before.

"The content has been factual, eye-opening, and challenging. The conclusion, however, is riddled with illogical thinking. Hear me, the resolution of the challenge before us will not be found in a poem written decades ago by a boy, John the Younger. The answer lies not in the destruction of that poem, but in the preservation of this man. As long as he is alive, you have nothing to fear. At the risk of sounding hallucinatory and obscene, the key throughout human history has always been a man. Today, this man is the key. The poem is not the key. No. This man is the key."

As he stood beside me Zarathustra pointed to the large number of medical tubes, machines and medical devices invading my body to keep me alive.

"He shall live that men shall not die."

Thus Spoke Zarathustra.

RESTORE POINT 29:

THE MENORAH

Seeing the unseeable. Hearing the inaudible. Stepping beyond the known – into the unknown. Peering beyond the veil that separates the visible from the invisible, the temporal from the eternal -- this is the stuff of fantasy, the stuff of fiction – of fact -- *of faith.*

"Truth is sometimes stranger than fiction," Emma once said. *"Sometimes, what actually happens is more bizarre than anything imagined."*

Stranger than fiction.

Such was my current situation. *Something stranger than fiction, something more bizarre than anything imagined began to happen* as I sat beside the *Christ Candle* peering into the *Defense Advanced Research Projects Agency facility.* Two realities that had begun to merge were now being separated, one from the other. It was as if massive unseen hands were prying the two apart, returning them to autonomy.

How else could I describe this obvious pulling apart of two realities?

The brightness of the *Defense Advanced Research Projects Agency* began to grow dim. The nearness of everyone and everything attached to that facility retreated, becoming more and more distant, eventually disappearing into darkness.

The winds grew stronger, rustling and blowing through the *labyrinth* that lay between the *Chapel of the Candle* and *Christ Cathedral,* signaling yet another storm. The green skies began to darken as grey-purple clouds gathered overhead. A faint echo of thunder rumbled in the distance.

The *Chapel of the Candle* vibrated again, making loud shuddering sounds.

The night was dark, and getting darker. Other than the skip of lightning across the sky, no light, only blackness. Inside the *Belfry Tower* the fragile, orange glow from the flickering flame of the *Christ Candle* created light shadows, but little light.

As I huddled close to the floor of the second story of the *Belfry Tower*, a light, an uncertain kind of light from outside the building began to gently flash across the inner walls through the stain-glass windows beneath the steeple. The noise, however, wasn't gentle. The noise sounded like a roar from heaven. At first I thought it was a helicopter, shining rescue lights. But it wasn't.

A bizarre pattern of light movements, flashing across the darkened sky, came into focus. The sky actually appeared to be broken. I don't know if it was a crack or a rip in the fabric of space, or a hole in the sky or a tear -- but something was wrong. Something was wrong with everything that was happening. Everything was familiar, very familiar -- *too familiar.* This was not an experience of *Déjà vu.* It was beyond that. It was as if I had been here, actually physically been here before – several times. *And I knew it. I didn't just feel it. I knew it.*

There was a loud convergence of sounds, whooshing sounds, overshadowed by sounds like that of a rumbling freight train, or perhaps the loud, rushing rapids of a waterfall, or of a roaring jet engine. It was deafening. There were whistling noises, whining, humming noises, and rattling sounds.

Somewhere, somehow, inexplicably, in the distance I heard a lonesome sound, the faint cry of a fog horn – the sound of a ship leaving port.

The *Chapel of the Candle* vibrated again, making loud shuddering sounds as a large section of the roof was suddenly peeled back and blown away into the *labyrinth.*

A series of loud creaking sounds from above caused me to turn, look up, and react quickly. The towering steeple with its three foot aluminum cross at the top was swaying, then separating from the roofless building. The steeple and cross were somehow being lifted high into the air, with the steeple splintering and coming apart as it was violently carried higher and higher, then suddenly it came crashing downward. Somehow, I don't know if it was intuition or instinct but I caught the cross just before it crashed into my head.

Suddenly, I was flying through the air, surrounded by the narrow column of circulating rectangles and squares, desperately holding onto the cross. Gripping the cross I closed my eyes tightly, leaving just a sliver of an opening, straining to see through the glare of light, rain and flying debris.

Everything around me was spinning, growing smaller and smaller as I was pulled upward, away from the *Belfry Tower* by forces that were greater than that of the swirling winds. The gravitational pull of the earth had dissipated, releasing me to a greater power, the power of a thin column of circulating rectangles and squares. I was inside that thin column, that tunnel of circulating squares and rectangles, surrounded by flashing colors.

"Truth is sometimes stranger than fiction," said Emma. "Sometimes, what actually happens is more bizarre than anything imagined."

Simultaneously, somehow, I could see myself from both inside and outside of the circulating column. From the outside, I actually saw myself, inside this thin, rapidly rotating column, holding onto the cross, safely seated inside a series of clear domes, one within another, that were within the rotating column. Again, I can't explain it – I can only attempt to describe it.

My vision blurred as the whirlwind, with increasing velocity, thrust forward, then upward, winding this way, then that, constantly increasing its powerful rotating flow. Rolling and pitching, forward, then upward, I was helpless, hurtling through an upward spiraling pathway.

I was being pulled up and away, faster and faster, upward, upward, then pitching and arching, being pulled out of, then over and then away from the planet's ionosphere. Bouncing back and forth, surrounded by flashing colors, rotating rectangles and squares, smelling nothing, nausea surfaced, then mercifully left as quickly as it came.

The English novelist and poet Thomas Hardy once said that "while many things are too strange to be believed, nothing is too strange to have happened.[110]"

In the distant darkness of space I saw a pale yellow gaseous shroud of a dying sun-like star. It cast faint shadows across open space with lingering strokes of faint pink, purple and gray. There, all around me, was space, the wondrous, massive, expanse of space filled with mystery – *and beauty.*

Beauty. Such Beauty.

On earth we often debated the question of *beauty. What constitutes beauty? What is its origin? What is its purpose? When is it present? When is it absent? And, why?*

Here, above and beyond the poverty of language, *beauty* is its own interpreter – needing neither man, mind, poem nor prose. Here, *beauty* speaks its own language, yet without words. It speaks aesthetically, in a language that creates a sacred hush – a sense of awe – *a stunned silence.* The aesthetic harmony, the sheer aesthetic harmony and *beauty* of the universe is beyond human imagination.

Strangely, while surrounded by *beauty,* I recalled an old Navajo chant. It stirred within me as I looked across the width, breadth and depth of the universe with wide-eyed wonder.

> *"Beauty is before me and Beauty behind me.*
> *Above me and below me hovers the beautiful.*
> *I am surrounded by it, I am immersed in it…"* [III]

I could never show anyone anything as beautiful as the *beauty* that was surrounding me. Like the Navajo I was *immersed in it, surrounded by it.* In the midst of this *beauty,* cosmic contradictions became contrasts, and contrasts became compliments, with each creating indescribable cosmic *beauty* and character. Who can comprehend these nuances of the cosmos?

In the midst of the *beauty* I could hear a faint, distant sound. It was the sound of voices, a chorus of voices, a mournful, nostalgic sounding choir of male and female voices, singing again in Italian the words….

> *"Te Deum. Te Deum. Te Deum. "Thee, O God, we praise"*
> *"Te Deum. Te Deum. Te Deum. "Thee, O God, we praise"*

As lightning flashed the chorus triggered memories of *Leitourgós.* I could see him and I could see the three horses hitched to what appeared to be large old wooden-wheeled wagons, funeral carriages. And, I heard *Lietourgós* voice and his words…

"The Noble Army of the Martyrs Salute Thee. TE DEUM."

Three tall men, wearing silvery-white cloaks and hoods, stood in silence beside each of the horses hitched to the funeral carriages. I heard *Leitourgós'* voice again….and a Scripture….

"It has begun."
"A voice was heard in Ramah, lamentation, and bitter weeping."[112]

Once again I could feel fear rising with me. The *voice heard in Ramah, the lamentation and the bitter weeping* triggered more memories – thoughts of *A Psalm of the Apocalypse…*

The Sound of Weeping
The Feel of Fear,
Jacob's Day of Trouble, Drawing Near

"It has begun."
Jacob's Day of Trouble. The Eschatos.
"It has begun."

My thin rotating column of rectangles and squares began swaying, backward, then forward, hurtling toward what I believed to be either a certain death -- or a certain destination. The sections of the rotating spiral pathway that I was passing through bucked and pitched, out of sync with both the previous section and the one which was approaching.

"Te Deum. Te Deum. Te Deum. "Thee, O God, we praise"
"Te Deum. Te Deum. Te Deum. "Thee, O God, we praise"

"It has begun." "It has begun." "It has begun."

Suddenly, my dome and I began to pitch upward. Tremors began to ripple, then rip, then rattle with particularly strong movements. Massive forces, greater than those that had propelled me thus far, began to build up and increase. Time and space began to bend and twist and fold back on itself more rapidly. I wondered, Is this a modern day version of Elijah's chariot that propelled him into the heavens?

The enormity of God's creation, splashing in and out of my vision, caused feelings of awe, feelings of euphoria -- then utter and compete terror. These anxious episodes, these bouts with fear, gave birth to troubling feelings of claustrophobia. The stress, anxiety and inward tension was unbelievable, almost unbearable.

"Te Deum. Te Deum. Te Deum. "Thee, O God, we praise"
"Te Deum. Te Deum. Te Deum. "Thee, O God, we praise"

Claustrophobic.

Once again I became nauseous. *Once again* I was losing my breath. *Once again* I felt as if I was losing my mind. *Once again. Once again.* How many times have I experienced this? How many times must I experience this yet again?

Once again. Once again.

I began squirming anxiously. There was pressure on my chest. My head was pounding, throbbing. My lungs were heaving heavily, stifled by constricting anxieties and fears which swirled within me, swirling as fast as the rotating rectangles and squares around me.

Anxiety. Fear. Anxiety. Fear. Once again. Once again. For as long as I can recall fear has been my nemesis-- with anxiety its troubling companion. I hate fear. I hate fear. I hate feeling this way.

I took several long, slow, deep breaths in an effort to calm myself.

"It has begun." "It has begun." "It has begun."

"Te Deum. Te Deum. Te Deum. "Thee, O God, we praise"
"Te Deum. Te Deum. Te Deum. "Thee, O God, we praise"

The Sound of Weeping
The Feel of Fear,
Jacob's Day of Trouble, Drawing Near

"It has begun."

The singing gradually faded, diminishing into the distance. It was as if some invisible conductor leading an off-stage orchestra had slowly brought his hand down signaling a *diminuendo.* In the distance I could hear the retreating, dull roll of thunder. Lightning once again flashed, a bluish-white stretching across the darkening night sky, from the east like long fingers reaching toward the west. As it flashed I saw myself seated in my dome clinging to the cross – *stunned into silence – by what I saw.*

Silence. Cosmic Silence. As I sat with wide-eyed wonder, stunned by what I saw, the only sound I heard was that of the cosmic wind.

I was *peering beyond the veil that separates the visible from the invisible, the temporal from the eternal. And, I was stunned. Stunned. Stunned into silence.*

I wasn't paralyzed with fear. The fear was paralyzed -- with astonishment. Stunned. Astonished. Amazed. Feelings of serenity washed over me, through me, within me. A spirit of calmness rushed through me as a sense of peace and well being worked deeply within me – *chasing my fear away.*

My eyes began to well up with tears. A tear, a single tear, crawled down my cheek. My fear was chased away by what I was seeing.

The entire firmament of the sky beyond the star group was blood red in appearance, stained with several large glowing pulsating orange-yellow splotches. In the distance, beneath the blood red firmament, stood a brilliant celestial display, the cause of those pulsating splotches.

I couldn't believe what I was seeing. Here was the most unusual, the most unanticipated sight – clear evidence of intelligent design -- a massive, colossal seven branched candlestick – *a terribly large ancient Menorah.*

I can't explain the inrush of euphoria. My arms started to tingle as I experienced amazing feelings of elation. The fear disappeared, quickly. I can't explain the feeling, the feeling that replaced the fear, other than to say that it was euphoric, ecstatic, exhilarating.

The *Menorah* was massive. It was tremendously large. It stood taller than the earth, planted on the earth, towering over the earth, with the earth its footstool. *This was no cosmic accident – this was not the work of man -- God did this. Only God could do this!*

The Menorah was – how can I say this? It was like a mighty inrush of faith. It was visual evidence of things hoped for….the substance of things unseen.

I was trembling. Weeping. If this is a dream – or, or as Edgar Allan Poe once said, *if all that we see is a dream within a dream*[113] – then, Mr. Poe, don't wake me. Let me dream. Let me dream the dream within a dream and let me remain a dreamer. But, this was no dream – *this was Peering beyond the veil…*

"It has begun." "It has begun." "It has begun."

I wept. I was seeing the unseeable. Hearing the inaudible. Stepping beyond the known – into the unknown. Peering beyond the veil that separates the visible from the invisible, the temporal from the eternal. I was in awe.

The pulsating orange-yellow splotches bouncing off the blood red firmament presented an unbelievably gorgeous spectacle. Simultaneously, radiant swirls of golden light streamed upward from the base of the *Menorah* like steam, creating a hot mist of flashing pastel-colored gases.

Astounded as I was by the sight of the *Menorah* I began to notice something peculiar, something really odd *about the earth* upon which the *Menorah* stood. The universe around me and the earth before me were mirror images of the earth and universe that I knew, yet this earth and universe before me, they were rotating counter-clockwise with reverse rotations. Consequently, both the universe and the earth had rotations that were operating in reverse, reflecting a mirror image opposite of what one would normally anticipate.

Another perculiarity was immediately apparent. In addition to being a mirror opposite in its rotation the position of the earth's axis was also strange, very strange. Most satellite imagery of the earth portrays the axis of the earth with a slight tilt. The earth before me, the earth that I was seeing had no tilt. Its axis was upright -- *the Menorah was standing on an earth which had an upright axis caught in a reverse rotation.*

Yes, Emma, "Truth is sometimes stranger than fiction."

The voices began singing again.

> *"Te Deum. Te Deum. Te Deum. "Thee, O God, we praise"*
> *"Te Deum. Te Deum. Te Deum. "Thee, O God, we praise"*

The placement and the shape of the continents were also strange, very strange. This reverse earth actually resembled a thirteenth-century crusader map that was once on display at the *New Orleans Metropolitan Museum of Art.* The crusader map was the work of Heinrich Bunting in his *Itinerarium Sacrae Scripturae.*

Bunting depicted the earth as a three-leaf clover, with each leaf representing one of three continents: Europe, Asia, and Africa. At the top of the earth the three continents were linked by several large global rings – rings within rings, wheels within wheels -- that were drawn around a city located at the very top of the earth, at the actual center of the earth. *Bunting identified that city as Jerusalem.*

The heavens became even more brilliantly illuminated as a large host of distant stars fell through the firmament like rain. As my eyes followed one especially bright star as it raced across the sky, I wondered, what of the *Star of David?* And, what of the *Star of Bethlehem?* And, what of the *Bright and Morning Star?*

Here. Before me. In some unknown region of the universe – here was a cosmic image of falling stars piercing a red firmament above what appeared to be Bunting's world map. Here, before me, atop the map, was a massive *Menorah* – standing on Jerusalem – the center of the earth. *This was not a cosmic accident. This was not the work of man. This was not the work of Bunting. Only God could actually do this.*

My voice, the sound of my voice, suddenly singing, filled my dome. Clinging to the aluminum cross I stood and sang an anthem of praise…

> *O Lord my God, when I in awesome wonder*
> *Consider all the works Thy hand hath made,*
> *I see the stars, I hear the mighty thunder,*
> *Thy power throughout the universe displayed.*

Then sings my soul, my Saviour God; to Thee,
How great Thou art, how great Thou art.
Then sings my soul, my Saviour God; to Thee,
How great Thou art, how great Thou art.[114]

As lighting cracked across the crimson sky I could not help but wonder, *Had Bunting once stood where I was now standing? Had he seen what I now see? What was the correlation between Bunting's ancient crusader world map and the vision that was before me? How could these things be?*

If the earth was standing on Jerusalem, the center of the earth, was this earth the center of the universe? Must Ptolemy and Copernicus do battle again?

An ancient *midrash*, preserved from antiquity, identified *Eretz Yisrael* as *the navel of the world.* It also declared that the city of *Yerushalayim* was *Yisrael's* center. *Bet ha-Mikdash, the Temple,* stood at the center of the city of *Yerushalayim,* with the *Holy of Holies* located at the very center of the *Temple.* The *Ark of the Covenant*, according to the *midrash,* was located at the center of the *Holy of Holies* and in front of the *Ark of the Covenant* stood the *Foundation Stone* on which the world was founded – and there before me stood the *Menorah,* on the *Foundation Stone* – at the very center of *Jerusalem,* the very center of the earth.[115]

On earth, yes, on earth there are many voices and many fingers pointed toward the supposed center of the earth. Some, like Bunting, say Jerusalem. Others say Mecca or Varaanasi, Benares. Still others say the Aral Sea. Some even say Venice in Italy. Several *Byzantine hymns* describe the Cross as being *"planted in the center of the earth."*[116]

On this reverse earth, however, the stunning image and the thunderous roar of the *Menorah* flames seemed to be God's final word.

The three continents. The three-leafed clover. Rings within Rings. Wheels within Wheels. The Seven Candlesticks. The Menorah. The Center of the Earth. Yerushalayim. The Foundation Stone. There is none other foundation than that which has been lain. [117] *This could only be of God.*

"Yes, Emma," I shouted, "Yes, Emma, Yes. Sometimes, what actually happens is more bizarre than anything imagined."

The chorus of voices continued singing, with greater force – followed by the whispering voice of *Leitourgós.*

"Te Deum. Te Deum. Te Deum. "Thee, O God, we praise"
"Te Deum. Te Deum. Te Deum. "Thee, O God, we praise"

"It has begun." "It has begun." "It has begun."

The roar of *Menorah's* flames thundered across the red firmament. *Menorah's* loud roar and the shaking, caused by the flames, rumbled repeatedly, methodically, rhythmically. It was a constant rumbling, a constant repetitious roar, over and over, again and again. Plumes of hot white gas flared upward. Rippling, swirling white smoke continued its dance around the base of the *Menorah.*

The flames were tall and moved swiftly, with raw power. Each of the seven flames created glowing orange-yellow splotches whose pulsations were reflected onto the red firmament. I had never imagined such as this.

The hum and hiss of a lonesome falling star – with the sound of eternity -- echoed briefly as it traced across then through the red firmament.

The main shaft or trunk of the *Menorah* was visually subdivided into four sections with each section separated one from the other by a large curved spindle wrapped around the shaft. The smooth curves of these spindles were overlain with a dark shade of burnished gold. They resembled the curved wooden rings that circle wooden spindles turned by a lathe on earth. Within each of the four sections there were fourteen smaller spindles, overlain with a lighter shade of gold with names written in Hebrew, etched and engraved on each of these fourteen smaller spindles.

"Te Deum. Te Deum. Te Deum. "Thee, O God, we praise"
"Te Deum. Te Deum. Te Deum. "Thee, O God, we praise"

Evidently the schematic of this *Menorah* was intentionally designed to bear witness to time, prophetic history and the unfolding historical sequence from earth's creation to its conclusion. Just as the four sections of the shaft of the *Menorah* pointed toward the first coming of Christ and the beginning of the church age so too did the seven branches proceeding out of the shaft point to His second coming and the ending of the church age.

The traditional ornamentation of the *Menorah,* with its original design of almond flowers, buds and blossoms, was retained. In other, more profound ways, the emphasis was on the fullness of time and its Messianic interpretation.

Fourteen smaller spindles in the lowest of the four sections of the *Menorah's* shaft represented fourteen generations from Adam to Abraham. The names *Adam, Seth, E'nosh, Ke'nan, Ma·hal'a·lel, Ja'red, E'noch, Me·thu'se·lah, La'mech, Noah, Shem* and more were engraved on each of these fourteen smaller spindles.

The second section also had fourteen smaller spindles with fourteen different engraved names representing the fourteen generations, from Abraham to David.

There were also fourteen small spindles in the third section representing the fourteen generations from David until the carrying away into Babylon; and, in the final section, fourteen small spindles represented fourteen generations from the carrying away into Babylon to the *incarnation,* the birth of Christ. The opening chapter of the Gospel of Matthew records the fourteen generational scheme.

"Te Deum. Te Deum. Te Deum. "Thee, O God, we praise"
"Te Deum. Te Deum. Te Deum. "Thee, O God, we praise"

Large flames, massive fiery flames, continued to leap from each of the seven branches of the *Menorah.* They shot upwards with a loud roar like that of a thousand Niagara Falls, then bent in horizontal submission to the cosmic winds, with the tip of their flames stretching horizontally from the eastern sky toward the west.

The flames atop each of the seven branches were massive, yet differed in width and length. The external dimensions of the flames varied, one from the other, but only slightly. They were not, however, measured in either metrics or miles – but in increments of time.

The duration or length of each flame represented a certain period or measurement of time as it pertained to the unfolding history of the New Testament church age from *Pentecost* to the rapture of the church. In some strange, inexplicable way the length of the flames flowing from this incredibly large *Menorah* represented the flames of New Testament church history. Here, in the length of the flames, was the eternal plan – the eternal plan for the church age – *from Pentecost to the end of the church age.*

"Te Deum. Te Deum. Te Deum. "Thee, O God, we praise"
"Te Deum. Te Deum. Te Deum. "Thee, O God, we praise"

Each of the seven flames flowing from the branches of the *Menorah* corresponded to seven churches who were recipients of seven letters recorded in the book of Revelation. The first candle had the name *Ephesus* engraved and etched in Greek lettering into its golden cap. The length of the flame passing through that cap, which was measured in time, represented the duration of the Ephesian portion of the church age, which began on *the day of Pentecost* and concluded, according to many Bible scholars, around A.D. 170. Many of these scholars view the seven letters to the seven churches as representing seven periods or sequential stages of church history. In this sense the seven letters are viewed as a hidden map of church history from its inception – *the Ephesian age* -- to it conclusion – *the Laodicean age.*

With this understanding some view the first portion of the church age as being symbolized by *Ephesus,* followed by a second portion of the church age symbolized by *Smyrna,* followed by a third portion symbolized by *Pergamum,* and so on. Each portion of the church age unfolding on earth reflects specific spiritual characteristics that corresponded to the descriptions described in the individual letters to each of the seven churches.

Through this interpretive grid some have discerned and deduced that the *Ephesian church age* emerged on *the day of Pentecost* then concluded in A.D. 170. Then came the *Smyrnean church age* which ended in A.D. 312. It was followed by the *Pergamean* portion which ended in A.D. 606. The *Thyaterian church age* then emerged then concluded nearly a thousand years later in A.D. 1520. Then came the *Sardisean church age* which lasted approximately two hundred years, ending in A.D. 1750. The *Philadelphian church age* which followed was of an even shorter duration, having ended in A.D. 1906.

According to this interpretation since A.D. 1906 the New Testament church has been in the *Laodicean church age*, an age which will end with the *rapture* of the church, a seven year *Great Tribulation – and the eschatos.*

Oh. God. Show me. Show me. Is this interpretation valid?

"It has begun." "It has begun." "It has begun."

The sky darkened, becoming deeper and deeper crimson. Expanding slowly the lower level of the crimson firmament mingled with pale violet misty gases, creating mystical brilliancy. Several super bolts of lightning flashed across the massive *aurora borealis* beneath the firmament. A moment later a large meteor passed by, tumbling over and over, spinning then disappearing into the dark distance of space.

"Te Deum. Te Deum. Te Deum. "Thee, O God, we praise"
"Te Deum. Te Deum. Te Deum. "Thee, O God, we praise"

There it stood – the massive Menorah. The seven raging flames, weaving and waving like gigantic fiery flags, traced wild shadows across the firmament.

This was no common fire. Common fire destroys. This fire purifies.

Great red-orange outer flames circled and spun forward, roaring as yellow-blue inner flames surged up then merged, then twisted into a fiery circular rotation. Fresh specks of white hot embers sparked upward then were swallowed by the circulating whirlpool of flames. Fire followed fire in the swirling rotation, forming a long, fire-filled, smoke-filled tunnel that ran the full length of *Menorah's* seven connected flames, from the first flame, the *Ephesus* flame, to the seventh, final flame, the *Laodicean* flame.

Fire and flames constantly shot forward, licking and shooting their way through the outer wall of fire, only to be caught in the rotation of the giant outer flames. This compression and constriction of fire caused hot smoke, sparks and fiery gases to fill and circulate through the tunnel as the fire raged.

Against that backdrop I heard spinning sounds, familiar spinning sounds like that of rotating rectangles and squares. There was a distant flash of light. I was staggered, overwhelmed by what I was hearing and by what I saw. My dome was being drawn closer and closer to the golden *Menorah.* The Italian voices resumed singing but with a greater urgency….

"Te Deum. Te Deum. Te Deum. "Thee, O God, we praise"
"Te Deum. Te Deum. Te Deum. "Thee, O God, we praise"

"It has begun." "It has begun." "It has begun."

As I was being drawn toward the *Menorah* I began to hear the sounds of fire, crackling sounds; popping sounds, like the repeated popping of a whip; hissing sounds, like the recurring hisses of a cat.

A clap, a powerful startling clap of thunder rumbled again. It was immediately followed by another brilliant burst of lightning. The lightning flash enabled me to see deeper into the flames. In the midst of the rotating tunnel of flames, I saw what appeared to be shadows; but, as I shielded my eyes to see more clearly….

"O God. O God. There are people in there. There are people in there."
…these are not shadows – but people.

People. People struggling for breath, struggling for strength as they raced through the flames. Some stumbled. Some fell. Some crawled. Yet, just as the Scripture said, "*no torment touched them*"[118] – "*neither were they burned*"[119] -- "*neither did the flame kindle upon them.*"[120]

I was horrified, horrified by what I was seeing. Uncontrollable surges of fright and fear welled up inside of me again. Here, before my eyes, was one of the most terrifying sights I could ever imagine. The people, the people in the flames were striving, straining, pushing themselves, pushing themselves physically, pushing themselves mentally, as hard as they could, to make it through the fire and flames – and each, in his turn, somehow made it through the tunnel of fire unscathed.

Some would stumble and fall, then get up. Others would crawl through the smoke, then, with God's strength they would get up and resume running. The image of the flames, the image of the people racing through the flames still burns in my brain.

"O God. O God. There are people in there. There are people in there."

I was too shocked to cry, too confused, too bewildered, too filled with fear to even think. Once again, I was stunned, simply stunned – this time not by *beauty* but by what I perceived to be pure *horror. I did not yet understand God's providence, the power of God to protect and preserve His people.*

In the midst of my fear-plagued mind I somehow recalled the calming testimony of Israel's King Solomon....

"the souls of the righteous are in the hand of God and no torment will ever touch them."[121]

A small portion of *A Psalm of the Apocalypse* shouted inside my brain....

Fiery Trial. Fiery Trial. A Hard Example.
Sacred Blood through Flames Trample.
Learn Patience Beneath their Altar
As they sing Retribution's Psalter
How long, O Lord, How long shall we wait?

"the souls of the righteous are in the hand of God and no torment will ever touch them."[122]

These people racing through the flames – these are the last group of martyrs, the Laodicean martyrs, slain during the New Testament age. Soon, very soon, as they completed with patience the race that was before them, they would take their place with the martyrs who preceded them in death, who had counted it a joy to suffer for Christ. They, like their brethren who had preceded them in martyrdom, would soon stand with other martyred souls under the altar.

As they ran, they appeared to struggle, struggle desperately for breath and for strength as they ran enveloped in flames. Fire was streaming into and through the shaft as biting flames attempted to devour the runners -- *without success.*

In many ways they were reminiscent of the burning bush that caught the attention of Moses while on the backside of the desert -- *the bush burned with fire, and the bush was not consumed – and neither were these people,* the Laodicean martyrs.

"the souls of the righteous are in the hand of God and no torment will ever touch them."[123]
"when thou walkest through the fire, thou shalt not be burned; neither shall the flame kindle upon thee"[124]

"Te Deum. Te Deum. Te Deum. "Thee, O God, we praise"
"Te Deum. Te Deum. Te Deum. "Thee, O God, we praise"

Monstrous waves of fire would periodically rise, covering the runners, making them appear as dull reddish shadows racing through the glowing haze. Even though they were surrounded by hot oceans of flames and smoke, they continued running – *victoriously shouting and praising God as they ran with patience the race set before them.*

I heard the words of *Leitourgós* again….

"The Noble Army of the Martyrs Salute Thee.
TE DEUM"

Then I heard my words and my memories of words spoken by *Leitourgós* at the *Defense Advanced Research Projects Agency*, in Blacksburg, Virginia

"I saw the Souls of the Martyrs under the Altar."
"White Robes. White Robes were given unto every one of them. White Robes."

"You reached the Fifth Seal, John, you reached the Fifth Seal."
"Choices have Consequences, John. Choices have Consequences."

As my memories of these words surfaced I realized that there was *no altar here in Menorah's flames. And, there are no souls of martyrs under any altar – at least not here. This tunnel of flames was not the fifth seal.* It certainly wasn't hell. Purgatory? No. There is no biblical basis for such a place as purgatory.

"Make a Faith Choice. John, Make a Faith Choice. Do not let fear hold you back."
"You must go back, John. You must go back, beyond the fifth seal."

"But, where are the souls of the martyrs? Where is the altar? And, what of the fifth seal?"
"The fifth seal is not yet, John, not yet. This tunnel of flames is that which is called *Bema.*

Bema. The Bema Judgment.

"Every man's work shall be made manifest: for the day shall declare it, because it shall be revealed by fire; and the fire shall try every man's work of what sort it is."[125]

SORT. Wood, Hay, Stubble. Gold, Silver, Precious Stones. the fire shall try every man's work of what sort it is

"Te Deum. Te Deum. Te Deum. "Thee, O God, we praise"
"Te Deum. Te Deum. Te Deum. "Thee, O God, we praise"

I watched, wide-eyed, as the last of the runners raced through the seventh, final Laodicean section of flames. Then, in the midst of swirling smoke and flames I saw a man running, one single man running back through the flames toward the first flame, the Ephesian flame. He had already run his race and finished the course that was set before him – *and now he was coming back.*

As I looked into his face I sensed familiarity. I had always wondered how the three apostles who were with Jesus on the *Mount of Transfiguration* recognized Moses and Elijah as they stood beside Jesus. The apostles knew Moses, though they had never met him They knew Elijah, though they had never met him. I once wondered how they knew – now I know.

This man, this man running back through the flames -- *I know this man. Though we had never met -- I know him.* He was the very first New Testament martyr, the first among many who had run through these flames. As he ran back toward the entrance of the first flame he seemed to curve his body downward then upward, working his way through the fire and flames. It was Stephen, the first martyr.

"The last will be first and the first will be last."

As Stephen reached the entrance to the Ephesian flame, the area where he stood was suddenly surrounded by cosmic dust. Out of the dust came a great fog, a great thick white fog that looked like a sandstorm filled with the glare of white haze.

Wisps of swirling light hovered around three tall men wearing cloaks and hoods who stood surrounded by white haze at the entrance to the tunnel of flames. Beside them were three horses. As lightning flashed yet again I could see that each of the horses were hitched to what appeared to be large old wooden-wheeled wagons, funeral carriages. Atop each carriage was a plain wooden casket. The horses stood, muscular and tall. And the men? They stood still, surrounded by haze and glare, and stared at me in silence. They stood across from Stephen who was surrounded by the glow and glare of fire.

My dome slowly moved toward the area where the men stood. At a certain point I stepped out of my dome, still holding my aluminum cross.

It was then that another man, a fourth, emerged from the haze that surrounded the three men and knelt down in front of me. His silvery-white cloak had an insignia, an insignia across the chest. The insignia featured an eagle, a winged man, an ox and a lion. As he knelt before me he spoke with a calm, firm voice, directly to me…

"The Noble Army of the Martyrs Salute Thee.
TE DEUM"

It was *Leitourgós.*

"Make a Faith Choice. John, Make a Faith Choice.
Fear held you back."

As *Leitourgós* stood before me he suddenly reached for and took my cross and held it high above his head. He then shouted a shout that filled the entire tunnel of flames, the *Menorah* and the earth below.

"In hoc signo vinces."
"In hoc signo vinces."
"In hoc signo vinces."

His triple shout echoed, again and again.

"In this sign you will conquer." "In hoc signo vinces."

He then turned to face me yet again….

"Make a Faith Choice. John, Make a Faith Choice.
Fear held you back."

As I turned from *Leitourgós* to face the flames, I thought of that which was written by the prophet Isaiah, thousands of years ago….

"When thou walkest through the fire, thou shalt not be burned;
neither shall the flame kindle upon thee."[126]

"In hoc signo vinces."
"In this sign you will conquer."
I was about to step beyond – my fear.

RESTORE POINT 30:

"IN HOC SIGNO VINCES."

"In hoc signo vinces."
"In this sign you will conquer."
I was about to step beyond – my fear.

I stood firm, resolute, determined – staring intently at the tunnel of flames. I was surrounded by the pulsating orange glow of fire. White hot sparks swirled around me. Hot wisps of gas wrapped around my legs, ankles and feet. Flames were licking upward then bending at the entrance of the rotating tunnel of fire.

I turned back toward *Leitourgós* – he was gone. So too were the three men who were with him; and the white horses and the funeral carriages. They too were gone. I then looked toward Stephen – he too was gone. One moment they were there. The next moment, they were gone. It was as if they were never really there.

Choices have Consequences.

The Bible speaks of the *"Valley of Decision."* This was my valley, this was my decision. *Leitourgós* knew that. So did Stephen. And, so did I. A decision had to be made. The choice was mine – and so were the consequences.

The prophet Joel, who spoke of the *"Valley of Decision"* cautioned that "the day of the LORD is near in the valley of decision." [127] In some strange way that was beyond my ability to discern my *choice* in my *"Valley of Decision"* was also linked to *"the day of the Lord."*

My face was hot – but not from the flames. It was hot, hot with the flush of fear. Oh. The horror. I trembled and trembled again. My fear returned with great vengeance. I was terrified, filled with trembling fear, so much so that I thought I was going to die of sheer fright rather than by fire. Doubt and hesitancy, like proud, arrogant, intimidating warriors, stood up inside of me – mocking me, working against me – stoking the fire of my fear.

I scanned the tunnel of fire as the rotating winds blew with greater and greater strength. Narrow thin ribbons of fire, like streaking tongues, licked at everything in its path.

"I cannot do this. I cannot do this. I can't. I can't."

My heart was pounding. My head was spinning. The flames, the raging flames, they seemed to be everywhere, spinning and rotating, faster and faster. Without taking a step I had already stumbled – faltered and failed. Fear stopped me even before I started. I began to weep. Surrounded by the roar of the flames I cried aloud, I cried out to God….

"Kyrie Boethei, Lord Help."
"Kyrie Boethei, Lord Help."
"Kyrie Boethei, Lord Help."

Nothing. No response. There was no monk with a shaved circle on the back of his head waving his arm, coming to my rescue. Nor did I hear the sound of the monk's encouraging French voice, *"Monsieur." – Sir. "Je vous aiderai." – I will help you.*

No. The monk did not come to my rescue – *but memory did.* And for some strange reason I recalled a small portion of a sermon I had preached at the Chalmette church….

> *"Know this: God has appointed a time, a place and a circumstance for faith to ultimately triumph over fear. When that time comes you will see that God has used every event and experience of fear to strengthen your faith – to enable you to Advance Through Adversity."*

I thought about that sermon and about the words of *Leitourgós*: This is *my appointed time.* This is *my appointed place.* This is *my appointed circumstance.*

"Make a Faith Choice. John, Make a Faith Choice. Fear held you back."
"In hoc signo vinces."

With my eyes tightly closed and my fists tightly clenched -- I ran as fast as I could into the raging fire, wild with fright. As I ran I heard a voice, shouting and screaming. It was my voice, my voice, once again crying out to God....

"Kyrie Boethei, Lord Help."
"Kyrie Boethei, Lord Help."
"Kyrie Boethei, Lord Help."

Large balls of fire, like fierce super-heated beasts snorting flames, breathing hot breath, consumed my works. I could smell the nauceous smoke of burning *wood, hay and stubble.* Fresh swirls of fire, rolling clouds of smoke and hot gases gathered above me, then rolled before me, then under me as I ran faster and faster. The *wood, hay and stubble* of my life were consumed by the flames while the *gold, silver* and *precious stones* were purified, glistening and gleaming.

White hot sparks and red hot embers shot upward, rushed forward, then fell on my hair, my neck, and my clothing, smoldering then burning through my clothes, sticking to my flesh. Strangely, as I continued running I felt no pain. Once again I though of that which was written by the prophet Isaiah, thousands of years ago....

"When thou walkest through the fire, thou shalt not be burned;
neither shall the flame kindle upon thee."[128]

"In hoc signo vinces."
"In hoc signo vinces."
"In hoc signo vinces."

The whole fiery ambiance, this super-heated environment, caused me to run even faster, fearful lest I faint, fearful lest I falter and fearful lest I fall. I ran so fast that I actually tripped, stumbled and fell. As I struggled to get up I stumbled and fell again.

"Not by might nor by power, but by My Spirit,' says the LORD of hosts."[129]

Falling…falling…falling…It seemed that I was constantly falling, stumbling and struggling to pick myself up, only to falter and fall yet again. Finally, exhausted, I yielded to a greater power outside myself, the power of God. Once again I was reminded of Moses on the backside of the desert -- *the bush burned with fire yet the bush was not consumed – and neither was I.*

Then, as I struggled to get up and resume running I saw something, something I had never anticipated seeing. I saw through the flames to the earth beneath the *Menorah.* Surrounding the earth, at the four points of the compass, four angels were preparing to blow *apocalyptic trumpets.*

Suddenly, their trumpets blared loudly. The trumpets sounded, repeatedly, creating a sacred symphony unlike anything ever heard on earth. Haunting voices with a poetic cadence whispered several portions of *A Psalm of the Apocalypse….*

Seven, the Number of Perfection
And of Weeks
Daniel saw Seventy, of Years
One Disappears, Cut Off – Eternal Tears

One remains
Only One, One Week of Years
The Lamb, The Lion -- Final Tears
Jacob's Time of Trouble.
It now appears.

"Te Deum. Te Deum. Te Deum. "Thee, O God, we praise"
"Te Deum. Te Deum. Te Deum. "Thee, O God, we praise"

"It has begun." "It has begun." "It has begun."

These phrases *"one week of years"* and *"Jacob's Time of Trouble"* are direct references to the appointed time, the seven years of the *Great Tribulation.*

Several times when we talked *Leitourgós* would stress that...

"It has begun." "It has begun." "It has begun."

Daniel, in his great apocalyptic prophecy stated that the actual length of time of the *Great Tribulation* would be "one week of years" or "seven years" – Thus the warning of *A Psalm of the Apocalypse....*

It now appears" – thus "Final Tears."
"It has begun." "It has begun." "It has begun."

But, what is the source of *these "Final Tears?"* What is the source of *"Jacob's Time of Trouble?" The Battle of Armageddon!*

Blinded by fear, overwhelmed by a feeling of dread, confused and disoriented -- *I panicked.* The blaring sound of the trumpets was still ringing in my ears, reverberating through the tunnel of flames and echoing across the universe.

The shofar -- It would soon sound above all others. It would be the final trump. Then, on earth, there would be *"Tears," "Final Tears" and "Trouble," "Jacob's Time of Trouble."*

The Battle of Armageddon.

This frightening apocalyptic word refers to earth's final battle in the valley of *Jezreel, Merj ibn-'Amir,* the *Plain of Megiddo. Armageddon* is a very real place that has become a symbol of the final conflict between God and the forces of evil. That battle, which will occur near the end of the seven year *Great Tribulation,* will precede the *Great White Throne Judgment.*

Jezreel. Jezreel.
Stained with Blood. Graves, Open, Bone-Filled.
Widen their jaws.
A Gathering of Armies. Falling Stars.
Merj ibn-'Amir, the *Plain of Megiddo.*
War Men at the End of Time

One Week Remains, Singular. Alone.
Earth's Final Judgment – The Great White Throne

Once again I panicked. The tension was great. So was my fear. *The Trumpets. The Flames. The Final Trump.* History's final seven years. The *"one week"* – the *"one week"* of *Great Tribulation* – *"Singular."* and *"Alone."* – It had begun. And, beyond this apocalyptic event, looming on the horizon, at the end of the *Great Tribulation* was....

Earth's Final Judgment – The Great White Throne

I cried, in my anguish, I cried with a frightful, trembling voice. The wind blew with ever increasing strength. Rolls of smoke covered the length of the tunnel, swirling with the rotation of the flames. The flames were tall, moving swiftly. I continued running, running as fast as I could with the strength that God gave.

The firmament above was still crimson, a deep blood red crimson, as far as the eye could see. The light from *Menorah's* seven flames bounced off the blood red sky, staining the firmament with several large glowing pulsating orange-yellow splotches, eerie reflections of *Menorah's* seven flames.

In the distance, near the edge of the red firmament I saw a door, a door opened in heaven. As the sound of blaring trumpets continued filling the universe, the long, loud sound of a single *shofar* overwhelmed the sound of the trumpets – causing them to immediately become silent.

The blowing of the *shofar* was long, loud, and shrill, a high, long piercing sound -- a summons. The *shofar* seemed to be talking, saying...

"Come up hither." "Come up hither." "Come up hither."

And, the redeemed people of God – *both the dead in Christ and those who were alive* -- were doing just that – *going up hither from the four corners of the earth.*

With the sound of the *shofar -- that final trump* -- one of the greatest miracles of history happened, instantaneously, in the twinkling of an eye: *dead believers in Christ on earth were raised, raptured, caught up to be with the Lord in the clouds. And, immediately following them were those believers who were alive, who had not yet died. They were also raptured, and caught up together with them in the clouds -- meeting the Lord in the air.*

"It has begun." "It has begun." "It has begun."

The time is fulfilled.
Final Trump.
Shiv`a.

My heart was pounding, pounding hard, and the tightness in my chest, it felt like…it felt like the stage was being set for a massive heart attack. I was astonished by all that was happening – astonished by what I was seeing, astonished by what I was hearing. And, astonished that I was still battling fear.

I couldn't catch my breath -- hyperventilation. The struggle for breath intensified. I felt like I was going to suffocate. My fear was so intense that it was making me struggle to breath.

In the distance I could hear the roll of thunder. Lightning once again flashed, with bluish-white streaks that pierced through both the red firmament and the fiery flames of the circulating tunnel of fire.

I struggled frantically to catch my breath and get to my feet. I became dizzy, disoriented and stumbled yet again.

Questions began to race through my mind: *Where was Leitourgós? Where was Stephen? Why was I alone? Why was I not caught up as the other believers when the final trump sounded?*

I continued running.

See, The Just Man –
Struggling For Breath
Running to Certain Death
He, a Martyr, the Last, Runs, Yet Not Alone
Nor for sin does he Atone
But for Fear
It crawls down his cheek, a tear
At his death, *Eschatos* appears.

The Italian voices singing TE DEUM gradually faded. It was as if some invisible conductor leading an off-stage orchestra had slowly brought his hand down signaling a *diminuendo – the TE DEUM was replaced by brilliant flashes of lightning, thunderings and voices singing a new song…*

Thou art worthy, O Lord, to receive glory and honor and power….
Thou art worthy, O Lord, to receive glory and honor and power….

The massive tunnel was filled with flames that were rumbling and roaring as they were pushed and whipped into the circular rotation with increasing velocity, power and strength. In the distance I once again saw the open door. The sound of the voices singing the new song was coming through that open door. Someone shouted, *"The seals. The seals. Who is worthy – Who is worthy – Who is worthy to open the seals?*

Thou art worthy, O Lord, to receive glory and honor and power….
Thou art worthy, O Lord, to receive glory and honor and power….

War Men at the End of Time
Broken Seals. An Ancient Rhyme.

The Seven-Sealed Scroll.

Each of the seven seals unleashed sequential episodes of God's judgment. The unleashing of that judgment began with the *Four Horsemen of the Apocalypse.* My rapid breathing seared my lips, tortured my tongue, and blistered my mouth. The constant breathing of hot air caused my lungs to feel like pot belly stoves, filled with fire. I could feel, I could actually feel my blood, my hot blood coursing through my veins. It was boiling hot, my blood was boiling hot, making it feel as if volcanic lava was working its way within me. Everything seemed red, red with fire.

I then heard the distant sound of hoof beats racing across the red firmament -- and saw four evil riders, each riding a different colored horse – The first horseman was riding a white horse. The second horseman rode a red horse. The third horseman sat upon a pale horse and the fourth horseman sat astride a black horse. They suddenly stopped near the *Menorah* awaiting the appointed time before heading toward *"the twisted land" – the earth.* Voices, eerie voices that sounded like *"burning winds"* once again whispered a portion of *A Psalm of the Apocalypse*...

The horsemen. The horsemen.
Four in number.
Apocalypse. Apocalypse.
Do not slumber.
Burning Winds. Twisted Land.
Waters Rise and Rage.
Eschatos. Eschatos.
The Lion. The Lamb. The Cage.
Avel.

The Horsemen. The Four Horsemen of the Apocalypse.

History bears witness to diabolical, cruel, evil world leaders. History also testifies that these evil leaders at first appear to be loving and compassionate. Evil masquerades as something other than what it actually is by wearing deceptive disguises. Sometimes evil leaders wear the mask of savior. Disguised with the mask of goodness, they and their empty promises deceive many. Evil, masqueraded as goodness, has often been enthusiastically and blindly followed by the populace. Such was the case of the first of these four horsemen.

The distant noise of thunder rumbled as the *first seal* was opened. Then I heard the sound of approaching hoof beats. I saw the rider of the first horse, the white horse. He had a bow in his hand -- *a bow with no arrow*

– signifying false peace. I saw him – and he saw me. I knew him – and he knew me. *It was Secretary General Antiochus Zarathustra.*

Antiochus Zarathustra. He promised peace, global peace -- peace on earth and goodwill for men – but it was a false peace – and a false promise. He indeed was a....

War Man at the End of Time

Zarathustra
An Image – A Symbol -- Who will understand?
Six thrice, the Number, the Beast, a Man
Shiv`a.

Antiochus Zarathustra was not simply one of a long litany of evil leaders to appear on the stage of human history. He was evil personified and bore the number of both man and a man, a specific man.

Six, Imperfection, the Number of Man
Six thrice, Woe unto the Earth, the Beast
In the Latter Day, his Feast –
Six, Imperfection, the Number of Man
War Man at the End of Time
Zarathustra

This man, this evil one personified, he has been called by many names. *The Lawless One. The Evil One. The Anti-Christ.* He is the most evil leader in all of human history. *He is the Beast.*

Zarathustra
An Image – A Symbol -- Who will understand?
Six thrice, the Number, the Beast, a Man

Here is wisdom. Let him that hath understanding count the number of the beast:
for it is the number of a man; and his number is

Six hundred threescore and six [130]

War Man at the End of Time
Zarathustra
An Image – A Symbol -- Who will understand?
Six thrice, the Number, the Beast, a Man
Shiv`a.

My legs were jiggling and my hands were trembling as the evil *Antiochus Zarathustra* galloped across the face of the earth -- *Antiochus. That Swine.*

I struggled to get up and continue running through the flames. Once again, I felt like I was going to faint. I felt dizzy and strange. The worse of it was the fear, the unrelenting fear, the fear that I was going to die, consumed by the swirling hot flames. *Self-immolation.*

The voice shouted yet again, *"The seal. The seal. The second seal.* After the *second seal* was opened the *third seal* and then the *fourth seal* were opened in sequence -- unleashing *hunger, war, pestilence and death* to savage the earth.

Small columns of fire shot high into the air above me then flared into larger flames, followed by swirling smoke that was immediately engulfed in and absorbed by the larger flames.

The circulating winds of the fire storm added fresh swirls of smoke, embers and sparks – forcing me to run even faster. The smoke, sparks and embers were driven by a mad whirl of constantly swirling hot gases that carried millions of sparks, deeper and deeper into the fiery tunnel of flames.

My heart was pounding, harder and harder. Once again I lost my balance, stumbled and fell. I couldn't breathe. I felt like I couldn't run any further. I couldn't go any farther. Staggering from one side of the tunnel of flames to the other, fear, like a menacing monster rose up, growling -- at me -- within me – against me. As I strained and struggled I once again began shouting and screaming….

"Kyrie Boethei, Lord Help."
"Kyrie Boethei, Lord Help."
"Kyrie Boethei, Lord Help."

For seven days I ran like this, falling, stumbling and falling, overcoming exhaustion, excessive heat, fire and flames, until all the *wood, hay and stubble* were burnt away and all the *gold, silver* and *precious stones* were totally purified.

Then, suddenly, I was there – *at the fifth seal* – standing before *the altar of the martyrs.*

John, the last living apostle once stood here, on hallowed ground, before this very altar. He wrote about what he saw in the book of Revelation....

I saw under the altar the souls of them that were slain
for the word of God, and for the testimony which they held
And they cried with a loud voice, saying,
How long, O Lord, holy and true, dost thou not judge and avenge
our blood on them that dwell on the earth [131]

The great apostle saw *the souls under the altar.* He did not see a symbol. These people -- *the souls under the altar* -- are real people. There is no *symbolism* here. These people are not *metaphors* nor are they *abstractions.* They are real flesh and blood people – *martyrs* – who gave their lives during both the Old Testament and New Testament age. They were stoned, sawn asunder, slain with the sword, crucified upside down, drowned, fed to wild animals and worse.[132] Yet, they ran with patience the race that was set before them, endured affliction, running by faith through the flames of martyrdom. They resisted unto blood as the fiery trial of their faith unfolded. And John says that he saw them. He said that he saw these people. He *"saw under the altar the souls of them that were slain."*

Fiery Trial. Fiery Trial. A Hard Example.
Sacred Blood through Flames Trample.
Learn Patience Beneath their Altar
As they sing Retribution's Psalter
How long, O Lord, How long shall we wait?

A shudder, a trembling shudder, ran through me as I realized that I was standing where the aged Apostle John once stood; and, I was seeing what he had once seen. Even though I was heavily medicated at the time I distinctly remember saying, while I was at the *Defense Advanced Research Projects Agency facility in Blacksburg, Virginia* that…

"I saw the Souls of the Martyrs under the Altar."
"White Robes. White Robes were given unto every one of them. White Robes."

A second shudder ran through me as I realized that, though I was standing where the Apostle John once stood – seeing what he had seen -- I was also seeing something that he had not seen. Above the altar was the handiwork of *Leitourgós*. He had strategically placed, above the altar – *an aluminum cross – my aluminum cross* from *The Chapel of the Candle.* A golden plaque was attached to the cross with the following inscription engraved upon it….

"In hoc signo vinces."
"In this sign you will conquer."

I was suddenly surrounded by swirls of white cosmic dust. Out of the dust came a great fog, a great thick fog that looked like a sandstorm filled with the glare of white haze. As the dust cleared I saw Stephen. His skin was white as snow as was his hair. He was wearing a white robe.

Next to him stood *Leitourgós*. Wisps of swirling light hovered around both Stephen and *Leitourgós*. Behind them stood the three tall men wearing white cloaks and hoods. Beside them were three horses. As lightning flashed yet again, I could see that each of the horses was hitched to what appeared to be large old wooden-wheeled wagons, funeral carriages. Atop each carriage was a plain wooden casket. The horses stood, muscular and tall. And the men? They stood still, surrounded by white haze. They stared at me in silence.

"The Souls of the Martyrs under the Altar. Stephen, the first martyr. Leitourgós.

Leitourgós walked through the haze and knelt down in front of me. His silvery-white cloak had an insignia, an insignia across the chest. The insignia featured an eagle, a winged man, an ox and a lion. As he knelt before me he spoke with a calm, firm voice, directly to me…

"The Noble Army of the Martyrs Salute Thee.
TE DEUM"

"You are now at the Fifth Seal, John, you have reached the Fifth Seal."

"I saw the Souls of the Martyrs under the Altar. White Robes. White Robes were given unto every one of them."

"Make a Faith Choice. John, Make a Faith Choice. Fear held you back.
You must move beyond the fifth seal, John – move beyond the fifth seal."

"The old man is dying. John, the old man is dying."

"The three caskets. What are these three caskets?"

"One, the casket in the middle, is for him, the old man who is now dying. He is the last living martyr of the New Testament church age."

"What of the other two?"

"In the first is John from the isle of Greece. He died many years ago. In the second is Cosmas, the son of John from the isle of Greece. He too died years ago. They are *absent from the body and present with the Lord.* [133] They are now raptured and in heaven."

"How are they connected to this old man who is now dying? And, who is this old man that is now dying?"

"He who is now dying is John the Younger, now grown old. He, as a child, wrote *A Psalm of the Apocalypse.* His father, Cosmas, and his grandfather, John, from the isle of Greece, witnessed the writing and transcribed seven original copies onto seven smaller parchments.

"When you burned the sixth of seven original parchments in your church office, the smoke from that burning triggered the start of a series of events, catastrophic, eschatological end-time events. In the *Belfry Tower* of the *Chapel of the Candle* you burned the final copy – triggering the *unavoidable, inevitable, irreversible eschatos.* That final burning sealed the destiny of John the younger. He is now an old man and he is dying. According to the foreordained counsel of God, He is the last martyr of this, the dispensation known as the New Testament church age."

"The last martyr?"

I heard the soft voice of John the Younger, racing through my brain.

"I-I-I am you; and, you are me. Op-Op-Open your eyes; and, you will see. A ri-riddle—A mystery. I-I-I am you; and, you are me."

"The last martyr?"

I was once again stunned, stunned into silence. I couldn't think. I could only stand and listen. I couldn't believe what I was hearing.

"Of this dispensation?"

"Yes. The other men, the two standing beside the horses and caskets behind me, are the two witnesses, God's end time prophets who will prophesy for twelve hundred and sixty days, clothed in sackcloth, then they will be killed, martyred, during *the time of Jacob's trouble*. They are the first of those who suffer martyrdom during *the time of Jacob's trouble, the Great Tribulation.*"

"Who, who, who is the last martyr?"

"John, the Baptist, was the last prophet of the Old Testament age
And you, John, are the last martyr of the New Testament age.
You, John, are John the Younger now grown old."

RESTORE POINT 31:

DEFRAGMENT-DISSOLVE

"Code Blue. Code Blue. Code Blue."
"GET THE CODE CART. GET THE CODE CART.
"

Nurses. Doctors. – Shouting. Shouting. Shouting. – Nurses. Doctors.

HE'S TACHYCARDIC. HE'S TACHYCARDIC. HIS BP IS DROPPING RAPIDLY. HIS SATS ARE LOW – TOO LOW. GOING LOWER.

Shouting. Shouting. Shouting.

GET SOME MORE HELP IN HERE... ANESTHESIA...

"Brain Embolism. Brain Embolism."
"He's thrown a blood clot. Blockage. Hemorrhaging."
"He's Flatlined. He's Flatlined."
Flatlined.

"Dr. Rieux, this is Zarathustra. We have ten minutes. Ten minutes."

"Ten minutes for him to be restored."
"Ten minutes."

"Count Down Activated."
Defragment-Dissolve 10:00... Defragment-Dissolve 09:59... Defragment-Dissolve 09:58... Defragment-Dissolve 09:57... Defragment-Dissolve 09:56... Defragment-Dissolve 09:55...

"In ten minutes everything and everyone in our world will begin to dissolve."
"Dissolve. Defragment. Disappear."
"We have ten minutes."

Nurses. Doctors. – Shouting. Shouting. Shouting. – Nurses. Doctors.
Defragment-Dissolve 09:07... Defragment-Dissolve 09:06... Defragment-Dissolve 09:05...

"We must have that Apocalyptic Psalm. Do something Rieux."
We stand at the very edge of that abyss.
Annihilation. Extinction. Non-existence. Oblivion. Nothingness.

Defragment-Dissolve 06:04... Defragment-Dissolve 06:03... Defragment-Dissolve 06:02...

"We must have the Apocalyptic Psalm, Dr. Rieux. We must have the Apocalyptic Psalm.

Nurses. Doctors. – Shouting. Shouting. Shouting. – Nurses. Doctors.

"Mr. Grand. Paging Mr. Grand. This is Dr. Bernard Rieux. Grand, what is the Restore Point?"
Defragment-Dissolve 03:57… Defragment-Dissolve 03:56… Defragment-Dissolve 03:55…

Large circular glass panels shattered and exploded into tiny pieces,
Falling onto my circulating platform.

Defragment-Dissolve 01:57… Defragment-Dissolve 01:56… Defragment-Dissolve 01:55… Defragment-Dissolve 01:54… Defragment-Dissolve 01:53… Defragment-Dissolve 01:52…

My body bounced violently as if it was being shaken by invisible hands.

"Rieux. This is Grand."
"There Is No Restore Point."

Defragment-Dissolve 00:04… Defragment-Dissolve 00:03… Defragment-Dissolve 00:02…

"He's Dead."
"He's Dead."
"He's Dead."

Defragment-Dissolve 00:00

RESTORE POINT 32:

THE METAPHOR

I died. My body is now incorruptible. My spirit has been set free. I was the last martyr of the New Testament age. I, John, died by the hand of *Zarathustra.* It was there, in the wretched underground facility of the *Defense Advanced Research Projects Agency* in Blacksburg, Virginia, that I died.

I died. Yes, I died – and I, even I, am now a *soul under the altar.* My body is now incorruptible. My spirit has been set free. But my transformation is not yet complete.

And so – here I stand. Above me – a crimson firmament mingled with pale violet misty gases, creating mystical brilliance. Several super bolts of lightning flashed across the massive *aurora borealis* beneath the firmament.

Yes. Here I stand. Above me – a crimson firmament. Before me -- an altar -- and, above the altar, an aluminum cross placed their by *Leitourgós.* And, beneath the altar, people, not ordinary people but martyrs, *souls under the altar.* And I, yes, even I am one of their number. Standing here, beside the altar, looking beneath the altar -- It is as if I am outside myself looking at myself, seeing myself see myself.

The number of *souls under the altar* was great, so great that no man could count. This great cloud of witnesses, this massive multitude of martyrs had the appearance of a great sea, a great rolling milky white sea. They rose and fell, then rose and fell again, and again. This living sea, flowing, like massive, slow moving waves of water was comprised of a sea of milk-white faces blended with white robes. This sea, this sea of *souls under the altar,* had the appearance of white, pure white, pristine white, blended with flowing white and white shadows. This was a vision of things not seen – *a vision of things eternal.*

The Bible relates that "Eye hath not seen, nor ear heard, neither have entered into the heart of man, the things which God hath prepared for them that love him." [134] And, what can be said, what can be said of these *souls under the altar?* What can be said of these martyrs? John, who wrote the book of Revelation, wrote of some who "loved not their lives unto the death." [135]

These souls, these *souls under the altar,* they did not cherish their life when they came face to face with martyrdom. The loveliness above them and the loneliness within them caused a longing – a longing within each soul that no man could satisfy. Mysterious and inexplicable, the obscure white faces of the martyrs saw the secret of their sea. Like waves beating out the passage of time they did learn its secret, yet, just as *John the Younger* wrote, they did learn…

Learn Patience Beneath their Altar
As they sing Retribution's Psalter
How long, O Lord, How long shall we wait?

As I looked at the massive sea of faces, one face, one face among the multitude of white faces retained the natural color of flesh. I could see that familiar face clearly, very clearly – and was stunned by what I saw -- *the soul with the flesh face was me.* Though I was now one, one with this multitude, one with the martyrs, and though I had indeed died a martyr's death -- my transformation was not yet complete.

I was now a *soul under the altar* surrounded by other *souls under the altar* -- but my transformation was not yet complete.

And so, here I stand, beneath a crimson firmament, beside the altar, looking below the altar – seeing myself, a *soul under the altar* surrounded by myriads of *white faced souls under the same altar.* Again, it was as if I was outside myself looking at myself, seeing myself see myself.

The color of my drab flesh in the midst of the sea of white -- it was as if I were a dying caterpillar, a chrysalis without a cocoon surrounded by beautiful butterflies. I was alive yet not yet fully alive – my transformation was not yet complete.

Around me – *souls under the altar.* Above me -- *the altar.* And, above the altar an aluminum cross – *and an engraved inscription…*

"In hoc signo vinces."
"In this sign you will conquer."

A fragrant breeze wandered up from the patient sea of faces. I took a deep breath. My chest expanded as my heart started thumping strongly. Above, high above the *aluminum cross*, I saw images, eternal images, images of a Throne surrounded by a large circular rainbow, a rainbow with no beginning or end. Seated on that Throne was One like unto *the Lamb of God – the Lion of Judah -- high and lifted up.*

His face, the face of God, was veiled. I could not fully see His face – my transformation was not yet fully complete. His feet, which had the appearance of fine brass, were resting on the earth, which served as His footstool. An upward gesture of blessing, made by his right hand, had two fingers pointed upward, the traditional medieval symbol of reward and blessing.

Beneath Him, surrounding the earth, at the four points of the compass, the four angels had ceased blowing their apocalyptic trumpets. They were now shouting shouts of victory.

On earth tombs were opened. Graves were emptied. The dead in Christ who had fallen asleep were raised. The sea gave up the dead who were in it. Then those believers who were alive were caught up to be with the Lord forevermore.

"O Death. Where is your sting."
"O Grave. Where is your victory." [136]

Then, He that sat upon the Throne opened the Sixth Seal.

Eschatos. Eschatos.
"It has begun." "It has begun." "It has begun."

When the Lamb opened the *Sixth Seal* in the distance I could see the earth as it shuddered and shook with great violence -- *an earthquake.* Volcanic ash and great rolling grey-black clouds and smoke caused by earthquake eruptions covered the sun with darkness. The moon, which was barely visible, became red, blood red. Then, in the midst of the chaos, the *Lamb* opened the *Seventh Seal.* There was stillness and silence in heaven about the space of half an hour, then I heard the sound of…

Seven Final Thunders
The Nations, They Shudder, They Cry
Mountains fall on us, Lest we die
Seven Heads Turn, Seven Crowns Fall
Seven Kings Weep – Earth, Final Call

Seven angels which stood before the Throne were then given seven trumpets that would sound *"earth's final call."* They readied themselves to sound what Bible scholars call *the seven trumpet judgments.*

The *seven seals, seven trumpets,* and *seven bowls/vials* are three successive series of apocalyptic judgments from God. The judgments increase in intensity, becoming more and more devastating as the end times progressed.

The sky above me was still crimson but it appeared to be moving away from the chaotic earth. It seemed to be gradually drifting toward the distant horizon, which was inky black. Inexplicably, at the same time, the horizon seemed to remain at a fixed distance. It was as if there was movement – *but there was no motion.*

As I stood there staring at the distant horizon, swirls of thick fog, heavy with the glare of white haze, suddenly surrounded me. As the white gas and dust settled and cleared, Stephen appeared. He was surrounded by the swirl of white fog. His skin was white, and his hair, his hood and his robe. *Leitourgós* stood beside him. At first I did not see him. The white rolling fog was so thick. He stepped out of the haze, walked toward me, then, again, as was his tradition, he knelt down in front of me

"The Noble Army of the Martyrs Salute Thee. TE DEUM"

"And I salute Thee, *Leitourgós*, I salute Thee."

As *Leitourgós* rose to his feet I gave a second salute.

"And I salute Thee, Stephen, I salute Thee."

Stephen then stepped forward.

"Important changes must be made within us, John. Changes within me, within you and within all of the martyrs. Unlike those who died a normal death we are not yet fully prepared for the complexities of eternity. Our bodies are now incorruptible and our spirits are indeed free. However, the transformative process we began on earth through sanctification, the renewal of our minds and our martydom must continue because our...."

"...transformation is not yet complete," I heard myself say, finishing his sentence.

Leitourgós then spoke...

"The martyrs, in their present state, cannot yet inherit the kingdom of God. Even though your body, like their bodies, is incorruptible, and even though your spirit is indeed free -- your nature, John, and Stephen's nature, and the nature of all of the martyrs is still not completely suited to the eternal. The human mind in its present state is yet too earthy to endure the exceedingly great, eternal weight of glory."

As they continued speaking I thought of Jesus raising Lazarus from the dead. Jesus cried with a loud voice, "Lazarus, come forth." And Lazarus, who was dead, was raised from death. He came forth; but, he was still bound hand and foot with grave clothes: and his face was bound about with a napkin. Even though Lazarus was now raised from the dead and alive his transformation was not yet complete. He was still bound by the garments of death. In a very real way, so was I, and Stephen, and the martyrs, *the souls under the altar.* Our transformation is not yet complete.

"We have put on new bodies," added Stephen, "and new spirits. Now we must put on a new mind – the eternal mind of Christ -- by completing the sanctification process that began on earth."

"It's like being a butterfly," added *Leitourgós*. "You, and the martyrs, began as a caterpillar and now are like a chrysalis within a cocoon, alive yet not fully alive. Butterflies, my friend, actually hatch from a chrysalis to become a butterfly. For the butterfly, being alive in the chrysalis stage is being alive but not yet fully alive. You, and Stephen and the martyrs are yet in that stage."

Alive yet not yet fully alive. I was alive yet not fully alive. The thought of that raced through my mind.

"The martyrs, like butterflies, are *alive yet not fully alive,"* added *Leitourgós. "They must be metamorphosed, fully sanctified, transformed fully, transformed completely -- glorified -- by the eternal renewing of the mind."*

"Each of us must take this path," added Stephen, "and, in accordance with biblical chivalry, conduct and courtesy -- *The last shall be first and the first last."*

"What does that mean? I asked.

"You, John," added *Leitourgós,* "It means you will lead the way. You – *the last martyr of the New Testament age – you shall be first.* Then these, *the souls under the altar,* will follow, with Stephen – *the first martyr of the New Testament age – being last."*

"Each of us, however," added Stephen, "must pilgrimage alone – in solitude."

The sound of that word – *"solitude"* – led me to recall a portion of A Psalm of the Apocalypse…

In – in the darkness
A slender flame leaps – in solitude.
Like a Sheep led to Slaughter
He Died for His Own

In solitude. Christ. The Slender Flame leaps. The Light of the World. In our darkness. Like a sheep led to slaughter. He died. For us. He died for His own. And, now we must follow Him – Follow His Steps – in Solitude. Alone.

Stephen then quietly walked toward me, drawing me away from memory and meditation. He placed his hand on my shoulder then offered one final thought concerning the remainder of my journey.

"John, do you remember what Jesus said concerning the eye of the needle?"

"Yes, he said it would be easier for a camel to go through the eye of a needle, than for a rich man to enter the kingdom of God," [137]

"This is true, John. But, remember, He also added that with God nothing is impossible. Remember that, John – the eye of the needle – nothing is impossible with God. When you're facing impossibility – when you can't. God can."

Stephen then handed me the aluminum cross and read aloud the engraved inscription.

"In hoc signo vinces."
"In this sign you will conquer."

He then slowly knelt down in front of me and gently spoke words normally reserved for *Leitourgós.*

"The Noble Army of the Martyrs Salute Thee. TE DEUM"

Leitourgós said nothing. He was silent. Without uttering a word he simply stood there, staring at me, slowly nodding his head as a single tear crawled down his cheek. It was a sweet tear. Then, as he looked intently into my eyes, he nodded his head one final time, then smiled a sly knowing smile – and winked – and I winked back. – *Déjà vu.*

Then they were gone.

The sky above was still crimson. It seemed, however, that the pace of the gradual drift toward the distant dark horizon had quickened.

Then I heard spinning sounds, familiar spinning sounds like that of rotating rectangles and squares. Once again I was caught up in the air, in my now familiar dome, streaking across the crimson firmament. Several super bolts of lightning flashed across the massive *aurora borealis* beneath the firmament.

A distant flash of light, shining in the midst of the dark horizon seemed to beckon me. I began what I knew would be the last portion of my journey, hearing different sounds – voices – voices singing in Hebrew, the language of God. I heard ancient, strange sounding words, words that echoed the sentiment and revelation of the sacred *Trisagion.* The chorus was sung over and over, repeatedly, in unison by the heavenly choir…

Thrice Holy. Thrice Holy. Thrice Holy Is Our One God.
Thrice Holy. Thrice Holy. Thrice Holy Is Our One God.

Outside, the universe was spinning, faster and faster; *yet there was no motion.* Once again, I cannot explain it. I can only struggle to find words to describe it. There was movement, rotating movement -- *but there was no motion.*

There was something else. I could also hear the familiar sound of a great, ceaseless breath, the breath that had carried me across the universe on several earlier occasions. As I was carried along, once again, space, and time, seemed to twist and bend, turning back on itself, folding in upon itself, meeting itself, then rippling back to its original time and place. There was neither silence, nor sound – only time – and timelessness -- and space, the wondrous, massive, expanse of space – yet space seemed to be constricting.

Gradually, as my journey continued, contrasts, inexplicable, insensible, incomprehensible contrasts, began to emerge. I remember now how I wondered if these experiences were real. *I now know in my spirit that they were real – even more real than anything I'd ever experienced on earth.* I was about to embark on a *Thought Journey* -- intentionally designed to change false patterns of thought that were shaped within me by life in a fallen universe.

Initially, I anticipated that the focus of this *Thought Journey* would be on ethics, morals, values and such. Instead, the focus was on cognitive concepts, perspectives, mental constructs, prejudicial biases, perceived notions and unchallenged assumptions, all generated by and shaped by life in a fallen universe.

The Thought Journey. Complexities. Simplicities.

"Truth is sometimes stranger than fiction…."

I was Seeing, actually seeing, the unseeable. Hearing the inaudible. Stepping beyond the known – into the unknown. I could not believe it – but I did believe. I did believe. Such is the overpowering nature of faith.

I wondered, *How can one explain the inexplicable?* The inexplicable is just that – *inexplicable.* How can words, meaningful words, thoughts and concepts that we all embrace suddenly become empty of meaning while other meaningless words, thoughts and concepts are instantly transformed, overflowing with new powerfully profound meaning? And, how does one communicate that to others who have not shared the experience. Its like trying to explain the taste of peppermint to an aged man who has lived his entire life in a jungle, away from civilization.

It doesn't make sense; but, everything I am describing happened. As I was carried across the great expanse of the universe -- *these things were happening.*

I was Seeing the unseeable. Hearing the inaudible. Stepping beyond the known – into the unknown.

To my left, in the distance, hot orange stars at the edge of an immense interstellar debris field were sending ripples of radiation into long stretches of space. Beneath the debris field bright rectangular slabs of white light, like light flowing from open fields of beautiful light, flared against a backdrop of pale stars and stardust. A twisting ribbon of glowing reddish-green gas wound its way through the stardust. Beneath the ribbon was an eerie blue glow that formed a thin column of pale blue swirling cosmic dust.

Words, thoughts and concepts raced through my brain. Like a mirror they reflected an image of long held cherished understandings of reality. Yet, just like a mirror the image was reversed. Everything was a reflection of an opposite. *It was inexplicable.*

Then, incomprehensibly, the mirror would suddenly shatter, reflecting and flashing bits and pieces of even newer understandings in totally different, unanticipated ways. Metaphors, similies symbols and more, flittled like butterflies, as language took on differing, profound meanings. Multiplied bits and pieces of new meaning, profound and deep, like shards of shattered glass, were flying everywhere. And, just as quickly, the mental mirror became whole again reflecting the old, yet retaining the new, while revealing opposing imagery, and new, previously unknown images. There was power, a strange new kind of power, infused into the metaphors and similies. This cognitive process, designed to create new paradigms, perspectives and understandings happened many times, repeatedly. Each time, as I saw different angles, different perspectives, I gained a clearer understanding of myself, of life and of God. A doxology of praise exploded within me -- *the foolishness of God is wiser than human wisdom.* [138]

Somehow, in the midst of one of these cognitive cycles I recalled a prayer by J. B. Phillips. I remembered that, while on earth, I prayed that prayer often, with the conviction that God's answer to that prayer in my life and in the life of His children was of great value. I chose to call that prayer, though J. B. Phillips did not label it as such, "The Reality Prayer." It is a very short, very concise, very simple prayer: *"God, Help me to see the world as it is, myself as I am; and, Thou as Thou art."* [139]

That prayer, when I prayed it on earth, was a prayer for truth; a simple request for the ability to understand, for discernment, for wisdom; for the gift of seeing life unencumbered by the many illusions that distort our perceptions, cloud our understanding and hinder us in our pilgrimage through life.

Hustling across the emptiness of space a bright white ball, a comet, was followed by a long trail of yellow gas. As it raced, rolled and twisted oddly, the sparkling red and blue veins of a tattered lime green nebulae stretched across its path.

Something bizarre, something stranger than fiction began happening. It was again inexplicable.

That which was, was no longer, yet remained. Stability became instability, yet remained stable. Everything became topsy-turvy. Up was down and down was up – yet everything remained right-side up. That which was stained was suddenly pure and that which was pure was suddenly purer still, pristine. Old became new and new became old – *without aging. Freedom* and *Determinism* merged, yet maintained *autonomy. Universals* and *Particulars, Diversity* and *Unity* – everything was melting together, becoming one, then separating, becoming many – yet maintaining unity, remaining one, yet without *monism.*

At the close of each of these conceptual cycles I sensed a greater sense of inward serenity, a heightened sense of awareness and a greater appreciation concerning how we are, as the Bible says, *"wondrously and fearfully made."*[140]

Then the cognitive cycle repeated – sometimes focusing on mental concepts; at other times focusing on philosophical issues and a great deal of time focusing on theological concerns…

Predestination. Providence. Law. Grace. Works. Spirit. Flesh. Regeneration. Justification. Sanctification. Glorification. Revelation. Inspiration.

Nothing was ignored. No stone was left unturned.

Augustine vs. Pelagius. Calvin vs. Arminius. Luther vs. Erasmus. Christology. Soteriology. Angelology.

The pale rainbow colors of several constellations swirled tighter and tighter together, forming a colorful well-defined spiral. Wisps of pale green gases on the outer edge of the constellations struggled, without success, to escape the magnetic pull of the spirals.

It was then that I began to notice that the universe, the entire universe, was spinning, actually spinning, faster and faster -- *yet there was no motion.* Stars and distant galaxies came near, then joined the ever constricting narrow spiral – *yet there was no motion.* Great movement, perpetual planetary and galactic movement, cosmic movement, rotated throughout the tightening expanse of space -- *yet there was no motion.* I wondered, *'How could this be?' Is motion an illusion? Is time an illusion?* Time, as we know it on earth, is an emergent effect of motion. *Yet, around me, there was no motion.*

Inexplicably, there was neither silence, nor sound – only time, and timelessness, the ethereal music of the spheres, and the laboring breath of cosmic winds. An invisible, unseen bridge between what was and what was to be was collapsing. Yesterday was irrevocably severed – *finished.*

Who can comprehend these nuances of the cosmos? I could not. Yet, there was a sense of knowing, a knowing that was working deep within me – and with it a competing sense, an overwhelming *sense of not knowing. Contradictions. Contrasts. Compliments. Cosmic Character. Order. Disorder. Stability. Instability. Freedom. Form. Determinism. Responsibility. Disorientation. Clarity.*

Just as a mirror image of a galaxy rotating counter-clockwise would have clockwise rotation so too was everything in this portion of the universe operating as a mirror image opposite. I was witnessing a breakdown of symmetry, or, in the language of physics, *a parity violation* of cosmic proportions. *Cosmic expansion and contraction* were simultaneous events with the *"either/or"* perspective an illusion. The *"both/and"* position was the more prominent perspective – but not the preeminent perspective. God's ways and God's thoughts are higher, infinitely higher than any could ever imagine.

In the midst of the contradictions and contrasts I saw the birthplace of stars. I could not explain it but it harbored the seeds of both stellular life and death. There, in the cosmic incubator of stars, was the unthinkable -- a dual seeding of opposites, of competing forces, of life struggling against death and of death waging war against life. It was as if the inanimate elements of the universe were slanted toward cosmic conflict. Such is *the mystery of iniquity.*

The iniquitous effect of this cosmic conflict was most apparent in the dark empty hollow galaxies. They had evidently lost the battle for life and were defeated in their struggle. Like lost sinners separated from God by their sin, these empty hollow galaxies were stained with sorrowful, bittersweet colors of despair and traveled cold lonesome paths, floundering in darkness. The emptiness around them was filled with howling, violent winds that echoed an eerie hollow sound, the sound of weeping, a bitter lament. Dark gray cosmic clouds, above, beneath and beyond each of these empty galaxies served as their bleak backdrop.

Everything rotated at an apparently steady rate in a constant rotating direction, following a circular path that gradually descended toward a dark, narrow, unseen center. As I spiraled deeper into the darkness of the distant narrow center, the bright colors of the universe began to fade, with all light and color being absorbed by the darkness. Larger constellations, varying in brightness, attempting veering angles to avoid the dark center, eventually succumbed to the pull of the dark center. Descending deeper into the dark spiral I could see distant lights flare up, momentarily. Protesting the darkness, they and their light were soon extinguished.

Everything became black, very black – and silent. There was no sound, none whatsoever. Yet, something was heard -- the distant, whispery sound of the Menorah's flames of history. It was a profound reminder that God has a time table.

There was no sense of space, nor was there any sense of time. It was as if I was locked in a void, an empty black void filled with nothing and nothingness. It appeared that I was in a region of the universe where spatial distances and sequential intervals are so brief that the very notion of time and space break down.

At the *Defense Advanced Research Projects Agency* in Blacksburg, Virginia, AC4 spoke of the abyss of *nothingness,* the mystery of mysteries that he said was looming on the horizon before us. He spoke of the very edge of extinction, of annihilation, of non- existence -- that mystery of oblivion. And he warned that a cataclysmic, momentous and violent conclusion of humanity and history loomed on the horizon. Then, I remember, he asked, "Who among us is wise enough for this hour?"

Wise enough. It is impossible for me to describe the absence of light, or the deep blackness of *nothingness,* or its emptiness. Who among us can define or even describe with coherence such things without using the language and vocabulary of time and space. It is challenging, very challenging, to define or describe absence, especially the absence of the fundamental dimensions of time and space. Nevertheless, both were disappearing before my very eyes. But, what I was seeing was the great womb of time giving birth, not to *nothingness – but to newness.*

Yesterday was being irrevocably severed from today. Old years, the old centuries, the old millenniums – *finished.*

Then, in the far distance I saw a tiny dot of light, just a speck, a very, very small tiny pinpoint of light. Such is the poverty of language. How can there be spatial distance when there is no space? Initially the tiny dot did not appear to move, but there did seem to be a slight erratic variation in its brightness as it began to shift its position, slowly – *yet there was no motion.*

Dark cosmic cloud banks and their dusty shadows hanging low on the horizon temporarily blocked my view of the tiny pinpoint of light, then, as it emerged from behind the dark clouds it slowed to a halt, and remained stationary for a brief period of time. Then it slowly began to rise and shift its position, once again, flickering slightly and irregularly. Then it gradually seemed to gain speed, then it gradually slowed.

The blackness around me suddenly began to take shape, the shape of a tunnel, an ever narrowing tunnel. I could see movement, circulating movement, but no motion; yet, out of the stillness, out of the silence and out of the darkness of nothing and nothingness -- something was taking shape, something inexplicable. I felt myself traveling, faster and faster through the blackness, winding my way deeper into the dark spiral. I began to sense that I was moving through the stillness at an even greater speed, rushing toward the tiny dot of light -- *yet there was no motion.*

Once again, the pinpoint became still. Then, suddenly rising, it moved laterally, still flickering but it was now gaining speed, then, just as quickly it came to a sudden stop. It appeared that the pinpoint of light was positioning itself in relation to some distant object. This was puzzling, yet I was puzzled even more, startled with great surprise, by this dot of light -- the light stood still then suddenly divided into two tiny lights – *two separate pinpoints of light.*

As I continued to watch what were now two pinpoints of light, both lights flickered, then divided again -- becoming four. Shaking my head in disbelief I looked again toward these multiplying tiny dots -- they divided again, then those divided yet again, and again and again -- *eventually filling the distant blackness with millions of tiny pinpoints of light.*

Suddenly, the swirling blackness around me was filled with flashes of light. Sound, distorted sound -- voices, whispering voices, voices singing in Italian, voices singing in Hebrew, choruses -- merged together in symphony, breaking the silence. Images, above me were images, twisted, bending, taking form, then dissolving, then appearing again.

As I stood looking upward at the images I trembled with fear -- not negative, anxious fear – but reverence. I had reverent fear in what I was hearing and reverent fear in what I was seeing -- *a mighty weeping angel.* The weeping angel had huge white feather wings, towering high in the heavens. The weeping angel held an open book, the *Lamb's book of Life.*

The *Great Tribulation – Jacob's Time of Trouble – Daniel's seventieth week, the final, singular week that remained, alone on the prophetic time table* – that final remaining week had come to an end.

Somehow, surly by God grace I saw deep into the future – and saw the *Great White Throne Judgment.*

One Week Remains, Singular. Alone.
Earth's Final Judgment – The Great White Throne

The names of the redeemed of the ages were written in that book – *the Lamb's Book of Life.* Seven other angels with trumpets, signaling judgment, were behind the large weeping angel. They had sounded their horns in fulfillment of ancient prophecies -- to distribute divine retribution.

A sense of awe, and contrasting feelings of fear, dread and trembling overwhelmed me. I wanted to fall on my face but there was no room in my small dome to do that. And, so, I sat there, clinging to my aluminum cross – the emblem of my salvation. My eyes were fixed on the totality of what I was seeing.

The weeping angel holding the open book had another arm, a long, outstretched arm, with its hand and a long finger pointed downward, indicating judgment and banishment. Beneath the angel's frightening outstretched hand stood a condemned heretic, an atheistic philosopher, and behind him, two of his atheistic peers.

The first philosopher cowered and trembled, his face wet with tears, filled with eternal fright. *His name was not written* in the *Lamb's Book of*

Life. There was something sad and something pathetic about this atheistic philosopher – *I felt like I knew him. And I did.*

I also knew his two peers -- the other two atheistic philosophers, who, with equal fright, fear and trembling, stood behind him. Here, cowering before the *Great White Throne* was…

Three. Three. Shaped by the Pen.
Recurrence. Recurring, Again and Again.
Philosophers Three – All Agree
What Ill Hath Befallen Thee
Camus' Foul Sons, Foul Sons Thou Art
Who are, will be, yet are not --
A Devious Plot.
He Who Has Eyes, See.
Unholy Trinity. – Unholy Three.
Avel.

Here stood Dr. Rieux, Joseph Grand and Jean Tarrou, philosophers three. Shaped by the pen of Camus. Their lives recur, again and again, every time someone reads Camus' book, *The Plague.* They are indeed, *Philosophers Three – All Agree*

Rieux represented and embraced *Atheistic Pragmatism.* Joseph Grand pursued and promoted *Atheistic Materialism* and Jean Tarrou was an adamant proponent of *Atheistic Secularism.* Each of them were not only affected but infected *by Atheistic Existentialism – the philosophy of despair* -- that absurdist philosophical school of thought which believes that all efforts to find inherent meaning in life will ultimately fail.

To the right of the weeping angel the righteous were standing beside the Judge. On the left of the Judge a large group of Old Testament believers were standing beside their leaders represented by the twelve tribes of Israel. On the opposite side, in a similar position another group of New Testament believers stood beside the twelve apostles.

Both groups were clothed with white robes. In the midst of the great crowd I could see, barely see, a man waving his arm, trying to get my attention.

"Monsieur. Monsieur. Monsieur.

It was the monk, the one with the shaved circle on the back of his head. Beside him was Dr. Castel. He turned, looked at me – and smiled. A sense of awe and inward reverence overwhelmed me as I saw, not too far behind them a rather sickly looking old woman with tired, yellowed eyes. She glared at me as she slowly and carefully placed one foot in front of another marching with the redeemed. As she received her white robe from the angels she smiled a simple smile. Then all I could see was grinning teeth as she became young again.

My eyes were so fixed on the totality of the *Great White Throne* that I could not move. I could only look, and wonder – and search the sea of faces. Then. Then. Then I saw her. My Emma. My Emma. She was waving. Smiling at me. Then she pointed to someone, a man standing next to her.

He was standing there, holding onto an aluminum cross, looking at the Great White Throne -- I was stunned. It is as if I am outside myself looking at myself, seeing myself see myself.

In the midst of this unbelievably ecstasy of the moment the heavens suddenly closed and the heavenly vision disappeared.

Before me, once again, was blackness, only blackness – *and the still multiplying tiny dots of light. They filled the blackness with millions of tiny pinpoints of light.*

Then, simultaneously, with great speed, each of the tiny dots of light flew pass me, so rapidly that they appeared as a fast moving spinning blur. As my head quickly turned to follow them it appeared that each one was drawn to one of the martyrs behind me. It was as if each tiny dot of light was assigned to a specific martyr.

In front of me, in the distance – was the one, singular, original pinpoint of light – that first, tiny, speck of light seemed to be assigned to me. As it hung in the blackness of space before me it was still surrounded by that circle of perfect blackness – blacker and darker than any black I had ever encountered -- but the circle was smaller now, more intense and tighter. Gradually all light, even the *tiny pinpoints of light* behind me vanished.

Surrounded by darkness, I felt myself traveling, faster and faster through the blackness, winding my way deeper and deeper into the dark spiral. Still flickering, the tiny speck of light was spinning faster and faster, round and round, then, just as quickly, it came to a sudden stop. It appeared that the pinpoint of light had positioned itself in relation to me and my trajectory.

Completely still, the tiny speck of light was completely still, as I was carried even deeper and deeper down the black spiral. I could feel a narrowing of the spiral. Its slope was swerving, going further and further downward. In some inexplicable way space was being constricted, contracted, and compressed, becoming a tighter and tighter spiral, whirling in the midst of the darkness. It was so dark and spinning so fast that I could no longer discern even the outlines of the narrowing spiral.

In front of me, still, in the distance – was that one, original dot – that tiny, speck of light – still surrounded by that circle of perfect blackness. As the speed of the downward spiral increased the spiral was becoming smaller, terribly smaller, narrower and narrower, tighter and tighter. I could feel the spiral edges tightening. The circular lines of the spiral began to curve and tighten. I began to feel numb as if I was crumbling and being crushed by massive, circulating forces that were beyond my control. I was weakened, very much weakened, yet still spiraling downward, downward toward the tiny, pinpoint of light.

I remembered the words of *Leitourgós*, "You, and the martyrs, began as a caterpillar and now are like a chrysalis, a chrysalis within a cocoon, alive yet not fully alive." I felt as if I were a dying caterpillar, a chrysalis being crushed in a collapsing cocoon – *alive yet not fully alive – nearly dead.*

I was descending, deeper and deeper. It was getting tighter and tighter, darker and darker. My ability to speak was gone. I could not cry out – my voice was silenced. My ability to think was weak and weakening – even my thoughts were like slurred speech. I was at the end of my senses. I was being squashed into and through a single point of infinite density… words dribbled from my mouth in a rush of barely distinguishable syllables.

Then, in the dark silence my protective dome collapsed onto itself.

I felt as if I were a dying caterpillar, a chrysalis being crushed in a collapsing a cocoon… a dying caterpillar, a chrysalis being crushed in a collapsing a cocoon… a dying caterpillar, a chrysalis, in a…. in a… crushed…crushed…, a chrysalis… Co, co, cocoon…my, my life is over…this is im, im, impossible…

The Speck of Light.
The Eye of the Needle.
I can't. I can't. This is impossible. I can't. I can't.
God can. God can.
I can't. I can't. I can't.
God can.
Grace.

"In hoc signo vinces."
"In this sign you will conquer."
I was about to step beyond – my fear.

Look… Look… A Metaphor.

It's Beautiful.
Look. On God's Finger. Look.
A Butterfly.

ENDNOTES

1 George Gordon, Lord Byron, *Darkness,* http://www.strickling.net/byron_darkness.htm

2 Wikipedia free encyclopedia. *Four Evangelists.* https://en.wikipedia.org/wiki/Four_Evangelists

3 Thomas Hardy, *Quotes About Writing,* http://www.rhettaakamatsu.com/writingquotes.htm

4 Is 65:25 KJV

5 C. S. Lewis. *C. S. Lewis Quotes.* http://www.goodreads.com/author/quotes/1069006.C_S_Lewis

6 Is 53:3 KJV

7 Je 14:8 KJV

8 Mt 4:16 KJV

9 T. S. Eliot. *T. S. Eliot Quotes.* http://www.goodreads.com/author/quotes/18540.T_S_Eliot

10 Ps 34L17 KJV

11 Ps 83:1 KJV

12 Corrie ten Boom. *Corrie ten Boom Quotes.* https://www.goodreads.com/author/quotes/102203.Corrie_ten_Boom

13 Vincent van Gough. *Vincent van Gough Quotes.* http://www.goodreads.com/quotes/773113-looking-at-the-stars-always-makes-me-dream-as-simply

14 Ps 119:105 KJV

15 Ibid.

16 Henry David Thoreau. *Henry David Thoreau Quotes.* http://www.goodreads.com/quotes/8202-most-men-lead-lives-of-quiet-desperation-and-go-to

17 1 Tm 1:18 KJV

18 1 Tm 6:12 KJV

19 1 Cor 15:58 KJV

20 T. S. Eliot. Ibid.

21 Ps 22:1 KJV; Mt 27:48 KJV

22 Ps 119:105 KJV

23 T. S. Eliot. Ibid.

24 Ps 41:8 KJV

25 Ps 22:1 KJV; Mt 27:48 KJV

26 T. S. Eliot. Ibid.

27 Mt 7:7 KJV

28 Ibid.

29 Ibid.

30 Unknown Author.

31 T. S. Eliot. Ibid.

32 Ibid.

33 Mt 7:7 KJV

34 Ibid.

35 Ibid.

36 Albert Camus. *The Plague Translated from the French by Stuart Gilbert.* (The Modern Library, New York, 1948), 88.

37 Mt 10:16 KJV

38 Albert Camus. *The Plague Translated from the French by Stuart Gilbert.* (The Modern Library, New York, 1948), 73.

39 Mt 10:16 KJV

40 Ec 3:7 KJV

41 Rene Descartes. *Rene Descartes Quotes. http://www.goodreads.com/quotes/3922-cogito-ergo-sum-i-think-therefore-i-am*

42 Ibid.

43 Albert Camus. *The Plague Translated from the French by Stuart Gilbert.* (The Modern Library, New York, 1948), 41.

44 Ibid.

45 Ibid.

46 Ibid.

47 Ibid.

48 Ibid.

49 Ibid.

50 Ibid. 92.

51 1Tm 6:12 KJV

52 1 Cor 15:58 KJV

53 Rv 2:17 KJV

54 1 Cor 15:58 KJV

55 Albert Camus. *The Plague Translated from the French by Stuart Gilbert.* (The Modern Library, New York, 1948), 41.

56 Ibid.

57 Albert Camus. *The Plague Translated from the French by Stuart Gilbert.* (The Modern Library, New York, 1948), 92.

58 Ibid.

59 Ibid.

60 Ibid.

61 Albert Camus. *The Plague Translated from the French by Stuart Gilbert.* (The Modern Library, New York, 1948), 92.

62 Socrates. *Socrates Quotes. http://www.goodreads.com/author/quotes/275648. Socrates*

63 Lewis Carroll, *Alice in Wonderland Quotes.* http://www.goodreads.com/work/quotes/2933712-alice-s-adventures-in-wonderland

64 Ibid.

65 Ibid.

66 Ibid.

67 William Shakespeare. *Shakespeare Quotes.* http://www.goodreads.com/quotes/541758-all-the-world-is-a-stage

68 Lewis Carroll, *Alice in Wonderland Quotes.* http://www.goodreads.com/work/quotes/2933712-alice-s-adventures-in-wonderland

69 Rene Descartes. *Rene Descartes Quotes. http://www.goodreads.com/quotes/3922-cogito-ergo-sum-i-think-therefore-i-am*

70 1 Cor 1:20 Holman Christian Standard Bible (©2009)

71 Wikipedia free encyclopedia. *Criticism Of Christianity.* http://en.wikipedia.org/wiki/Criticism_of_Christianity

72 Wikipedia free encyclopedia. *Aristotle.* http://en.wikipedia.org/wiki/Rhetoric_(Aristotle)

73 Quintus Septimius Florens Tertullian. *Tertullian Quotes.* http://www.goodreads.com/author/quotes/ 319733. Tertullian

74 Os Guinness. *The Dust Of Death.* (InterVarsity Press, Downs Grove, Illinois, 1973), 337.

75 Immanuel Kant. *Kant's Antinomies.* http://en.wikipedia.org/wiki/Kant's_antinomies

76 William Ernest Henley. *Invictus.* http://www.poetryfoundation.org/poem/182194

77 Augustine of Hippo. *What is Time? Or, Just What do Philosophers of Science Do?* John Norton, University of Pittsburg. http://www.pitt.edu/~jdnorton/Goodies/What_is_time/index.html, December 23, 2012.

78 T. S. Elliot. *The Four Quartets: Burnt Norton.* http://allspirit.co.uk/norton.html

79 Mt 9:17 KJV

80 Wikipedia free encyclopedia. *Four Evangelists.* https://en.wikipedia.org/wiki/Four_Evangelists

81 Rv 19:11 KJV

82 Rv 11:4 KJV

83 Albert Camus. *The Plague Translated from the French by Stuart Gilbert.* (The Modern Library, New York, 1948), 88.

84 L. Frank Baum. *The Wizard of Oz Quotes.* http://www.goodreads.com/work/quotes/1993810-the-wonderful-wizard-of-oz

85 Ps 46:1 KJV

86 Jo 20 KJV

87 Jo 3:4 KJV

88 Ex 27:2 KJV

89 Jl 2:28 KJV

90 Is 40:31 KJV

91 Ps 42:7 KJV

92 Dn 2 KJV

93 Dn 8:26 KJV

94 Jas 1:6 KJV

95 Unknown Author.

96 2 Cor 5:7 KJV

97 Dn 4:7 KJV

98 Wikipedia free encyclopedia. *Four Evangelists.* https://en.wikipedia.org/wiki/Four_Evangelists

99 Dn 9:24-27 KJV

100 Jer 30:3-4 KJV

101 L. Frank Baum. *The Wizard of Oz Quotes.* http://www.goodreads.com/work/quotes/1993810-the-wonderful-wizard-of-oz

102 Ibid.

103 Ibid.

104 Ibid.

105 William Blake. *William Blake Quotes.* http://www.goodreads.com/quotes/227256-the-cut-worm-forgives-the-plow

106 Genoud, François, ed. (1961). *The Testament of Adolf Hitler: the Hitler-Bormann documents, February-April* (London: Cassell), 1945.

107 Franklin Delano Roosevelt. *Franklin Delano Roosevelt Quotes.* http://www.goodreads.com/author/quotes/ 219075.Franklin_D_Roosevelt

108 T. S. Eliot. *T. S. Eliot Quotes.* http://www.goodreads.com/author/quotes/18540.T_S_Eliot

109 William Blake. *William Blake Quotes.* http://www.goodreads.com/quotes/679982-thou-art-a-man-god-is-no-more-thy-own

110 Thomas Hardy, *Quotes About Writing,* http://www.rhettaakamatsu.com/writingquotes.htm

111 Navajo Chant. (Northwest Choral Publishers, 2013) http://nwchoral.com/beauty-is-before-me-thomas/

112 Mt 2:18 KJV

113 Edgar Allan Poe. *Edgar Allan Poe Quotes.* http://www.goodreads.com/author/quotes/4624490.Edgar_Allan_Poe

114 Carl Gustav Boberg, "How Great Thou Art" (No. 10) in The Baptist Hymnal (Convention Press, Nashville, TN), 1991.

115 David Holzel. *Journey To The Center Of The Earth.* http://www.mindspring.com/~dbholzel/maps.html

116 Wikipedia free encyclopedia. *History Of The Center Of The Universe.* http://en.wikipedia.org/wiki/History_of_the_Center_of_the_Universe

117 1 Cor 3:11 KJV

118 Is 43:2 KJV

119 Ibid.

120 Ibid.

121 Ibid.

122 Ibid.

123 Ibid.

124 Ibid.

125 1 Cor 3:13 KJV

126 Is 43:2 KJV

127 Jl 3:14 KJV

128 Is 43:2 KJV

129 Zec 4:6 KJV

130 Rv 13:18 KJV

131 Rv 6:10 KJV

132 He 11:36ff KJV

133 2 Cor 5:8 KJV

134 1 Cor 2:9 KJV

135 Rv 12:11 KJV

136 1 Cor 15:55 KJV

137 Mt 19:24 KJV

138 1 Cor 1:25 KJV

139 J. B. Phillips. The Wounded Healer by Edwin Hanton Robertson, Vera Phillips (William B. Eerdmans Publishing Company, January, 1985), 57.

140 Ps 139:14 KJV

Encouragers

Special Thanks to the Encouragers listed below
for their financial and prayer support

Anonymous Memorial Gift in Memory of
Cosmas Jeffries

Doris Jeffries
Cosmas Sean Jeffries
Sheri Jeffries Bankson
Courtney Jeffries Geoperopolis
Glenn and Linda Jeffries
Rick and TerryAnn Jeffries Fielding
Scott and Cathy Jeffries
Mark and Kelly Jeffries Bates
Elizabeth J Clark
Cathy Denning
Laurie Flanagan
Nancy Brashear Ford
Malynda Guarisco
heartwood
Shannon Nevels
Jake and Kim Schiro
Tina Schiro
Cory Shaw
John C Tucker Sr
Elyn Walker

www.ingramcontent.com/pod-product-compliance
Lightning Source LLC
Chambersburg PA
CBHW050506110726
47899CB00005B/1345

* 9 7 8 0 6 9 2 4 5 5 5 3 1 *